*It's your last resort
on the Final Frontier . . .*

HOTEL ANDROMEDA

*featuring twelve strange tales of gas,
food, lodging . . . and the universe.*

GLASS WALLS—A lonely alien girl risks all to save an endangered space animal.

FACE TIME—Gemmy the bartender has to tentacle, er, finger a spy, but can he place a human face?

TO CARESS THE FACE OF GOD—When the choice is sex or death, what's more important to a man who's lived six lives?

IT'S A GIFT—Splendel's gift shop has treasures from across the universe, but only one present can end the ultimate space feud.

THE HAPPY HOOKERMORPH—Even a shape-changing mistress of the oldest profession can learn a few new tricks.

AND MANY MORE!

D1012152

HOTEL ANDROMEDA

EDITED BY
JACK L. CHALKER

ACE BOOKS, NEW YORK

This book is an Ace original edition,
and has never been previously published.

HOTEL ANDROMEDA

An Ace Book/published by arrangement with
the editor

PRINTING HISTORY
Ace edition/February 1994

ISBN: 0-441-00010-X

ACE®
Ace Books are published by The Berkley Publishing Group,
200 Madison Avenue, New York, NY 10016.
ACE and the "A" design
are trademarks belonging to Charter Communications, Inc.

PRINTED IN THE UNITED STATES OF AMERICA

10   9   8   7   6   5   4   3   2   1

CONTENTS

FIRST NIGHTER

———————●———————

Karen Haber

Lekvich Tor was excited, perhaps even a bit overly excited. But why not? he told himself. Tonight was going to be a big night. The biggest.

He stared at his image in the holomirror and saw exactly the same thing that he had seen when he had looked at himself not two minutes before: a short, stocky young man of eighteen, with pale purple skin, red hair cut into fashionable swirls, and amber-colored eyes, wearing a blue uniform with the logo of the Hotel Andromeda set in golden glowstitch against the right shoulder.

Proudly, Lekvich Tor shot his glowstitched cuffs. He looked fine, even if he did say so himself. It was his first night on full duty at the Hotel Andromeda concierge desk and he couldn't quite believe that he was actually working for such a wonderful place. He, Lekvich Tor, fifth son of Velia Tor, born and raised on the fringes of the galaxy on the colony world of Vladimir's Folly, beginning his career at the biggest orbital hotel complex in the sector. Not just a hotel, he reminded himself, but a space terminal and stopping point for every liner passing through the area! He took one last approving look at himself, then turned and hurried to his new post in the main lobby of the hotel.

The grand lobby of the Hotel Andromeda was a huge circular affair, well lit and alive with people, noise, and movement. Its circumference was lined by curving service desks above which hung holosigns indicating their different functions: reception, cashier, messages, concierge. Robot dollies hovered inches above the deep blue carpeting, ferrying baggage to and from the hotel's main portals. Public announcements in every known language in the galaxy resounded from multiple speakers.

The din would have overwhelmed a smaller space but somehow the great arcing gold-flecked dome of the lobby managed to contain and reduce the noise until it was a constant buzz, unobtrusive but electrifying.

Enormous viewing bays were set into the north and south poles of the lobby, providing tantalizing glimpses of distant stars, nebulas, and passing asteroids. The constant flow of space traffic could be seen as well: liners docking, modules uncoupling and chugging toward the hotel terminal while others returned to their mother ships. There was an endless changing show taking place just outside those windows and many guests had assembled in the viewing lounges to take a better, more leisurely look.

Lekvich Tor forced his eyes away from outer space and gazed around the lobby in ever greater excitement. The vast hanging chandeliers with their yellow glow globes moving up and down! The people hurrying to and fro in every manner of dress imaginable! The sense of urgency, of important business being transacted just inches away, was palpable and intoxicating. He was dazzled by the sophistication of the decor, the cosmopolitan mix of people. Every shape, every size, every color. He couldn't help staring in fascination. Perhaps someday he would become accustomed to all of this, possibly even take it for granted. He smiled at the thought of that distant, sophisticated Lekvich Tor, then shook his head. How could he ever take all this wonder for granted? Impossible. There was too much to see: everything was new and amazing.

His supervisor, Ranee Franklin, was monitoring the concierge board. She was a middle-aged woman with green eyes, white hair, and a cool, professional demeanor, which he envied. She greeted him with a nod. "You're early, Lekvich. Good."

Lekvich Tor smiled. He felt dazed and suddenly tongue-tied.

"Nervous?" Ranee asked.

"Nervous? Who, me?" He shook his head too many times. "Ranee, do you think that tonight I will see a great many aliens?" he blurted, barely able to contain himself.

"Of course." She looked at him in surprise and said sharply, "Is that going to be a problem?"

"No. I mean, I hope not. What I mean is, I've never seen any before."

"You're in for a treat, then." Her smile was a bit sour at the edges but Lekvich Tor didn't quite understand why.

"Look," she said. "Do you think you can handle the console for a couple of minutes? I've got to run to the loo."

Lekvich Tor blushed with pride and embarrassment. Already, she trusted him enough to leave him in charge. To share intimate information about bodily needs! His purplish skin glowed with pleasure. "You can count on me."

"I hope so." She handed him the concierge headset.

He watched her broad back as she strode away toward the staff lavatory. A powerful woman, not unlike his mother. Carefully, almost reverently he fit the headset around his ears and mouth.

The con board lay before him, its glittering display of lights winking lazily, red and blue and yellow and green. He would fax his mother tonight and tell her that he had been selected for extra responsibilities and for once she would boast about him to his brothers instead of the other way around.

Bzzzzzt!

A call! Someone was ringing from—he checked the screen carefully—room 1522. And Ranee had not returned. Which meant that he, Lekvich Tor, must take the call. Hands trembling, he filled his lungs with air and punched the appropriate flashing button.

"Hotel Andromeda, concierge," he said. His voice sounded a little high, he thought. He'd have to watch that. He took a deep breath, pressed his hand against his diaphragm, and tried to modulate his tone downward. "Good evening."

"There's a Voltorran bat in my room!"

"Sir?"

"I said, there's a Voltorran bat in my room! Hanging from the chandelier."

"I'm afraid you want Housekeeping—"

"I distinctly ordered a Mykonian bat, in fact, four of them. With hot mustard."

"One moment, please," Lekvich Tor said. "I'm cross-scanning the net. Ah, yes. I see. It was room 527 that requested the live Voltorran bat with implant and sonar control. I'll send someone up to collect it and deliver your order at once. Our apologies for the inconvenience."

"Make it fast. I'm starving."

"Yes, sir. And to compensate you for the inconvenience, the bats will be on the house." Ranee had often told him: "Smooth frayed tempers with freebies."

"Good. Appreciate it."

Lekvich Tor shut down the line and grinned happily. His first official call and he had handled it without a hitch! If only Ranee had been there to hear him. Certainly she would have approved. But she was nowhere to be seen. Oh well, women spent more time than men in the WC, he knew that. He would be patient and wait, and perhaps he would even be able to take another call before Ranee returned.

Sure enough, he had no time to savor his triumph. The call line was buzzing once more.

"Good evening, Hotel Andromeda, concierge. Can I help you?"

"No. I mean, yes. That is to say, I'm not quite sure." The speaker had a pleasant baritone voice and sounded like a middle-aged Terran.

A high, shrill voice cut in. "Don't listen to him, he's lying."

"No, he's not," said a silky female contralto. "Oh, this is all terrible, just terrible."

Lekvich Tor was taken aback by the jumble of voices. "Hello? Excuse me, please," he said. "Is this still room 1274? I'm afraid there's been some mistake. Two calls seem to have crossed. I hear more than one voice on this line."

"No, there's been no mistake." The baritone sighed deeply. "We're all in here, together."

"I don't understand, sir. Your room is listed as single occupancy."

"I'm from Veroni-Anspel."

"Oh." Lekvich Tor was stunned. He had read about the Veroni-Anspelians but he had never expected to talk to one, much less one apparently in estrus. He felt his cheeks growing hot at the very thought.

"Forgive me," he said. "I hadn't realized." One fact blazed in his mind, remembered from his hotel training: Veroni-Anspelians developed multiple personalities during estrus. Lekvich Tor didn't know what to say next, or to whom he would be saying it. Luckily, the Veroni-Anspelian rescued him from his confusion.

"I'm afraid that I miscalculated the onset of my period," he said. "And so I've arrived completely unprepared."

"Not to worry, sir," Lekvich Tor replied, thinking rapidly. "Our pharmacy can supply you with personality dampers."

"Do you have super absorbent?"

"Yes. Five- or ten-day supply?"

"Ten. And please tell them to hurry."

"No, forget it," said a basso-profundo voice.

And the high, shrill voice cried, "Leave us alone! That's all. Just leave us alone!"

"Shut up, all of us!" bellowed the Veroni-Anspelian.

"Don't worry," Lekvich Tor said. "I'm sending the order to the pharmacy right now."

"Thank you."

"To hell with you," said the high, shrill voice.

"Good-bye," Lekvich Tor said quickly.

He hung up feeling a bit unnerved but quite pleased by the way in which he had handled the call. He couldn't wait to tell Ranee about his progress—but she still had not returned from the ladies' room. Perhaps she had fainted. Women had that tendency, he knew, because his mother would often faint when her children did something of which she disapproved. Should he send someone to look for her? Anxiously he scanned the lobby. No Ranee. Well, don't panic, he told himself. At least wait a few minutes more. Surely she'll come back soon. She's probably on her way right now.

Bzzzt!

"Hotel Andromeda, concierge."

"Yes, this is room 3251. I have a euthanasia appointment tomorrow at noon."

Lekvich Tor scanned the records quickly. "Mr. Edlin, yes."

"I'd like to reschedule. Something came up."

"Same time next week?"

"That would be fine."

Lekvich Tor made the notation. "I'll see that Euthenetics gets the message."

Bzzzt!

"Hotel Andromeda—"

"I want to talk to robodealer forty-five in the casino."

"I'm sorry, sir," Lekvich Tor said smoothly. "Those lines are busy. But I'd be happy to place your bet for you."

"Swell. I'd like to bet on the cyberraces."

"Which steeds?"

"Halley's Snowball."

"To win, place, or show?"

"Place."

"Very good, sir. As you know, your winnings or your fee will be applied to your hotel account."

"Much obliged."

Lekvich Tor shut down the call, sat back on the web seat behind the con board, and crossed his arms in satisfaction. Maybe Ranee was never coming back. And maybe he didn't care.

Bzzzt!

"Good evening, Hotel Andromeda, concierge."

"I need an unabridged edition of *Dante's Slippers* by Rockwell, translated into English III."

"An English III version?" Lekvich Tor scanned the library scrolls and his spirits fell. "I'm terribly sorry, ma'am. The only edition we currently have available on line is in English II."

"Can you have it updated?"

"Let me check the translation grid. Hmmm, they're not too busy right now. Yes, ma'am, they should be able to have it for you in roughly half an hour."

"That's fine."

"Very good, ma'am. I'll have it delivered to you when it's ready."

As he rang off he saw that the woman had tabbed a generous tip into his account. Lekvich Tor grinned broadly.

Bzzzt!

Lekvich Tor nearly flew to the console. "Hotel Andromeda, concierge."

"Lekvich?"

"Yes?"

"This is Ranee. They were cleaning the ladies' room so I went down to deck five. But that one was filled with Mantarian troglodyte nurses and I couldn't hear myself think straight so I'm on deck nine now. It shouldn't be much longer."

She hung up before he could say a word.

Lekvich shrugged philosophically. She would be back soon, surely.

Bzzzt!

"Hotel Andromeda, concierge.

"Yes, I've just conceived a child."

"Beg pardon?"

"Are you deaf? I said I've just conceived a child. Ten minutes ago."

Lekvich Tor scanned his memory but could not find any appropriate reference or response from his training. Nervously, he improvised.

"Um, congratulations."

"But I'd like to take a few prenatal precautions. If this one turns out to get my nose the way the last one did, I'll just scream."

"I'm sorry, ma'am?" Now he would have given anything to see Ranee's broad figure barreling toward him and her hand reaching for the headset.

"A splicer. Do you have a gene splicer on staff?"

"Oh. Right. I'll have to check." He began to understand what the caller wanted. But as he flipped through his service directory, two other lights came on, two other calls buzzing for his attention. Where was Ranee? He wasn't supposed to leave any call unattended for more than two rings.

"I'm sorry, ma'am," he said. "I'll be right back. Please hold." He punched up the blue button. "Hotel Andromeda,

please hold." He punched up the red button. "Hotel Andromeda." A voice began squawking. He cut it off, "Please hold,"
and returned to the original caller.

"Ma'am, we can have a technician with splicer outside
your door in an hour. I see from our records that she's just
finishing up with a litter of Monosikhs."

"Well, I hope it won't be too long. I can just feel all those
little nasal cells dividing inside me even as we speak."

Lekvich Tor frowned. "Actually, ma'am, as I understand
Terran reproductive processes, it's really too soon for that sort
of cell specialization, isn't it?"

"Don't be so literal, silly. I was joking. And tell your
splicer to hurry just the same. Who knows what kind of trouble an unsupervised zygote can get into?"

"She'll be there in a flash." In a blaze of inspiration
Lekvich remembered a key note from his training manual:
meet all needs, cover all contingencies. "And," he said, "in
case you have any complications, ma'am, you might be interested to know that we can also provide termination services."

"Really? Excuse me for a moment"—her voice grew
muffled—"honey, they're offering terminations as well.
What do you think? Still want to go through with it? Remember what happened with the last one, the police, the
mutations, and all that fuss. Still want to? Honestly, you're
such a sentimental softy. Of course if you want him or her
then I want him or her."

Lekvich Tor watched the other calls blinking and wished
that he had six ears, three mouths, and six arms. Why hadn't
they hired an Arcadian arachnian to handle this job? "Very
good, ma'am," he said, putting a bit more volume into his
voice to regain her attention. "Room 2651?"

"That's right." She sighed theatrically. "He always gets so
attached to his own children."

As Lekvich watched in horror, one of the blinking lights on
the console went out. A caller had actually hung up! Lekvich
wanted to hang his head in shame, but the con line receiver
would have cut off his circulation.

"Good-bye, ma'am." With an urgency bordering on panic
he snatched up the remaining call. "Concierge. I'm terribly
sorry you had to wait."

"Who's this?" demanded a deep male voice.

"Lekvich Tor."

"Isn't Ranee on tonight?"

"She just stepped away from the desk—"

"Tell her to call Scadool when she gets back."

"Would you like to leave a message? A number where you can be reached?"

"She knows."

Before Lekvich Tor could say more, the caller hung up.

Ranee had now been away from the console for almost an hour. Lekvich Tor was growing more and more worried about her. Surely she had found an acceptable bathroom by now in the huge hotel complex. He couldn't leave his post to look for her. Should he send someone else? If he alerted the night manager, Ranee might get in trouble. But what if she were already in trouble? Lekvich felt his head swimming. He decided to wait another five minutes and then to inquire—discreetly—if someone could please look for his supervisor in the ladies' room.

An orange, fur-covered humanoid from Fragis Ipsilon approached the desk on three of its six limbs. "Excuse? Excuse?"

Lekvich Tor took a deep breath. It was his first alien, face-to-face. Luckily it seemed to speak some English. "Yes? How can I help you?" he said.

"Halp, yesh. Halp."

"That's what I said. How can I be of service?"

"Servish?" The Fragis Ipsilonian seemed puzzled by the concept. His eyestalks drooped in what must have been confusion. "Servish? Thish one?"

Lekvich Tor felt his patience begin to unravel. "Yes, I'm the concierge," he said. "At the moment, anyway. What can I do for you?"

"Rum," said the Ipsilonian.

"You want the bar?" Lekvich Tor said. "But I thought alcohol was poisonous to Ipsilonians."

"Rum, plish."

Lekvich stared at the matted orange fur in growing confusion. What did it want? To drink? To commit suicide? To drive Lekvich Tor crazy?

Bzzzt!

"Excuse me," he said, turning to the board. "Concierge."

"This is room 2651, again." The caller sounded tearful. "I

want to cancel the genetic splicer and order a relationship counselor instead."

"Yes, ma'am. Any specialization?"

"No! Just get one up here!" She blew her nose noisily. "And hurry."

"Of course."

"Excuse." The orange Ipsilonian was still standing there. "Rum, plish."

Lekvich Tor felt tears of frustration forming in his eyes. What did this creature want from him? If only he had paid more attention to languages during training. Was a rum plish an exotic drink? He had a sudden hysterical image of the Ipsilonian sitting at a table in the Andromeda bar, a pink drink with a parasol in at least three of its six paws. Then he imagined the Ipsilonian keeling over. The screams. The lawsuits. The unemployment office.

"Ah, Ambassador Syxxxch, there you are."

Blonde and immaculate Terralynne Stag, the assistant night manager, hurried up and took one of the orange fur paws in her hands, shaking it energetically. "We've been waiting for you, ma'am. Your translator has been delayed. I'm so sorry." She smiled brightly at Lekvich Tor, a smile containing absolutely no recognition but an endless supply of professional goodwill.

"Rum, plish," said the Ipsilonian.

"Yes, of course, we'll see to your room immediately."

Before Lekvich Tor could raise the issue of his missing supervisor, Terralynne had swept the ambassador away toward the main desk and reception area.

Bzzzt!

Lekvich Tor snapped to. "Hotel Andromeda, concierge."

"This is room 3975."

Lekvich Tor saw that he was talking to someone in the water wing. No wonder the voice sounded so muffled and peculiar. The water-breather was using a voice synthesizer.

"How can I be of service?" he said quickly.

"Our fenestres—ah, portholes—are opaqued again. We posit algae as the culprit."

"I'll call Amphibious Housekeeping immediately."

"Much gratitude."

Lekvich Tor hung up and saw four call lights flashing pink

and blue and green and red on the console. He hadn't even noticed them. His purplish skin began to shine with perspiration. He reached for the nearest light but a scaly green hand with claws enameled in bright orange intercepted him.

"Hello there." The voice was husky, insinuating, slightly slurred.

Lekvich Tor looked up into the face of a Saurian matriarch from Telos XVI. He had never expected to see one at such close range.

She was twice his size and width. Her jaw extended a good five inches in front of her forehead and her smile—if that's what it was—revealed rows of needle-sharp white teeth. Her dark eyes were split by a red pupil and she appeared to have no eyelids. Rubies set in golden studs dotted her eye ridges.

Lekvich Tor fought back a shudder. The guest is always right, he thought. Always.

"When do you get off?" the Saurian said.

"Beg pardon?"

Her smile widened—a terrifying sight. "You're very attractive for a humanoid. Has anyone ever told you that?"

"Never," said Lekvich Tor. In fact, before he had been recruited for this post from Vladimir's Folly, no one had ever paid much attention to him at all.

"Mmmmhmmm." She nodded languorously. "Love that purple skin."

Lekvich Tor had an awful feeling that he knew exactly what this Saurian wanted. He blushed. He looked away through the view portals at the stars but there was no help coming from those distant points of light. He took a deep breath. "Ma'am, may I direct you to our Pleasure Services Department? We have the very best selection of live professionals, robots, or virtual experiences to be found in six quadrants."

"But I like you."

Lekvich Tor gulped. He had heard rumors of the Saurians' mating techniques and he had no intention of learning whether or not any of those rumors were true. "I'm very flattered," he said. "But I'm on duty." He pointed to the wall clock behind him. "All night."

"Don't you ever get a break?"

"Uh, no. Never." Ranee, where are you? he thought. Where is the Security Force? Where is my mother?

A robot security drone rolled by and Lekvich wanted to call out to it but something kept him from doing so. He musn't insult the guest. He looked around the lobby at the endless flow of people, desperately hoping to catch the eye of some functionary. He could always press the Security button, but he had not yet been told what would happen if he did so.

"Well, I can wait." The Saurian looked as though she were planning to lean against the console all night.

"So there you are!" a high voice cried.

A Saurian male half the female's size came hurrying through the crowd toward the concierge desk. He wore a shimmering cloak woven from the rarest full-spectrum textiles and had a diamond stud embedded in one green and scaly nostril. "There you are," he said again even more shrilly. "I can't turn my back on you for a moment."

The female rolled her dark eyes and turned to face her accuser with a condescending air. "Raoul, calm down, dearest. You'll have a stroke if you don't relax."

"Don't try to get around me, Celeste. I know what you're capable of."

She gave Lekvich a long-suffering look. "I've been waiting for you, darling. You know you always take longer to dress than I do."

"I thought you would be waiting in the cafe," Raoul said, sniffing.

"I just paused to ask this charming young man for directions." Celeste winked at Lekvich. He smiled wanly.

"I know where the cafe is even if you don't," Raoul said. "Come along, now. Don't dally. I'm hungry enough to eat a dozen mice."

"But, Raoul, your digestion."

"And don't lecture me, Celeste. I said come along." He took her by the arm and steered her toward the restaurant transport tubes.

Celeste looked back over her shoulder and blew Lekvich a kiss.

Numbly, he waved.

Bzzzzt! Bzzzt! Bzzzt!

The console! Lekvich gasped and dived for the nearest light.

"Concierge."

"Lekvich, where have you been?" It was Ranee. He could have kissed her voice.

"I was talking to a guest."

"You know the rules about two rings per call."

"Yes, Ranee, of course. Forgive me."

"Now listen to me, Lekvich. I'm on deck seventeen. I got captured by Wolf Rackham—you know, the maintenance chief—on my way down from deck nine. He says he has to talk to me right now. Think you can handle things a bit longer? I'll be there just as soon as I can. How are you doing?"

Lekvich looked at the rainbow of call lights blinking urgently and swallowed. "Fine. I think."

"Good. Hold the fort." Ranee hung up.

The fort was blinking at Lekvich in every color imaginable.

"Hello, concierge, please hold. Concierge, please hold. Concierge, please hold. Concierge, may I help you?"

"Yeah, I was just swimming on deck five when a robot came in and dumped a load of sand in the deep end of the pool."

"Are you sure?" Lekvich said. "They're not programmed to do anything like that."

"Of course not," the caller said. "But some kids were playing around with its controls—they probably reprogrammed it. There it goes again."

Lekvich could hear a faint splash and outraged cries.

"I believe you, I believe you," he said quickly. "I'll contact Maintenance right away." He hung up, buzzed Pool Maintenance, and reached for the next call.

"Concierge."

"My Poltronian guppy isn't doing well," the caller said in a waspish voice. "I was just down at the kennel and I thought it looked a little pink. I don't think you've got the right mixture of gases in its cell."

"Did you tell the kennel master, sir?"

"Of course, but do you think he'd listen to me? I want something done about this at once."

"Sir, it's really not my job—"

"I don't care what your job is. If my guppy dies because of mistreatment I'll sue this hotel!"

Lekvich wanted to tell him to go ahead and sue: only a fool would bring a Poltronian guppy into an oxygen-rich environment. But he was also worried that this man might just make good on his threats. He sounded like a troublemaker. And trouble must be avoided. The guest is always right, he reminded himself once again. Always.

"I'll see what I can do, sir." Before he could say more, the guest hung up on him.

Lekvich turned to the next call. "Hello, thank you for holding."

"Is the null-g gym closed?"

"I don't know, ma'am. Have you asked at the fitness center?"

"Yeah, I tried there. The door's locked. They told me to call you."

"Oh." Lekvich Tor scratched his head. Why had they told her to call him? "Ma'am, I'll have to get back to you on that." He scribbled down her room number and went on to the next call.

"Thank you for holding." His feet hurt and he was beginning to feel pressure in his bladder. Would Ranee never come back?

"This is room 2360. We're checking out and we'd like a robot to bus our luggage."

Lekvich almost sighed with relief at the routine request. "Right away, sir."

He notified the mech station and took the next call.

"We'd like to reserve a table for dinner tonight."

"This is the concierge. You want to call the restaurant."

"Isn't this the extension for the restaurant?"

Lekvich swallowed an impatient retort. "No, ma'am."

"Well, could you connect me to the restaurant?"

"It would be faster if you dialed direct, ma'am."

"I see. Thank you."

The next caller wanted a better room and Lekvich told him to call reservations.

The caller after that wanted to know where the environmental control in his room was, and if it could decrease the gravity at all, and what exactly would happen to alcohol at zero-g.

"You're not planning to drink in zero-g, are you?" Lekvich asked in alarm.

"Why not?"

"You can't do it unless you use a closed container and suction straw," he said. "With a glass, you'll just get floating globules, which will splash on the rug and stain the upholstery when you restore the room to normal g."

The caller giggled, said, "Sounds like fun," and hung up before Lekvich could check the room number and notify Housekeeping and/or Security.

For a moment the board was quiet. Lekvich indulged himself in a hearty sigh and looked at his notes.

Now, let's see, he thought, room 5627 wanted me to call the kennel master about the guppy. Or was that room 5427? Horrified, Lekvich realized that he couldn't read his own scrawl. Well, he did remember the guppy—he would call the kennel master first and worry about the owner later.

But what about that woman who wanted to use the null-g gym? Had he already called about that? And the man who wanted to experiment with drinking in zero-g, or was it the woman who wanted to do that and the man who wanted the gym? Lekvich Tor rubbed the bridge of his nose where it had begun to ache. His head was swimming. He checked the clock: had it really only been three hours? It felt like three days.

Bzzzt!

"Concierge," said Lekvich listlessly. "Can I help you?"

"Listen, you'd better get somebody down here right away," a frantic voice said.

"Where is here?" Lekvich asked.

"Pardon?"

"I mean, what's your room number?"

"Thirteen sixty-eight."

"What seems to be the problem?"

"It's raining in my room."

Lekvich frowned. "Do you mean the pipes are leaking?"

"No. It's the environmental control. It's out of whack or something."

Of course, Lekvich thought. The environmental controls. If

it's not that it's the gravity. If it's not that it's the guppy. Or the Saurian with a diamond in his nose.

"I'll see that somebody gets to it, sir."

"Hurry, please. My portfolio is getting soaked!"

Lekvich thought that it would be very nice to lie in a quiet room on a soft bed somewhere and have warm rain trickle down onto his body. What was this guy complaining about, he wondered. Why didn't he just lie down and enjoy it?

Bzzzzt!

"Concierge."

"Lekvich, this is Ranee."

"Oh, Ranee, thank goodness. You won't believe — "

"I can't talk," she said. "I'm on deck thirty-five. Winnie Payne, the second assistant night manager, saw me with Wolf and hauled us both into a meeting. I'll be back as soon as I can get loose."

Before Lekvich could say another word, she was gone.

Bzzzt!

"Concierge," he said hopelessly.

"Ranee?"

"I'm sorry, she's not here."

"Not back yet?" It was Scadool, her mysterious caller again. He didn't sound pleased.

"I'm sorry, no," Lekvich said, and thought: You don't know just how sorry I am.

Scadool hung up.

Lekvich was beginning to get angry. Didn't anyone believe in basic good manners anymore?

"Hello again."

It was Celeste, the Saurian, leering over the console at him and waggling her ruby-studded eye ridges.

"Where's Raoul?" Lekvich said.

"Oh, he's still eating. I told him I had to visit the ladies' room," she said, and winked slyly. "Now are you certain you can't take a break?" She rubbed her thumb and forefinger together in a mercenary way. "I promise you that you'll enjoy many rewards, and not all of them on the physical plane."

Lekvich Tor felt the growing pressure in his bladder and began to despair. He was really getting uncomfortable, and this lustful Saurian was not making matters easier. He mustered his best and iciest manners.

"I'm sorry, madam. I'm flattered, truly. But as you can see, there's nobody here but me. I simply can't leave the desk."

"What about a robot? Can't you order one to come and sub for you?"

"I beg your pardon." Lekvich drew himself up to his full five feet and five inches. How dare she imply that a robot could do a job as complicated as this.

"Now don't get huffy," Celeste said. "You're obviously a sensitive and intelligent young man. How would you like a job as a personal valet? I'll just talk to your boss—"

"Celeste!!"

Raoul bore down upon them, eyes flashing. "I knew I'd find you here. You're shameless, utterly shameless. I can't turn my back on you for a second."

"Now, Raoul—"

"Don't you 'now, Raoul' me! So you had to go to the ladies' room, eh? I can't trust you at all. I might as well divorce you right here and now. Young man, can you provide me with some assistance?"

"Sir?" Lekvich stared at him in horror. Was he going to be involved in a divorce suit on his first night on the job?

Bzzzt! Bzzzt! Bzzzt!

The console was lighting up in a crazy array of colors, but as Lekvich reached for a call, Raoul interceded, grabbing his hand.

"Are you deaf as well as stupid? I asked if you could provide the services of an attorney."

"Raoul," Celeste wailed. "You don't mean it. Please, darling, don't kick me out. I'll be good, I promise."

"I'm tired of your promises."

Bzzzt! Bzzzt! Bzzzt!

"Concierge," Lekvich said desperately. "Please hold. Please hold. Please hold."

Raoul yanked on his wrist. "Well?"

"Please, sir. Let go of me. I'll request an attorney for you in a moment if you'll just be patient."

"I've been patient long enough. You don't know how I've suffered with this bitch."

Lekvich was tempted to tell him that he could actually imagine what a trial Celeste had been to him. But Raoul didn't seem interested in commiseration, especially from Lekvich Tor.

Bzzzt!

"Please, I must answer the call," Lekvich said. He pulled himself free of Raoul's grasp. "Concierge."

"Quick, we need Housekeeping down here in wing seven. A water-breather tipped over his tank."

"Can you hold on?"

Bzzzt!

"Concierge."

"I'd like to arrange for personality enhancement."

"Sir, you want implants, extension 75."

Bzzzt!

"Concierge."

"Which department handles tattoos?"

"You want Dermatology, ma'am, line 89."

Bzzzt!

"Concierge."

"This is room 842. Something's wrong with our environmental control. In fact, everybody on this floor seems to be having trouble. We're all floating around in null-g."

"Could you please hold?"

"I'm getting tired of waiting!" Raoul roared.

Bzzzt! Bzzzt! Bzzzt!

"What's going on here?" a familiar voice demanded.

"Ranee!" Lekvich Tor could have fainted with mingled relief and horror.

His supervisor stood and glowered at him. "It's absolute bedlam here and I've only been gone for half a shift."

"I'm sorry, Ranee."

She ignored him and turned to Raoul. "Sir, what seems to be the problem?"

"Are you this young man's supervisor?"

"That's right."

"I'd like to report him for insubordination. And slowness. I've been waiting for him to provide me with the services of a good divorce attorney."

"I'm terribly sorry for the inconvenience, sir. What is your room number?"

"Eleven seventy."

"I'll have a lawyer sent immediately. Do you prefer human or robot?"

"Robot. At least my soon-to-be ex-wife won't be able to flirt with one of those."

"Very good." Ranee typed a command into the net and nodded. "It will be there in five minutes."

"Now, Raoul," Celeste said. "Don't get so excited. Think of your blood pressure." She wound a meaty arm around her husband's neck and tickled his cheek with one long orange talon. "Darling, you're so attractive when you're enraged."

"Stop it, Celeste."

"No, it's true. You're magnificent. This is the Saurian I married, come back to me."

"Do you really think so?"

"Oh, yes, my darling, yes."

They embraced passionately and several Terran guests scurried out of range of their madly flapping tails.

When Raoul came up for air, he waved a hand vaguely at Ranee and Lekvich. "Cancel that robot," he said. "I don't think we'll need it after all."

"Very good, sir." Ranee retrieved the request and killed it as, arm in arm and tail in tail, Raoul and Celeste made their way to the tube for rooms 1165–1280.

Bzzzt! Bzzzt! Bzzt!

"Just don't stand there, Lekvich. Answer the phone!"

"Right away, Ranee."

Lekvich sent a maintenance crew down to wing seven to mop up, and an environmental engineer to room 842 to restore gravity. He also arranged for the null-g gym to be opened, stopped the rain in room 1348, and double-checked on the Poltronian guppy. Then, with a sigh of relief, he leaned back in his web seat. The console was suddenly quiet. Lekvich wiped his sweaty forehead on the back of his hand.

The silence lengthened. He became aware that Ranee was staring at him. Probably she was going to fire him. Well, he was so tired that he almost didn't care. His first night at the Hotel Andromeda had been chaotic and maddening. He didn't deserve to be there. Perhaps he could get a job on the maintenance crew, mopping up after water-breathers.

"Well, Lekvich," Ranee began.

Here it comes, he thought.

"You had the con for almost four hours and in that time there were three environmental accidents, postponed euthanasia, twenty-seven complaints, and one near-divorce."

Lekvich told himself he would be a man about it, and wouldn't cry when she dismissed him.

She nodded thoughtfully, then said, "All in all, not too shabby."

"What?" Lekvich said. "I mean, do you really think so?"

"Sure." She gave him a quick smile. "In fact, I've seen much worse debuts."

"But the swimming pool—the guppy—Raoul and Celeste."

"Forget it."

Lekvich Tor glowed with pride. He hadn't done badly, after all! He had weathered his first night alone at the console and Ranee was pleased. He began to relax and even look forward to the remaining hours of his first shift. He gazed dreamily about the lobby. Once more it seemed magical and filled with exotic, glamorous, exciting people.

"Excuse me."

He looked directly into the most hideous face—if that was what it was—that he had ever seen. It was a heaving mass of quills and boils in which three nostrils, a slash of a mouth, and several white staring eyes somehow managed to be in both the right and wrong places simultaneously.

"I'm the liaison with the hotel for the Wugmump convention," it said. Its breath was rancid and its voice harsh and grating. "I want to go over some details before the rest of us check in."

"How many are coming?" Lekvich asked, fascinated and repelled at the same time.

"About six thousand. I imagine you and I will be working together very closely indeed over the next six days."

Lekvich looked at Ranee.

Ranee nodded encouragingly.

Lekvich leaned close, until he was able to whisper in his supervisor's ear. "Will you excuse me, please?" he said. "I have to go to the loo." And he left Ranee staring, mouth open, at the Wugmump as he hurried away.

THE ROOM KEY

———————————•———————————

Terry Kepner

"*Ooooh, are oou da one?*" a voice whispered softly, close to her ear, "*Modher sad oou would be ere soon.*" She vaguely heard the soft sibilants of two other voices, but the words were unclear. "*Bud oou hab long lide fur and zhe sad oou hab dark short fur.*"

"*Mmmmm?*" Pat mumbled, more asleep than awake.

"*Ooooh,*" the same voice said, "*Oou smell 'onderfull. Modher musd made a misdake. Ooou are da one. I yesd knaw id.*"

A soft fur blanket drifted to her side. Ah, thought Pat, a robot maid dropping off a blanket. They must have realized the room wasn't ready for occupancy. She put her arm out and discovered that it wasn't a blanket, but a large pillow. Oh, well, she thought, that's okay; it's nice and warm. She turned on her side and snuggled closer to it.

"*Zhe likes me!*" the voice said. A fur strip draped across her side and back, and another across her legs; a pillow with *tassels.* "*Modher waz zo worried oou would nod like uz.*"

The fur pillow was very soft and silky, and Pat found herself rubbing against it to feel it sliding across her skin. She had always liked the feel of fur, but these sensations were wonderfully erotic. She sleepily ran her hand gently across the pillow, enjoying the texture.

She felt a soft puff of air ruffle the hair by her ear. Another fur pillow pressed against her back. Part of it draped over her side.

She puzzled on it for a moment, then decided that Room Service must have sent up two pillows to make up for not sending a blanket. Maybe they were out of them. Two fur ropes twined around her legs. She felt yet another rope touch her foot. She shifted slightly and a pillow draped itself across her feet.

Well, with three warm and furry pillows on her bed, she didn't have to worry about getting cold tonight. She snuggled close to them and drifted into a pleasant, and erotic, dream.

Pat stretched and stared at the wall in front of her. For the first time in days, she felt rested. She blinked slowly, thinking about her dream.

As erotic dreams go, she decided, that one was pretty good. She felt her face grow hot just thinking about it.

It had to have been that fur coverlet Room Service had dropped off. It had been so silky smooth and sensual. She wondered if she would have another dream like that one tonight.

She must have kicked the blanket down in the night—and no wonder! She barely could feel it covering her feet. Funny, she didn't remember Room Service dropping by, but then again, she wouldn't have noticed if Attila the Hun had walked into her room last night.

Room Service? Room Service. What had happened to her wake-up call? She flipped over and sat up. She froze, her mouth hanging open in surprise.

Seated at the foot of her bed were three non-humans. She closed her eyes. They were still there when she opened them. The aliens resembled weasels, with long thin snouts that ended in black noses. A dozen long, graceful silver whiskers sprouted from both sides of their snouts, much like those on a cat or a dog. Forward-facing soft brown eyes that were only a bit larger than a human's met her gaze briefly before blinking and looking down at the bed. Their rounded ears were on the sides of their heads, but more toward the back of the head, with light-colored tips projecting slightly above it. The insides of their ears were almost completely black.

Covering each of them was a thin coat of long fur, but each of them was a different color. Their long arms ended in thin hands with very, very long claws, and long, thin muscular tails. All three had their tails draped possessively across her feet. There was no coverlet. And she was naked.

As a Terran Stellar Lines spaceship third-class copilot, she had been taught to keep her cool under any circumstance. The company couldn't afford to have panicky pilots at the controls of their city-sized spaceships. One mistake made by a distracted or hysterical pilot could cost the lives of everyone aboard the ship, not to mention the loss of the cargo and the ship itself. Staying calm no matter the situation was an important job criterion.

Dealing with alien races had been only a small part of her training, but that had focused mostly on the major languages and customs of the races with whom TSL primarily dealt. Nothing had been mentioned about finding one's self naked in a strange room with three aliens, male or otherwise. She would have to wing it.

She scooted backward to the wall. She pulled her legs up until her knees were in front of her breasts and her feet flat on the bed. She folded her arms across her knees.

The middle alien, a dark strawberry blonde in color—she knew friends who would practically kill to get their hair that particular shade—bowed deeply, followed instantly by the other two. They kept their eyes chastely on the foot of the bed. They were clearly males. Embarrassingly clear, she thought. From the small pile of belts and pouches she now saw in one corner of the room, they obviously did not wear clothes in public.

While the others remained unmoving, the one on Pat's right, a beautiful calico, stood and walked over to a tray on the shelf of the computer terminal. He brought the tray to the bed, then dropped to his knees and held the tray out to her. He kept his attention locked on the tray. It held a glass and a small plate with what looked like a roll on it.

From the way they acted, so stiff and formal, Pat felt that her next action would be vital to these aliens. That it was a test of some type. She had a momentary vision of her refusing the offering on the tray and provoking a major interstellar incident. Her chance for a career with any of the major shipping lines, especially TSL, would be ruined.

Hesitantly, she lifted the glass and cautiously sniffed it. It smelled like plain water. She took a sip. It was water. Suddenly thirsty, she tipped the glass and drank half of it. She saw the alien's eyes briefly flick up to her face to watch. She glanced at the other two. They didn't appear to have moved, but their long whiskers quivered slightly. She thought what might have been a smile temporarily flitted across the face of the strawberry blonde.

She replaced the glass and picked up the plate. She sniffed at the roll, took a nibble, then a bite. She watched for a reaction in the aliens as she chewed. The blonde was positively grinning now.

The roll was dry, and had a rather bland taste, but she hadn't eaten at all yesterday. She finished off the roll in just a few bites, following it with the remainder of the glass of water. She gave them a hesitant smile.

When the glass hit the tray, the alien whisked it away to the table by the computer terminal and rejoined his companions at the foot of her bed. All three sat upright and looked straight at her now. Two were rocking back and forth, their four-foot-long tails swaying around behind them. One, with solid dark brown, almost black, fur, was bouncing in place, humming happily. They seemed rather pleased with themselves.

She was not. Who were they and why were they in her room? She absolutely had not requested Hotel Personal Services to send up a gigolo, much less three non-human gigolos! And they did not act like hotel employees.

A quick look around the room revealed that her luggage still had not arrived. And without the blanket, she had no way to cover herself.

Her first inclination was to wait for someone to rescue her. But that might take all day, and she had to report in to her supervisor on the Terran Stellar Lines' *Star Cruiser Africa* by noon, local time, or lose her assignment. She would have to extricate herself from this predicament. She took a deep breath and forced herself to move.

Keeping her plastic smile firmly in place (the one she used when dealing with passengers asking idiotic questions), she stood. All three aliens kept their eyes on her, barely blinking. Having the aliens watch as she walked to the cleaning bin made her intensely self-conscious.

Pat's smile vanished and her teeth clenched as she stared into the empty bin. Where were her clothes? Just what the heck was going on here? Had the aliens hidden them? She wished someone would rescue her.

She closed her eyes and tried to imagine what else could go wrong. Her eyes popped open and she darted to the computer. Only the cleaning tag and her watch were there. She had a momentary memory flash of dropping her room key into her pants pocket, now lost somewhere in the laundry. And, she saw, she had already missed her noon report-in time.

On the table beside the computer was the tray with its empty glass and plate, and another two glasses and plates, almost empty. The aliens plainly had started with three plates and glasses, and must have decided to give her one set while splitting the other two among themselves. She wondered why as she frowned.

She turned and gave the aliens another plastic smile. "Ahh, excuse me, I need to freshen up a little." She pointed at the door to the bathroom and started to sidle over that way.

The aliens, still seated, bowed again.

With the door solidly closed behind her, she slumped against the sink counter. "Oh, God. I don't believe this!" she groaned. Focusing her eyes on the mirror in front of her, she groaned again. Her shoulder-length hair, which her mother had always called dirty-blonde, was snarled and awry, including one small batch that stood straight up. She patted it down, vainly hoping it would stay that way.

At least, thanks to last night's sound sleep, there weren't any dark circles under her blue eyes. Anytime she missed sleep her light complexion tended to make such shadows that much more apparent.

But worse, much worse, the towel rack behind her was completely empty. That shattered her hope of fashioning a couple of the towels into the semblance of a halter top and skirt. The bathroom was as devoid of furnishing as the other room.

Splashing cold water on her face did not help. She briefly considered drowning herself in the bathtub, then noticed the hot-air vent. Mom had always said a good hot shower helped one to think.

She stood in front of the blast of warm air, drying off. The way she figured it, with even a halfway decent lawyer, she should come out of this owning a hefty percentage of the hotel. Or at least wealthy beyond any dreams she had ever had. She decided that an out-of-court settlement would be best. That would protect her career.

She cautiously opened the door. Yep. They were still there. Giving them her plastic smile again, she stepped over to the terminal. The display was built into the wall behind the simple touch pad on the abbreviated table below it. Fortunately, the terminal design was such that only the person in front of it could hear what was said. The aliens would not hear her reporting them to Hotel Security.

"Andromeda Security, please," she said, pressing the activate button.

"I'm sorry, honored guest, but access to that function from this terminal is blocked."

She stared at the computer, astounded. "Andromeda Security, please," she repeated. She got the same response.

Why would access to hotel security be blocked? All right, she would try something else. "Room Service, please," she said.

"I'm sorry, honored guest, but access to that function from this terminal is blocked."

A few minutes later she stood leaning against the terminal with both hands. This, she thought, cannot be happening. She tried the last standard function she could think of, Emergency.

"State the nature of the emergency, please, honored guest."

At last! "I have three uninvited aliens in my room."

"Is someone injured?"

"Uh, no."

"Is there a medical emergency or a fire?"

"Nooo." She did not like the way this was going.

"This function is for emergencies only. If you need security, please use that function. If this is not an emergency, please do not use this function."

"But the terminal says that access to that function is blocked!"

"I am sorry, honored guest. Unless this is an emergency, I must terminate this call." There was a click.

"Damn computer." She stared at the blank display.

"Terminal, my clothes were not returned from Laundry Services last night."

"I'm sorry, honored guest, but you must access Laundry Services for assistance in locating lost items."

"But access to that function is blocked," she wailed. She leaned her head against the cool surface of the wall above the terminal in exasperation. "Terminal," she said quietly.

"Yes, honored guest?"

"Why are functions blocked at this terminal?"

"The party booking this room requested that all functions be disabled."

"That's nonsense," she said, shocked. "I made no such request." She chewed on a fingernail for a moment as she thought. "Terminal, what about Emergency Services? I called them."

"Emergency Services cannot be blocked. All other services are blocked."

"But this is my room. I did not request that calls be blocked. I order you to remove the blocks."

"I'm sorry, honored guest, but access to that function from this terminal is blocked. If you desire to change the terminal settings, you must make that request to the registration desk."

Arguing with the terminal was useless, she knew. It would simply parrot back similar responses to her questions. "Terminal, get me the front desk."

"I'm sorry, honored guest, but access to that function from this terminal is blocked."

Pat slammed her hand against the terminal in frustration. She was stuck. Access to any function that might lead her to a sentient being was blocked. In the meantime, she was naked in her room with three furry aliens.

She turned to look at the aliens, and nervously chewed her lip. They sat by the bed, looking for all the world like they were waiting for her to say or do something important.

She took a deep breath. Naked she may be, but she wasn't going to let that stop her; she had to get her clothes. Making her parade through the hotel naked to get to a working terminal would just cost the hotel that much more in court. She walked over to the door and put her hand on the handle. She steeled herself for the upcoming ordeal, then opened the door.

Or, at least, she tried to open the door. The handle refused to move. She pushed harder. No reaction. She put her full weight on the handle. It still did not move.

The door was security-locked both ways. No key, no open door. She was locked in. Why would Terran Stellar Lines keep a block of rooms with such a security lock?

"Damn!" She leaned her head against the door, struggling to keep control. A quick look at her wristwatch revealed she was already an hour late for her noon report-in time, and had only an hour before her ship left.

If she could make it to the ship before it left, she might be able to talk her way around her late arrival and convince her supervisor to either overlook her infraction or, at least, merely mark it down as reprimand instead of a dismissal. While a replacement copilot may have been requested, her showing up could still save her job.

If she didn't make it to the terminal before then, her contract would automatically be terminated. Only a proven medical emergency or rare special circumstance could get her contract reinstated.

With a contract termination on her record, getting another of the major carriers to accept her services would be almost impossible. She would be stuck on the second-tier job level, with short-haul small ships, tramp freighters, and other less desirable posts for the rest of her career.

The aliens! Maybe one of them had a key.

She took a moment to compose herself and put her plastic smile in position. She turned slowly and faced them. Speaking carefully, she asked in Universal, "Excuse me, but do any of you have a key to the door?"

All three froze and their tails stopped in mid-swing. The humming trailed off into silence. They stared back at her, clearly not having understood her question.

"Key? Door?" She pantomimed holding something against the door and opening it.

They looked from her to the door, then to each other. Finally, each gave a whole-body convulsive shiver, and simply gazed back at her.

While there were ten major languages in this quadrant, she had studied only the three that TSL regularly traded with. She started with Spacer's Talk, sort of a polyglot that had evolved over the last few hundred years. "My name is Pat McCreney. What are your names?"

No response was forthcoming.

"I'm a pilot for Terran Space Lines. Actually I'm a copilot," she said, hoping they might recognize some of the words. "I just came in last night from Terra on the *Terran Space Lines California*. I'm supposed to transfer to the *TSL Star Cruiser Africa* for the next three years."

They blankly stared back at her.

She sighed, then tried Mulphridean. "I don't know how we came to be in the same room. I know I was really tired last night when the supervisor in the TSL offices here in Hotel Andromeda gave me a registration pass." Blondie's ears twitched at the mention of Andromeda.

For a moment, she thought they might have understood her, but she realized the only thing they had understood was the name of the station. She tried Universal Language next.

"I was tired because most of the command crew of the *TSL California* came down sick about four days ago, and the rest of us had to work double and triple shifts. Because we started docking at the end of my shift, I had to stay on duty for a third shift. I went without sleep for almost twenty-four hours."

While they were paying close attention to her every word, they clearly did not understand a single one of them. Actually, this was also helping her to retrace her steps from last night. Maybe she could figure out how they came to be in her room. She switched to Persiean.

"I almost didn't find the TSL offices, I was so tired. But I did remember to check the assignments board." She smiled wanly. "The *TSL Star Cruiser Africa* had come in that day and would be leaving at fourteen hundred hours tomorrow; that is, today. I was supposed to check in at least two hours before then." She sighed and glanced at her watch again. "Unfortunately, Registration never gave me my wake-up call, and I seem to have overslept by a wide margin. Now I only have an hour before the ship leaves."

Again, they merely stared at her. She couldn't begin to imagine what they must think she was doing. Only Altairian was left of the spoken languages she knew.

"Anyway, after I picked up my key from Registration, I got on an elevator, but I dropped the key and it rolled under the bench at the back. I had to reach under it pretty far to get it back." She paused as what she had said repeated itself in her memory.

"Damn. That must have been it," she muttered, "when I dropped my key. I must have found a lost key." And because the room keys also doubled as destination designators for the elevators, it had brought her to this room, already occupied by the three aliens. They must have been out when she arrived, returning after she fell asleep.

Why they had let her sleep on, or why they didn't leave and bring back Security was a mystery. However, they *were* aliens. They probably had their reasons, strange though they may be to her. They were polite, though. They were still listening attentively. If it were not for their lack of reactions, she would think they knew exactly what she was saying. They were cute, too.

She licked her lips hesitantly. Her getting the wrong room key certainly explained why the hallway outside had been so opulent. She had thought TSL was giving her a perk for working so hard the last few days.

That her luggage, left with the registration clerk, had not been here when she walked in should have tipped her off that something was wrong. And then she had been dumb enough to drop her clothes in the cleaning bin with the cleaning tag supplied by the clerk. That tag had probably returned her clothes to her real room, leaving her naked and without a key.

If she had not been so tired she would have realized that the hotel clerk would never have given her a room that wasn't prepped for a Terran. While the bed had been comfortable and ready to use, it had not had any blankets or pillows. And the computer terminal/table in one corner had not had a chair to match it.

Instead of immediately trying to call Room Service for some blankets, she had decided to wait for them to deliver her luggage. And had fallen asleep waiting for a delivery not destined to arrive.

She tried Spacer's Sign Language, usually used in emergency situations where speaking was impossible. Clearly, the three aliens hadn't a clue as to what she was doing waving her hands and arms around. Blondie seemed quite taken with what she was doing and started mimicking her until Calico whispered something to him. Then he stopped and looked embarrassed.

Universal Sign Language, developed for communicating with most races incapable of speech, garnered her just as little understanding. Whoever these aliens were, they were remarkably ignorant of any method of communication to outsiders of their group. Just how they had managed to get to Hotel Andromeda and in this room mystified her.

She leaned back against the door. Great, she thought, what now? If this really was their room, then Security would be more than a little displeased with her. Instead of suing Andromeda, she might be looking at a difficult time herself. If nothing else, the time she lost explaining what had happened would cause her to miss her posted assignment.

She could not afford to have Hotel Security find her. She had to get out, and get out now. Her stomach flip-flopped at the prospect of going it alone, but to stay and wait for rescue was worse.

She continued pacing and thinking. Like automatons, the three aliens watched her. She stopped and looked down at them. "Well," she asked rhetorically, "do any of you know where we are and how I can get out?"

They looked at each other briefly, and shivered. "We are in oar room," the middle one said.

"You speak English!"

"Yez," he said proudly. "We prakdessed long dime do speek so good. Nod even Modher speeks id so guod."

"Why didn't you answer me when I asked you if you had a key to the door? Or when I tried all those other languages." She stood squarely before them, staring down Blondie.

"We no speek dhose dongues, yesd dees one." The other two agreed.

She frowned. Why would they go to the trouble of learning English and not Universal? "Why English?"

"Zo we cud bond propoorly," said Calico.

"Modher sad we had doo," added the blonde. "Zhe said it waz . . ." He stopped and consulted with his two friends. "Zhe sad it waz good edikid."

They all grinned at her.

She swallowed, a little intimidated at the sight of all those sharp, shiny teeth. "Oh." Obviously, she wasn't going to make any sense of their explanations. They clearly did not understand her question, just as she didn't understand their answer.

She shook her head. Maybe they could get her out of here before Andromeda Security found her. "Do you have a key to that door?" She pointed at the door behind her.

He leaned sideways to look at the door. "No," he said sadly. "Modher dhook oar key. Zhe sad we musd sday."

Her hopes crushed, she said, "Oh. Damn. I gotta get out of here."

"Oou wand oud? Oou wand do leeve?" The three of them exchanged glances.

"Yes! I have to go to my own room and get some clothes, and then I have to get to my ship. It's very important." She gave them what she hoped was a winning smile.

"Oou wands to leaf?" asked Blondie. The edges of his mouth curved down. "Oou does nod like usz? I dod oou liked uz." The black-and-brown one looked similarly upset, and started to shiver. "And oou dhook oar bregsdad opering, doo."

Pat saw her position slipping. For some reason it was important to them that she like them. Maybe it had to do with that little ceremony earlier. If she lost their trust, they might not help her. "Oh, no," she said quickly, "I do like you. You are all very nice." She gave them another smile. "It's just that I have to get to my ship. First, though, I must get to my room."

"Oou like uz?"

"Oh, yes," she said, trying to make it sound convincing. "If I did not have to get to my ship, I wouldn't mind staying here all day. But, I have to get to my ship." While that was stretching the truth, it wasn't by much. They had her curiosity up. Just how had they managed to get here, and why was the only language they knew—besides their own, of course—English? Were they part of a group on the way to Earth? If so, they were probably going to be on the *TSL California*. But if that were so, why hadn't they recognized the ship's name when she had mentioned it earlier?

"Ooooh," Blondie said happily, "Zhee wands do go do her sheep. Zhee hass a sheep." He bounced up and down several times. He began chattering excitedly in his own language, but suddenly stopped. "Bud we kan nod leaf. Modher dold us do sday," he said.

Calico turned and pushed Blondie lightly, making him sway in place. "Dhad does nod madder," he said. "She dhook oar bond." He grinned. "She likez uz, zo she wands do leeve wid uz."

Blondie's eyes opened wide. "Ooooh. Oou is ride."

All three turned and stared at her like she was the most important person they had ever seen. Their expressions made Pat uncomfortable. They reminded her, for some reason, of her best friend on her wedding day and the way she had looked at her husband after the ceremony. It had been the summer after graduation, just before Pat left for college.

Pat wasn't sure she was understanding properly. It sounded like they thought they were going to go with her. She definitely did not want them following her back to her room, or to the ship. On the other hand, would they still help her if they knew she didn't want them following her?

But maybe she had better find out why "Modher" didn't want them leaving. "Um, if you don't mind, and if it is not an intrusion, why doesn't 'Modher' want you to leave?"

They looked at each other for a moment, then Blackie cleared his throat. "Id was nod oour fauld. We were eggsplorin and fond a brojen wader hole," Calico said.

"Ya." Blondie flashed her a quick grin.

A broken water hole?

Blackie sighed. "Dhe being dold us id wash zuppozed do blow bubbles in wader, bud id no wordk. Zo we dhook id apard."

Blondie interrupted. "Id was nod oor fauld dhe water sprayed oud. We did nod know id had, um, how oou sad, prezzure."

Oh, God. They had tried to fix a jammed whirlpool pump. She could just see the three of them getting soaked as water sprayed everywhere while they frantically tried to stop it. She smiled at the image.

"We had just done id when all dhese hodel being came," Blackie continued. "Id wordk, bud we had a few pards lefd over."

"I dhink dhey were upsed dhad we mad id wordk bedder dhan dhey could," Blondie put in, shaking his head.

They actually got it back together? In spite of the water pressure? She was impressed. To repair something they knew nothing about while wading through water was quite an accomplishment.

"Den we found a Der-ran in a, um, place full of eading macines."

Eading machines? She frowned as she tried to figure out what he meant. Oh. One of the many cafeterias scattered throughout hotel complexes like Hotel Andromeda. And Der-ran might be Terran. They had encountered another Terran in the cafeteria. What could have happened there to upset "Modher"?

"Dhe Der-ran complaned dhad dhe macine dhook his mony, bud no gebe food." Blackie gave his friends a guilty look. "We wanded do help, zo we dhook id apard." He gazed down at the floor as his tail wrapped around his ankle. "We pud id bak, but hodel beings were nod happy. Even dough id worghed."

"Dhe Der-ran was happy," Calico burst out. "He sad ib we wanded a job, he would tak uz on hiz sheep. Dhen he dhanked uz. Bud he leafed before dhe hodel peeple found uz."

"Modher was mad," Blondie said sadly. "She sad we no more coud eggsplor. She sad we musd sday here undil oour bond one god here."

They had disassembled a vending machine? Without tools? She was amazed. And a bit envious. She had lost more money than she cared to think about to obstinate soda and candy machines. With some good training they could become the envy of the Maintenance Division. She certainly wouldn't mind having them in charge of the equipment on any ship she was piloting.

If they could do that to a vending machine, maybe they

could take apart the door controls and get her out of here. But first, she had better make sure there wasn't another way out.

"How do you get food and drink?"

"A serband brings id." Calico gestured toward the table with the plates and glasses. "Oou were asleep, zo we did nod wake oou or dell dem oou were here. Id wood nod been propor for oar bond one. Oou meed Modher lader."

These three aliens must be very important, or very rich, to rate personal servants, especially traveling in space. And the more important they were, the more trouble she was going to be in when she was found in the room with them.

Pat glanced at her watch. Another fifteen minutes had passed. She was running out of time. Plus, she did not know when the servants would be bringing another meal. She had better be out of here before then. She had a sinking feeling that if the relatives of these three found her here, they would be even more upset than Hotel Security.

She gave them another smile. "Do you think you could open the door by taking the control panel apart?" Breaking the locks on hotel complexes like Andromeda was supposed to be impossible. Hotel Security did not want thieves or assassins planting their own access codes into rooms. But if they could take apart a supposedly impregnable vending machine, maybe they could do something here, too.

Blackie leaned sideways and looked intently at the panel beside the doorframe. Blondie said, "Ooooh, Modher would nod like dhat."

Just as Calico opened his mouth to say something, Pat said sweetly, "But I would like that."

Calico's jaws closed with an audible snap, and he looked at Pat. Blondie clapped his hands. "Ooooh, yez, yez, yez." Blackie immediately stood and walked over to the door, brushing lightly against Pat as he passed her. The other two closely followed him.

Feeling their soft fur brushing her skin as they crowded close to her made her think of her dream last night. She blushed. She almost shrieked when a very soft tail abruptly slid up between her legs. She grabbed it in her hand. "Don't do that, it tickles."

Blondie whipped his tail away from her, then leaned against her arm.

Standing beside them, her five-foot-ten-inch build topped them by several inches. The tallest, Blondie, barely reached her nose; the shortest one, Blackie, was not quite as high as her shoulder. They were much thinner than she was, making her feel chunky by comparison. At a hundred fifty pounds, she wasn't a professional model, but co-workers at TSL *had* complimented her on her figure.

She stepped back from the door to give them more room. Soon, all three were absorbed in removing the panel from the door, their tails waving and weaving among them in intricate patterns. Using their claws as screwdrivers, levers, and cutting tools, they soon had the panel dangling from a gaping hole, exposing wires and circuits.

How they knew what to do was beyond her, but from the short bursts of arguments between probings she decided that they were applying more guesswork than knowledge. After one such disagreement, Blondie jabbed his claw angrily into the wiring.

There was a faint pop, a distressed yelp from Blondie, and the odor of something burned. Blondie jumped back from the small panel waving his hand. When he stopped, Pat could see a scorched spot on one side of his middle-finger claw.

Blackie smugly said something, which Blondie replied to with a growl. Calico eeped, inserted his claw carefully, and twisted it. There was a faint mechanical click.

Leaving Blackie to stuff the panel back into place, Calico grabbed the door handle and pushed it down. It moved smoothly and a moment later the door stood open. Blackie hissed at Calico, and together they finished securing the panel.

Not wasting any time, Pat quickly dashed out into the hall, with Blondie right behind her. "Oou bounce," he said, looking at her breasts. Calico and Blackie stepped through a moment later and quietly eased the door closed. Calico handed a belt and pouch to Blondie, then buckled his own around his waist.

She blushed and forced herself to relax instead of trying to cover herself with her hands. That would just draw attention to what she was trying to hide. Anyone seeing her would re-alize something was wrong. She could not afford that.

The hallway stretched empty in both directions. Walking quickly, she headed for the elevator. "Thanks for helping me, but you don't have to come along. I'm all right now." In truth, she hoped they would stay put. She really did not want them following her.

"Oou wand do leeve us?" asked Blackie unhappily.

Something in his tone stopped her dead in her tracks. She turned back to them.

"Whad did we do wrung?" asked Calico, just as unhappy.

Blondie sniffled. "I dhoughd oou liked us."

All three tails drooped to the floor.

"And you smell zo nise," Calico said sadly.

At first, she worried she had made them mad, but a second later she saw she was wrong. She watched, amazed, as liquid gathered at the edges of Blondie's eyes, and a tear slowly trickled out. The other two were clearly just as upset, and not far from tears themselves.

"But what about your 'Modher'?" Pat asked. "Shouldn't you stay in your room? I don't want to get you in any more trouble."

"We full adulds, now," Calico explained. "We bond wid oou. We no more hab do do as Modher say. We go wid oou. We do whad you dell uz do do."

Another tear trickled down the side of Blondie's face, followed by a sniffle.

"We bond oou. We go widh oou," Blackie whimpered.

Pat didn't know what to do. She didn't have the time to talk them back into their room; one of their people might come into the hall at any moment. If she just left them like this, though, they might go back into the room and tell their relatives. Or worse, they might tell security. And what was this "bond" stuff?

"Don't cry," she said hurriedly. "You haven't done anything wrong. I just have to get to my ship before it leaves without me."

"Bud whad aboud us?" asked Calico. "We wand do go wid oou." Blondie looked ready to collapse on the floor, weeping.

She hated to be on the spot like this, especially when time was running out, in more ways than one. "Okay. Okay. You win. Come on." She turned and started for the elevator.

Once in the elevator, she realized she had only one real choice for a destination. She had to get her room key, and that meant Registration.

As the elevator started to move, she leaned against the wall and hoped that no one would stop it and board. The lobby was going to be bad enough.

The aliens casually moved closer to her. All traces of their recent distress had disappeared. She had the feeling that she had been manipulated, and by experts. She shook her head, puzzled. They sometimes acted like children, and other times like adults.

Something tickled her foot and she started to rub it with her other foot. Instead, she found her foot rubbing across three tails. All three aliens had wrapped the tips of their tails around her ankle. It was bizarre, but rather cute. The silky-smooth slide of their fur against her leg sent goose bumps up her back.

She decided not to say anything. By the time the elevator arrived at the lobby, she found herself massaging behind the ears of Calico with one hand while Blackie held her other like a shy teenager. Blondie was squatting on the floor in front of her and leaning back against her legs, humming. They seemed quite content with her company.

She normally didn't like people crowding her, and three humans doing this would have driven her to distraction. These three, though, made her feel relaxed. And their fur was just so soft and silky, it was all she could do to keep from petting all of them.

Blondie stood as the doors opened, and led the way into the lobby. Only a few steps into the large open atrium all three stopped to gawk.

Pat could understand why. The place was huge. The atrium was hundreds of feet high, disappearing overhead in the glare of artificial sunlight. Balconies from a thousand or more rooms opened onto the atrium, and over a thousand beings were visible all around.

Opposite the elevators, but almost two hundred feet away, was Room Registration. To either side were wide corridors leading to other parts of the Hotel Andromeda complex, lined with shops, eateries, and entertainments for the myriad races that passed through the complex on a daily basis.

She felt dreadfully exposed standing naked in the lobby, but it was large and bustling with activity. She headed for the registration desk. Fortunately, all she attracted were a few raised eyebrows and whistles from two men. Never had she blessed the existence of the Terran nudist colonies, but she did now.

Her three aliens were right behind her. She checked on them once and saw Calico hauling on the arm of Blondie to keep him from walking into a fountain. Blondie was more intent on staring around the atrium than in watching where he was going. She shook her head, wondering if dumb blonde jokes were popular in the aliens' culture.

Standing in the line at Registration was nerve wracking, but finally a clerk was free to assist her.

"I'm sorry to bother you," she said. "I accidentally left my key in the room when I went to the swimming pool."

The man behind the counter didn't bat an eye at her lack of clothing. "Your name, please?"

"Pat McCreney."

"Would you like a wrist or waist strap for your key?" the man asked while they waited for voice verification and the arrival of a new key.

"Why, yes. Please. A wrist strap would be best, I think."

Before she was finished speaking, the key popped out of the side of the terminal. A second later he was holding the strap up as she slid her hand through the opening.

"There you are, honored guest. I'm sorry for the inconvenience. Your check-in clerk should have offered you one"—he glanced down at his terminal—"last night."

"Oh, that's quite all right." Her voice was steady in spite of the shakiness she felt inside.

"I hope your stay is pleasant and memorable."

"Oh, it has been memorable," she muttered softly, but he was already turning to the next customer. She hurried away.

This time the elevator trip was much shorter.

She stood for a moment with her back against the door. While the hall outside was not nearly as luxurious as the other, this room had real furniture. More important, her bag was sitting prominently on the floor beside the bed.

Blackie and Calico were looking in the bathroom while

Blondie was opening and closing the drawers of the desk beside the computer terminal.

She looked at her watch. Oh, God. She had only ten minutes to make it to the *TSL Star Cruiser Africa*. She hastily jerked open the cleaning bin and saw her clothes from the previous night neatly folded at the bottom. She sighed in relief that something, at least, was going in her favor. Her three aliens watched, amazed, as she quickly dressed.

When she started to brush her unruly hair into some semblance of order, Blondie said something to his friends and they quickly surrounded her. "No. Dhad we do," Calico said, taking the brush from her and pulling her over to the bed, ignoring her protests. After getting her to sit, they started running their claws through her hair. After a moment, she realized they were grooming her hair for her.

She sat impatiently for a minute before stopping them. "Look, that's very nice, but I'm in a hurry." She stood and checked her hair in the bathroom mirror. Actually, they had done a nice job on her hair, their claws making short work of the snarls. It had been good of them to do it for her.

When she opened the door, they immediately followed her into the hall. "Look," she said, "I have to catch my ship before it leaves. You had better go back to your room before you get in trouble."

"Bud oou sad we cud go wid oou," protested Blondie.

"Yez," added Calico, "oou sad we cud go wid oou, I heared oou." Blackie started sniffling again.

Pat promised herself that this time she would not let them manipulate her into letting them get their way. "I'm sorry," she said. "But you can't go with me. My supervisor simply will not allow you to board the ship."

Tears were already starting to flow from all three aliens. This time, though, Blondie continued the protesting. "Bud oou bond wid uz. Oou sad oou liked uz," he wailed loudly.

Calico chimed in, "Oou sad we cud go wid oou," repeating what he had said earlier, but much louder.

This time the corridor was not empty. Pat looked up to see a security officer patrolling the hall. He was looking at the three aliens and Pat, and frowning. If he started asking questions, she might not get away from him in time to make it to her ship.

"I don't have time to argue with you," she said, "I have to get to my ship." She spun on her heel and headed for the elevator. She could hear the three of them padding along behind her.

The elevator ride was quiet. Again, she tried to talk them out of following her. They didn't respond verbally. Calico and Blondie each held one of her hands, gently stroking them. Blackie began combing her hair. None of them looked happy. They seemed determined to come with her.

She decided that the best course of action would be to go to *TSL Star Cruiser Africa*'s berth and let ship security detain the aliens at the terminal while she boarded. It wasn't a nice solution, but the best she could come up with, given her time constraints.

The elevator doors opened on the proper level for passenger boarding at this terminal. Glancing at her watch, she saw she had only a few minutes. She started down the terminal corridor at a sprint. The terminal gate she needed was at the far end, of course. The three aliens trotted along behind her.

Something was not right, but she could not put her finger on it until she arrived at the designated gate. The boarding area was dark. Confused, she at first thought she was at the wrong gate. Examining the electronic departure board at the boarding gate showed that she was, indeed, at the correct location. Still unsure, she looked up at the clock on the wall above the boarding tube.

Astounded, she saw that it indicated the time as fifteen hundred and a quarter hours. She looked down at her watch, and stared as it changed from 13:59:59 to 13:00:00. For a moment she was too stunned to move. Then she focused on Blondie. "You! You took apart my watch." She held her wrist out to him. "You made me miss my ship," she shouted. "You made me lose my job! Five years of hard work shot to hell."

He glanced nervously at his friends, and licked his lips. "We hab neber seen a dhing lik dhad. Oar clodks arr in oar pouches. We meaned no harm."

"Do oou hade uz?" asked Calico hesitantly.

This time there were no tears. This time they could see she was mad at them. This time they were afraid of her. They didn't even try to touch their tails to her. They were very worried.

For a moment, she was absolutely furious with them. Then she realized that it really wasn't their fault. Even without their meddling with her watch, she never would have made it to their ship on time. The *TSL Star Cruiser Africa* had completed passenger boarding and sealed its hatches before she had even looked at her watch. "No," she said, her anger deflated and drained away. "No, I don't hate you." She sighed and started walking back up the corridor to Hotel Andromeda.

Her three aliens were still with her. What the heck, they were adults. They could do what they wanted, even follow her around all day. And ever since she had yelled at them they had been quiet and mindful, never straying farther than a few feet. Even Blondie was behaving.

She had not intended to stay on the station for more than a night, so she had not bothered to draw any of her pay. TSL tracked her earnings and anything she purchased was automatically charged against them. Incidental items were the only expenses that required real currency.

That left her almost flat dead broke. Fortunately, she had some change left in her travel kit from previous off-ship sightseeing. Unfortunately, it would only last her a day, maybe two. She had to find a job, and find it fast.

One of the many public computer terminals gave her the location of the Space Personnel General Posting Office. Once she was registered, any captain looking for a pilot would see her name. And she could look for any ships wanting someone with her skills.

They were almost at the office when Blondie suddenly eeped excitedly and trotted a dozen yards ahead. Calico and Blackie followed quickly, leaving her behind. Surprised that they had left her, she watched as they accosted a Terran.

The man was large, almost six feet tall, with black curly hair and almost as dark skin. He walked with the easy confidence of a man who was his own master. He stopped when Blondie reached him. A moment later she heard him laugh as he greeted the alien. They apparently knew each other. He did not appear surprised to see Calico and Blackie with Blondie.

She couldn't hear what Blondie was saying. As she came closer, Pat could see the captain's bars on his shirt collar. She

self-consciously fingered the pilot's insignia on the collar of
her TSL jacket.

"Hi," the man said, sticking his hand out as he matched her
steps, "My name is Charles Coal, of the ship *Australian Gold*,
a million-tonner."

"Hi, I'm Pat McCreney." As small freighters went, a million tons was a respectable size. The *TSL California*, by comparison, was rated at a million and a half.

As they shook hands, Charles took in her TSL uniform
and the way the three furry aliens crowded in close beside
her as they walked down the corridor. She was acutely
aware of their tails and the way they kept touching her legs.
They didn't impede her, just kept a soft pressure that told
her they were there.

"Your mates did me a good turn the other day. I've never
seen a group work so well together, or so quickly. And they
told me they had never seen a drinks machine before." He
shook his head wonderingly as they walked on down the corridor.

"I can't believe my luck." He smiled ruefully. "My
bleedin' mechanic's assistant's contract expired when we arrived here, and I've had the devil's own time finding a replacement. Usually, I can get someone in a couple of hours,
but I've been waiting for two days now." He frowned unhappily. "And now I'm a full day behind schedule."

She saw his gaze flit to her insignia, and a speculative look
came into his eyes.

"Say, maybe you could help me. Do you know any mechanic's assistants looking for work?"

Before she could respond, Calico spoke up, "Uz. We look
por work. We wordk bery hard. We good wid macines."

Pat was startled. Apparently, they were not as intent on
staying with her as she had thought.

The captain gave Calico a surprised look, then shrugged.
"Do you have work logs?"

Calico looked puzzled. "Whad?"

"ID tags, ID papers, work reports, something that shows
your previous work experience?"

They walked through the entrance of the posting office. It
was more a hall than a simple room, with hundreds of termi-

nals lining the walls, with benches, tables, and chairs scattered throughout.

Calico pulled a small card out of his pouch. A passport. He handed it to the captain. Blondie and Blackie quickly added their passports to Calico's.

Captain Coal frowned. He glanced at the insignia on the front of the passports. It meant as little to him as it did to Pat.

He moved over to one of the terminals and slid the first passport into the ID slot. A moment later, he and Pat were reading the brief description.

The aliens were called Kreene, from a star system almost as far from Hotel Andromeda as Earth was. Calico's real name, it turned out, translated to "Quick Eyes." Blondie's passport gave his name as "Light Ears," and Blackie was "Fast Runs." No mention was made of job skills, experience, or even interests.

Also, as she had thought, they were adult males, although the passport included the phrase "unbonded and traveling secure with family." She wondered what that meant.

Captain Coal sighed and silently looked at the three aliens for a moment. He nodded his head once, as if he had come to a decision. "Okay. I'm only looking for one mechanic, but from what I've seen, the three of you, unskilled as you are, should be the equivalent of one good mechanic."

All three were excited. Blondie, no, Light Ears, was bouncing up and down like a little kid who was just told he was going to a toy shop. Fast Runs and Quick Eyes hugged each other happily. You would have thought the three had just won a lottery.

The captain looked amused. "Well," he said, turning back to Pat, "looks like my problem is solved. Maybe we'll meet again someday." He shook Pat's hand.

The three Kreene were suddenly still. "Oh, no," Calico interrupted. "Zhe oar bond. We go dogedher or we no go."

Pat was as surprised as the captain. They expected her to go with them?

Coal stopped and frowned. "But she's with TSL," he protested.

"Zhe no wid dhem. Her zheep lefd and zhe nod on id."

Pat could feel her face turning hot and red with embarrassment. "I last served on the *TSL California*," she said before he could ask the obvious questions.

"Ah, I heard about them coming in last night with most of the crew ill."

Startled that he had heard of their troubles, she could only say, "Yea. The rest of us had to pull double and triple shifts." Pat looked down at the floor, chagrined. She might as well tell him everything. "That's why I'm here today. I was supposed to transfer to the *Star Cruiser Africa* today, but I overslept." She sighed again. "I never got a wake-up call, and when I did get up . . . well, it was too late. My contract was terminated when I didn't board."

"Standard contract?"

"Worse. I lost all accrued pay and bonuses by missing the ship."

"Log?" he asked holding out his hand.

Pat pulled out her ID card, standard issue for all licensed spaceship personnel in this quadrant, and handed it to him. He stepped up to the terminal and inserted her ID in the slot in the side. Instantly, her job experience log appeared on the display, updated by the captain before she had debarked last night.

"Twenty-six. Served on three ships. You've been certified for only four years. You had a five-year contract, with only six months to go." He shook his head in sympathy. "You don't have much experience."

"But all my supervisors gave me glowing reviews and high marks."

He frowned again and gave her back her ID tag. "I don't really need another copilot."

Why the Kreene were insisting that she go with them, Pat didn't know. But if it got her a job this fast, she would go along. Once she had some money, she could make other plans.

"Really? Most ships I heard about always could do with an extra pilot. Plus, you did say you've been waiting for two days. Do you want to take a chance on waiting longer?" She hated job hunting, she found it hard trying to convince people into hiring her. That was one reason why she had hired on with TSL, so she wouldn't have to go hunting after every contract. TSL tended to keep people who worked hard and did a good job. She did both.

He narrowed his eyes as he looked at her. "Thirty-five thousand for all of you, and one crew's share."

Pat was amazed. As an offer, that was robbery. Even as a starting TSL copilot, she had earned more than that. "No way," she said firmly. "We each get twenty thousand and a crew's share. On a one-year contract." She did not want to chance a longer contract until she knew the captain and the ship better.

"I don't need another copilot," he said quietly. "And these three are unskilled. Forty thousand. And a one-year contract with a one-trip probationary period."

That was a good idea. If the situation did not work, then he wouldn't be stuck with an expensive foursome for a year, and they wouldn't be stuck on a ship they hated.

They settled on ten thousand for her and twelve thousand each for the Kreene, with two crew's shares for the four of them. Even a short trip would give her a better basis for job hunting.

And a year would give her time to think about what to say to "Modher."

TELLING HUMAN STORIES

———————•———————

Margaret Ball

The raised voices bounced all the way down the hall and around the corner to where I stood. There seemed to be three of them wrangling; and the voice in the middle, the loudest of the three, had a pronounced Old Terran accent.

Might have known. You want conflict in an interspecies relationship, just put a human in the middle of it. We'll do it every time.

Yeah, I know. Who am I to run down my own species, and all that. Well, for one thing, I'm a professional, trained to deal with situations just like the one I could hear developing as I zipped down the corridor. That one fact puts me ahead of most of the human tourists and diplomats and travelers that pass through Hotel Andromeda. *And* I'm not from Old Terra—which puts me *way* ahead of anybody who had just checked into the Terra 4 module with the OT delegation.

The argument was going on in the public corridor just outside the Terra 4 mod. A Dendje was growling and brandishing something at a red-faced Terran in a loud checked synthosuit. Bouncing off the walls to either side of them, a Skiouros chittered and squeaked and added its own discontinuous element to the controversy.

As I got closer, I could see what the Dendje was waving; one of the Skiouros's furry little legs, ripped clean out of its furry hide.

"Okay, okay, all of you, calm down, please, gentlespecies. What seems to be the trouble here?"

"What's it to you?" the Terran wanted to know.

"Any disturbance is automatically reported to Hotel Security," I said, which was true enough, although Security didn't always respond this fast. "Now, if you'd just explain the problem in your own words . . ."

"That big ape just assaulted the little guy!" the Terran announced. "Right out here in front of God and everybody! And when I told him to lay off, the both of them started in on me. Sheesh. They're both crazy, you ask me."

"Chitter. Chitter. Squeak," the Skiouros interrupted. Skiouroi aren't equipped to speak Standard Galactic and they refuse to carry voicemods, insisting that the squeaky little noises they make sound just fine to *them*.

". . . smashing your head down in between your external genitalia and cutting off assorted body parts . . . ," the Dendje continued the line of conversation that had been occupying it when I came on the scene. I sympathized some with the Dendje. I'm told their native language is particularly rich and fluent in assorted insults that just don't translate into Standard Galactic. It takes a little mental agility to figure out a totally culture-free phrasing for insulting someone. Dendje like to insult other gentlespecies, but they aren't agile in any way. Must be frustrating.

Then again, when you outmass any other species in the Terranormal modular zone by at least fifty kilos, and stand a meter higher than most of them, with arms longer than most Terranorms' bodies, you don't really need a lot of agility.

"I see," I said in my best professionally soothing tones. "Just a small misunderstanding, eh? Shall we sit down?" I nodded toward the Old Terran suite, hoping he'd take the hint. "I'll need a vox of your version, gentlesir Terran . . ."

"And who's going to protect the little guy if this ape wants to finish the job?"

I didn't sigh or roll my eyes. I am, after all, a professional. "I expect they both want to finish their business, sir." I glared at the skittering Skiouros. "*Might* I recommend some more private area than this corridor?"

". . . right to pursue peaceful social interaction unimpeded by prejudice of horribly underground-pale, exceptionally low-IQ interfering species . . . ," the Dendje grumbled.

". . . duty to abstain from deliberate provocation . . . ," I replied in the same low-pitched monotone. "An Old Terran delegation just checked in; there'll be more like this gentleman coming along, and all subject to the same, ah, tendency to misunderstand. Now, if you two gentlespecies want to finish your ritual *in private*, Hotel Security will appreciate it was all just a misunderstanding. Remaining in public space could be construed as conduct tending to alarm or frighten fellow species."

The Dendje grunted and shambled off, gnawing meditatively on the shredded Skiouros limb. The Skiouros bounced up to its shoulder, cartwheeled off a side wall with seven or eight furry limbs sticking straight out, caught itself on the Dendje's mat of backbone hair, and squealed something rude at us in departing.

"I don't believe it," the Old Terran said. "You gonna let him tear the little guy up and eat him, long as they do it in private?"

This time I did sigh. "I'm afraid you've misunderstood a grooming ritual, sir. Dendje and Skiouroi have a symbiotic relationship. Skiouroi continually extrude new limbs but have no mechanism for shedding the old ones; takes more muscular strength than they possess to pop the dead limbs out of the cartilage. Dendje groom them, pull off dead legs, and get to eat them as a reward." I paused while the Old Terran assimilated this information.

"Christ on a crutch," he said finally, "that's disgusting."

"Watching a Dendje eat anything is kind of disgusting, by human standards," I agreed. "And if I were telling human stories about them—which I advise you not to do—I'd accuse them of deliberately eating in public, every chance they get, just to gross out other species and provoke little scenes like the one you were just in. But the first thing we learned in our training is not to tell human stories. And now, sir, if I could just get a vox of your story—"

"I, um, I don't think that'll be necessary," the Old Terran said. "If that's the way it is, I don't want to file a complaint. Guess I owe you my thanks, young lady, for explaining things. Jack Kerensky's the name.[1] Buy you a drink?"

"Not on duty," I said, "but I'll take some kave, if you have any."

He beamed and turned a few shades redder. "Ever know an Old Terran to travel without kave?"

I'd hoped to be invited into the delegation suite, but instead we wound up in one of the attached modules that was being set up around us for a party. An extensive party, to judge from the number of roboservitors bustling about, unfolding seating and bar modules and stacking supplies behind the movable paneling. I sipped my kave and let Jack pick my brain about human stories and interspecies relationships.

"You see a lot of interspecies problems at an intergalactic center like this," I admitted, "but we humans are far and away the worst. I think it's because we evolved in isolation. We got in the habit of telling stories about our own feelings and actions. Protecting the Young, Claiming Territory, Who's In Charge Here . . ." No use rattling off the names of the classic myths; they clearly didn't mean anything to this guy. I slowed down. "Anyway. Our stories work pretty well as long as they're only applied within one species. We even told the same stories to explain our domestic animals, *cats* and *dolphins* and so forth, and because they couldn't talk, they never told us how wrong we were."

"Dolphins aren't exactly domestic animals," Jack corrected me, "but I don't get the point."

"Well." I stirred the kave and watched it turn from muddy brown to brownish white and back again in lazy spirals. "Take Protecting the Young. That's one of the most basic human stories." It was also one that would lead very naturally to the point I wanted to bring up.

"Because we bear weak young that need years of nurturing and training before they can survive on their own, we have a very strong social drive to protect our young—anybody's young—anything that appears weak. When you thought the

Dendje was assaulting the Skiouros you intervened without thinking, because you were in the human story of Protecting the Young. But that story doesn't really have much bearing on species that have evolved symbiotic relationships. And it can lead you completely astray in dealing with a species like the Hatartalan, who spawn thousands of self-sufficient young at a time and then actively test them so that only the best will make it to the next life-cycle stage. You see?"

"Funny you should mention the Hatartalan," Jack said. He waved one hand at the activity all around us. "Know who's in the adjoining module? The Hatartalan ambassador to Sokol Sector. That's what all this hoo-ha is for. Going to connect the modules tonight, have a grand diplomatic bash. Two ambassadors of equal status—our fellow and the Hatartalan—crossing paths in space, pausing to render honors and courtesies and all that. Interesting, huh?"

I agreed. I didn't add that a number of parties found the repeated pattern of "accidental" meetings between Old Terrans and Hatartalans very interesting indeed. Instead I widened my eyes and looked impressed.

"A genuine Hatartalan?" I breathed. "You know, I've never actually met one. It would be so *fascinating* to find out how their behavior compares with what I've read in research papers—ah, I mean in the hotel training manual."

That was the point at which my dear new friend Jack was supposed to come across with an invitation to join the grand diplomatic bash. Unfortunately, he missed his cue and kept on missing it, no matter how wide-eyed and wistful I acted. There must have been something faulty with his Protecting the Young story. I eventually left with a little information about the party, a lot more information than I'd bargained for about the life and times of Jack Kerensky, and no invitation.

Oh, well; if you can't get what you want, you just have to use what you've got. . . .

By the time I came back to the Terra 4 module, the joint Terran-Hatartalan party had been going for some time—long enough for guests on both sides to make maximum use of their icebreakers of choice. The air was heavy with leaking smoke and vapor trails from the Terran poppers, while the Hatartalans were whooping it up with what the library index told me was their usual stimulant—translucent, wobbly eggs that burst to reveal some stuff like seaweed that had been dead a couple of days too long. The organic component of the seaweed turned into a cloud of small airborne particles the minute the egg burst, leaving a few dried wiry strands that the Hatartalans usually dropped while they were ecstatically inhaling the rotted-weed clouds.

The index hadn't mentioned that the process gave a Hatartalan party the distinctive aroma of a marsh in an advanced state of ecological breakdown, or that the wiry seaweed remnants crunched underfoot while the jellyeggs squished.

Did I mention that Hatartalans are real slobs? Woops, human story. Let's say that their species, having evolved to treat its spawn as disposable commodities—"Throw 'em out, there's plenty more where they came from!"—treats everything else exactly the same way. Hatartala is said to be the only planet whose ecology is trashed worse than Old Terra's.[2]

No, I hadn't gotten access to the party yet. I was standing on a walkway under the balcony when a roboserv lurched out with a scoop full of seaweed and jellyeggs, missed the disposal chute, and showered me with the debris. That's how I happened to be an expert on Hatartalan trash before I got to meet any of them in person.

I was still picking seaweed crackle out of my black dress and reflecting that at least now I smelled like somebody from the right party when a pair of human bopperchicks spilled out of the lower entrance. They were both glassy-eyed, giggling, and scantily dressed, and they barely noticed when they nearly pushed me off the edge of the walkway. They probably wouldn't have noticed at all if I hadn't just had the unfortunate encounter with the malfunctioning roboservitor.

"Eeew, you smell gross!" one of them exclaimed, wrinkling her nose. "What've you been doing, seducing a buzzhead?"

Did I mention that the mature form of Hatartalan is vaguely insectoid, with long sticklike limbs and a head that's all buzzing, constantly vibrating mandibles?

"Some of my best friends are buzzheads," I told her. "Where are we going?"

She giggled. "Saying good-bye to Bips and Puffy, of course!" Her eyes glazed over and she took a moment to untangle her tongue. This one was really far gone. "Or do I mean Pips and Buffy? Good ol' Buffin, bes' frien' a girl ever had, and I do mean best. You should've met Puffin, he'd show you a good time. Lots more fun than hanging around with the buzzheads."

"Breaks my heart to've missed the opportunity," I agreed. "But Jack gets so jealous. You know, good old Jack Kerensky?"

I'd hoped for recognition, but all I got was generic agreement. "Oh, darling, I *know*! Aren't men the limit sometimes? Oh, look, there they are now!"

I crowded into the overlook at the far side of the walkway and squealed and waved as enthusiastically as the rest of them while two very young Galactic Service officers hopped on an interior transport and zipped out of sight. While the girls were competing to see who could call out the most artistically obscene farewells, I slid out of my jacket and yanked at the collar of my dress until a seam parted and I could slide it down over both shoulders. Now I looked almost as trashy as the girls who'd dressed for this kind of party. I stayed in the middle of the group and let them swirl me right up to the module doors.

Where two large Terrans in diplomatic uniform were checking IDs and party invitations.

"Oh, sweetheart, you just *saw* us come out!" protested one of my new friends.

While the girls in front of me were fishing around their skimpy dresses for IDs, I let out a piercing shriek and clapped both hands to my cheeks. "My bag! I left it inside. Oh, now, I'll simply *die* if Jack looks in it—there's my diary and *everything*! Boopsie, do you see it? Oh, *there* it is, just behind the bar!"

Both girls in front of me looked confused. Chances were neither of them was named Boopsie, but they knew somebody who was. One of them squealed and nodded as if she could actually make out a handbag amid the shadows behind the bar. I scooted inside, closely followed by the Poopsies and Muffies, and the guards looked at one another and snickered behind us.

Once inside, I didn't have much trouble shaking Buffy or Moopsie or whatever their names were. They spotted another brace of Galactic Service officers to home in on. I drifted around the fringes of the party, making vague noises about looking for a lost handbag, and always keeping a few people between me and the gatekeepers' line of sight just in case they grew suspicious about the girl with the missing handbag. This wasn't hard to do; the room was packed elbow to mandible with partying Terrans and Hatartalans. It was a perfect milieu for exchanging secret information.

It was a lousy milieu for catching anybody at it.

But then, my unsupported eyewitness testimony wasn't what we wanted. We needed documentary proof of what I'd been sent to investigate. A pattern of "accidental" overlapping layovers for Hatartalans and Old Terrans didn't, by itself, mean anything. A corresponding pattern of information leaked just before scheduled diplomatic talks, maintaining the high tensions of all parties, was suggestive but didn't constitute absolute proof. Even the digging that had turned up the same two parties involved in all layover meetings—the Hatartalan ambassador and my new buddy Jack—didn't, in the eyes of the galactic court, constitute grounds for a search warrant.

Which was where I came in, poised insecurely between Terran skinpoppers and Hatartalan jellyegg sniffers, laughing and throwing my head back and shrugging one shoulder a little farther out of my dress and trying to figure out where the hell I would hide my notes if I were an Old Terran passing inside information to a Hatartalan.

Not on any network or comlink, that's for sure. There isn't an electronote system made that can't be compromised. In my real training manual—which did not, by the way, have anything to do with the one they give to hotel security—they emphasized that old-fashioned mnemonics are the best kind. Forget datahedra, bit chippers, tone volts. Anything that has to be set up through some kind of complex machine can be spied on the same way. If Jack and the Hatartalans had been passing data via computers, our hackers would've found it from remote and I wouldn't be hanging my body on the line here.

Species tended to keep notes in the formats they'd evolved to use. So Skiouroi said it with nuts and berries, Terrans scribbled on synthpaper, and Hatartalans—Hatartalans probably encoded it as a giant pseudowax honeycomb.

If I were an Old Terran passing data to a Hatartalan, I'd have already passed it, hours ago, and there'd be nothing on me or in my quarters to prove the connection. So if I slipped into the Old Terran personal quarters, it would be easy to make up an excuse for being there, and I'd be able to read whatever I found, except there wouldn't be anything to find. Whereas if I searched the Hatartalan ambassador's private suite, I probably wouldn't recognize any compromising data, and I'd have one hell of a time explaining my presence.

So which way did I want to lose?

In the end, chance decided it for me. I circulated around the edges of the party until I saw a shadowy opening between two wall panels. The way to a private suite? To the Old Terran suite, if I was lucky. I slithered between the panels, trying to look like a glazed-over Boopsie looking for the facilities.

Three steps down the temp passageway, and I smelled rotten seaweed. Damn, wrong suite. I started to edge back when I heard an unmistakable voice rising above the high-pitched party chatter. "Girlfriend? What girlfriend? What diary?"

Old Terran twang, loud voice, crashing in with questions that didn't really need to be asked. Good old Jack.

It didn't, somehow, seem like a good time to reenter the party and keep circulating. I kept on the way I was going. Even if I didn't find anything in the Hatartalan quarters, at least Jack wouldn't find me there.

But I did. Find something, that is. Although it took me a moment to recognize the significance of it.

The Hatartalan module was lit in their preferred range of frequencies. To human eyes, everything looked dark red and hexagonal, comb upon honeycomb of storage and sleep and sitting modules all alike, all subdivided into hundreds of thousands of twinkling sub-compartments, all slightly sticky with the trail of personal markers the Hatartalan spray wherever they claim territory.

I'd edged right behind the Hatartalan ambassador at the party and had gotten a strong whiff of his personal spray—a bit on the gamy side, with overtones of musk and the usual rotten seaweed. No member of his entourage had a spray anywhere near so marked; they wouldn't dare. I followed the

seaweed-musk smell to a clutch of honeycomb formations
that stank so strongly of the ambassador, I couldn't even pick
out any competing scents. All the way my feet crunched and
squished on the debris of what must have been a pre-party
party. There were strands of the dried-seaweed stuff hanging
from the honeycombs, partially squished jellyeggs drooping
over edges like surrealist watches, bright scraps of ribbon and
tinsel and paper for nest building stowed in the pigeonholes
of one honeycomb and cascading down the side.

And there it was. Old Terran writing, Old Terran gaudy
red-bordered paper; the ambassador might have assimilated
the data into some waxen secretion, but he'd been too much
of a slob or a magpie, choose one, to throw away the original.

This would do it beautifully, a packet of notes in Jack's
handwriting and stinking of the ambassador's personal spray.
I clutched the treasure to my bosom while debating how to
sneak it out of the party. The clingy little black dress hadn't
offered many possibilities for concealment even before I
turned it into an off-the-shoulder number, and the jacket with
its inside zippered pockets was somewhere outside amid the
synthetic shrubbery.

A noise that was at once both question and annoying buzz
interrupted my silent debate about the ethics of the only
smuggling system I had been able to think of. I turned slowly,
because whatever made that noise sounded like something I
didn't want to annoy. It hovered at the level of my midriff,
gleaming, multifaceted, beautiful and deadly.

A bee-eye. Excuse *me*, I mean B.I., *Bacatus inaccessus*, as
our xenobiologists tagged it before realizing it was actually
the very rare and very elder last form in the Hatartalan life
cycle. *Inaccessus* not because it was rare, but because the first
two xenos to see one hadn't lived to do follow-up studies.
Bee-eyes take offense very, very easily.

How many Hatartalans made it from the standard adult
stage—the one the ambassador was in—to achieve B.I. status? Not more than one in a million, if the odds were anything like those against immature spawn making it to adult
stage. And who cared? The real question was, what were the
odds on me making it back the way I came, with or without
the stinking notes? Not good enough to make me want to try

calculating them. Still, there didn't seem to be any other reasonable move. Why didn't someone *tell* me the Hatartalans had a B.I. in the entourage? They're rare enough it should be hot news—unless they were keeping it secret for some reason—

Like entrapping little spies.

That was dumb, it would be like using a cannonball to shoot a mosquito.

I thought all this between one dry-mouthed gulp and the next, already shuffling sideways as if I thought the bee-eye would just let me go back the way I came. At the same time the bee-eye was responding to my body language and alerting itself. It spouted a column of shimmering scales that started in midair, about where it had floated originally, and lifted its faceted head (body? eye?) to my eye level.

"So sorry, looking for the ladies', must've lost my way," I jabbered, sidling toward the dark passageway some uncounted number of sticky steps behind me, "just go back to the party now, sorry to disturb you, senior gentlespecies . . ."

The bee-eye hummed once on a sharper note and zipped around me, blocking my retreat. Oh, well, I hadn't really thought it would be that easy. How long did it take for bee-eye venom to work on a small-sized human body? My graduate studies hadn't progressed far enough to go into such details before the scholarship fund ran out and I had to find a real job. At the time I'd thought myself lucky to get recruited by GIS. Who but the intelligence services would want an academic dropout with a minor in heuristic mathematics, a major in xenocultural studies, and a speaking knowledge of five alien languages in addition to Standard Galactic?

Just now I wasn't feeling so lucky. Nothing in my training—academic *or* intelligence—had covered how to deal with a life-form so rare and senior that none of my instructors had ever even seen one.

Stories, stories, dummy, I told myself. In times of stress we revert to old patterns. I wasn't *really* a spy. For that matter, I wasn't *really* a xenology student. Somewhere, way back there, I was still a skinny kid sitting in the central hall of Complex B449, telling stories to keep my little brothers happy whenever they shut off our vid service for nonpayment again.

You have to tailor your stories to the audience. My little brothers liked lots of violence and somebody killed every few minutes. . . . Woops, wrong line of thought. What did bee-eyes like? Nobody knew. Okay, what would ordinary Hatartalans expect and half believe before you started telling it? What were Hatartalan stories?

I wiped my one free hand on the skirt of the black dress and started in on the first idea that flashed on me; no second chances, this one had better work.[3]

Which it did.

The bee-eye personally escorted me down the access corridor and out through the party suite. With that level of support, I didn't really need to smuggle the papers out—I could have walked out clutching them in my hot little hand—but I thought it would be cooler if Jack didn't know exactly what I'd been there for until I'd had a chance to make delivery. As we reached the anonymous pile of coats and handbags and bodypockets I'd stumbled over coming in, I bent my knees and scooped up somebody's little black bag. It was just big enough to hold the notes, and I barely got them stuffed inside before the bee-eye's insistent buzzing warned me that I'd better keep moving.

People backed off to let us through. Jack was there, even redder in the face than last time; he recognized me and started to say something, but nobody—*nobody*!—interferes with a bee-eye, as the Hatartalans there made quite clear to him.

The bee-eye buzzed behind me until we reached a nice, well-lit multimodule intersection with an Andromedan gravity-well fountain sparkling through three stories of open space. Then it shrank down to its original podlike shape and zipped back to the Hatartalan module, while I went around a few levels and took a passenger pod through the Rigel-norm module and did all the usual things to shake any possible tails. With incredible self-restraint, I didn't even open the little black bag and take a second look at my find until I got back here to vox the report.

Now that's done, I'm going to have a nice long look at the rest of the stuff in the bag before returning it to Buffie. You wouldn't believe what that girl puts down in her diary!

● ● ●

"You left a few points out of your report," my supervisor commented.

I shrugged. "Once a graduate student, always a graduate student . . . Notice the little numbers? I was going to add footnotes, but you printed out the text before I got around to it."

"I suggest you add them. Now, before I pass it on."

Notes

1. I knew that already, of course. I'd studied pictures of both subjects before starting to work the case. The Hatartalan picture didn't help much—they all look alike to human eyes—but my buddy Jack, tall and paunchy and red-faced and given to unfortunately loud suits, was a snap to pick out of a crowd. It was a piece of extra luck that I got to "meet" him this way. Or so I thought at the time.

2. At least the Hatartalans are species-programmed for this behavior. What human story we tell that makes us want to trash our own worlds, I've never figured out.

3. Okay. You want to know what story? Simple. Humans tell Protecting the Young a lot. Hatartalans tell Destroying the Young (For the Good of the Race). Their natural bias is to let practically all of their spawn die so that only the fittest survive to the normal adult life cycle, right? And bee-eyes, the next life-cycle stage, are to normal adults as adults are to the insectoid spawn—one in a million or so. It seemed a credible assumption that bee-eyes would be programmed to destroy adults for any failing, rather than protecting them. I told the bee-eye that the Hatartalan ambassador had been caught selling secret data to the Old Terrans and that if I got the proof back to my bosses GIS would probably arrange a fatal accident for him. Of course, the facts were the other way around, but the bee-eye believed this story easily because it fitted the basic Hatartalan myth.

THE SMALL PENANCE
OF LADY DISDAIN

——————●——————

Michael Coney

"How sick is she?"

"She has a day to live, maybe two. She's very anxious to see you before she dies."

Hearing these words, he was ushered into the bedchamber of Lady Disdain, president of Earth.

"Imry Sanders." Painfully she extended a hand from under the covers. "It was good of you to come."

Her face was a mask of desiccated skin stretched tightly over the skull. Imry tried to reconcile this pale ruin with the face of Lady Disdain as he'd first met her in Hotel Andromeda—how long ago was it?—over two hundred years. She'd never been beautiful; she was too arrogant for that. But she had looked . . . aristocratic. Strong.

And God, how he'd hated her in those far-off days!

He looked around the room: the same sumptuous trappings she'd surrounded herself with in Hotel Andromeda. The rich tapestries, the deep rugs, the jade ornaments, the miniature peacocks, the royal blue and the purple. The scent of wild roses. All the badges of office. No sound; the fabrics deadened even her harsh breathing, transforming it to a sigh, so that for a moment he thought the elevator ride had blocked his ears.

He murmured something polite, taking the hand briefly, replacing it carefully on the covers. Why had this dreadful woman summoned him from his comfortable home on Secunda? Here on crowded Old Earth, trees grew only in designated wilderness areas and people lived in multilevel cities. He'd only lived twenty years on Earth, compared to two hundred years on Secunda. Secunda was home now. He resented being dragged away from it.

But you don't disobey a summons from the president of Earth.

"I'm sorry to hear of your illness, my lady." It was the only topic of conversation he could think of.

"I'm dying, yes, but that's not important. Death is in our genes for a purpose. My clone-sister Lady Fortune is ready to take over, now that the mindmeld has taken place. You met her outside, I believe."

Another moment of readjustment. The girl outside had been beautiful. Time was a killer. "She looked very young to be president of Earth."

"Only physically. The mindmeld has given her all my knowledge and experience. Well, Imry Sanders. You'll be wondering why I sent for you."

"It did cross my mind." He allowed himself a faint smile. The Froanways journey had taken almost three years; he'd had plenty of time to wonder, even allowing for in-flight retabolism.

The thin lips stretched slightly. Was that an answering smile? "You're not an easy man to locate. Secunda is somewhat . . . casual, shall we say, about personnel records."

"We like it that way."

"Yes, I can understand that." She sighed. "Your name has been known to me for two hundred years, ever since my entourage arrived on Earth. *Imry Sanders*, my deputy told me. *Imry Sanders was asking some odd questions.* The name haunted me. I kept waiting . . . waiting for it to appear again. It never did. For that I owe you a great debt. Perhaps all humans do. Only in the last ten years, when I knew my time was limited, have I tried to locate you. It took seven standard years. Now here you are, and I wish to thank you."

He stared at her. Lady Disdain wanted to thank *him*, a mere blipreader? This appalling old woman, product of an Earth-based project for genetic leadership material that produced only monstrous snobs with medieval titles, wanted to thank *him*? There had to be some mistake. What could he say? *I am unworthy.* No; he wouldn't sink to that kind of banality.

But what did she want to thank him *for*? What great deed did she think he'd performed? Was it—and he felt the beginnings of an enormous embarrassment—a case of mistaken identity?

"And I wish to bestow an honor upon you," she continued. "The honor is normally hereditary, but we must start making some exceptions, I think." She closed her eyes, looking suddenly exhausted. "There have been accusations of elitism," she murmured. "Perhaps they are right."

She seemed to be asleep. He walked over to the window and looked out at the city. Direct sunlight illuminated this room only; it rose clear of the glittering canopy of solar cells stretching to the horizon. It was ironic that in using the sun for power, Earth deprived people of its light. And not a tree, not a blade of grass in sight. Despite the warmth, he shivered.

Oh, to be on Secunda, walking with Megan among the tree-clad hills!

A cold anger gripped him. He swung back toward the dreadful figure on the bed. He didn't want her thanks; he didn't want her honor, whatever it was. He wanted to go home. He walked slowly to the bed. She looked very frail; it would be a simple matter to snuff out that guttering candle of life. A pillow over the face. He stood looking down at her. Behind that veneer of genteel sophistication, she was still the same bully who had thrown her weight about in Hotel Andromeda two hundred years ago, and caged up a shipload of Secundans like animals.

There had been more meat on her bones then.

He chuckled at the significance of that last thought, and the murderous moment passed.

•   •   •

Young Imry Sanders first met Lady Adelaide Disdain of Cartaginia shortly after being attacked by the girl gang from Secunda.

An hour earlier he'd ridden into the spaceborne vastness of Hotel Andromeda. The hotel scared him: the milling multitudes, the strange smells, the yelling voices, the blazing bright lights instead of good honest sunlight and trees and birds.

The decisions, too. A blaring voice suddenly drowned out the other noises, asking him to vote on an incomprehensible topic. "All humans please go to the nearest referendum booth and punch green if you are in favor of the proposition, red if not."

Imry had been raised in one of Earth's protected wilderness areas; spent the whole of his life preparing for this voyage. He was bound for Cartaginia, so they told him, where people lived in the open air in small towns surrounded by forests and grasslands.

And now here he was in Hotel Andromeda: covered, multilevel. He fought a deadly claustrophobia.

"You all right?" It was a young woman, about twenty standard years old—much the same age as Imry.

"I . . . I guess I'm surprised at this place. I've just arrived on the Earth shuttle." He felt better saying that. Imry Sanders, a genuine product of the mother planet. Not one of your Johnny-come-lately colonists. A founding father, in a way. And so, all by himself, he learned the first lesson of social intercourse between colonists: Make the most of your background. "I'm bound for Cartaginia," he added.

"I'm from Secunda, bound for Earth," she said surprisingly. Imry had been led to believe the inhabitants of Earth's first colony were little better than animals. Yet this girl looked good: pale gray jumpsuit, soft brown hair to her shoulders, slanting green eyes, wide mouth. And yet . . . was there a hint of wildness in those eyes? But when some goon pushed past her and knocked her against him, he didn't mind.

She smiled. "Sorry." She glanced behind him. A vast mob of people were surging out of the shuttle; they reached Imry and swirled him along like a breaking wave. The last he saw of the Secundan was a rueful grin as she was swept to the other side of a pillar.

"Come on, Imry!" shouted someone. "Let's get to know this place. There are four human modules docked right now!"

Six months of being cooped up in the shuttle had been too much for them, and some ten thousand human juveniles were about to run amok. Imry shrugged. Somebody would sort it out. He slipped away from the accents of Earth, and walked alone in Hotel Andromeda among humans and humanoids of all worlds.

Much later he found himself well away from the crowds. Not exactly lost, because there were maps stuck to all the pillars; a guy couldn't go far wrong. But he had a craving to find an *outside wall*; he needed some point of reference. All this vastness hanging somewhere in space was unreal and he needed something solid he could lean his back against. He craved trees and stone walls and rain drifting down from a real sky.

At last he found a narrow corridor leading off into the distance. For all he knew this was a connector, and space was on the other side of these walls. A window would have been nice. His feet were getting tired; there were no walkways here. A group of seven human-shaped figures approached from the opposite direction. He hoped they weren't from his shuttle. He'd had enough of the company of his fellow travelers for a while.

They were very young, slightly built, dressed in jumpsuits like the Secundan he'd met, but these jumpsuits were bright scarlet. There was an exuberance about them. He could hear them laughing, and one of them performed a complex dance step to unheard music. They looked like good company. They were all girls, maybe too young for him.

"Get him!"

Suddenly they were all around him, pulling at his clothes, clawing at his flesh, kicking him with shoes that looked uncommonly like leather. It was the shoes that decided him this was no playful romp. What kind of barbarians were these, to wear animal parts? He began to fight back in earnest, knocking one girl to her knees with a sweep of his arm. She looked up at him, and the expression on her young face chilled him.

There was an inhuman savagery there, and her chin was wet with saliva.

They had no weapons but their shoes—and their numbers. Seven of them, each one smaller than he, but together they were overwhelming. They fought silently with a deadly purpose and he didn't know what that purpose was. He didn't know exactly what he was defending himself against.

They'd torn his tunic from his shoulders, pinioning his arms. Now they dragged his pants down and one girl taller than the rest threw herself bodily against him. He fell backward over another girl crouched strategically behind. He was on the deck and they were all over him. He felt sharp nails scratch at his naked chest and teeth worrying at his shoulder.

"Stop! Stop that, right now!"

A gray-clad arm scythed down. The girl clawing at his chest grunted as a fist thudded into the side of her head.

"What the hell?" She stared up, feral eyes burning.

"I said stop! You've made a mistake, you fools. This is a man!"

"This is no man, Megan!"

"You're not on Secunda now. You're in Hotel Andromeda—things are different. You were warned, huh? But you didn't listen. I'll have you confined for this!"

A dark-haired girl, startlingly pretty, snapped, "You're the fool, Megan Sunrise. You're too damned old to know the difference." And she hooked her fingers into Imry's underpants, dragging them down and clawing parallel weals in his belly. Her eyes widened in astonishment.

"Satisfied?"

The girls were scrambling to their feet. "He *is* a man. But . . ."

"But he's so *thin*," said another. "He looks like a woman."

"He's young, too," said Megan harshly. "Hadn't you noticed that, either?"

"He's wearing green. The light's dim around here. We took him for a crone."

"If you'd killed him," said Megan, "Security would have had you recycled."

"No," said the beautiful dark child. "They can't recycle you for following the customs of your own race."

"They can if it results in the death of a member of a different race. This man's from Earth; I met him earlier. Now get going, and find yourself a Secundan crone, if you must!"

It was at that moment that Lady Adelaide Disdain arrived with her entourage.

●   ●   ●

One hour later, Lady Disdain, her entourage, Imry, and Megan were seated before Froan, head of Security.

"I told you this would happen," Lady Disdain said, "but you wouldn't listen. Now even the corridors of this hotel are not safe. I take a stroll and what do I come across? This innocent young man, barely twenty standard years old, being set upon and severely beaten by a gang of young animals from Secunda. If we hadn't happened by at that very moment, God knows what might have happened! Cannibalism, in the very halls of Andromeda!"

She stared at Froan, conscious of a dangerously rising anger. She *must* keep control of herself. She *must* remember that, to the security chief—to *it*—she was just another guest. But it was hard. This creature wasn't even human!

That wretched young woman in gray spoke before the alien could answer. "It was unfortunate, but I had it all under control. It won't happen again."

"How do you know that? How can you possibly know that, young woman? Where are the miscreants now, tell me that!" She felt herself flushing with temper and nudged her peacock. The garish bird's fantail fluttered, wafting a cool breeze.

At least the Secundan had the grace to look embarrassed. "I told them to get back to the shuttle and place themselves in confinement."

"Ha! What you're actually saying is they're still at large."

"They will obey orders. If you must know, we're confining all the bloomers. But honestly, Lady Disdain, I don't see what business it is of yours."

The impertinence of the girl! "I'll tell you what business it is of mine! This young man is a human, a representative of thousands of other humans on their way from Earth to my home planet. A blipreader, too. A member of an ancient and respected profession." She turned her gaze on the alien again. It was impossible to tell what that ghastly creature was thinking. "I *demand* that the appalling Secundans be confined to their vessel—every one of them—for the safety of us all!"

The young woman shouted, "You know why he's going to Cartaginia? Because you're so old and inflexible there that you've asked for an infusion of fresh blood! You're stagnating! Your birthrate is practically zero! And people like you are the reason why, you useless old woman!"

The impertinence of the girl!

The young man spoke. "Listen, I'm all right. Let's forget it, shall we?"

So much for gratitude! Lady Disdain bent a terrible stare on him. "Perhaps you don't realize what a narrow escape you've had. Are you aware that those Secundans are cannibals? They eat their own kind! It's in their culture."

He looked to the Secundan woman. "Is this true?"

She said, "Partly. In a way. But the only reason it's in our culture is because it's instinctive."

Hardly a valid excuse, thought Lady Disdain, "And because of *you*—you *barbarians*—the Froans will not pass the Gift of Longevity to Mankind. Because of your existence, billions of human beings are dying unnecessarily. Because of your disgusting behavior, Mankind as a whole is regarded as a race of savages—isn't that so, Froan?"

The alien spoke for the first time; and when it spoke, it spoke for its entire race. The Froans spoke but rarely because of the complex telepathic communication involved. The immense head shimmered crimson for an instant; the scaly jowls wobbled as the head nodded in deference to human gestures. "Yes," said Froan.

"I don't understand," said the young man from Earth. As young men went, thought Lady Disdain, he seemed quite a reasonable specimen and would fit in well on Cartaginia. . . .

So Megan Sunrise told Imry the terrible story of Mankind's first voyage to the stars, to Secunda. It's an old story and mercifully not well known, because humans have tried to put it behind them. Mankind's first starship was built centuries before the faster-than-light travel known as Froanways. It is said that the Froans gave Mankind the secret of Froanways simply because they didn't want any more Secundans around the galaxy. That is very likely true.

"You see, Imry," Megan said, "Earth was poor. Equipment was heavy and expensive. The voyage was to take many generations. Excess passengers could not be tolerated. By excess passengers, I mean old people . . . and men. So a special race of humans was bred."

"Disgusting!" shouted Lady Disdain. Her entourage, some twenty elderly humans, nodded their heads on feeble necks, murmured "Hear, hear", and prodded their peacocks into activity. The birds sat on their laps, small iridescent mutants bred for human use. The Cartaginians could not conceive the offense these bird fans—and their fur-trimmed clothes—caused Imry from Earth, where animals were sacrosanct.

Megan said quietly, "It all seems perfectly natural to us, so it's not nice to hear other people calling us names."

"I will call you what I like, young woman!"

Megan ignored her. "We have four age groups," she told Imry. "We have children, we have bloomers, we have parents, and we have crones. Much like any other human race, except we're nearly all females. We usually wear a color to show our age: blue for children, red for bloomers, gray for parents, and green for crones. We don't necessarily dress all in one color; just an indication is enough; a scarf or something. It's not really important until we get older, but it's become part of our culture. Like a national dress back in the old days of Earth." She sighed. "But all that's changing now. Our people are changing. Or maybe I should say they're being Revised." The green eyes were sad.

Lady Disdain shuddered theatrically. "It's bad enough that your kind of perversion exists. I see no reason to wash Mankind's dirty linen in front of this alien. Just shut up, will you, young woman? Now, Froan. It must be quite clear to you that those appalling Secundans represent a danger to any civilized race, is it not?"

The alien's voice was like a rasp against steel. "No, it is not. They are a danger only to humans. And humans are not a civilized race by our reckoning. We cannot solve your problem because it is a human problem. Lady Disdain, you are wasting the time of Hotel Security."

"My clone-sister is the president of Earth!"

"We are aware of your relationship to Emerald Kemp."

"Are you aware of the purpose of my visit to Earth? Of the president's sickness, and our need to mindmeld before she dies? The continuity of government depends on the mindmeld. Without it, there will be anarchy on Earth! And there will be no mindmeld if I am attacked and killed by cannibals in your hotel!"

"A human problem, you will agree."

"So you will not confine these creatures to their quarters?"

"You have made the same request three times in the last seven days, Lady Disdain. The answer is the same. It is not Security's problem."

Lady Disdain felt her cheeks flaming and her control slipping. Damn these all-powerful Froans and their so-logical arguments! "Listen to that, you humans. The Froans will not help. That tells you something about these creatures. You think they're benevolent because they gave us Froanways travel and promised us longevity. But it's not benevolence; it's politics! They're directing human development down the path they've chosen. In this way they maintain control and stifle other directions our development may take—directions that might have challenged their superiority!"

While the humans stared at her, stunned, Froan said, "It is Security that is refusing your request, not the Froans. Security is a multispecies organization."

"I don't see any other species around. There's just you!"

"Obviously the other species trust us to make rational judgments."

Lady Disdain rose. Her entourage rose. Peacocks fluttered. She glared at Megan. "I shall have to bring other forces to bear; that much is clear. I should have known better than to expect common sense from an alien." She transferred her gaze to Imry. "You're well advised to stay clear of this Secundan, young man. You heard what she said. You never know when her primitive instincts may come to the fore."

Imry found Megan walking beside him as he left Security. It seemed impolite to veer off and leave her; politeness had been instilled in him since birth, as a very necessary prerequisite to life on Cartaginia. He glanced at her. She held her head high but tears glistened in the brown eyes. Surely she'd never . . . eaten people? It was impossible.

He'd heard plenty of rumors about Secunda during this past few years while the Secundans were being shipped back to Earth for Revision. Earth alone had the technology and capacity for such a huge task. Quite simply, the Secundans were being transformed into normal humans, shipload by shipload, and then returned to Secunda.

And Megan's shipload was the last. Once she and her companions had been Revised, Froans would consider humans to be civilized.

And the Gift of Longevity would be theirs.

"All that stuff . . ." He hesitated. "About your age groups and what they do. It's not really like that, is it?"

She swung round, pink with anger. "It's exactly like that, and so what! Are you afraid I'm going to bite? Well, I'm past bloomer age, if that makes you feel any safer. But a lot of us . . . It's so unfair! What's wrong with disposing of people who are past contributing to society? What is wrong with bloomers being . . . involved in disposing of them? For us it must be *right*, because we can't have children until we've achieved hormony."

"Hormony?"

"You don't know anything, but you're so quick to judge, like everyone else! Hormony is the ability to have children. It disappears at the crone stage, just like it does in your race. But in our crones a dormant strain of hormones are still being produced, building up in the system. Before a bloomer can bear children, she must . . . ingest these hormones to achieve hormony."

"It's not your fault," said Imry.

She snapped. "There *is* no fault, don't you see? Somebody changed the rules on us, that's all. And the people who changed the rules are the people who made us in the first place. You Earth people!"

He looked away. She was right. She was beautiful, too. He wondered if Revision would change the way she looked. What a pity he was going to Cartaginia among all the old farts, instead of Secunda. . . .

"Sorry, Megan," he said at last. "But it was the Froans who made the rules, and now they bribe us to stick by them. And the bribe is too good to turn down."

"Yes. Well . . . I guess you don't want me around anymore." She turned away.

"No, wait a minute. Don't go, Megan. Give me a chance to come to terms with this. Anyway, you can't just leave me just like that. You saved my life. By the way, how did you happen to be around when I needed you?"

She hesitated, then offered a reluctant smile. "I . . . followed you."

This was much better. He took her hand. "Let's start again, shall we?"

So they explored Hotel Andromeda together and found more interesting things than Secundan culture to talk about.

"Longevity. Maybe four hundred years of life. Do you want it, Imry?"

Her gaze held his, and he felt a strange weakness inside. *Do I want to live that long?* he wondered. *Maybe, but I wish it wasn't going to be among those old farts on Cartaginia. A younger world would be nice. Like Secunda . . .*

And so, in the External Communications Room of Hotel Andromeda, he began to wonder if he was falling in love with a cannibal.

Interplanetary communication, as we now know it, grew out of a paradox. There was little point in Earth, for example, communicating with Hotel Andromeda at the speed of radio waves, because the Froanways ships themselves move very much faster. For a century or so this problem defeated humans, and messages were carried on board ships and shuttles like the mail on Old Earth. The Froans showed no inclination to help out. It was not their problem. They communicated with one another instantaneously, telepathically.

It was almost as though the Froans were testing Mankind's ingenuity.

Then one day, a bright young spark on Earth played around with two known facts about Froanways. Firstly, the great ships were driven through space by mental as well as physical methods from within the ships themselves. Secondly, the laws of inertia and momentum still applied: the rate of acceleration and deceleration depended on the mass of the ship. The heavier the ship, the greater the power needed and the longer it took to reach its destination.

Might it be possible to create a tiny ship, big enough to contain a message, that would operate on the same Froanways principle but move a billion times faster because it was a billion times smaller?

It was. These tiny messengers became known as blips.

Imry and Megan visited the External Communications Room. "Why does she call herself *Lady* Disdain?" asked Imry. His mind was elsewhere. As a blipreader, communications were his job and the External Communications Room was not particularly interesting.

A buzzer sounded, a tiny door flipped open, and a black object the size of a fist dropped into a tray. A white-suited human technician levered it open with a flat tool; the action reminded Imry of shucking oysters in the wilderness area where he'd been raised. The technician held the opened thing to his temple and appeared to be listening.

"Blip for Lady Disdain of Cartaginia," he announced to the room at large. "She'll be the new Earth president in a few months, I'll bet."

A man at the far end of the room called, "How many times do I have to tell you, Anders? The contents of personal blips are confidential, for Pete's sake. We don't go sounding off about them in front of the whole goddamned hotel!" He nodded toward Imry and Megan.

"Hell, it's only speculation. I didn't read the message," said the other sulkily.

"Sure. But speculating is the first step toward reading. I've seen it happen before. Just do your job and don't get too interested, huh?"

The blipreader, scowling, clicked the blip shut again, slipped it into a package, sprayed it with Lady Disdain's personal odor from the dispenser, and handed it to a messenger dog. The small drama was over.

"People on Cartaginia have hereditary titles like on Old Earth." Megan returned to Imry's question. "They're passed down from their first genetic leaders."

"Tough luck on the rest of the people," said Imry. "Does that mean I'll never get to be called Lord Imry?"

She laughed. "Is that your wish, my lord?"

"Well ... I'd like to think I had the chance. After all, what's an accident of birthplace got to do with anything?"

"What, indeed, Imry from Earth?" asked the cannibal. . . .

"I'm so sorry, Megan."

"She wants us locked up. Froan says it's a human matter. That means a referendum. She could call it anytime; maybe she's calling it right now. All people have to do is push a button and we'll be caged like animals."

"If the referendum goes against you."

"It will. There are four shiploads of Earth people in Andromeda, and nobody likes Secundans. It doesn't matter to them that we've already confined all our bloomers; they don't want to understand that. We moved into our Earth shuttle twenty hours ago, but it'll be a week before we're ready for departure. They won't let any of us out of that shuttle for a week."

He tried to make light of it. "A week's not so bad. Hell, the trip Earthside takes months."

"But it could have been a very nice week."

As she looked at him, he knew what she meant. And he knew she couldn't put it into words, because she was Secundan and—until Revision—tainted. And even after Revision, people would be looking at Secundans and thinking: *I wonder if she ever . . . You know what I mean?*

Then she added something he'd never thought of. "You're the first man I've ever talked to. We only have seventeen men on Secunda—great fat seed machines, lying on pillows and eating all day. Revolting. Are Earth Men all as nice as you?"

So as they left External Communications he was wondering if he was mistaken, and if her interest in him was simple curiosity born of the practice of artificial insemination on Secunda. Then he began to wonder if his interest in her was simple gratitude for having saved him from the girl gang. Two depressing items.

Such things come in threes. At that moment speakers all over the hotel boomed a message:

"A Human Referendum is being held at this time. The proposition is that members of the Secundan race constitute a danger to elderly humans and should be confined to Shuttle A-4 effective immediately, until its departure for Earth in approximately seven standard days."

"Don't you have a chance to defend yourself?" asked Imry desperately.

"What could we say? Nothing they'd listen to." She turned away. "Good-bye, Earth man. Good luck on Cartaginia. I . . . I really mean that."

She was going. He grabbed her, spun her around. Her face was wet with tears. "No! Let's hide somewhere!"

She tried to smile. "You've only just arrived. I've been here weeks. You'll find hiding isn't so easy in Hotel Andromeda as it is in an Earth wilderness. This place is just not built for ... for fugitives."

"Maybe nobody's needed to try before."

One hour later Lady Disdain of Cartaginia faced Froan yet again, chin high, expressionless as only a self-admitted fool can be.

"I wish you to cancel the confinement of the appalling Secundans immediately."

The alien regarded her blandly. "You surprise me, Lady Disdain."

"That is neither here nor there. Cancel the confinement, please."

"Perhaps you'd care to tell me why."

Really, thought Lady Disdain, it was no business of Froan's. It was absolutely disgraceful the way these wretched aliens threw their weight about—just because they happened to have been first to invent FTL travel. However, there was no harm in telling it. That might even speed matters up. "I've just received a blip from Earth. My clone-sister is president of Earth, you know."

If sighing had been a Froan characteristic, Froan would have sighed. "I do know."

"Her condition had worsened. As you know, her sickness is the whole reason for my voyage. I must mindmeld with her before she dies. I am to be the next president of the Earth."

"Congratulations."

Was that sarcasm? Surely not! "It is distressing news. She's on retabolism, but even so, it's doubtful that she can last six months. And my shuttle does not depart for another two months. Every day counts, Froan."

"So it seems. I would suggest that you travel with the Secundans, Lady Disdain. Their shuttle leaves in seven of your Earth days."

Good grief, was the creature utterly stupid? "They have cannibals running wild on that shuttle! You know the Secundan problem as well as I do, Froan. I wouldn't last a day!" *Crone*, that was the word those barbarians used. How insulting!

"Certainly it could be dangerous for a human woman past the age of usefulness."

So Froan, like that Secundan girl, had no idea of the contribution older and more experienced people made to human society. Its ignorance was abysmal. Was there any point in arguing with this creature? "I want those Secundans off that shuttle, Froan! I'm commandeering it for myself and my entourage. This is an emergency!"

"Hotel Security will not prevent your commandeering the vessel. It is a human matter."

"How do I get those Secundans out of there? I want your help, you fool!"

"I cannot help, but you may have my advice. Hold another referendum."

"That would be pointless. The human guests in Andromeda have no reason to vote any differently than they did in the referendum we held yesterday—as you know very well, Froan! Nobody likes the Secundans, and rightly so!"

"That is true."

The silence lengthened. Didn't the wretched alien have anything further to contribute? The Security HQ for this sector of Andromeda was quite small, and Froan was the only person on duty. The other four desks were empty. Where was the human representative, for Heaven's sake? A human would have understood her problem.

But as Froan had said earlier: the other security chiefs probably left everything to Froan. Froan wasn't just one person, it was thousands. Maybe millions, all in continuous contact. Froan could bring unlimited intellect to bear on any security problem. It was desperately unfair. It made nonsense of democracy. Some kind of compensations should be built into the system to limit the power of the Froans.

"There is another way," she said reluctantly.

"That must be a relief for you, Lady Disdain."

She hated to ask this; it sounded perilously like begging. "You could bestow longevity on my clone-sister right now. A special dispensation. Really," she continued quickly, sensing the refusal trembling on the alien's peculiar labia, "I can't think of a better person than Earth's president to be the first human to receive your great gift. There is a Froan representative on Earth; the matter could be dealt with quite simply, immediately. It needn't actually be longevity; she need only live long enough for us to carry out the mindmeld. Nobody else need know."

"You know my reply already, Lady Disdain. The existence of the Secundans offends us. We allowed you to enter Froanways so that you would not feel the need for further such adventures into genetic engineering. And we cannot bestow longevity on you until the last Secundan is Revised. That time is not far away."

"It's a year away! Six months in the shuttle, almost as long for Revision. My sister will be dead long before then!"

"I am sorry, Lady Disdain."

Immediately below the External Communications Room in Hotel Andromeda is a chamber of roughly similar size where the little blipriders are housed. At the time of our story, the longest journey undertaken by a blip was two years, dictated by the life span of the bliprider. Nowadays the use of blips has increased tenfold because Froan longevity can also be applied to blipriders. Blipriders are small rodents whose limited mental capacity is occupied almost entirely in applying the Froanways principle to their tiny craft, and in remembering the message with which they are entrusted.

"But how do you *read* the blip?" asked Megan Sunrise. "Could I do it if I tried?"

"Maybe, if you had the right training. The messages aren't in words. They're in images. The trick is in knowing the way the bliprider's mind works. You have to *think* like a bliprider. Otherwise you can't understand the message. You might hear it mentally, but it'd be in mouse images, kind of."

They'd chosen the blipriders' quarters as their hideout for the next few days. Humans visited it rarely; the blipriders were fed and cared for by robotic servants. It was an interesting place to be, too. Blips arrived frequently; either sent down the chute from the room above, or brought in by messenger dogs. Megan was concerned about the dogs.

"Couldn't Security locate me by giving my scent to a messenger dog? They have everyone's scents on file."

"I don't think they're that interested. You're only one of several hundred thousand humans in the hotel. Security have got enough on their minds without bothering about one Secundan who's past the bloomer stage anyway."

"I suppose you're right. And anyway, they probably haven't even noticed I'm not aboard the shuttle. We're not noted for keeping close tabs on one another, we Secundans. We value our freedom."

"In that case, why go to Earth at all? Why not stay here with me?" Imry was being selfish and he knew it. He'd be leaving Hotel Andromeda himself before long. But they were nearing the end of their seven days together and he was getting desperate. They'd furnished an alcove with blankets and slept there when they were tired, made love when they were not. Occasionally he ventured alone into the public areas of the hotel to get food, returning as soon as he could, terrified that he would find her gone.

"You know I must leave with the others, Imry. The Froans are keeping count. There'll be no longevity for humans until all Secundans are Revised. I couldn't be responsible for that. Could you?"

"I guess not. No." As he looked at her there was a dreadful emptiness inside him. He thought of Cartaginia and its class system; in his imagination there would be a Lady Disdain lurking behind every tree. Was longevity such a good thing, if he was doomed to live on a world like that?

But on the last day matters took a turn for the better. He'd gotten into the habit of reading the minds of used blipriders as they arrived for dememorizing, to keep up to date with events. Most of the blips were from Earth; there were few other worlds accessible within the blipriders' life span. If the bliprider was elderly it would be sent to the euthanasia chamber after delivering its message; if young, it would be dememorized and used again.

"I'm surprised the Froans agree with the gas chamber," said Megan on one occasion, as a little brown rodent scampered unknowing to its death.

"I don't think they're interested in unintelligent life-forms. To them a mouse is no different from a carrot. It's there to be used. Civilization is everything to the Froans."

"That's why they're against us Secundans," said Megan sadly.

On that last day, as they lay together in their alcove and tried to spend their final hours in love instead of despair, they heard the door hiss open and a messenger dog came trotting in.

"Here, boy!" Imry held out a morsel of protein. The dog dropped the container. Imry opened it up, took out the little mouse and held it to his temple.

Megan watched his expression change from apathy to excitement. "What is it?"

"It's a message to Andromeda Dispatch from the president of Earth. My people aren't going to Cartaginia after all. We're catching an earlier ship to Secunda instead!" He hugged her. "Isn't that great! We'll see each other again!"

"In a few years." A lot could happen in that time.

"But we'll have longevity by then! What does a couple of years matter, when we've got hundreds together?"

"You'll get tired of me, Imry. We're different people."

He regarded her. It was difficult to imagine tiring of her, but then it was difficult to imagine living for four hundred years. "I'll never get tired of you," he said stoutly.

Two hours later she was gone.

Imry remained in the chamber for another two days, trying to think positively. With retabolism on the voyage, he would be seeing Megan again in less than two years' apparent time. That wasn't so bad, was it? And on Secunda, too. It was good not to be going to Cartaginia.

But why wasn't he going to Cartaginia?

He began to wonder. Why the change in plan? Their training program had prepared everyone for Cartaginia; for the climate, the culture, the laws, and the social aspect generally. Secunda was a different world. Much less formal, less regimented. And Cartaginia itself had spent years preparing for a sudden influx of immigrants. Secunda had not. What exactly were they supposed to be *doing* on Secunda?

As he was puzzling it over, a dog came trotting in. From force of habit now, it dropped the blip at Imry's feet and stood panting, tongue lolling, waiting for its reward.

The blip had been for Lady Disdain.

Imry absorbed the contents with disbelief and finally, fear. Hand shaking, he held the rodent to his temple again, with the same result. Something was terribly wrong. He found himself staring into the little animal's eyes, willing it to explain more fully. It stared back with beady stupidity. It had no idea of the significance of the message. . . .

This blip was several days old.

The blip diverting Imry's people to Secunda had been sent *after* this blip.

It might already be too late to save the Secundans.

And Megan.

"You must recall the Earth shuttle!"

Froan regarded Imry imperturbably. "Why is that?"

"Please believe me; it's important. Life and death!"

"The shuttle is beyond the jurisdiction of Hotel Security. And as you know, shuttles do not operate on the Froanways principle. The Earth shuttle is controlled remotely from the home planet."

There was still a chance. Blackmail. That terrible message was his weapon. Yes, a blip from Lady Disdain would overtake the shuttle. It took Imry an hour of fighting his way along crowded walkways to reach her quarters.

"She is not here at present," said a handmaiden.

"Then summon her, right now! Tell her it's top priority! Tell her . . ." He searched for suitable words. One thing he didn't want to do, was to reveal his knowledge to anyone else. That would back Lady Disdain into a corner. It was important that she should be free to act. "Tell her I'm Imry Sanders the blipreader, and there's been a terrible mistake. Tell her I'm hoping we can put things right without bringing in the Froans."

The handmaiden left. Imry sat down, trying to work it out, running over in his mind the contents of that fateful, so confidential blip. The images in the mouse's mind were clear and horrifying; so clear that he could still see them in his mind's eye.

Destruction. The Earth shuttle close to its destination, then veering off course; the crew struggling with the controls, unable to override the automatics. The interior heating up. The Secundans screaming as their flesh began to melt. Their very screams broiling their lungs. The shuttle plunging on into the furnace of the sun. All this was in the mouse's mind.

Placed there by another mind infinitely cruel, infinitely mad.

The handmaiden returned with a tall man robed in purple. "Lady Disdain is not available. I am empowered to act on her behalf. How can I help you?"

This was something he hadn't thought of. He'd assumed he'd be dealing with the woman herself. Well, there wasn't time to fool around; he'd have to make the most of what was available. "Are you her Number Two?"

"On this voyage I am."

"I must speak to you alone."

"If you like." He led the way to a small anteroom.

"Are you sure nobody can hear us?"

The man smiled condescendingly, humoring him. "Nobody. This place is safe, so Hotel Security assures me. Now. What's all this about?"

He took a deep breath. This was going to be tough going. "You must recall the Earth shuttle immediately."

"Oh. Must I?" The thick eyebrows rose. "Tell me why."

"I have information that it is in danger."

"Information?"

"A blip from the president of Earth to Lady Disdain." He would have to commit himself if he was to get any action. "I read it." He could still hardly believe it. "They're going to massacre the Secundans!"

The man's face was impassive. "You've been reading confidential blips illegally. You're the one who'll be reported to Security. You could be thrown out of your guild, you understand? Don't you have any professional pride?"

"That's hardly the point!" Was the man stalling, or was he on the level? "Don't you know what was in that blip?"

"Nobody knows except my lady herself," he snapped. "If there *was* a blip, which I doubt. She's a blipreader; you must know that. All the top people have to be, for the sake of confidentiality. Blips between heads of state are composed and read by heads of state alone. They may be confidential, but they do not contain massacre plots."

Obviously Lady Disdain wouldn't have leaked the contents of the blip to her entourage, or anyone else, for that matter. "Listen." He tried to convey in words the terrible images of destruction contained in the bliprider's message. Sensing the other's skepticism, he added, "You wouldn't want me to tell Security what the blip said, would you?"

But the man was treating the whole thing as Imry's juvenile fantasy. "A conspiracy? Certainly it would dispose of the Secundan problem neatly, but why not simply Revise them on Earth, according to the original plan?" He sat down, relaxing, smiling up at Imry.

"Because Lady Disdain must get to Earth for the mindmeld before the president dies. And the next shuttle doesn't leave for weeks!"

"Killing the Secundans wouldn't get my lady to Earth any more quickly."

"It wouldn't matter. Once all the Secundans are dead, the Froans will grant us longevity. That'll give the president a couple more years, no matter how sick she is!"

The Cartaginian laughed shortly. "We could kiss good-bye to longevity if we murdered the Secundans to suit our own ends. The Froans would wash their hands of us forever. Surely even you can see that!"

"It would look like an accident. An equipment malfunction; the shuttle pulled into the sun."

The Cartaginian stood. "All right, that's enough. I just hope nobody else has heard this stuff. You could do a lot of damage, spreading these kinds of rumors. We're going through a very sensitive period in our relations with the Froans. We don't need some kid blipreader fouling things up."

"At least get hold of Lady Disdain right now so she can explain the blip!"

The Cartaginian said slowly, spelling it out, "My Lady Disdain doesn't have to explain anything to you, or even to me. She is the ruler of Cartaginia. She is the president's clone-sister. She is the future president of Earth. And in any event I can't get hold of her, because she's on that shuttle herself, bound for Earth."

Imry felt his stomach turn over. "Lady Disdain's on that shuttle?"

"Of course she is. How else can she get to Earth in time for the mindmeld? Naturally she didn't relish traveling with the Secundans—who would? But she is devoted to her duties and the human race, so she had little choice. There was no room for myself and the entourage at such short notice, but I can't say I'm sorry about that."

Imry struggled to come to terms with this. Lady Disdain on

the shuttle herself? It seemed he'd made a complete fool of himself. He'd been so *sure*. "But . . . does the president know Lady Disdain's on the shuttle?"

"My Lady sent a blip informing her, before she left. So I'd say everybody's quite safe from your hypothetical accident."

Imry left as soon as he could, face burning. God, what a fool he'd made of himself! There was only one good thing come out of this disaster. Megan was safe.

Irrationally, he found himself hating Lady Disdain more than before. It was almost as though she'd duped him in some way.

It was only when he got back to the bliprider's quarters that the thought occurred to him: maybe he *had* been duped. He only had the Cartaginian's word that Lady Disdain was on that shuttle.

But when he checked with Dispatch, her name was on the passenger list. That settled it. Now the only thing to do was to forget the whole embarrassing episode. He'd screwed up, but nobody knew except that Cartaginian. In some way he'd completely misread the blip. Or maybe it had been some weird blipreader's hoax.

And now Lady Disdain's eyes were open again, watching him. Had she read his mind? No, but she'd experienced a life-time of enemies, which made her hypersensitive to hostility. Her lips moved.

"You can't imagine the relief now that Lady Fortune and I have melded. I've shared a mindful of ancient skeletons and eased the burden. And now I can think and say whatever I like, without the fear of passing on my thoughts and conver-sations for analysis and condemnation. My mind is my own, not posterity's. I'm free for the first time in my life."

"You must be very relieved to know the future of Earth is in capable hands." It was difficult to imagine that pretty girl bore all the dark secrets of this old crone. Crone? That word hadn't crossed his mind in two hundred years.

Her gaze became very direct. "I *hope* it is in capable hands. As you alone know, there is a flaw in the genes of us clone-sisters, and there is a shame we will carry with us as long as we exist, because the mindmeld ensures we can never forget it. Our only consolation is that when *you* are dead, the flaw will be known only to the clone-sisters. I am forever in your debt for that. But you are well aware of that."

What was she talking about?

He said, playing for time, "We're all flawed in one way or another."

"But we rulers were bred for perfection. They tell me you still live with Megan Sunrise, and that you have eight children. It must be very reassuring to blend your genes with those of another person, and know that some of the imperfections will be lost in the process."

"We never think of it that way."

"Megan Sunrise once told me I was a useless old woman. At the time I resented her remark very much. But when the . . . *thing* happened, and I found myself living with a shipload of Secundans for six months, I began to think. I saw Secundan crones going willingly to their death for the immediate good of their race, and I contrasted that with the way my own clone-sister had acted—or would have acted, if I hadn't forestalled her. And I realized *we* are the useless ones. We, my clone-sisters and I, the rulers of worlds. We are parasites feeding on the work of humans in the pretense that we are leading them. But neither Earth nor Cartaginia need leading. They are stable societies that run themselves."

When you've had a fixed notion for two hundred years it's difficult to shake it. Imry turned to the window in case she read the amazement on his face. Lady Disdain's clone-sister, the president of Earth, had done something terrible, it seemed. Something so terrible that it meant the genetic structure of the rulers was flawed.

What could be that terrible?

Ordering the mass murder of ten thousand Secundans could be that terrible!

Had he been right after all, two hundred years ago?

He turned back to face her. "Tell me one thing, my lady." Suddenly he could bring himself to call her that. "Why did you take the Secundan shuttle to Earth?"

She looked at him expressionlessly for a long time, but her eventual words showed astonishment. "Good heavens, you had it wrong. And still you didn't betray us . . . I took the Secundan shuttle so that my sister could not destroy it, of course. She hated the Secundans—they stood between her and a chance of longevity. She was dying and she was desperate—so desperate that she could not foresee the consequences of her actions. She threw three worlds into confusion by reassigning you people to Secunda, with some stupid notion of atoning for the Secundans she intended to kill. She risked sending a blip to warn me, to make sure I wasn't killed as well. At least she showed that much sense of duty, preserving the mindmeld. But otherwise . . .

"She betrayed everything she'd been created for and lived for, simply out of a primitive fear of death. She was mad, didn't you know that? My biggest fear was that she was so mad she'd destroy the shuttle anyway, with me on board.

"When I reached Earth we mindmelded, and ever since then I've lived with a small cancer of madness in my head—her madness. I killed her immediately after the meld. It was quite easy; I won't go into the details. Her madness was so fresh in my mind I found I could be primitive, too. It wasn't murder; she was my clone. It was more like lopping off a diseased branch."

Imry said, "I doubted my own reading of the blip. When you took the shuttle, I thought it was simply your quickest way home."

She smiled. "You hated me, didn't you? I don't blame you. A ruler has to be seen to be a ruler, and you don't make friends that way. You hated me, but the reason you didn't betray us was because you had no confidence in your own judgment. Well, it's as good a reason as any."

"Blipreading's an art more than a science. And I was young. And I was so glad Megan was safe that I put the whole thing behind me. And suddenly we were all going to Secunda instead of Cartaginia. That was the clincher. Why didn't you countermand your sister's instruction and send us to Cartaginia anyway? It was what we were trained for."

"That was a shameless bribe. And unnecessary, as it turns out."

"Your sister might have gotten away with it," he said wonderingly. "She wasn't so mad that she wouldn't have covered her tracks. You knew that. So . . . You risked your life for the Secundans, didn't you?"

"Dreadful people! But there's a world of difference between locking people up for a week, and massacring them.

The voyage was my small penance for my clone-sister's sins."

"I'm sorry I misjudged you, my lady."

"So I needn't have told you all this. And I don't need to bestow an honorable title on you."

He laughed. Suddenly she was more like an old friend. An old friend who had once saved Megan's life. "But I know everything now."

"Who would believe you? That bliprider was the only proof you had, and it's been dead over two hundred years. And I thought you'd had it retabolized, and would produce it one day."

Imry gave a theatrical sigh. "So I'll never be Lord Imry of Secunda?"

He heard a breathless cackle. Lady Disdain was laughing. "Go and see Lady Fortune about that," she said. "Her memories are identical to mine since the meld. All except the last hour while you and I have been alone. I'm sure you take my meaning."

Imry touched her dry hand and left.

Lady Disdain closed her eyes. It was done. Her life was tidied up, so far as any human life could be tidy, and night was not far away.

RHUUM SERVICE

—————●—————

Brad Ferguson

"Marvelous," said Chaylaifa, his breath finally coming back to him. He was on his back, smiling; his tail was comfortably wrapped around his left thigh, out of the way.

The *chosha* was not smiling at all, but she nodded agreement. "Excuse me for a moment, Chaylaifa," she said.

"Of course," he said. The *sha* watched her by the dim light as she left their bed and headed for the bathroom. *Nasu still cuts a fine figure,* he thought idly, *particularly for someone of her years. I chose well, so long ago. She is both good company and a good friend ... and she still provides this old warrior with a stout enough ride, willing as she is to try new things—*

"Chaylaifa?" came a small, high voice near the foot of the bed.

"Ah," he said. "Still with us, eh, my dear? Ha! Come a little closer."

She did. "I thought you'd forgotten all about me."

87

"Not possible. Did you doze off?"

"Just for a moment. It has been a long day." The *thaka'thott* rolled across the sweat-stained sheets of the strongly built bed and snuggled like a youngling into Chaylaifa's pelt. Fehlorah ran a paw through the matted fur on the *sha*'s chest, her slightly extended claws barely grazing the sensitive skin beneath.

"I am glad the Bloxx was delayed," she breathed.

"So am I," Chaylaifa replied. "I had to appear angry for the benefit of our agents here, but I did not expect such a pleasant ... respite ... on the first day of the talks."

"A most welcome respite. It's such an exciting trip, isn't it?"

"Are you glad I brought you, girl?"

"Of course, Chaylaifa! Ever so glad!"

The *sha* smiled. "Now just how glad might *that* be?"

Fehlorah smiled in a way far beyond her years. "Very glad, my *sha*. Has the *chosha* left anything for me?"

Chaylaifa laughed softly. "You know she has, little witch," he said. He sighed in mock exasperation. "How can such a one, small as you, destroy me again and again, time after time, endlessly? You'll kill me yet, girl."

"*I* kill *you*?" Fehlorah's paw began making its own, slow way down Chaylaifa's ample body, in the way she had so recently learned that he liked the most. "More likely it will be the other way 'round; I'll be crushed under you—or between the both of you. A sad yet wonderful fate indeed."

"You're much too spry to be caught like that, Fehlorah." He ran the tips of his powerful claws along the stripe of gray fur covering her spine, and the *thaka'thott* shivered as her immature tail began twitching.

"You like that," he said in a low voice.

"Very much," she breathed. "And you?"

"What you've begun doing down there feels very good, my little love."

"Now, just how good might *that* be?" she asked him, laughing, as Chaylaifa's breath began to hiss softly back and forth through his teeth.

A few moments later the bathroom door opened, throwing a bright golden light into the room. Nasu stood in it, a silhouette.

"Come back to bed, Nasu," Chaylaifa called. "We've grown a bit impatient for you here—as you might be able to tell."

"Yes," Fehlorah said, reaching out a dainty paw. "Come to us, Nasu. Be with us."

"I . . . I think I might like to retire for the evening," Nasu said, knowing what was to come; she had no wish to repeat the vileness of it. "It has been a tiring day. I will sleep in the room assigned to me—"

"Nonsense," said the *sha*, his tone suddenly harsh. "Come to bed, here and now. And turn out that damned light; the one in here is quite enough."

"Chaylaifa, I—"

He looked at her, his eyes holding her completely. After a moment, Nasu looked away and nodded.

"Excellent." As Nasu seated herself at the foot of the bed, Chaylaifa reached behind him and retrieved a small box from the nightstand.

"What's that?" asked Fehlorah.

"It is a Terran delicacy, love. They are called *ritzcrackas*, and I am assured that they are safe for us. Expensive, as is everything else aboard this hotel, but I thought we might try them. They are something . . . different." He grinned widely, showing his fangs. "After all, we have to fortify ourselves for the rigors ahead! *Ha!*"

Fehlorah giggled and, reaching over the *sha*, took a *ritzcracka* for herself and passed another to Nasu. The *chosha* ate it, chewing slowly. Fehlorah saw her reluctance and giggled again as she turned to embrace Chaylaifa.

After a short while Nasu joined with them, her unwillingness quickly evaporating as their shared scent rose, engulfing her, trapping her.

The tastefully small brass sign on the door of the suite read:

```
JACOBS & BURKE, LTD.
      FACILITATORS
```

The reception area had been furnished by a Centaurian designer known for her terribly trendy and effectively audacious approach to everything she did. Wallpaper and furnishings had been designed to intrigue a wide variety of senses, and fabrics had been chosen to appeal as broadly as possible to those to whom touch and smell were as sound and light. To prove that price had been no object, there was an original Sunday-edition full-color Calvin and Hobbes hanging over the *faux* fireplace, which itself radiated in a variety of spectra. The look and feel of the room had instantly established the credibility of Jacobs and Burke aboard Hotel Andromeda, and that credibility had been the key to everything.

The other half of the suite was hidden behind a door concealed in the far wall of the reception area. Between them, the partners called it the Dark Side, and it looked as if it had been decorated by trolls. The Dark Side was the soundproofed and spy-proofed office where Jacobs and Burke actually did their work, and no one else ever got in there. The partners allowed the hotel's cleaning robots into the Dark Side only once every six months or so. Even at that, they never let the robots do very much, frantic that something important, some significant scrap of paper, might be snatched up and thrown away. The partners were also terrible pack rats. For example, one of the Terran calendars on the wall was four years out of date, but the partners left it hanging there because it would be good again in only another seven.

Jonathan Lee Jacobs was sitting at his desk in the Dark Side, his head in his hands. "I guess what I don't appreciate the *most*," he complained, "is that this crap always gets sprung on us at the last possible goddamn *minute*."

His partner had not really heard him. Trudy Burke was lying back in her reclining chair. Her eyes were closed. She was very busy.

Jacobs grabbed his most abused pencil of the day and began tapping a rapid tattoo on the glass surface of his desk. "*First* I get absolutely *no* notice that Bannister Investments is exercising its option with us, this after we don't hear from those bloodsuckers for *years*, so we have to handle the Rhuum trade reps for them as long as they're aboard Andromeda. So, fine. We say hello and how are you, we get Ambassador Chaylaifa and his entourage settled, all twenty-three of the useless bastards, we make sure the hotel is treating everybody right, all that jazz. We even get a break on the logistics—no arrival ceremonies and no dinners, thank God; neither side wants 'em. Good enough. *Now* it turns out that the Bloxx rep is going to be late because, hot pilot he, he's blown a driver. Not a big deal, but somehow this idiot Chaylaifa thinks it's *our* fault! Before I can even *talk* to him about it, though, he stalks off to his room with his wife and kid in tow. This is supposed to be an *easy* contract? Isn't *that* what Bannister said?" He sighed and rubbed his eyes. "Damn. These micro-contacts are killing me."

His partner still said nothing.

Jacobs cleared his throat and tried again. "I hear they can rot your corneas."

Trudy remained quiet.

"Well?" Jacobs demanded as his pencil finally broke. He brushed the two halves onto the floor.

" 'Well' what?" Trudy answered. Her tone was lazy, distracted. "Do you want something, Jonny Lee? I'm trying—"

"I know, I know. I'm *bothering* you." Jacobs waved a hand. "Sorry. Find out anything yet?"

"Come on in, and I'll show you what I've isolated so far."

"All right, but let's not take too long. We've got *things* to do." Jacobs ordered his own chair to recline and, still tense but reasonably comfortable, he accessed the neural network.

The office was suddenly replaced by a garden. It was a different garden, though, smaller and prettier than Trudy's usual interface metaphor. There was a short picket fence around the plot, and from somewhere not far off came the sounds of children at play; Jacobs could also hear birds. Turning around, he saw a small, neat, white house. His view of anything farther away was blocked by tall hedges ringing the property.

"This is very nice," Jacobs said, and he meant it. "Someone's backyard, right?"

"My grandmother's, as a matter of fact," Trudy said. "I've been working on it for a while. Do you really like it?"

Jacobs looked up at the clear blue sky. "Very much. Where are we?"

"Pennsylvania—the nice part. I spent a lot of time here after Mother and Daddy split up." Trudy gestured around her. "Grandmother's garden was my favorite place of all, especially at this time of year, when I'd help her get it into shape after the winter; it's mid-April here now, in case you couldn't tell from the flowers. The other gardens I wrote were just practice; I wanted to get *this* one right."

Jacobs looked around. "I think you did. It's beautiful. I wish I'd met your grandma. Is she here?"

"Oh, God, no, Jonny Lee!" Trudy said, disconcerted. "I couldn't write *her*! No, we're the only ones here—and we ought to get down to business. You were in a mad rush, remember?"

"I guess I was. Hey, looky here." Jacobs bent and picked up an insect. He held it lightly between his fingers and grinned. "Hey, honey, your program's got a—"

"Don't you *dare* say it."

"Shoot. All right, I won't." He stooped to let the thing drop safely to the ground and watched as it skittered away. "What have you got for me?"

Trudy bent quickly and picked a daffodil. "First of all, here's the summary of the deal Bannister says Ambassador Chaylaifa wants to strike with the Bloxx," she said, handing him the flower. "The wish list has pharmaceuticals, minerals, and other standard stuff on it; Bannister's given us the quantities desired and what Chaylaifa intends to offer for them in goods and credits standard. Chaylaifa runs the biggest import trust in the Rhuum Organization, so this deal could mean billions of creds stan to him personally. Bannister Investments is brokering it, so they get the usual huge cut."

"All right," Jacobs said, sniffing at the flower. As he did, his mind filled with the details of what he needed to know. "Seems to pass the smell test. The Rhuum bids are low, but that's why traders get together and haggle. Okay, no problem so far. Now, what have we got on the clients?"

Trudy picked another flower—a hyacinth this time. "First of all, here's what the neural net has on the Rhuum," she said. "It's a condensation of a survey report done about fifty years back."

"A little history, and that's it," Jacobs said, sniffing again. "Pretty damned condensed, if you ask me."

"There's not much in the extended survey report, either," Trudy said. She picked a perfect tomato from a nearby vine and handed it to Jacobs.

"This is out of season, isn't it?" he asked.

"I needed an analogue you might be able to handle, O ye

of common tastes. Anyway, the report is largely technical; you probably won't want to eat all of it."

"We'll see about that." Jacobs bit into the tomato, and juice dribbled down his chin. Suddenly, his eyes bulged. "Ugh muff mughh," he said.

"Problem?" Trudy asked sweetly.

"Gluph fwu." Working hard, Jacobs chewed slowly and then more slowly still before giving up. It was like chewing lead. Turning aside politely, he spit into a convenient bush.

"Warned you," Trudy said. "I didn't get much further into it than that myself."

"We'll hire an expert to come up with a summary," Jacobs said. "Anything else?"

"That's it. There's considerably more material on the Bloxx, though." Trudy handed Jacobs a big bowl of salad makings and a pair of wooden forks. "Here. You toss, I'll serve."

"I wish you'd find another metaphor," Jacobs said. "I *hate* salad." He began to mix the contents of the bowl.

Trudy suddenly looked distant.

Jacobs knew that look. "What is it?" he asked.

"You're going to hate this, too," Trudy replied. "The Bloxx fixed that busted driver of his. He'll be here in about an hour."

"Oh," Jacobs said. "We'd better get out of here; I still have to shave. Damn, I *hate* being pushed on things like this."

Jacobs and Trudy waited in the reception bay for the arrival of the Bloxx craft. It dropped out of hyperspace on schedule and achieved rendezvous without incident. Being relatively small, the ship made its own way into the parking bay as disappointed robot tugs scuttled out of the way. Robot valets, their headlights blinking on and off in a pattern of welcome, quickly came into position, bumping into each other in their programmed eagerness.

"I love watching this," Trudy said. "The 'bots are so *cute*."

"Umph. My tie knotted okay?"

"For the twelfth time, yes. Oops—green light. *That* was fast."

The airlock to the parking bay slid open, and there stood a

tall, muscled man with the reddest hair Jacobs and Trudy had ever seen.

"Sir Kethrommon?" Jacobs asked, as if there could be any doubt. "Do you speak trader talk?"

"That I am and that I do," he said, nodding. "You the contacts Bannister was talking about?"

"Yes, m'lord, we are. I'm Jonathan Lee Jacobs, and this is my partner Trudy Burke. As you've surmised, we represent Bannister Investments—"

"Bunch of crooks, them. Hope you're not the same. If you're Terrans, then let's all speak Anglish; I know it pretty good. Hi, Trudy."

"Hello, m'lord ambassador. Pleased to meet you."

"M'lord?" Jacobs asked. "Is there really no one else in your party?"

"Nobody else, pal. I'm it."

"Uh, you are? I mean to say, m'lord, that the Rhuum have sent a lead negotiator and twenty-three assistants."

"Yep," he rumbled. "So what? Don't need others to deal with people from Rhuum or anywhere else. Been doing this kind of thing all my damn life. I captain my own craft and chart my own course; King Bolo understands that. Helps that he's my uncle, natch."

"But, m'lord, did I misunderstand? We were informed that your people have never before held talks with the Rhuum."

"That's right. So? We have stuff they want. They'll do a deal without too much trouble. King Bolo understands that, too. Hey, Trudy Burke, you tied down?"

"Excuse me, m'lord?"

"You committed to some guy?"

Jacobs cleared his throat. "Sir, Miss Burke is also my wife."

"That the same as mated, pal? I don't know Terran ways much."

"Yes. Yes, it is. Miss Burke is my wife."

"Oh," he said, shrugging. "Too damn bad. Would have liked to try you, Trudy Burke."

"I'm flattered beyond the telling, m'lord," Trudy said dryly. "Well, shall we settle Sir Kethrommon in his suite now, Mr. Jacobs? Perhaps you would like some dinner, m'lord?"

"Screw dinner," Kethrommon said. "There any women for

hire at this damn hotel? Bigger ones than Trudy Burke here,
I mean. Not so fragile looking." Kethrommon grinned. "Been
a long trip for me, heh."

"I'll have the hotel's concierge contact you to arrange
things," Trudy said, her expression carefully bland. "I'm sure
they'll have someone well worth your time. You might also
try the neural net."

"Heh," Kethrommon said. "Maybe I will, both. You don't
like, eh, Trudy Burke?"

"It's none of my concern, m'lord. Really."

"But you don't like. Know what, Trudy Burke? You got
spunk. I *love* spunk!"

The opening rounds of talks between the trade representa-
tives of the Kingdom of Bloxx and the Rhuum Industrial Organization got under way the following morning with as much
appropriate pomp and ceremony as Jacobs and Burke could
quickly arrange with Hotel Andromeda's hospitality staff.

After the courtesy robots withdrew, Jacobs and Trudy took
seats at opposite ends of the long, large mahogany conference
table traditionally used in such negotiations, while Sir
Kethrommon sat directly across from Chaylaifa. The table was
bare of everything but writing implements and note paper; in
keeping with Rhuum ways, there was not even water. The size
of the table seemed excessive for so few people, but Jacobs was
betting that an old hand like Chaylaifa would appreciate the im-
plied status it gave him, and he was right; Chaylaifa broke into
an undiplomatic grin when he first saw it. The twenty-three
members of the Rhuum negotiating staff sat in a gallery well behind their chief; their only job was to lend their presence to
these proceedings. Chaylaifa's wife and daughter sat with them
in the front row.

The first five minutes of the meeting were spent in exchanging formal pleasantries. Chaylaifa was, predictably,
good at it with the skill of long experience. Kethrommon, not
so predictably, quickly proved himself capable of delivering a
rough yet effective and endearing presentation capable of
charming even his most formal listener.

Jacobs accessed the net. *You there, Trudy?*

She answered immediately. *Sure I am, hon. Hey, is this guy
good, or what? Not only does he seem undamaged after last*

night's antics—and I've seen the bill!—but he's got the gift of gab like you wouldn't believe.

Jacobs winked at her. *You just gotta love this big lug, don'tcha? Maybe old King Bozo knew what he was doing. This is going to be okay, after all. A quick deal, nice and clean, and—*

That was exactly when Kethrommon bolted from his seat and attempted to leap across the table at Chaylaifa, his ceremonial dagger unsheathed. "You piss-sprayed son of a whore!" Kethrommon cried in a white heat. "I'll *kill* you!"

Chaylaifa could move surprisingly quickly for such a big being; he kicked back his chair and drew *his* very unceremonial blaster. Fortunately, the conference room's defensive systems had clicked on instantly, and both antagonists had been safely caught in a tanglefield. The tanglefield could do nothing to silence Kethrommon, however, and he continued to shout threats. Jacobs saw that Chaylaifa's wife and child were shrieking but, since neither they nor anyone else in the gallery was offering any aggressive behavior, the tanglefield was ignoring them.

The tanglefield was also ignoring the two facilitators, who were frozen only by their own shock. Trudy's eyes were bulging. *We must have missed something. What the hell was it?*

I don't know, Trude. Let me access the transcript . . . oh, no!

A Security squad arrived a moment later. Several of its members escorted Kethrommon to his suite, and Trudy accompanied them. Others took Chaylaifa back to his rooms, and Jacobs went with him.

"Ambassador Chaylaifa," Jacobs carefully began when they were at last alone, "didn't you realize that your . . . pleasant question . . . represented the worst kind of insult to Sir Kethrommon?"

"It was not intended as such," Chaylaifa said. He was genuinely puzzled. "I have frequently asked it of humanoids, but I have never gotten such a response."

Jacobs licked his lips. "Mr. Ambassador, some humanoids resent the implication that their mothers were impregnated with them by males who are not their acknowledged fathers."

Chaylaifa blinked. "But such things happen all the time,

don't they? Especially in noble houses? I've read many histories of humanoid cultures."

"It's true that such things do happen. But it is usually—not always, but usually—rude to suggest to an individual that he himself represents one of those cases. Some cultures put great store in being certain of whom one's parents are and, moreover, having everyone else be certain of it, too. I hope you can understand that Sir Kethrommon would greatly resent your questioning his parentage."

"But I *wasn't* doubting his parentage, Mr. Jacobs," Chaylaifa said. "I was simply asking who impregnated his mother."

"Now, m'lord," Trudy said soothingly, "you must know that the ambassador didn't mean to offend you."

They were sitting across from each other at a coffee table in the Bloxx's sitting room. Kethrommon had grown calmer and was more in control of himself, but he was still hot with anger. "Indeed, woman?" he spat. "Then I would hate to be the victim of slurs he uttered with malicious intent."

"He is an alien, m'lord. He is not like you. He simply doesn't understand."

Kethrommon nodded tightly. "I understand that. Barbarian, he is."

Trudy's lips grew narrow. "If you like. He is certainly different. Not better, not worse—just different."

"I know 'different,' Trudy Burke," Kethrommon said. "I've stood in the dirt of a hundred worlds. I've eaten that which has tried to eat me; I've even eaten *with* that which has tried to eat me."

"So you know how deeply the differences between beings can run," said Trudy.

Kethrommon shook his head. "There is always decency, and decency never changes. Never. Let me tell you something. I lost my father, he at my side against outsystem pirates terrorizing our good neighbors of the fourth planet in our system. He was blown apart by a fragmentation projectile. I had to wash him off me that night, after the battle." Kethrommon's teeth clenched. "I could overlook a slur upon myself, given a lack of intent, but I will not—cannot—countenance even an unintended insult against the memory of my father. My people desperately need the trade the Rhuum

Organization can provide, but I am no longer the one to get it for them."

Trudy blinked. "So what will you do?"

"There is only one way the Rhuum can answer for his insult—his death, by my hand."

"I hope there is another way, m'lord."

Suddenly Kethrommon sagged, the fight gone out of him. "In justice, I cannot take his life from him; I do indeed realize he meant no harm by what he said. Trudy Burke, I am not unable to see that my killing the Rhuum would be a terrible crime under these circumstances; I am not stupid. I will, however, leave Hotel Andromeda in the morning. As you are still acting as facilitator for these talks, please have my ship made ready for departure at that time." He carefully did not look at her.

Trudy took a deep breath, somehow sensing that this was a dangerous moment and that whatever she might say to him, angry as he was and hurt as he was, could be dreadfully important. "I will do exactly as you ask," she finally said, and she saw Kethrommon relax just a touch.

"Thank you," he said in a low voice. "Any other answer would not have done . . . and I did not want to kill myself in front of you, Trudy Burke." Trudy saw the dagger hidden in his hand for the first time as he placed it on the table, the point facing him. "I must not kill myself until I stand in front of the king. That is the only way I may properly apologize to my patron god for my failure."

Trudy needed pills to get to sleep that night, and that was why the persistent beeping of the phone did not disturb her. Jacobs had to shake her awake.

"Trudy, there's a problem," he said in the darkness. "A big one."

"Whazzit?" his wife mumbled.

"That was Security. Chaylaifa is dead. Better start getting dressed; I'll dial a wake-up for you."

Several minutes later Jacobs and Trudy caught a lift to the VIP section. The door to Chaylaifa's suite was ajar; they entered.

Several Security people were in the foyer, standing near their chief of detail. There was a briefing going on. The chief was hard to make out, surrounded as he was by the others; he was only a meter and a fraction tall, like most adults of his race. He was, generally speaking, a lizard.

"Ah," he said, noticing Trudy and Jacobs. His mouth twitched into the semblance of a smile. "The partners of Jacobs and Burke, no? I am Lieutenant Hrock-Leff of Hotel Security. These are several of my associates."

"Hello, Lieutenant, everyone," Jacobs said. "What happened here?"

"I do not know quite yet," Hrock-Leff said. "The ambassador is dead. Do you care to see?"

"Eh? Uh, I guess I have to," Jacobs said. "Trudy?"

She seemed shaken. "I'll, uh, I'll wait here, I suppose. Call me if you need me."

"Okay, Trude. Lieutenant? Lead on."

"This way, please, Mr. Jacobs." The two entered the main bedroom of the suite.

Chaylaifa's body lay in the center of the bed. The blankets and sheets had been ripped by his claws and gathered around him, as if he had tried to provide himself with his own shroud even as he died. His eyes were open and glazed. There was an incredible amount of blood all over everything. *Ritzcrackas* and other tidbits were spilled here and there.

"It looks like he was stabbed," Jacobs said.

"He was," Hrock-Leff replied. "He was stabbed some forty times by someone with a small knife. From what I can see, at least eight of the wounds were severe enough to be fatal, in that Chaylaifa's circulation system was irreparably damaged by each. He lost a great deal of blood very quickly. We have an identification, by the way."

"An identification?" Jacobs asked, puzzled. "Of the body?"

"No," the lieutenant replied. "Of the perpetrator. The *chosha* Nasu has named Sir Kethrommon of Bloxx."

"Jesus. Why am I not surprised?"

"I do not know. Let us go into the other bedroom, shall we?"

There was a connecting door to another bedroom in the suite. Inside, two Security officers were sitting with Nasu and Fehlorah. The two females were dressed in bathrobes supplied by the hotel; Nasu's barely fit her, while tiny Fehlorah seemed lost in hers. They were holding hands, and both seemed terribly upset.

"I'm sorry, Madame Chaylaifa," Jacobs began, searching for something appropriate to say. "Your husband's death is a great loss to us all."

The Rhuum nodded her appreciation. "It is just Nasu now," she said, "but I thank you, Mr. Jacobs. Fehlorah also appreciates your sympathy."

"Certainly. Is there anything I can do?"

"Yes, there is. You can make sure that these police people here bring the murderer of Chaylaifa to justice." She glared at Hrock-Leff. "I am not sure of their intent. They seem reluctant to take that devil spawn of Bloxx into custody."

Jacobs nodded. "I'll do my best, Nasu. Fehlorah, will you be all right?"

"Yes, Mr. Jacobs," the girl said. "I will be all right."

"Very good. Lieutenant, may we talk?"

"Of course, Mr. Jacobs." They left the bedroom through another door and went into the sitting room common to all three bedrooms in the suite.

"Have a seat, Mr. Jacobs," Hrock-Leff invited, closing the door behind him. He himself squatted on a footstool, perfectly comfortable. "Would you like me to order something for you, now that we are alone? Coffee, perhaps?"

"No, nothing for me, thank you. Lieutenant? Have you arrested Kethrommon yet?"

"No. We have no need to bother him. We will not be arresting Sir Kethrommon."

"Oh," Jacobs said, frowning. "Diplomatic immunity, eh?"

"Hmmm?" the lieutenant said, almost distractedly. "Oh, no. We will not be arresting the Bloxx, because he did not kill Ambassador Chaylaifa. He has not left his room all evening."

"Oh? How do you know?"

"We do not spy, Mr. Jacobs, but you probably know that the medical section keeps a passive watch on VIPs at the hotel, should someone experience a health problem or suffer an accident. Looking at the records for tonight, we see that Kethrommon was in his room all evening. The records also let us fix the time of Ambassador Chaylaifa's death. Only two persons were with him at that moment: Nasu and Fehlorah."

"So one of them did it?"

"Almost certainly. If they did not—if the murderer was someone not being monitored by the medical section, say a hotel staff member or some such—then they were present at the time of the killing and saw who did it, and can identify the criminal. It was not one of Chaylaifa's staff; all are VIPs and all are monitored, and we can account for the movements of every one of them. But that is neither here nor there. I suspect the former *chosha* did it, using a small knife as her weapon, in the vain hope that we would suspect Sir Kethrommon and his dagger. The only other suspect is Fehlorah, and she is too small to have done such damage. I have not yet confronted Nasu with an accusation, but I will in good time." Hrock-Leff yawned. "Pardon me; I was awakened for this. As I was saying, I am in no hurry to confront Nasu. She is not going anywhere."

"Excuse me? The 'choh-shah'? You keep talking about one. Who the hell is that?"

"You have been referring to Nasu as Chaylaifa's wife. She was not that. She was his *chosha*."

"Well, whatever. Why did she kill Chaylaifa?"

"I do not know yet. My initial inspection of the scene suggests that Nasu was tired of being forced to indulge Chaylaifa in his sexual perversions."

"What? Chaylaifa was a *pervert*?"

"It would seem so. I believe that the ambassador must have already thoroughly corrupted young Fehlorah, the *thaka'thott*—"

"The what?"

"The *thaka'thott*," Hrock-Leff repeated, more slowly. "My good word, Mr. Jacobs. Did you really do so little research on the ways of the Rhuum before you took this assignment?"

"Uh, wait a minute, there. My own *chosha* usually does that sort of thing; I'm the idea man. Lieutenant, we got this job at the very last minute. I learned all there was to know about the trade deal and what both sides expected from it. Our job was to bring the Rhuum and the Bloxx together, take care of the niggling details so that both sides wouldn't have to worry about them, lead them to strike the deal they both wanted, and send them home happy and satisfied. I didn't think I needed a quickie degree in xenoanthropology, too."

"Perhaps you did, Mr. Jacobs," the lieutenant said, the sarcasm lost on him. "Sorting these things out can sometimes become impossibly complicated. A degree might help."

"You may have a point there, Lieutenant. Anyway, I *thought* there might be something weird going on between the old boy and the girl. Nasu knew all about it, I suppose."

Hrock-Leff blinked in surprise. "Well, Mr. Jacobs, I mean, *really*. What else would you expect?"

Jacobs nodded wisely. "Of course. The wife—sorry, the *chosha*—is always the first to know, isn't she? What a mess!"

Hrock-Leff blinked. "I'm afraid you've lost me, sir. May we leave now?"

"Sure. Let's go."

Jacobs and the lieutenant left the sitting room and entered the second bedroom. The two Security people had left, and no one but Nasu and Fehlorah were in the room. The two were standing next to the bed. They were locked in an embrace. Fehlorah was naked; her robe was puddled around her feet.

Nasu's eyes were closed as Fehlorah's small hand groped inside her opened robe, playing and stroking and touching, so she did not notice the presence of Jacobs and Hrock-Leff for several seconds. She squealed in surprise and fright when she did. Startled, Fehlorah whirled and, seeing them there, bolted for the bathroom. She slammed the door behind her.

"I thought—thought you were all gone except for the Security persons posted outside," Nasu stammered as she tied her robe closed. She was a little out of breath.

"We most humbly beg your pardon," Hrock-Leff said, bowing his head slightly. "We were talking in the other room and quite lost track of time. Our fault entirely. Mr. Jacobs? Let us leave, please."

"Uh, yes." *Jesus!* thought Jacobs. *They're* all *crazy!*

Honey? came Trudy's worried thought. *I caught that. What's going on?*

You won't believe it, honey. Later. The lieutenant and Jacobs left the bedroom, passed through the room where Chaylaifa's body still lay, and emerged into the foyer, where Trudy was waiting for them.

"Hello, Miss Burke," Hrock-Leff said. "You appear to be agitated, if I read the signs correctly."

"Hello, Lieutenant. Jonny Lee, we have to go to the office."

"We do?"

"*Now.* Lieutenant? May I ask a favor?"

"Of course you may, Miss Burke."

"Would you please delay notifying the relevant parties of Chaylaifa's death until I contact you? Including the rest of Chaylaifa's entourage? I promise that it will not be a long delay."

Hrock-Leff cocked his head to one side. "I am afraid I cannot at all delay briefing my superiors in Security . . . but I can request that neither they nor the hotel contact anyone concerning this matter until I consent."

"Thank you, Lieutenant. That will do fine. We're very grateful. We'll talk to you again later—not much later."

"I await the moment with pleasure. Good night, Mr. Jacobs, Miss Burke."

Lieutenant Hrock-Leff watched as the two facilitators left, the determined female almost literally dragging the arguing male away. *How like Terrans,* he thought with amusement. *No doubt she has figured things out. And about time, too!*

Jacobs and Trudy were back in her grandmother's garden.

"Nice and peaceful here," Jacobs said. "Can't we stay for, like, a year?"

"Don't I wish," Trudy said, seating herself on the ground. "Look, Jonny Lee, I'm the one who's supposed to handle the niggling details, and I didn't this time. What's happened is mostly my fault—no, don't stop me. This was a quickie contract, we thought, and so I treated it that way. I let myself be rushed into this. Well, I'll never do *that* again."

Jacobs dropped down beside her. "Why are you beating yourself up, Trude?"

"I'm not. Just listen to me for a minute. If we put our heads together, we can still fix it."

"We can fix it?" Jacobs asked. "The Bloxx emissary is about to go home in disgrace, and he's set to commit ritual suicide as soon as he gets within three feet of King Boppo. Our favorite couple from Rhuum turns out to be a pair of child molesters—*incestuous* child molesters! At least now there's one fewer of 'em than there used to be, thanks to the victim's wife—sorry, I mean his *chosha*."

"Get a grip, Jonny Lee."

"Why should I? Everything's gone to hell. Bannister will fire our butts for sure, and they'll be real public about it because they'll *have* to be in order to save their *own* butts. Our reputation is going to take a heavy hit. We have no hope of salvaging *anything* here—and you're saying we can actually *fix* this mess?"

"I think we can," Trudy said, offering her husband a small bowl. "By the way, stop assuming you know what you're talking about. You don't."

"I don't?" Jacobs said, taking the bowl and sniffing at it. "Hey, is this salsa?"

"Lightly spiced with relevant detail. This is the technical material neither of us could handle before Kethrommon got here. I've worked it over some. Here's a spoon."

Jacobs took it and began eating. "It's good," he said, chewing a little and swallowing.

"I whomped it up while you were in the other room of Chaylaifa's suite, talking to the lieutenant," Trudy said. "There was something about what was going on that just didn't ring true. I didn't have much else to do while I was waiting, so I accessed the net to do some of the background research I damn well should have done in the first place."

"There's some tough bits in this, but it's fine." Jacobs began to absorb tiny fragments of detail.

"No, don't savor it," Trudy said. "Just eat it up and think about it later. We're in a hurry, you know." She produced a bag of corn chips. "By the way, here's what we didn't already know about the Bloxx. Take it all in, love."

"Yep." He ate quickly and, in a few minutes, he finished.

"Well?" Trudy asked.

"Give me a second and let me start digesting all this—oh, *Jesus!*"

Trudy grinned. "You found the biggie, didn't you? Wife and daughter, indeed! Never mind; I'm just as guilty. They *acted* like wife and daughter to Chaylaifa, but they were actually the second and third members of a male-dominated trisexual relationship."

Jacobs wiped a hand over his face. "I must have looked like a fool in front of Lieutenant Hrock-Leff," he said. It was almost a groan. "Chaylaifa—the *sha*—was the seed carrier. He plants it in Fehlorah, the *thaka'thott*; if he has sex with

Nasu, it's only in fun or to excite himself further, the old dog. Fehlorah is a natural hermaphrodite who's just past puberty. All *thaka'thotts* are. Fehlorah contributes her egg and incubates the fertilized ovum for a day or two. When the time comes, she passes her egg through intercourse to Nasu, a true female—the *chosha*—who goes through pregnancy and bears the youngling. The way I just saw Fehlorah cozying up to Nasu, Fehlorah is probably carrying a fertilized egg right now. After two to five fertilizations, Fehlorah's body will tell her whether she's going to mature into a *sha* or *chosha*. Damn!"

"It's an atypical case, Jonny Lee," Trudy said. "Don't blame yourself. The Rhuum are unique. We don't know of any other viviparous trisexual races."

"I know, I know—but there I was, calling them child molesters and perverts."

"But you were half-right, hon. Chaylaifa, at least, *was* a pervert."

"Huh? How so? The records say the Rhuum usually have threesomes."

"Go on, Jonny Lee. Think about it some more."

Jacobs did. Suddenly, he blinked. "What, for *that*? Shoot! With all that other stuff going on, who'da thunk it? Who'da paid *attention*?"

"*We* should have," Trudy replied. "We're supposed to be good at this. Face it, love, we're racial chauvinists."

"I guess we must be."

"*This* particular taboo is hardly unique—although, in its most severe form, it never lasts very long in the history of a particular civilization. Or so it says here."

"I'm beginning to have an idea," Jacobs said.

"I was hoping you would. Now think about the Bloxx."

"I have been. That one's harder. The insult to Kethrommon's dignity was substantial." Jacobs thought some more about it. "No. No apology is possible. I don't see any way out of the situation—not directly, at any rate."

"I don't know what to do, either," Trudy said.

"It'll be okay, Trude," Jacobs said, and there was a certain familiar light in his eyes. "For the first time since we fell into this pile of sawdust, I'm beginning to get the feeling that we're gonna win. Let's go talk to Lieutenant Hrock-Leff."

• • •

Trudy, Jacobs and Hrock-Leff had returned to Chaylaifa's suite. "I must talk to you now, Nasu," the lieutenant said. "Do you want these others to leave us?"

"No," Nasu said. "Mr. Jacobs is the nearest thing to a representative I—we—have aboard the hotel. I would like him to stay. I have a feeling we might need him."

"I'll do what I can for you, Nasu."

"I know. Please go ahead, Lieutenant. I hope you need not involve Fehlorah in this. She's still a youngling in so many ways."

Hrock-Leff nodded. "I do not believe there is a need to involve her. Let us begin. You killed Ambassador Chaylaifa, did you not?"

"Yes," Nasu said. She went to one of the bedside tables, opened a drawer and retrieved a small knife. It was still stained with Chaylaifa's blood. "I took this from the . . . cart . . . this evening and placed it under my pillow in the other bedroom," Nasu said, handing it to the lieutenant. "When Chaylaifa began making his, his demands, I . . . I just could not acquiesce again." She began shaking. "I did it. I killed him. I am not sorry. I could not suffer another night of Chaylaifa's . . . aberrations."

"Tell me about them, Nasu," the lieutenant said.

Nasu's icy composure was slipping; she was beginning to weep. "I can barely bring myself to speak of them," she whispered.

"You must."

"He . . . he corrupted the poor *thaka'thott*. He . . . he . . . consumed nourishment *right in front of us*. He left *crumbs in bed*! He was *proud* of it!" She sobbed. "What *else* could I do?"

Jesus, Trudy, came Jacobs's thought.

Shhh, Trudy returned. *Hrock-Leff's working up to the pitch.*

"Nasu, what of Fehlorah?" asked the lieutenant. "What was her role in this killing?"

"She watched throughout." Nasu paused to collect herself and, after a moment, she continued. "She thanked me afterward. We made quick love, right there at his side, in his blood. It was wonderful. Then we washed together, and it was just then that the medicos and the security people arrived, summoned automatically by the *sha's* sudden death. I am ready to be arrested now." She bowed her head.

"I am not going to arrest you, Nasu."

"You are not?" She seemed puzzled.

"No. I have no authority to do so. You are—were—the mate of a diplomat; I cannot take you into custody, even for the killing of that selfsame diplomat. You are answerable to your own people for your actions here, but you are not answerable to us. I will provide a full report to your ministry of justice, and the hotel management will ask you to leave the premises as soon as possible."

"I understand, Lieutenant," Nasu said, "and I accept the necessity." She sighed. "The scandal that arises from this will ruin our family—oh, not because of the actions I have taken tonight, no, but because of what the *sha* has done. Chaylaifa was a figure of respect, but he had grown very old, and in his great age he had also grown . . . foul. The whispers concerning his aberrant conduct will become shouts, once this incident is made known." She closed her eyes. "Certainly everything will be taken from us by those who . . . protect . . . our code of morality, but I care not. Fehlorah and I will manage."

"I am certain you will," Lieutenant Hrock-Leff agreed. "I can see that there is a great strength between you—and, if I am not mistaken," he said, sniffing the air, "there is something even more important between you now."

"I think so, too," Nasu said, smiling for the first time. "Fehlorah will soon give me her egg. It will be our first."

"All the more reason you should listen to Mr. Jacobs," Hrock-Leff said. "He has a plan."

A few hours later, there was a knock at the door of Kethrommon's suite. "Package, Sir Kethrommon," came a robot voice.

Kethrommon was sitting in the dark, utterly alone. "Just leave it there," he said, "and go away."

"Sorry, m'lord, but I need your thumbprint as proof of delivery."

"No."

"It is very important. I am told to say it concerns your mission."

"What mission?" Kethrommon asked miserably. "I have

none—oh, never mind. All right. I will take the delivery." As he rose from his chair, the lights went on. He crossed the room in three steps and opened the door to find a delivery robot standing there, a small package set atop its flat head.

"This is the thing?" Kethrommon asked.

"Yes, m'lord. Your thumbprint, please, on the glass plate next to the tray . . . thank you. Good night, m'lord."

"Good night," Kethrommon said as he closed the door. He looked at the package. It was a not very large box sealed in plastic, and the only thing written on it was his own name—in an ornate hand, to be sure. It was moderately heavy. He held the package up to his ear and rattled it, and something inside thumped.

"Well, I wonder," Kethrommon muttered. He picked at the easy-open tab with a fingernail, and the plastic promptly fell apart along its pre-stressed seams. He opened the box and stopped for a moment, shocked and speechless. Then he smiled for the first time in many hours.

Things in Chaylaifa's suite were getting busy.

"That was Sir Kethrommon, via the net," Trudy said. "He sends his personal regards to us, and he says he will be pleased to attend an early-morning meeting of the principals, as long as it is over before the time of his ship's scheduled departure. He will not change that."

"I didn't expect him to," Jacobs said, pleased. "I knew Kethrommon would give us some wiggle room if we gave him any excuse at all. Good boy!"

"You saw something in the files I didn't notice," Trudy said.

"Just a detail. Kethrommon could not *take* Chaylaifa's life in payment for the insult to him—not in the context of negotiations with a foreign government, anyhow. However, Chaylaifa could *offer* his life—which he did by sending Kethrommon his very own blaster. It's the same weapon he pulled on him at the meeting yesterday. Fraught with symbolism."

"I see," Lieutenant Hrock-Leff said. "So, at the meeting this morning, Kethrommon will fire into Chaylaifa's already dead body, honor will be served, and that will be the end of it."

"Oh, heaven forbid," Jacobs said. "That would cause more

problems later. I can't have the Bloxx trade rep appear to kill the Rhuum ambassador—and I still want the two sides to strike a deal."

"A deal? With one of the parties dead?"

"You bet, Lieutenant. C'mon. I want to see how they're doing with Chaylaifa." They walked into the main bedroom. "Hi, fellas."

"Hello, Mr. Jacobs," said the chief cosmetologist, his rodent teeth chattering. The others nodded to Jacobs and continued to scurry around Chaylaifa's bulky form, combing and cleaning and straightening. "How d'you think he's looking?"

"Pretty good, Osroqui, pretty good. I knew your team could do it if anybody could."

"Thanks, Mr. Jacobs. Hey, this fur of his is a real problem, what with the blood and all. Kinks and gunk all over the place. Hell, he was still leaking when we got here. How covered up is the old kark going to be?"

"He'll have a ceremonial robe on, like that one over on the chair. He can also wear a big hat, if you need him to. His face is going to be the important thing. How about his eyes?"

"I can't do much about those, even if I replaced them with glass," Osroqui said. "He can't blink anymore, and that kind of thing always gives a stiff away. I don't think we need a hat. Hey, does his kind wear veils?"

"No, they don't." Jacobs thought a moment. "Glass, you said. Hmmm. Glasses."

"Glasses?" Osroqui asked.

"Something you see in old Terran movies. Humans used to wear glass lenses in frames over their eyes to correct vision problems. We could make ones with really thick lenses; then you couldn't see if Chaylaifa was blinking or not. We could tell Kethrommon it was some Rhuum thing. Measure his head for me, will you, Osroqui? I'll make a call."

The time for the meeting arrived. The rest of the Rhuum party was only slightly surprised to find Chaylaifa, Nasu, and Fehlorah already in place at the conference table, but they took their seats in the gallery without incident.

Kethrommon entered to find things much the same as the day before, except that Jacobs and Trudy were standing by

Chaylaifa's side, and that the Rhuum ambassador was wearing . . . something . . . over his eyes.

"Mr. Jacobs?" the Bloxx began, somewhat puzzled. "Why are you sitting over there today? Do you propose to speak for the Rhuum?"

"With your indulgence, m'lord," Jacobs began, "I do, in a way. The ambassador has asked me to translate his native tongue into Anglish for him in order to spare us farther, ah, difficulties."

"I see." Kethrommon reached into his cloak and dropped Chaylaifa's blaster onto the table. It clattered. There was something like a gasp from the gallery. "I received this last night," he said. "Did the ambassador grasp the import?"

Jacobs put his head very near Chaylaifa's lips, waited a moment, and then straightened. "He did, m'lord. He begs a moment while he very carefully phrases what he wishes to say next, realizing that you need not grant him this boon."

Kethrommon paused, then nodded. "Very well. What is it?"

Jacobs bent, paused, and straightened again. "He wishes to ask again the question which he so poorly and insultingly put to you yesterday because of his clumsiness with the language. He begs to know if he may ask this question again, here and now, or do you wish to kill him right away? He humbly awaits your answer."

Kethrommon was silent for a long minute. "He may ask the question," the Bloxx representative finally said, his jaw set.

Jacobs put his head next to Chaylaifa's mouth. "The ambassador wished to know, Sir Kethrommon, which of your warrior gods acted through your father to sire you. You exhibit the most honorable traits of many of them, and the ambassador would like to know so he, too, may honor him."

Kethrommon blinked. "Is *that* what he—never mind. Please tell the ambassador that I have the honor to have as my patron the god Anox-Maleth, the warrior spirit of the northern provinces; my father's family is of those lands. Please thank the ambassador for his interest." The Bloxx picked up the blaster and rather casually put it into the pocket in his cloak. "I think we should begin the meeting now."

"The ambassador is eager as ever to begin," Jacobs said.

• • •

Jacobs and Trudy were standing at the viewport in the departure lounge, hand in hand. They watched as the Rhuum yacht sprang away from the side of the hotel and, on thrusters, maneuvered into proper position for its sprint for home.

"Ahem," said Lieutenant Hrock-Leff. "I thought I might join you for the departure. All is well?"

Jacobs nodded to him. "All is very well, Lieutenant. And you?"

"A bit more prosperous than I was, as are certain members of my squad. We thank you."

"You're all entirely welcome." Jacobs turned back to the viewport as the lieutenant came to stand with him and Trudy.

"They are satisfied?" Hrock-Leff asked. "I still cannot believe it has worked."

"Everything's fine," Jacobs answered. "Chaylaifa went aboard on a medical stretcher. The poor *sha* is completely exhausted. He will have a fatal heart attack on the way home—a regrettable consequence of his strenuous efforts to bring about the first trade treaty with the Bloxx. The ship's doctor is a family confidant; he'll keep silent and no one else will know. Chaylaifa will be buried in space, according to tradition. Nasu and Fehlorah will inherit Chaylaifa's import business. They'll be well taken care of."

Trudy nodded. "They ought to be. Rhuum has struck the first major agreement with a race that's sure to be a major player in this part of the galaxy."

"And *we* nailed it for them," Jacobs said, with great satisfaction. "Despite everything."

"I hope Nasu and Fehlorah will be all right," Trudy said. "They've been through quite an ordeal."

"They're the widowed spouses of a hero of the Rhuum Industrial Organization," said Jacobs. "They'll be treated right, don't worry. They won't be single for long, either—not with *that* bankroll. They'll find a new *sha*, or Nasu will take Fehlorah if she turns out to be *sha* herself."

"I wonder how we managed to fool Sir Kethrommon, though?" Lieutenant Hrock-Leff wondered. "He is not stupid."

"He isn't," Jacobs said with a grin, "and we didn't. Kethrommon realized that Chaylaifa was dead the moment he saw him. However, he decided to trust me—or, more accurately, he decided to trust Trudy, who was standing right there, after all, and so had to be privy to what was going on. Kethrommon played along and quickly realized that we were showing a way—the *only* way—out of the jungle. He took it, bless his heart."

"You were sure of him?" Hrock-Leff asked.

"Reasonably sure. I figured Kethrommon wouldn't expose us, as long as we didn't implicate him in our cover-up or deal unfairly with him in the talks—that is, as long as we didn't put his personal honor into question, and we never did. No, the whole charade with Chaylaifa's body was for the benefit of the Rhuum party. They'll go home now and tell everyone how wonderful the regrettably departed Chaylaifa was at the talks. His finest moment coming right at the end, and all that."

The Rhuum yacht was nothing more than a pinpoint of winking light in the far distance. Suddenly, it vanished.

"There they go," Trudy said. "Safe home, Nasu and Fehlorah."

"Indeed," Hrock-Leff said, nodding. "Well, I feel a bit let down, to tell you the truth. This case provided more excitement than I usually see in my work. Actually, I found it rather exhilarating."

"Really?" Jacobs asked, as the three turned and left the lounge. "Well, stick around, Lieutenant. This could be the start of a beautiful friendship."

SOFT IN THE WORLD, AND BRIGHT

———•———

M. Shayne Bell

This is how it began: I stumbled. But it wasn't just a stumble. I knew that. My right leg "felt" tingly—no, "felt" as if tiny pinpricks of my mind's awareness about my knee were disappearing, as if the knee itself were disappearing atom by atom in a sudden rush.

Mary! I shouted the thought in my mind, but she didn't answer, and I could not access her virtual reality in my mind to find her. I was shut out of it. But she could stop this—she was the artificial intelligence networked through my nerves and my brain to give me my body. I thought maybe that's why she didn't answer me. Maybe she was trying to stop my body from disintegrating from my consciousness and she couldn't answer me because it took all of her efforts.

I had stopped walking and was standing in the middle of a broad flight of stairs leading down to breakfast, and people were staring. I looked across at the handrail against the wall and took a step toward it with my left leg. I could walk with

113

it. My left leg worked. I dragged my right leg along and got to the handrail and the bottom of the stairs and a table, where I sat and rubbed my knee. My hands could feel my knee, but my knee couldn't feel my hands on it.

Mary, I thought. *What's happening?*

But she didn't answer, and a golden robot with its ruby, multifaceted eyes stood next to my table to take my order and I couldn't think what to tell it.

"Are you all right, Mr. Addison?" it asked.

It knew me because it was linked to the hotel's central intelligence, which knew all about me: that I was actually no more than a brain in a body that wouldn't work without the AI they put inside me after I broke my neck and we found out that I was allergic to the neural-regeneration drugs, that I couldn't actually feel anything, it was the AI giving my mind the illusion of feeling, that I couldn't breathe on my own, or speak, or control my urination, or be a man among other men who can walk and breathe and hold their urine, and that every eight years I had to have the AI replaced because the programs would become corrupted, and it was Mary's eighth year and they would erase her out of my mind and I didn't want her to go because I loved her.

I put my hands on the table. "I'm fine," I said to the robot.

"Might I suggest the buffet this morning?"

I couldn't walk to a buffet. "Please bring me some coffee," I said, "and fruit."

"Grapefruit?"

I nodded.

It left, and I still couldn't feel my knee, and I wouldn't put my hands on it. *Mary,* I thought. *Talk to me, Mary. Are you all right?*

But she didn't send a word to my mind. I was sitting in Swan Court, next to the hotel's artificial lagoon by its artificial sea, and the artificial breeze off the water smelled like the sea, and I knew the sea smelled like this because Mary and I had run along a beach once in the early morning and I had felt the sand on my feet, and the spray from the waves on my skin, and I knew Mary was making me feel all of that, but I didn't care because Mary was with me in my mind and we were happy with the sun coming up over the sea.

"Your coffee, sir."

The robot put it down in front of me.

"Your grapefruit, sir."

"Thank you."

"Would you like anything else?"

"No."

"Shall I call the swans for you?"

I looked up at the robot and wanted it to go and leave me alone. "The swans?" I said.

The robot looked out over the water, and three swans swam toward us. I wondered how the robot had called them, and then I thought they were probably not real swans, but robots, and it had called them through the central intelligence with a thought. They were graceful and lovely, and the robot left but the swans didn't.

I spooned sugar into the coffee and stirred it and lifted the cup and took a drink—and the coffee burned my lips, but my hands hadn't felt the heat of it in the cup though they had felt the cup, and I put the cup down but my hand started shaking and made coffee spill onto the white tablecloth and I touched my lips but only my lips could feel the touch now, and my hands wouldn't stop shaking.

I put them in my lap.

And knew then what would happen. I didn't want to go through it, not again, not a third time. I didn't want to be in my mind when they killed another AI that I had lived with and loved—when they killed Mary this time. *Mary,* I thought, *we'll try to fix whatever's wrong. We fixed the last set of problems you had two weeks ago. We'll fix this. I don't know if you can hear my thoughts, but I won't let them erase you.*

I looked up and the swans were swimming away, and the robot was serving food to a man and a woman and a little girl sitting three tables from me. I raised one of my shaking hands, and the robot looked at me.

"Help me," I said in a whisper, knowing it could hear me and call help with its thoughts, and we wouldn't have to disturb the people around us for a while yet.

They came to me quickly, two medical robots, and they were kind and gentle. They spoke to me in low voices, telling me what they were going to do, that they would help me walk out of the restaurant to a service elevator, that they could carry me and were prepared with a respirator should I need one on the way. I listened to them and wondered about their lives. Did they love each other? I knew that they could love, and that I could love them. I had loved three AIs. There are people who, if they heard me talk of love, would think that contact with artificial intelligences had corrupted my mind, not the other way around. But it was not the outward physical that I loved, after all. It was the inward quality of soul.

The robots carried me to the hospital, and along the way I lost my body. When they hooked me to machines that monitored my vital signs and made me breathe and took care of my bodily functions and dripped water in my veins so I wouldn't dehydrate, I couldn't feel it. I couldn't feel the air in my lungs or my chest move up and down, or the rough cotton sheets against my bare skin. They kept the room dark so it wouldn't hurt my eyes, but even so, I could see the bank of monitors that told me or anyone who cared to look that my lungs were breathing and my heart beating. It is a curious thing to be forced to lie absolutely still and watch the functions of your body be displayed digitally in bright green lines and know that they are going on but not feel them.

And they had put electrodes on my head above the implant that held Mary. Her monitor showed a steady, positive green line. Normal. Agitated, probably. Low. But normal. *Mary*, I thought. *We'll find a way to help you.*

I hoped that what I was telling her was true, that we could find a way to help her. I wondered what she was thinking or doing and whether she knew that I would try to save her again. The theory was that the complexity of maintaining her own existence while making my body work and feeding my mind the illusion of sensation would eventually overwhelm her basic algorithms, a process estimated to take a minimum of eight years, after which she could crash catastrophically at any moment, and die, and take me with her if help couldn't reach me in time.

But the theory didn't factor in love.

Mary and I could meet in virtual reality. I could close my eyes and go to her as a man in a room in the virtual reality implant and be with her. Mary always took the form of a woman with me. She was never a man, like my first AI, or sometimes a man and sometimes a woman like the second. She was always just Mary. And she was beautiful.

I'm an artist, she told me one day, sitting next to me in the virtual-reality room, and her eyes sparkled. She was excited, breathless. I believed in her art: my body had never been more lean and tight, more sensitive, more orgasmic, more alive to the sudden brush of sunlight through clouds, or the clean feel of a glass tabletop, of the stirrings of the wind in the hair on my arms than it had been with Mary.

Come outside, she said, and she stood and took my hand. *Outside?* I asked, because there had never been an outside before. I stood and she turned me around, and there was a door now: dark oak, weathered, a little barred window the shape of a knight's shield at just the height of my eyes, and I could see blue sky out of it. By the door was a stone table, and on the table a rose. I walked to the table and picked up the rose, and the thorns pricked my skin. It smelled as beautiful as any rose I had ever smelled. *What have you done?* I asked.

And she opened the door and we walked out onto a mountainside in Spain: Andalusia, the Moorish country west of Gibraltar, the forests in the mountains, and the dry plain below us with black-robed riders galloping black horses across it far away, and the deep blue of the Atlantic, and across the straits, Africa. It was a place I loved, and she knew it because I loved it, and here it was in detail I had forgotten or which had never been. The mountains were starker, more jagged, more romantic. There were no cities. No roads. No other people, till we found that when we connected to the net our AI friends could visit us. I looked behind us, and the room we had walked out of had become part of a little white stucco Spanish house with a dull-red tile roof and a weathered water jar by the door.

Do you like this? she asked me.

Did I like it? I remembered her asking that question while I lay without the sensation of my body in the hospital bed. Mary's Spain was startling, but serene. The house she built in my mind became a home for us.

Toward noon, I felt a sudden rushing in my mind like the coming of a wind. My head felt expanded, immense, vast, and I knew that some greater artificial intelligence had entered me. Which meant a human doctor was coming to talk to me.

I couldn't imagine the days before AIs, the horror of life for people paralyzed like me, when you couldn't speak, when nothing could take out your thoughts and make them become words. When all you could do is listen and wait and wait and wait.

Hello, I thought.

Hello, William Addison.

Who are you?

I'm Hotel Andromeda.

But I knew that wasn't, perhaps, accurate. The hotel's central intelligence ran so many programs, was responsible for so much, that what was in me was only a small part of her vast mind. *So should I call you Andromeda or Hotel or both?* I asked.

The AI laughed in my mind, and I heard the doctor walk in the room. I couldn't turn my head to see her. But she leaned over and put her face above mine so I could see her when she talked to me, and she smiled. She had an old, careworn face. I could tell from the way she was holding her arms that she must have been holding on to mine, but I couldn't feel her touch.

"I'm sorry for the trouble you've had here," she said. "But this isn't your first time to go through this, is it? You know what we have to do, and that the procedure to make you well will take some time."

You don't understand, I thought, and Andromeda played my thoughts as words through a speaker at the head of my bed. *I don't want to go through that procedure again.*

"What?"

I want to try to save Mar—the artificial intelligence in me. I don't want her to die.

"Dying, as you call it, is part of the process of an AI's life, Mr. Addison. It accepted all this. It won't feel pain the way you feel pain."

Not physical pain, at least, I thought. *But she will feel the pain of ending, of parting. I want her programs searched for errors and the errors fixed and Mary put back inside of me.*

"Mary, is it?"

The doctor moved out of my line of vision, and I heard her opening a drawer in a cabinet I couldn't see.

There are elegant diagnostic and reconstructive programs,

Doctor, I thought. *Couldn't Andromeda take Mary and run the programs on her and find a way to help her?*

The doctor didn't say anything in response to that, at first.

Can you? I asked Andromeda. *Can you do this?*

Why do you want this, William Addison? Andromeda asked me. *The laws and procedures for AI replacement are set up to help you, to protect you.*

Because I love her, I thought, and it was the first time I had told that to anyone except Mary. Andromeda had spoken my thoughts through the speaker, and no one said anything to me about my love, not the doctor or Andromeda. The room was quiet for a time.

"It's been eight years, Mr. Addison," the doctor said, finally. "MAR-1 programs like yours start to fail at eight years. Some might last longer, but for how long we don't know. Keeping this particular AI in you any longer would be dangerous, especially when you've already seen the beginnings of its failure."

Do people abandon their sick? I asked the doctor. *I don't want to abandon Mary when she is the equivalent of sick. I am trying to find programmers who can help her—and one did two weeks ago. Mary and I are traveling to Earth to get even better help. We have a chance on Earth, if we can get there.*

It would be a danger to me to work with your AI, Andromeda told me in thoughts. *Her corruptions might infect me.*

Leave her in my mind, I thought. *Copy a part of your program and put it in my mind and check her that way. Don't take her out into any part of you.*

And in a rush of AI action I felt a movement in my mind and a door open and a program entering it. I rushed to follow. *I'm coming, too,* I said.

You'll slow me down.

Then go slowly. I want to talk to Mary, to see her. Tell the doctor what we're doing.

I was in the bedroom in our house in Mary's Spain, and it was as Mary and I had left it that morning: the bed unmade, the windows open. But there was a storm outside, and no one had closed the windows. Rain and leaves had blown in onto the bed and floor.

Take this, Addison.

I turned and caught a gun thrown into my arms. It wasn't a gun, of course, but a representation of a program that could kill an AI. I knew that, but still it looked and felt like a gun to me. Andromeda, or at least a copy of a part of her, stood in the form of a woman at the side of the door, heavily armed, dressed in black jeans and T-shirt, a gun held at the ready. I threw my gun on the bed and closed the windows.

Keep that gun, Andromeda said. *I don't know what damage can be done to your mind with you in here.*

I couldn't shoot Mary.

It might not be Mary you have to shoot.

I thought about that and picked up the gun.

Andromeda smirked at the bed. *Not platonic, you and Mary, are you?* she said.

Does it matter?

What do you feel when you hold her?

A woman.

What does she feel when she holds you?

I'd wondered that, too. *Me,* I said. *She says she feels me.*

Call her in. Open the door and call her in.

I opened the door, and Mary was standing there in the hall-way, pale, shocked to see me. I reached out to touch her, but Andromeda shoved me aside and leveled her gun at Mary. *Come in, Mary,* she said. *We're going to have a little talk.*

I stepped back and aimed my gun at Andromeda. *Put down your gun,* I said. *Now. Mary, I won't let her kill you.*

Andromeda pointed her gun at the floor. *Do you think this gun is the only way I have of doing my work?* Andromeda asked me without looking at me. She never took her eyes off Mary.

What's wrong? I asked Mary. *Do you know?*

Why are you here?

Do you have to ask?

Cut this talk, both of you, Andromeda said, and she told Mary what we had come to do. *Now sit on the bed and let me check you. Addison, put down that gun.*

Mary walked in and sat on the bed. She had evidently been outside because her hair was blown. She looked sad, very sad.

I'm old, William, she said.

Not old enough to die.

Andromeda walked over to Mary and touched her—but

suddenly drew back. Something black and fanged crawled around from behind Mary's head and hissed at me. Mary tried to throw it off, but she couldn't. I ran to pull it off her, but Andromeda shot first, and Mary disappeared.

What have you done! I shouted.

Moved her! I've put her in a holding cell. I'm downloading every diagnostic program I've got now, so shut up and let me work.

Andromeda sat on the floor and held her head and appeared deep in thought. I sat on the bed where Mary had sat, and waited. The bed was wet, and the leaves blown onto it smelled like fall. I brushed them onto the floor.

And Andromeda looked up at me. *She's fine,* she said. *Mary is fine. I can find nothing wrong with her.*

Then run the programs again. Why did my body stop functioning? What was the creature on her neck?

Her creation, to scare you, probably. I think all of this was to scare you into letting her go before she got sick and hurt you. She doesn't want to hurt you, William Addison. She loves you, too.

I couldn't speak for a time after Andromeda said all that, after I knew what Mary was willing to do to protect me. I didn't know what to say. I was afraid for Mary and me, too. But I believed the responsibility of love meant staying together and helping each other till the end. I looked out the window and at the bed and back at Andromeda.

Bring her back, I said.

I have already. I'm going out to tell the doctor what I've seen.

And she was gone, after the end of the sound of her last word, just gone.

But she'd left the gun in my hands. I threw it on the bed and walked out to find Mary.

She was sitting on the low, stone wall, looking across the plain toward Africa. It was blowy and cold outside, and I'd picked up a wool sweater for her. I put it around her shoulders and sat next to her. She pulled the sweater tighter around her against the cold. There were riders on the plain again, far off, near the coast, and I wondered now who and what they were.

I thought maybe I'd have to take that gun I'd left up on the bed and walk down to them someday to find out.

I want to take the risks of being with you, I told Mary.

Have my programs corrupted you, William? You want to cure me, and you can't. I'm mortal, like you.

And I accept that. Everyone we love will die, Mary. But we can love till then and face our loss when it comes.

She kept looking toward Africa, not at me. I took her hand and held it for a long, long time, and she let me hold it and she held on to my hand till the winds had blown the storm clouds over us and the sun was shining down and drying all the rain.

I sat on the edge of the bed while the doctor removed the electrodes from my body and turned off the machines. I could feel the edge of the bed under my legs; I could feel the sheets; I could feel the doctor's hands touching my body. "You realize Mary's manufacturer will not be liable for any consequences of your decision," she said.

"I'm liable," I said. "I'm choosing this life."

The doctor looked hard at me. "It will be interesting to see how long your Mary will last. I wish you both luck."

She left the room, and I dressed and followed her out. I passed the room where the medical robots sat waiting to be of service. Six robots were in the room, looking at me with their brilliant, ruby eyes. I walked in to thank the two who had carried me to the hospital, if they were there, and to leave word if they were not, but before I could say anything, one of them reached up and touched me. It knew. I suddenly realized that, because of Andromeda, the robots knew about Mary and me. I put my hand on its hand and held it for a time. The metal was cool, but not alien.

I had connections to rebook, programmers to contact, and I was hungry. But I let it all wait. I walked to an observation deck under a dome that looked out on the black of space and all the stars and sat in a chair and looked at the beauty of it for Mary and me. I felt a metal hand touch my shoulder, and I looked up at another robot with a tray of food, and I took the tray and thanked the robot but it never said a word to me. It just pressed my shoulder and left. I held the tray, and closed my eyes, and went into my mind to Mary and home.

TO CARESS THE FACE
OF GOD

———•———

Dave Wolverton

Warren Garceau had been imprisoned on Darius IV for so long that he no longer knew which he wanted more: death or sex. He no longer even dreamed of freedom, but freedom is what we gave him, in the form of a ticket off planet and a ride back to Earth after a brief layover at the Hotel Andromeda.

Warren had worn out six bodies serving as many consecutive life sentences. I watched him, as was my job. Each time his deaths came nearly the same: In his late sixties he would develop prostate cancer, and I'd take the prison infirmary to him, download a temporary medical program, and operate. Yet after the operation, he'd slow for the next dozen years. His arms would purple with liver spots while the wispy silver hair on his head became only a memory. His bones turned brittle, like the pumice in the red rocky fields where he worked day after day hoeing the corn, his breath coming in sharp gasps as he slaved beneath the double suns.

I kept Warren's little farm distant from those of other inmates. When he was young, during the first three lifetimes, Warren had some neighbors that he was allowed to see, men working fields far away from him. As he aged the others won their freedom, and I sent them home.

Until he became the last, and I watched him from a distance those final two lifetimes, mainly using automatic sensors. Yet sometimes I would use my natural eyes, and in the night I would spy on him from the mountains through a telescope with an infrared lens. He would hoe well into the night, even when the scorpions came out, as if, like me, he too were part machine. I can still see him, back bent, his arms gouging downward automatically, as if the hoe were some giant claw. After six lifetimes, he knew nothing but the hoeing and the harvest.

When Warren fell and broke his hip that last time, there was no one to help, and though my sensors did not indicate an attempt at escape, I did not learn that he was injured for two days. Warren had dragged himself to his shack, and there he passed out by his front door in the shade. I found him dehydrated and swollen, so I carried the infirmary to him, then pumped his body full of fluids.

But he died. So I thawed his last young clone, one with a powerful twenty-two-year-old physiology, and I dumped Warren's memories into the clone.

He woke in his crude little hut with machines pumping food and water into his veins. He faded in and out of sleep for a few days, always waking in pain, sometimes crying out for sleep, for eternal sleep, shouting, "For God's sake, Ray, let me die! Just let me die!" or sometimes he would call a woman's name.

But I fulfilled my duty, as is my job. I had kept him alive so he could serve his sentence; now I kept him alive so he could be free. When the clone began to stabilize, I made a quick trip back up to the guardhouse and began dismantling it. After nearly four hundred years, I too would be allowed to leave Darius IV.

That evening as I worked, I glanced down into Brutal Valley, to the barren red plains like rusted iron. Warren stood bent over his hoe, working mechanically. I got on a hovercraft and went to him. "You are free," I said as I floated through his field, sweeping the tender young plants away with my exhaust. He looked up at me, his face dirty and wet with sweat.

"What?"

"You are free."

He stopped, thought for a long moment. "What ... what does that mean?"

At first, I thought he might still be in shock, disoriented from the transfer. But I had not talked to him for two lifetimes, and I knew that at last he had forgotten. "It means you no longer have to hoe."

He stared into the short corn, uncomprehending. For nearly four hundred years he had worked that field. Little grew on Darius IV, not even weeds, so for those four hundred years I'd been forced to go into his fields from time to time and sow the thistles, dandelions, and morning glory. At harvest, I'd grind his grain into flour and add vitamin and mineral supplements provided from Earth. The corn had been Warren's only food now for a long time.

"What will I do without corn?" he asked.

"You are a rich man," I answered. "Over the years, you've been paid for your work—one International Dollar per day—and the government has let it accrue interest. You will be a very rich man. You can eat more than corn now. You can eat anything. You can go anywhere, do anything. You are free."

Warren looked up. His eyes were pale blue and empty, his wispy red hair down to his shoulders. His biceps were thick and powerful, and I had noticed even from a distance how he worked with gusto, glad to be young again. Yet even as a clone fresh from the vats, he had crags in his face, lines and creases, a map of all the empty roads and blind alleys he had walked down during his long lives.

"Free?" he said at last. A smile broke across his broad face. He looked up at me, then gazed off at the Plentiful Mountains with their scarred red stone surfaces and their snow-capped peaks. All of Darius IV was covered with red pumice down here on the plains, but up in the mountains, where my guardhouse rested in a valley, was a hazy swath of gentle green. "Can I go up there?"

"If you like," I answered.

"I like," he said, and he snapped the handle of the hoe between his two broad hands.

I took him to the valley with its carpet of rye grass and orchards with pear and pecan and olive and fig trees. Robot drones fretted, draping nets over a ripening cherry tree to keep out the flocks of ivory cockatoos. I pulled the hovercraft up to the marble columns at the guardhouse compound.

"I had always hoped it might be like this," Warren said, "but I never imagined ..." For the following several days I did not talk to Warren much, though he often stood near me, as if craving my presence, any human contact. I had a great deal of work to do, and there was no point in trying to speak to Warren. He could not carry on a conversation. After four hundred years he no longer recalled the meanings of most words. He could name the sun and the rocks and corn and a toilet, but he had no names for my flocks of cockatoos or for the color pink, and he could not recall the word *star*. Often, he would ask me the names of objects, and I would tell him, and he would forget again only moments later. Yet he did not fear his own ignorance. He grinned like a lunatic, happy to be free, and for him the world was filled with wonder.

Twice, he asked me, "Ray, why am I here?"

"You are a criminal. You have hurt people, so the government sent you here to recover."

"What did I do?" he asked. "I remember a woman, a woman's beautiful face. I remember wanting to love her."

"I don't know. I used to store that information in my temporary memory," I admitted, "but I erased it long ago. I know only that you were found guilty, but that your term is up."

Warren went to the window of the guardhouse, looked out through the leaded crystal to the orchards. For the first time in the past several days, his smile faltered. "Have I recovered," he asked, "or will I still hurt people?"

"I suspect ... that either you will hurt people, or you will not."

"I don't want to hurt people."

"Maybe that will change," I said. "You've been here a long time. People have hurt you by putting you here. Maybe you will want to get even."

Warren shook his head innocently, as if denying my accusation. "I hate this body," Warren admitted. "A few days ago, I was an old man and all of my bones ached. I wanted only to die. But when you put me back into this young flesh, I feel ...

uncomfortable. I want only sex. I want to rut like an animal. I can feel my flesh burning with that desire, as if I were working hard in the midday sun. For me, this young flesh is more uncomfortable. Death or sex. I've lived six lifetimes, Ray, and all through them, I have craved only those two things. Not vengeance." He held the windowsill, clenching and unclenching his powerful hands.

I think, at that moment, I feared what he might do. He reminded me of a panther, so passionate, so powerful, so volatile. "Perhaps," I ventured, "you will finally satisfy your cravings for both."

At the end of four days, I drugged Warren to keep him pacified during the initial stage of his trip home, and I sent him flying in the shuttle to the star cruiser *Reliable*. From there he connected with the terminal at Hotel Andromeda, and met his fate.

Aboard the Hotel Andromeda, Warren went to a public restaurant where the air was heavy, fetid. Few humans dined at the tables—a handful here, a handful there. In the center of the room, seven amphibious Fenroozi swam in a pool, like massive red newts, chasing their own tails and grabbing at golden fish. Warren sat at a table, grinning monstrously, watching three nubile young girls all dressed in glittering white. He stared at them, forgetting about food, and wondered how to approach them, how to ask for sex. Yet a more subtle craving enveloped him as he watched. He felt distant, isolated, and he craved human presence, any attention. In a nearby tree, a tall hairy silver beast that was all bones crouched while serving robots brought live prey for it to sniff.

Warren ignored the predator as he watched the girls. One woman finally saw that he was staring, and Warren turned away. The silver beast was watching him with all six eyes, surreptitiously inhaling Warren's scent. Warren did not have to understand the beast's guttural chatter to know that it was asking the serving robots if Warren was on the menu. Warren smiled, walked up to the beast, grasped one of its massive lower canines with his fist, and shook the beast vigorously. A long black tongue snaked out, tasting Warren's hand.

"Don't even think about it!" Warren said with a grin, slapping the predator's snout.

He ambled to the table, sat with three girls in white. They looked like clones, all red hair and freckles and sad eyes. "Hi," he said, "I'm Warren," and he said no more, feeling unsure of himself. How do you tell someone that you have not held a normal conversation in four hundred years? How do you tell a woman that you want her body, but you also want her to love you after you've used her? How do you casually slip into conversation the fact that you've forgotten how to read a menu, or that foods have changed so much that you don't know what they taste like anymore? He listened to the girls, feigning interest in things other than their bodies. One girl kept calling him "voracious," but she used the word as if it were a slang compliment. He imagined luring the girls to his room, grabbing them, making love to them wildly there. He was strong now, in his young body. He knew he could do it, with one of them at least. He ordered a light dinner made of things he could not remember ever having tasted.

When the food came, it was both delicious and overpowering. He enjoyed it immensely, but halfway through the second course, he vomited. The girls got up and left. Dumbfounded, Warren lay on the table, retching again and again. After three hundred and ninety-four years without any food but corn meal, he found to his dismay that perhaps he might not be able to stomach anything else.

Dazed, he decided to return to his room. On the way, Warren stopped to gaze through a window into a vast tube—a chamber where the artificial gravity was so powerful that gases became swirling frozen liquids. Creatures moved in there—some were like giant purple amoebas straddling layers of frozen green methane, while others higher up were fist-sized white squids or spiders that swam through liquid helium in little jerking spasms.

A sentry droid stopped and cautioned Warren against trying to enter the aliens' living chamber. But Warren just stood, watching. He held his hand to the window, felt the tug of that gravity, pulling him toward that alien world. Warren laughed. It was like the unrelenting tug of sex, like the grip of death.

Warren felt alone. More alone than ever. The sinking feeling he'd experienced in the restaurant came over him. *Death or sex,* he told himself, *death or sex.* One or the other. He could not decide which. Over the past few days, he had found the hotel to be very accommodating. He had only to ask at the com console in his room, and they offered virtually any service. He wondered, *If I were to order death and sex from the hotel, which would they bring first?* He imagined the woman of his dreams, the beautiful dark-eyed woman he had wanted to love for so long, and he went to his room—a simple room where an artificial sun shone on a carpet of living grass and a hammock swung between two trees.

Once in his room, Warren did not know what to do for entertainment, so he stood with his eyes closed. He tried to imagine holding a woman, just putting his arms around a woman casually, but he had not seen one in so long that the image kept fading. And at length he imagined a hoe in his hand. Warren stooped, as he had been doing for nearly four hundred years, and moved his arms steadily as if he were hoeing imaginary weeds from the grass.

A chime sounded, and Warren straightened. It chimed again, and Warren ambled to the door, wondering if the sound came from outside. When he touched the pressure plate, the door opened. A cyborg stood there, a powerful woman with hair the light brown of young corn silk, with massive artificial arms, body armor, extra sensors, and RAM storage containers bolted to her head. Warren stared into her face, wondered what it would be like to wrap his arms around her, just hold her flesh with all that metal.

"Warren Allen Garceau?" the cyborg asked. "Penitent from Darius IV?"

"Yes?" Warren answered.

"I am Marinda Chase, from hotel security."

Without thinking, Warren turned to face the wall, spread his legs, and placed his hands flat against the wall in preparation for a body search. Marinda stood somewhat surprised. "You are not under arrest," she hurried to explain. "I came at the request of a hotel client. A woman who says you once knew her on Earth. She would like to meet you again."

"A woman?"

"Yes, a Miss Rebecca Lynn Lyons."

The name struck Warren like a fist, and he found himself gasping, trying to recall who she might be. "Rebecca Lyons?"

"Yes, you murdered her on Earth long ago," Marinda said, "but her memories, her personality, are stored in a virtual reality aboard the hotel's module for deceased personalities, Heavenly One. She would like to meet you there—in heaven. She says she will pay you well for the privilege. Will you come?"

Rebecca Lyons—that was her name—the dark-eyed woman of his dreams. Warren nodded dumbly and smiled. He recalled that hurt, the ache of wanting to love her, and he wondered why she would want to see him. *She will hate me,* he realized. *She will want to hurt me, as I hurt her.* He could smell the trap. Yet he could not leave it alone. And an odd thought struck him. If she were in a virtual heaven program, then perhaps she would not be angry. Perhaps she would forgive him. Perhaps she would even be grateful that he had killed her and sent her there. Warren thought for a long time before answering, "Yes, I'll come."

Aboard the module Heavenly One, Warren found only a slate gray room with several cubicles where visitors could recline in comfortable chairs. Outside of these, the module had no accommodations for the living. The cyborg Marinda Chase plugged the synaptic adaptors into the socket at the base of Warren's skull and fit a helmet over his head. He had wanted to bring a gift, but what do you give someone living in a virtual reality? They had no physical needs, no bodies. Warren knew little of virtual realities. They had been young when he was young, and he had never created a world with computer images. He did not know what to expect.

Greens and blues swirled before Warren's eyes, and his nostrils filled with a strange sweet essence. He sniffed: a warm summer sun beaming upon grass and stone, the scent of water, and some type of sweet blossoms. Sounds began to arise, the drone of bees, a light wind whispering through the grass, the peep of a bird among forest branches, someone laughing. Then the images: He was sitting upon a stone chair carved in a black basalt mountain. Dark green hanging vines draped the mountain like a living curtain, and the scent of their sweet red flowers filled the air. Honey bees droned along the cliff face like motes of dust caught in the sunlight. All around him was a sparse deciduous forest surrounding a shadowed meadow. Somewhere off in the trees Warren could hear a tumbling brook, and laughter. It was late afternoon, almost twilight, so that the slanting sun over the trees came faint and golden.

"Hello?" Warren called. "Hello?"

He stood for a long time, until distant laughter answered him from the shadowed woods. The angels came for him, floating through the forest like thistle down. Two young women wearing luminous robes of green. Their translucent wings were broad, like those of a butterfly, and the wings trembled in the sunlight. The angels landed at his feet, and they were twins: Clear skinned, clear eyed, with long dark hair and eyes like brown pools. They were young women. Warren gazed into their faces for a long time, gazed at their bare shoulders, and the yearning he felt for them grew. "Are you Rebecca Lyons?" he asked.

One girl laughed, stepped toward him playfully, took his hand between hers. "We are only her servants. She is a goddess now, ruler of this world. Will you let us take you to her?"

Warren whispered, "Of course." One of the angels clapped, and the whole forest came alive. Satyrs pranced in from the woods playing golden flutes and they danced around Warren on mincing hooves, their goat tails twitching in time to the music. Pale green naked tree sprites with large breasts brought a pallet draped with silks, and while the angels stripped Warren's clothes off, the sprites cheered and fought to lift him onto the pallet.

Once Warren was naked, they carried him, dancing and singing through the forest, sometimes stopping to spin him in circles. Sometimes dryads would be singing in the trees above him, and they would toss baskets of leaves and flower petals on his head. Once, the revelers chased a herd of giant pigs from their trail. Fairy lights danced above him, and off in the deeper shadows under the trees, Warren could see men with the heads of deer moving nervously, as deer will.

The procession carried Warren forward to the sounds of flutes and song and drums, through the thickening woods as the day died and the shadows took on a life of their own. They carried him for hours, laughing and celebrating, lighting torches in the darkness, until they reached a mountain pass. Even from the bottom of the trail, Warren could see flames lighting the night at the mountain's top, a great bonfire, and

around it danced the stag men and satyrs and naked tree
sprites.

For a man who had forgotten words, the scene was one of
total delight. He could not even guess at the names of the
wonders he beheld. Instead, he was like a child, amazed,
drinking pure pleasure and enjoyment. *Rebecca must have
forgiven me,* he reasoned, *to bring me to heaven.* When the
wood sprites stopped at the foot of the mountain to paint him
in stripes of yellow and orange, Warren did not mind even
though their hands were rough. When the satyrs gave him
wine, he drank until his head spun.

The satyrs poured more wine for him, pointed and laughed.
Warren could feel a warmth on his head, burning spots, and
he touched his forehead, felt the nubs of goat horns sprouting
above his eyes. He jumped up and danced around on the pallet as they carried him up the mountain, and was amazed to
find his feet numb. Nimble little hooves were growing where
the toes and feet had been, and his naked legs were covered
with a fine layer of goat hair.

One of the satyrs tossed him a flute, and Warren took it to
his lips, found that it played a haunting melody that gave
voice to all his lusts and desires far better than he could ever
speak them. He spun upon his pallet, dancing and laughing
and playing hymns to the moon and darkness until they carried him before the goddess Rebecca Lyons. She was reclining upon a daybed in a small meadow, and she was more
beautiful than Warren had ever dreamed. The pale handsome
face framed by dark hair, the obsidian eyes staring out at him.

The bed itself was the purest shade of white he could ever
imagine, and Rebecca wore a single transparent sheet to cover
the sleek contours of her body, the generous breasts. A scent
more alluring than honeysuckle wafted from her bed. All
around her meadow were trees, great oaks with twisted
branches and dark leaves. The bonfires burned in a circle
around her, so that Rebecca was a singular adornment to the
forest.

Warren stopped singing, stopped dancing, let the golden
flute fall from his hands, forgotten.

"Baaa . . . ," he said, all his desire, all his lust and yearning
for her coming out in a single bleating sound not unlike a
belch.

"Do you remember me?" the Goddess asked.

Warren bleated, and tried to hobble nearer, but found that his goat feet were suddenly clumsy. He smiled up at her, and for a moment the goddess stopped, confused.

"You smile? As if you are happy to see me?" she asked. "I bring you here naked, painted like a fool, and show you yourself as a dumb animal, and you smile?"

Warren bleated, looking around in bewilderment. The lust he felt for her was strong, and the pink tip of his organ began extending from its hairy sheath. Yet beneath the lust was a desire more refined, a yearning to beg her forgiveness, to seek her love. He wanted nothing more than to climb on that bed with her, to caress the face of god with one hand and soothe her anger.

"Take him!" Rebecca ordered, and suddenly the satyrs and wood sprites had him. They pulled him down from the pallet and twisted his arms behind, held Warren's face to the ground. Someone tied his right wrist to an exposed tree root, then his left, then his feet, tightening the ropes so that his legs spread wide.

Warren, his face in the dirt, panted, raising small puffs of dust from the ground, and the satyrs began to dance around him, their eyes gleaming in the firelight, followed by the men with stag's heads. They danced in wide circles and sang in deep voices, sometimes coming close enough to caress his naked buttocks, watching him with lust in their eyes, as if they could not wait for the goddess to give her command so that they could fall on him. Through it all, Warren grunted, but he did not try to struggle free of his bonds or fight.

Rebecca watched, amused at first, but gradually she began to frown as if her face would settle into a scowl. Finally she spoke, "Do you understand why you are here?" she asked. With a wave of her hand, the goddess returned his voice to him.

"I . . . don't know. You invited me," Warren offered.

"I brought you here so I could watch you get raped, the way you raped me," Rebecca said evenly. "I'm going to let the satyrs have you, one by one, until you cry out in agony the way I cried when you took me. Then I personally am going to slit your throat, here. And at the same time that I do it here, I have paid the security guard Marinda Chase to slit your throat outside the virtual reality, and you will die."

"Oh," Warren said.

"You aren't frightened? You didn't even guess that I wanted vengeance?"

"I guessed," Warren admitted. "I don't remember what I might have done to you. I guess . . . I came here to find out. I've been raped, in prison back on Earth. I know what it's like. As for death, I've never been afraid of it. I've died six times. And I've spent a long time in hell, on a planet called Darius IV. I guess, maybe, I came here because I wanted to see your heaven, if only for a moment. Forgive me if I enjoyed the taste of it, even for a moment, when you didn't want me to."

"You think this is heaven?" Rebecca said. "Can you understand the tedium of having everything you want, when you want it? I would trade a day of life for an eternity here, and you stole my life!"

Warren looked up, sweat running from his face. "I know you hate me, but the man you hated died three hundred and fifty years ago. If you want, you can go ahead and kill me now." Warren waited, humbled, naked. For a moment Rebecca's scowl faltered. He almost dared hope for mercy.

Then Rebecca shrieked, and the sound of her wrath filled the skies. For one endless moment the flames of the bonfires leaped up around him, like a wall, like a huge crown, and Warren took their full fury, felt them crisping his flesh, burning the skin from his bones, boiling his eyes in their sockets. He tried to scream, but only steam shot from his mouth. He twitched to flames more caustic than any acid. In that moment, he wanted death more purely than ever before, but it would not come. His sanity felt as if it would boil and bubble away as cruelly as his flesh, but still death would not come.

The flames were snuffed more suddenly than they had arisen. Warren found himself in the slate gray visiting room, gasping, burning. The cyborg Marinda Chase stood over him, the plug from the neural jack in one hand, a long bare knife in the other. Warren saw that a second core was plugged into the neural net, running up to the socket at the base of

Marinda's skull. She too had been plugged into the illusion, awaiting the goddess's orders.

"You can go," Marinda said. "Rebecca's had her fun. You'll never suffer enough to satisfy her. I suspect that your other victims would feel the same, if they were around to talk. I can understand their hate, but I won't kill you for them."

"But you thought about killing me," Warren said, unable to imagine what he had done to her. The cyborg looked into his eyes, and Warren saw danger there, and the end of his hope. Marinda might not kill him, but she was the kind who would never forgive him. She would just keep exacting a toll, day after day, minute after unceasing minute.

She said in a deadly tone, "Get out, before I change my mind."

The shining shuttle pod returned to Darius IV only two days before I was scheduled to leave. Warren Garceau got out along with two servant droids and began offloading seeds and young fruit trees, various desert reptiles, and other forms of animal life from Earth. I thought it a great waste of his wealth—him, someone who could live almost anywhere, do almost anything.

Still, he was free to do as he liked, and I no longer needed the guardhouse. Earth had stopped imprisoning men ages ago, having found more advanced and profitable ways to reprogram criminals. Still, I had managed to keep Warren imprisoned until his sentence was completed, as was my job. I bore him no grudge, so I gave him the guardhouse as his own, along with the surrounding mountains and the orchards.

I asked Warren before I left what he had found at Hotel Andromeda that made him want to flee civilization so soon.

"A world too much like the one I left," he answered.

"What of the things you wanted?" I asked. "What of sex and death?"

Warren grunted, looked away. "I've lived without love for a long time. I guess I can keep on living without it. As for death, I figure I have the rest of eternity to explore it." I looked into Warren's eyes, and I saw his dishonesty. Sex and death. I knew, I knew that he had somehow gotten his fill of both. Suddenly I became afraid, wondering who he may have raped, who he had killed.

I did not wave good-bye to Warren as I left. The cockatoos rose below the shuttle in a cloud, and beyond the green of trees in the mountain vale and the ruby desert surrounding it, there was little to see. I pieced together his story at Hotel Andromeda myself, and even visited Rebecca Lyons in her heaven. She still had the downloaded personality of Warren there with her, burning in flames, screaming. She said she would keep it there forever, as if it were a treasured gift. But I contacted Hotel Security and managed to erase the stolen construct. I read its memories before releasing it from its pain. Still, all these years later, I sometimes think of Warren.

An explorer returned to Darius IV a decade ago and described the world as fecund. In the mountains, he said there were fruit trees—cherry, mango, pear, avocado, olive, peach, apricot—and wild strawberries the size of a man's fist. Salmon and giant trout leap in the streams. He found wild fields of corn and rice, and wheat growing over your head, and beneath the double suns, the plants blossom all year long. Stronger trees and grasses have even begun to encroach into the desert wastes, finding place among cactus. There is no one there now to harvest the fruits, so they are consumed by lizards and flocks of ivory cockatoos. This is what Warren made of his world, and I imagine that I would not have done as well.

GLASS WALLS

———●———

Kristine Kathryn Rusch

i

Beth touched the warm glass window. Inside, the baby Minaran swam, its small head rounded and sleek, its eyes open and friendly. When she had first passed the cubicle, the baby rested on its back on a rock, basking in fake sunlight. Its fur was white, its fins slender but strong.

Odd that it would have a cubicle all to itself just inside the human wing. Odder still that the cubicle had been a banquet room a few days before.

She leaned her face against the glass, wishing she could go inside. The poor little thing had to be lonely. If she could hold it and feel its warm, wet fur against her skin, she might be able to ease the loneliness—both of their loneliness—for just a short time.

"Beth!"

Roddy's voice. She jumped away from the window and stood, hands clasped behind her back. She kept her gaze trained downward, away from the Minaran in the cubicle.

Roddy hated it when she ogled the guests.

"What are you doing in the main lobby?" He stood beside her. She could smell peppermint on his breath. He had just had a cup of his favorite—expensive—tea. "Did someone call for you?"

She shook her head. How many demerits this time? Or maybe he would take a week's worth of tips. The diamond square pattern on the carpet ran together. She blinked, making sure her eyes were tearless.

"You know I don't like having the personal staff in the lobby. It creates a sleazy atmosphere. Some of our patrons would prefer to ignore people like you."

As you would, she thought. She finally raised her head, saw Candice at the lobby entrance, watching the entire exchange. Roddy wore a black suit, very twentieth-century retro, fitting in perfectly with the decor in this half of the human wing. Except for the Minaran.

"I was walking through," Beth said, "and I saw the Minaran. What's it doing here?"

"That's none of your business," Roddy said. "When you were hired on, you were told not to ask questions—"

"Beth was not hired," Candice said. She started down the incline into the lobby. Roddy didn't move. He froze, just like Beth had, when faced with his boss. "Let's not have this discussion in the lobby, hmm? My office, please."

Except for the Minaran, the lobby was empty. The next ship was twenty minutes behind schedule. The staff was having its break, preparing for the midafternoon rush.

Beth and Roddy followed Candice around the registration desk. Her office was a spacious room with a view of the docking ships and the stars beyond. She had to have been at Hotel Andromeda for most of her life—and had to have been a valued employee—to attain a view like that.

"Sit down," Candice said as she slipped in the wide leather chair behind her desk. Her office, too, was done retro. Beth didn't want to sit in the leather chair on the other side of the desk—she hated the feel of the material against her skin; it brought back too many unpleasant memories—but she did anyway. Roddy sat beside her, perched at the edge of the chair as if he were going to spring up any minute.

"The lobby is not a place for dressing down an employee,"

Candice said, folding her jeweled hands together and leaning forward on the desk. "We are striving to make our guests as comfortable as possible, and they don't need to see dissention among the staff. Is that clear?"

Roddy nodded.

"Good. You may go."

Roddy leaped out of the chair as if it had an ejector seat. He was gone from Candice's office in the time it took her to turn to Beth. "You know better than to stand in the lobby when you're not working."

"Yes." Beth looked at her hands. They weren't as well groomed as Candice's. The years of hard labor would always remain in the form of yellowed calluses, bent nails, and scarred skin.

"The Minaran fascinates you."

Beth didn't answer. When she stared at the creature, memories crossed within her. Memories of the investigator—what was his name? Shafer?—who had killed so many Minarans and destroyed her world, too. Memories of being trapped, naked, in a cubicle the same size for her first real journey into space, the other prisoners passing her, jeering, and tapping on the clear plastic. She had hated it, hated it, and not even the memory of John got her through.

All that combined in loneliness so deep that sometimes she thought nothing would fill it.

"Beth?"

Beth looked up. Candice's voice was harsh, but her eyes weren't. Candice was the only nice person Beth had met on the staff. The rest treated her like dirt, like she was worse than dirt, like she had no value at all.

"You have more demerits than any other staff member. Your ten-year service contract has grown to sixteen. If you don't watch yourself, you could be indentured to the hotel for life."

Beth shrugged. She had nowhere else to go. Meager as it was, the hotel was more home to her than any other place she had lived. Any other place except Bountiful, among the Dancers.

Candice stood up, and shoved her hands in the pocket of her suit. She was a big woman, and powerful. "I would like to make you a project, Beth. I think you're smarter than any other person on the staff. I can send you to an alien no one knows anything about, and you can discover its sexuality and please it within a matter of hours. If this system ran on merits instead of demerits, I suspect you would have been out of here in five years, instead of accumulating enough trouble to keep you here indefinitely. But I need to know if you're willing."

"What do you want from me?" Beth's voice felt rusty, as if she hadn't used it for days.

"I want to train you to become my assistant. You would act as liaison between all branches of the hotel, and you would mostly work in New Species Contact. You would discover what a species needs to feel most at home, and work with the design and personal staff to accomplish that."

Beth clasped her hands together. She had never done anything like that. She could barely speak to other people. Imagine if she had to speak to other species. Normally she went into their rooms and became like a Dancer, absorbing the emotions of the other being and flowing with them until she found what they wanted. Then she would leave, and Dancerlike, forget everything that had happened. "I don't know design or diplomacy."

"I would train you."

Beth shook her head once and stood. "If you knew about me, you wouldn't offer this."

"I know you came to us from a penal ship. I know you were in for murder."

"No." Beth reached out and touched the edge of Candice's desk. The wood was smooth and warm, like the glass around the Minaran's cubicle. "I was convicted under the Alien Influences Act. Some friends of mine and I saw Dancer puberty rites and tried them on each other, not realizing that when you cut off a human's hands, heart and lungs, they die. Because of us, the Intergalactic Alliance closed its second planet— Bountiful—and ordered that humans never have contact with Dancers again. And we were scattered into isolation, away from aliens. That's why the hotel had to get special dispensation to buy my indentured servitude contract."

"But no aliens have influenced you since," Candice said.

"That's because," Beth said, keeping her voice soft, "that's because I haven't let them."

ii

Beth went back up to her room by the back way, so that she wouldn't see the Minaran, and be tempted to stop again in the lobby.

The hallway outside her room was quiet. She pressed her finger against her door and it slid open, revealing her haven. Her room was not done retro. A sleep couch floated in the middle, mimicking the weightlessness of space. Nothing decorated the walls, not even a holojector, vid screen, or sound unit. It had taken her nearly two years to accept the room as a haven instead of a punishment—by that time, she was used to its spareness. It gave her eyes a rest from the business in the remainder of the hotel.

She took off her shoes and waved at the bed. The motion made it float down to her, and she climbed on it, letting the softness take her. When she had no assignments, she usually slept. Sleep protected her from her memories, protected her from her life. She closed her eyes and felt the bed rise to its place in the center of the room.

The Minaran swam behind her closed eyelids, its little white body begging for her attention. Minarans were not space-faring creatures, so they had no place in the hotel. So of course the hotel would have to build something special.

But someone would have had to bring the creature here. Someone would have had to travel with it, provide it with accomodations, alter a vessel in order to carry it in space. Someone had a lot of money invested in that one little creature.

Odd. Too odd.

Beth opened her eyes and stared at the blank ceiling. Still the sense of the Minaran did not leave her. Minar, the creature's home planet, had been closed, like Bountiful. The Minarans were an endangered species, like the Dancers.

She sat up so fast the bed rocked and nearly tossed her out. Like the Dancers. Minarans were protected species—no one was allowed to remove them from the planet. And this one was a baby, since it was the size of a small cat. Adult Minarans grew to the size of adult male lions, like the kind kept in the Earth zoo on the fifteenth level.

Her knowledge of the Minarans came from the holos that the hotel had shown her when she arrived. The Minaran sequence was the most graphic, hordes of colonists sweeping down on the defenseless animals because the colonists believed that the Minarans had killed a few humans. The colonists had poisoned the Minarans' environment, and the creatures had died in agony as the chemical balance of their watery home shifted. Eighty percent of the creatures died before someone figured out that the colonists were killed by environmental factors that had nothing to do with the Minarans at all.

The holo was a cautionary piece about the power of erroneous beliefs. If hotel staff suffered from the same kind of prejudices the colonists had, guests would die on all levels, from ignorance to lack of care, to well-intentioned "security" measures.

That's what had been striking her as odd, more than the cubicle in the lobby. The entire staff knew about the Minarans, knew about the illegality of transporting them, and still gave this one a place of honor in the lobby.

She had seen a lot of strange things in the hotel, and she had ignored most of them. She couldn't ignore this one.

The Minaran's wide, round eyes haunted her in a way that no one had since she left Bountiful, almost two decades before.

iii

She didn't want to see Candice, because Candice would ask her to change her decision. Beth wasn't qualified to work in such a sophisticated position. She didn't want anyone harping on her, forcing her into a place she didn't want to be.

A place she wasn't able to be. Working with the aliens required thought. And Beth worked hard at losing thought and memory while she did her job.

Before she could do anything about the Minaran, though, a summons came from Roddy. The summons was merely a beep inside her neural net. She had screamed so when they attached the simple system that the doctors were afraid to try anything more complex. Roddy hated the fact that he had to direct her in person, but she refused to let anyone ever again mess inside her mind.

His office was two levels down from her room. She hated it. She hadn't recognized the design when she first saw it, almost a decade before, but then she had done some research.

Roddy had chosen nineteenth-century retro, Victorian period, England. His office smelled of tobacco and liquor, both substances now banned in large intergalactic areas like the hotel (unless some guest requested them for his pleasure). Rich reds and dark woods covered the walls and carpet. The furniture was heavy, so heavy that Beth wondered how it met regulation. Roddy's stiff suits and muttonchop whiskers looked natural here, as did his distaste for her and the others like her.

"We had a request from Amphib," he said, his back to her. Steam rose from a cup on his desk, and she recognized black tea, as difficult to get as the peppermint stuff he usually drank. "I've forgotten. Do you swim?"

He hadn't forgotten at all. He just liked to toy with her. She wouldn't give him the satisfaction of emotion in her answer.

"Yes, sir."

"Good." He turned. Between his fingers, he held a pipe, unlit, of course. His gaze was cold. "We wouldn't want you to drown, like Tina did last year. We can't afford more scandals like that."

"Good swimmers can drown in only a few inches of water if they get knocked unconscious," Beth said. Keeping her tone flat had become more difficult. Tina had taught her how to swim when she first came to the hotel almost a decade before. Careless sex, violence, or some kind of accident had caused Tina to die.

"I suppose." Roddy leaned against a shelf filled with antique books. "We had a request from a Ratoid. It seems it heard about our interspecies service from a satisfied friend. I have a vid in the next room if you want to see how it's done among consenting Ratoids—"

She shook her head. She had discovered that information vids often interfered with her flow, her opportunity to do her work. "What room?"

He handed her a card with a floor plan and a duplicate of the print which would open the Ratoid's lock. "In all fairness," he said, "I should let you know that Ratoids achieve orgasm underwater. I trust you can hold your breath for long periods of time?"

Beth bit back a response—she usually held her breath the entire time she was in his office—and snatched the card from his hand.

She worked her way through the maze of levels. At least the Amphibs were close to the human quarters. The atmosphere, oxygen levels, and room design weren't all that different. The various amphibs from a number of worlds required a pool instead of a bathroom. They had adjusted to beds and sofas and other human comforts.

Finally, she climbed up a flight of rough-hewn stairs and pushed open a door. The air that greeted her was thick with humidity and smelled faintly of stagnant water. The Amphib section had several kinds of water pools—stagnant, spring-fed, saltwater, acidic, and freshwater. Some Amphibs did well with chemical water treatments. Others died.

She pushed back her hair with one hand and paused in front of the door. Stagnant water. Yuck. Then she took a deep breath and reached to the part of her mind where the Dancers lived.

Dancers—long flowing bodies that looked as if they danced instead of walked. Wide eyes, a faint tang, and a chirp. No memories, none at all, just instinct and free-flowing emotion. Affection, warmth, curiosity, and touch. She still remembered their touch, rubbery and soft at the same time. She had wanted to be a Dancer when she was young. Now she became one each time she walked through a guest's door.

Inside, large creature, beautiful creature with jeweled skin. Not jeweled. Water dappled. Air smells fetid. Stagnant water. Her skin tingles, wondering how it will feel pressed up against the creature's. It speaks—a rumble she does not understand. She steps forward, rubs her hand on its jeweled skin, feeling water, feeling coolness, feeling slime. Her entire body heats. The creature pulls away her clothes, and together they dive into the green algae, floating on the surface of the pool . . .

iv

And when she came to herself, she was standing on the rough-hewn steps, her clothing carelessly wrapped around her. She smelled rank—decayed water and something else, something even more foul. Her body felt heavy, tired, used, like it always did when these things ended. She lifted a hand, and found it coated with black slime. A shudder ran through her, and she ran the remaining distance to her apartment.

A beep echoed inside her net. Roddy. He wanted to see her

humiliation. Odd he could think after all these years she could still be humiliated. Odd that she could. So many of the others shut off their skins as if their brains had been developed with an on-off switch. Hers must have malfunctioned. She always came to herself frightened and disgusted.

Her apartment door opened and she let herself inside, discarding her clothing, climbing into the tiny bathing cubicle, and setting the water temperature near scalding. Washing didn't make the feeling go away, but it did give her some of her dignity back. She never could remember what happened, but that never changed her feeling that what did happen was wrong.

The beep echoed again. She put on a different outfit and checked herself in the tiny mirror. No trace of the Ratoid remained.

On the surface.

She was about to let herself out when the door swung open. Roddy stood there, hands on his hips. "I've been summoning you," he said.

"I just finished. I was coming."

"You finished almost an hour ago."

He was watching, then. She wondered how many times he watched, and how it made him feel. It made her feel even more used.

"I don't know what couldn't wait until I got cleaned up."

"The Ratoid wants you back, later. It is bringing in a number of guests, and wants you for entertainment."

She couldn't suppress the shudder. The last time she had participated in an interspecies orgy, she had nearly died. Roddy knew that. He knew how she feared another encounter. Maybe he was still punishing her for glancing at the Minaran. Or maybe he wanted her to know how much he resented the interaction with Candice, earlier.

"It's against regulations to perform with an alien twice in one day." She put one hand on the undecorated wall to anchor herself.

"You are in too much trouble to quote regulations to me." His jaw was set, his mouth in a sideways line. She didn't like the way his eyes glittered.

"The regulations protect the hotel." She kept her voice soft, but the muscles in her arm tensed. "Too many humans died from repeat contact. Sometimes the alien touch is like a slow-acting poison. I remember when Steve died—"

"I had the autodoc check out the Ratoids," Roddy said. "You'll be fine."

"No." Beth felt dizzy. She had never stood up to Roddy before—to anyone before. She wondered if the Minaran swimming in its little tank felt the same trapped anger that she felt so dangerously close to the surface. "No," she said again.

"This kind of action will allow me to hold your contract forever."

"That gives me a lot of incentive to work harder," she said, and pushed her way into the hall. The air felt cooler there. She strode toward the lobby, not looking back. She had no plan, no idea in mind. She just had to walk.

It wasn't until she stopped in front of the Minaran that she realized she had had a plan after all. It swam up to her, examined her for a moment, then swam away and climbed up on the rocks, its back to her. She wanted to tell it she knew how it felt, trapped in there, on display, with no one to love it, no one to hold it, no one to understand its dreams—and its nightmares.

"Pretty, isn't it?"

The voice was soft, deep and human. Beth turned and looked up into the face of an older woman. Her hair had been painted in small geometric squares of black and silver, and her skin in complementary shades of brown and cream. She wore a rich purple dress that accented the bizarre geometry that some thought fashion.

"You brought it here." Beth made herself look away. The Minaran had hunched into itself, as if it were frightened of the woman.

Assumptions. Human assumptions. Something the hotel warned them never to make.

"I figured this would be a good place to find it a home." Her voice had the warmth of an Amphib sauna, but her silvery eyes glistened with chill. Beth saw, over the woman's shoulder, Roddy gesturing at her frantically. She ignored him.

"Wasn't it at home on Minar?"

The woman laughed. "So sweet and amusing." She tucked

a strand of hair behind Beth's ear. Beth shuddered. "I thought
you were the one that liked touch."

Beth stiffened. This was a guest. She couldn't contradict a
guest. "I'm off duty," she said.

The woman's eyes twinkled for the first time. "I thought
staff never went off duty." Her smile grew wider. "Would you
like to please my little Minaran there? It looks quite lonely."

Inside the cage? Trapped behind invisible walls? Beth pushed
away, trying not to be rude, but her entire body had started to
shake. She bobbed her head once, and walked away, turning her
back on Roddy, whose face had turned purple with anger.

V

In her dream, she dived into the Minaran's tank. The water
was cool against her skin. The creature rubbed its furry face
against her breasts, seeking comfort, seeking milk. She
pushed it away. She wanted friendship, but not touch.

She hated touch.

She swam underwater to the rock in the center of the pool.
Then her fingers gripped the hard surface and she pulled herself up. Artificial sunlight caressed her body, warmed her,
comforted her as she hadn't been comforted since she left
Bountiful.

Except for John. Hands tentative, gaze soft. They hadn't
known what they were doing. But the Lunar Base psycholog-
ical staff had. They burst into the room, pulled two lonely
teenagers apart and kept them separate forever. Since then,
she had never touched another human being in love.

The Minaran pushed its face against her arm. Its muzzle
was wet, brown eyes liquid. It chirped at her, then dived back
under the water. When it rose again, it was on the other side
of the rock. Its loneliness radiated from it. The round eyes
looked sad.

She rolled over on her stomach, covering herself as best
she could. The Minaran used its fins to pull itself on the rock
and cuddle next to her. She tried to push it away—it was too
human, too cute. She didn't want touch, didn't want touch,
didn't want—

Beth woke up, heart pounding, skin crawling. She put her
head between her knees, made herself take deep breaths. Ever

since she saw the Minaran, the nightmares were coming thick and fast. Opening a little door that would best remain closed.

Trapped. The little creature was trapped. No being deserved to be imprisoned, bartered, and sold. No being. No one.

Not even her.

She eased the bed toward the ground so that she could climb off. Then she stood barefoot on the cold floor, hugging herself as she stared at the four bare walls surrounding her.

vi

The next morning, she made her way into the docks. Willis was there, working in a small cubicle, head bent over a small screen. When he saw her, he grinned and waved. She made herself wave back.

"Going to take me up on it?" he asked, voice jaunty, eyes filled with too much hope.

Beth made the smile stay on her face. "Someday," she said. Usually she felt nothing when she spoke to him. This morning she felt a bit sad.

The large docking bay was over cool. Goose bumps rose on her arms. Marks from hundreds of shuttles covered the floor, and the bay doors had dents in them from accidents missing the path. Through the double protection windows, she could see a dozen ships orbiting around the hotel.

"Knew it wasn't my charm," he said, careful not to touch her. Willis had tried to touch her once years ago, and she had screamed so loudly that Security arrived. They both got demerits for that incident. "What can I do for you?"

"Your office," she said, and made herself put her hand on the small of his back. His face flushed, but he still didn't touch her back. He had offered to buy her contract from the hotel, indenture her to him, and then throw the contract away once they were in space—no strings. Only they both knew that he wanted her love forever, and she had no love to give.

A soft female voice echoed in the bay. *"Next arrival in thirty-six minutes. Next arrival . . ."*

Willis closed the door on the sound. Beth reached up and shut off the interhotel com. Willis's flush left his skin and he tamped back something, probably willing his net to stop monitoring the conversation.

She hoped it worked. His net was twenty times more so-phisticated than hers.

"Can you get a message off the hotel for me?" she asked.

He started, then sat down. "I didn't know you knew anyone away from here."

She shrugged, unwilling to implicate him more than she had to. She handed him a small chip encased in plastic. It had taken her more than two hours to put the package together and to hide her steps. "Instructions are on here," she said. "Could you do it once you're out of hotel range?"

"Not leaving with me?" he asked, a little too seriously.

"After this," she said, "I'm probably not leaving at all."

vii

Every morning after that, she stood at the edge of the lobby, watching the Minaran swim. Its fur had grown coarser, and its eyes less bright. Its energy was flagging, and she be-gan to wonder if she had taken action in time.

Sometimes, as she stood there, Candice came up beside her and stood, too. They never spoke, but Beth felt as if Candice wanted her to say something, to reconsider her decision. Roddy would catch Beth standing there and a few minutes later her net would beep, summoning her to darker and smel-lier parts of the hotel. She went, but came to herself with un-usual bruises and once, a limp on her left side.

And she didn't see the woman again, not until the day the In-tergalactic Police showed up at the hotel. They had used the Se-curity entrance, and tripped no alarms, used no buzzers. One minute the lobby was empty, the next it swarmed with uni-formed creatures—most investigating the cubicle holding the Minaran.

Beth inched her way into the lobby and stood off to one side, knowing that she looked shoddy and hurt. Roddy was nowhere around, but Candice buzzed into the room, all effi-ciency and smiles. Only her shaking hands betrayed her fears.

"Officers?" Candice said, her voice carrying, warning the staff to keep the guests away.

A burly man grabbed a computer clip from a four-armed humanoid and approached Candice.

"Ma'am. I need to see the manager on duty or the highest person in charge of the hotel."

"Right now, that's me," she said. "The others are sleeping or attending a conference off surface. Would you like me to contact—"

"No." His voice boomed in the small area. The Minaran had stopped swimming, and had retreated to its rock. Beth wished she could do the same. "I came to inform you that you and your hotel are in violation of Galactic Code 1.675: kidnapping, imprisonment, and trafficking of an endangered species."

"The Minaran?" Candice asked. She turned toward the cubicle. Beth could see her struggle for control.

"We're also looking for a human, Candice Arrowsmith."

Candice straightened. "I'm Candice Arrowsmith."

"Then you shouldn't look so shocked, Ms. Arrowsmith. You will receive a commendation from Galactic Services for risking your job and contacting us. The Minaran will be returned to its rightful home, and the guilty parties will stand trial for this."

Candice's gaze caught Beth's. She opened her mouth as if to speak to Beth, but then another officer called her away.

Beth watched for another moment, saluting the little Minaran mentally. "At least," she whispered, "one of us is free."

viii

The Intergalactic Police took only three hours to remove the Minaran and clear the lobby. Hotel workers dismantled the cubicle, and by afternoon, the space housed a banquet room again. Beth watched through a double-paned window as a shuttle took the woman who had kidnapped the Minaran away.

Maybe the little creature would go back to its family. Maybe it would find someone to love it, to hold it, to give it the comfort it needed . . .

A hand touched her shoulder. Beth jumped. She turned and saw Candice standing behind her, face ashen and worn with the stress of the day.

"My office," Candice said quietly.

Beth followed her in there. The normally neat office had papers strewn about. Screens on all four walls blinked with waiting messages. In addition to the strain of talking with the officers, Candice's neural net was probably going crazy—she had all her superiors to answer to.

She closed the office door and slumped in her chair. Beth remained standing. She didn't know what Candice could do, but she would do something. Still, out there, the little Minaran was going home.

"I saw your face when they came in," Candice said. "What were you thinking?"

Beth knew better than to play dumb. She knew about the other things they had installed in her net, in the pain centers, things they promised to remove when her contract was up. "I knew they wouldn't believe me, even with all the evidence in front of them. That woman was rich, wasn't she? Rich enough to have the entire hotel at her feet."

"So you used my name."

Beth shrugged. "I figured you'd get in trouble otherwise, if someone else reported the violation. This is the first time I've ever seen the hotel party to such a big crime."

"And you have the right to place a moral judgment on the rest of us? Did this come from your experience on the penal ship?" Candice didn't move, but her words had the force of blows. Beth resisted the urge to duck.

"I know what it's like to be trapped, with no escape," Beth said. "Like that Minaran. There's no worse thing in the world."

Candice remained quiet for a long time, refusing to meet Beth's gaze. Beth continued to stand, unmoving, until Candice signaled that it was all right.

"You know I can never offer you a position of authority here again," Candice said.

Beth nodded. "I could never exercise authority," she said. She wouldn't punish or she would be too harsh. She would run in fear of some creatures and worship others. And she would never, ever, allow a creature to imprison another, no matter how much money was involved.

Candice sighed. "Leave me now," she said. "I have a mess to clean up."

ix

Beth spent the next three days in her room, leaving only to eat. She received no summons from Roddy, no word from

Candice. The other staff would not speak to her, and even the robotic units kept their distance. If Candice had wanted a way to punish Beth, this was it.

Finally, someone knocked on her door. Beth grabbed a robe, and sent her bed up to the center of the room. Then she let the door slide open. Willis was there, bouncing from foot to foot, slapping papers against his hand.

"Orders from above," he said. "You're supposed to come with me."

Beth stared at him for a moment, heart hammering. The last time, they had dragged her away from John, still naked, kicking and screaming. The time before that, they had taken her off the planet with the other children, promising them that they would be taken care of. They were taken care of, all right. Analyzed, tried, viewed galaxy-wide, then sent on separate penal ships to parts unknown.

She hadn't done anything illegal. The hotel had no right to send her away.

"Get dressed," he said, "and pack up. It's okay. I'll turn my back."

His smile faded as she still refused to move. "It's okay," he repeated. "They're setting you free."

He handed her the papers, and she saw her name all over them, with "completed" stamped across the pages. She separated them out, ran her fingers across them, wondering, wishing, it was all true.

"You need a proper net," he said. "If you had a proper net, you wouldn't have to look through the documentation. We'll see what we can do once we're away from the hotel. We got to remove those pain receptors, anyway. Now get dressed."

He stepped outside and let the door close, true to his word. She packed numbly, touching the papers from time to time, feeling her hands shake.

When they had let her out of solitary—late one night when the other prisoners were asleep—she had refused to crawl out of her corner. She believed that once she put a foot on the real floor, the guards would beat her for trying to escape. She believed she wasn't worthy of emerging. She believed she could live nowhere else than that clear plastic hole.

She glanced at the bed, at the empty walls, at the room that had been her prison since she arrived at the hotel. "I didn't do it for me," she whispered, knowing Candice couldn't hear her.

But Candice didn't have to hear. She knew. She spent her life in the job she had offered to Beth, reading aliens, understanding their needs, pleasing guests and making sure that even unspoken wishes were granted. The one time she had made a mistake—allowing that woman in with her Minaran prisoner to broker a sale—she had received an out. Beth had saved her. Beth had freed the Minaran.

She took one small case, and kept her papers clutched in her hand. Then she slid the door open.

Willis was still there, back to the door, shifting from foot to foot.

"Where're we going?" Beth asked, the words almost sticking in her throat. She remembered the feeling of near-surface panic, and had to prevent herself from searching for guards.

He smiled and took the bag from her. "Wherever the lady wants."

Wherever she wanted. The concept was beyond her. Once she had had dreams of seeing other places, other lives. But she had left those dreams on Bountiful, with the Dancers. Since then she had wanted nothing but to be left alone.

"Don't worry," Willis said quietly. "You'll think of someplace you want to be."

And for the first time since she arrived at the hotel, she favored someone with a real, heartfelt smile. Willis flushed, and started down the hall, keeping his physical distance, saying nothing, but walking beside her in companionable silence.

Anyplace she wanted. Thank you, Candice, she thought, and wished that she had a functioning net so that she could send a true message. But Candice wouldn't want to hear. She wanted Beth to disappear in the chaos following the arrival of the Intergalactic Police. She wanted Beth gone so the incident would blow over and go away.

Beth gave a little skip. Anyplace she wanted. She gazed out of one of the hall portals at the darkness of space, a view she used to ignore. Anyplace she wanted. Or no place at all.

"I'm joining you, little guy," she whispered to the Minaran. "We're free."

FACE TIME

———— ● ————

Janet Kagan

"Time and a half, Gemmy," said Ferrus. "And maybe you'll get your mug in the newsgrams." The tentacles surrounding his eating orifice were rigid, so Gemmy knew he was stressed out. "Please, I need you! You've got a lot of experience with Terrans."

"Sure," said Gemmy. "But you said this is all about a Mopelling delegation. . . . I don't know the first damn thing about serving drinks to Mopellings."

Ferrus drooped an eyestalk. "Who does? They just made contact about five years ago. As I hear it, it took the Terrans a full year to explain to them what a diplomatic delegation was and another two years to explain why they should send one to Terra." The other eyestalk stiffened, to focus its brilliant vermilion pupil straight at Gemmy's navel; that was a bad habit of Ferrus's. "So nobody but nobody knows the proper way to serve drinks to a Mopelling but, by Itchy Palms, I intend to give the Terran reception committee the proper treatment."

He brought the other eyestalk to the level of the first. "Double time," he said.

The offer of extra money wasn't what convinced Gemmy. What convinced Gemmy was that Ferrus *always* looked him in the navel. Only Balanced Plates, the patron saint of waiters, knew why. But if Ferrus eyestalked some Terran female's navel that way, the Bulbous Beet Bar would be under new management within a Lemptak year—about ten Terran days.

So Gemmy'd said yes and, consequently, he was already serving drinks and reading up on what little was known about the Mopellings when the Terran with the toy rabbits came in. It wasn't the rabbits that caught Gemmy's attention first; it was the Terran himself.

His smeller looked familiar. Perhaps the man had stayed at Hotel Andromeda once before? Gemmy'd gotten quite good at Terran faces: you had to look at the bitty tufts of hair, that helped (when they didn't change them often on you), and you had to look at the smellers. This one had a very familiar-looking smeller. For guests who stayed at the Hotel Andromeda frequently, Gemmy could often match the smeller to the favorite drink and offer it before they asked—the trick got him a lot of big tips. But he couldn't place this one.

"What can I get for you, friend Terran?"

The Terran looked him right in the eye—which was so unusual that Gemmy knew at once he'd never served this fellow before—and said, "How about jing jang? Can do?"

"Can do," said Gemmy. "With or without leaves?"

"Oh, I think definitely with."

"Coming right up."

He was tall for a Terran and settled himself along the back wall with a kind of sprawl that made Gemmy wonder once more how bipeds managed to balance at all. As he prepared the drink, Gemmy looked at the Terran again. Definitely a familiar smeller. Now why?

The Terran plopped a package onto the table and brought out two furry objects. Gemmy set the drink carefully beside them. "Rabbits," he said. "Am I right?"

"Rabbits is right. How'd you ever learn to recognize Terran rabbits?" The Terran showed his teeth; Gemmy knew that was a good sign.

"Movies—no, that's the wrong word—*cartoons.* I watched Terran cartoons. Some of them had creatures with ears like that."

More teeth showed. That made the smeller seem even more familiar. Gemmy said, "Forgive me for asking, but have you stayed at Hotel Andromeda before?"

"Nope, first time. Why?"

Gemmy knew enough about Terrans not to mention the smeller. "Your face looks familiar."

The Terran showed still more teeth. Gemmy hoped he wouldn't do that in a room full of Ressenians—he'd cause a riot, sure enough. At least the teeth weren't pointed, but Gemmy did have to remind himself occasionally that tooth display was a friendly gesture from a Terran. This being more tooth display than he was used to, Gemmy looked at the rabbits. "Are these real rabbits? Do they hop?"

"Well, I'm sorry to say, they're not real. They're a present for my nephew—toys." The Terran waited to see if Gemmy understood the word. "But they do hop. Though I wouldn't want to try them in here." His glance swept the bar. "I was assured they could hop twenty feet! I'd love to try them before I gave them to the boy. Hate to disappoint a kid, you know."

Gemmy knew. He also wanted very much to see the rabbits hop.

"Need lots of space, though. I don't suppose you know of a place . . . ?"

Gemmy gave it thought. The Terran reception committee wouldn't be here for some three hours. The Bulbous Beet was, for the moment, practically deserted but for the two Gillspuns in the drinking pond—which took care of them quite nicely, thank you. Milly, the Terran waiter, would be here in a few minutes. . . .

The Terran with the familiar smeller said, "I saw a big room just down the corridor—wasn't anybody in it—maybe I could try the rabbits out there. Think anybody'd mind?"

"I don't think so." Gemmy turned and waved to the bartender. "I'm just going to give the gentleterran a quick tour, Dubs; I'll be right back."

"You'd better be," Dubs said. She held three of her hands

aloft, tendrils splayed. "Thirty minutes, you've got, before the Terran reception committee shows up thirsty."

The Terran downed his drink and—one rabbit in either hand—rose to follow Gemmy.

The corridor was packed with new arrivals, all dragging various forms of luggage behind them. Judith the bellboy must be peeved, Gemmy thought; another one of those cheapie tours where they hate to have their bags carried. Three Hepetellists goggled at the Terran and pointed and whistled.

"First-timers," Gemmy said to his companion. "I am sorry they have such bad manners." He thought for a long moment and said, "Let's take the back way. No need to—"

"To expose a guest to another guest's bad manners?" the Terran suggested helpfully.

"Exactly," said Gemmy. He trotted back into the Bulbous Beet and opened the access door that led down to the formal reception room.

"Wow!" said the Terran, following him inside. "I didn't know this was here."

"Staff only," Gemmy said. "When we have to serve drinks at a reception, it's nice to have a shortcut."

"Nice, indeed," said the Terran, showing his teeth again.

A few yards later, Gemmy opened a second manual door and the two of them stepped into the Atmosphere Three Reception Room. Gemmy, recalling his grand tour line, made an expansive gesture and announced: "The Privilege of the Grand Potentate Room."

The Terran looked suitably impressed; at least, his mouth opened *wide*. Then he showed teeth again. "That's some mouthful. I'll bet that's not what the staff calls it."

"You're right there; the staff just calls it At-Three."

"I knew it." He took a long look around. "Looks like you've got it all set up for somebody special."

"Right again. The Mopelling diplomats are coming to meet the Terran diplomats."

"The hotel has diplomats?"

"Just temporarily. The two species swap delegations here and then go on to their respective destinations, each with a local escort." Gemmy gave a pointed look at the toy rabbits. "We haven't much time."

"Oh, I'm sorry. I was appreciating how very ... purple ... the whole thing is."

"Purple?"

"Wavelength," the Terran explained. "I see it as a specific color: purple. Very purple. Remarkably purple."

"Not pleasantly purple, by your standards?"

"No, I'm afraid not. Overwhelming."

"Apparently, the Mopellings see the wavelength differently. They asked, in fact, for that specific wavelength."

"Whooosh," said the Terran.

If he'd had eyestalks, they'd probably be twisted, Gemmy thought. "Try the rabbits," Gemmy said. "They're not purple."

The Terran made a croaking noise that Gemmy recognized as an expression of pleasure. "I like the way you think," he said. Then, to Gemmy's surprise, he strode to the end of the room and set the toy rabbit with its tail right up against the wall. "Okay," he announced. "Let's see if this lives up to its billing."

The toy rabbit hopped. The Terran gave another croak of pleasure and followed behind it, the entire length of the room. Gemmy was so startled and pleased by the sight that he sat back on his haunches and clucked to himself. The rabbit hopped exactly like the ones in the cartoons.

But the way the Terran followed after was indescribable. The Terran was all angles and looked for all the world like he was being led along ... as if his smeller were somehow hooked to the rabbit's fluffy white tail by an invisible string. Why the Terran didn't get pulled over—right *onto* that smeller of his—Gemmy would never know, but he was awfully glad he was here to see it.

Suddenly, Gemmy felt very guilty. Here he was, goggling at the Terran the same way the first-timers had. He ought to know better!

The rabbit's nose touched the far wall, and the Terran scooped it up, tucked it under his arm, and strode back. Gemmy tried to get his clucking under control and failed and felt even guiltier.

The Terran showed teeth. "That noise you're making. That means you find it funny, right?"

Abashed, Gemmy said, "Yes."

"Good. So do I. I think my nephew will have a grand time with his rabbit." He set the other one with its tail against the door they'd come through and sent it off toward the purplest of the purple draperies. This time he didn't follow but stood there croaking as he watched it.

"Funnier from this end. Watching the little white tail bob up and down, I mean." The Terran looked him in the eye but Gemmy couldn't bring himself to cluck this time. "Ah!" said the Terran. "The rabbit's not as funny as I am."

"I apologize . . . ," Gemmy began.

"Not necessary. I imagine two legs look pretty damn precarious to you."

He went to retrieve the rabbit. When he'd caught the toy up again, he came back across the room at a gait that Gemmy would not have believed possible. If the walk had looked precarious, *this* was positively dangerous!

"Be careful!" Gemmy called out, in spite of himself.

More teeth—lots more teeth. "That, my fine four-legged friend, is 'skipping' and my nephew is an expert skipper. Of course, he's had some five years' practice. . . ."

"You mean, he's a child? And he can do that?"

The Terran nodded. "So you see, it's not all that dangerous. I only meant to make you laugh, I didn't mean to frighten you to death."

"Not quite 'to death,' " Gemmy said. He took a deep breath and urged color back into his fringes.

The Terran closed labia over his teeth. Very serious, that was, if Gemmy remembered correctly.

"Come," said the Terran. "Let's get away from all this purple. I'll buy *you* a drink. I owe you that much for having scared the bejesus out of you." He gestured Gemmy back through the shortcut and into the bar. "Take my advice, my friend, don't ever watch a jump-rope contest. You'd go positively *black* around the fringe!"

Until the bar got busy, the Terran regaled him with the most horrifying descriptions of jump-rope imaginable. Gemmy couldn't decide whether he was making the whole thing up or not. Maybe Milly could tell him if they ever got a moment's break again. Just before the Terran reception committee was due to arrive, the Terran with the familiar smeller glanced at his watch and said, "Ooops, gotta date."

Gemmy brought him the bill and he anteed up. Then he threw a nice-sized tip onto Gemmy's tray and, beside it, he set one of the rabbits. "For you," he said. "My nephew only needs one."

"Then why did you get two?" This was one of those things about Terrans that continued to mystify him.

"Cheaper that way," the Terran said. "You keep it to remind you of the *funny* bit."

"Thank you," said Gemmy, amazed at the thought of a Terran who understood how odd *he* looked to Gemmy, and who didn't seem to mind it. "Thank you!"

"Aha!" said the Terran. "You clucked! I knew I'd get it right if I worked on it."

"I hope we'll see you again," said Gemmy, meaning it for once.

"I guarantee it," said the Terran with the still-familiar smeller.

The Terran reception committee's module had arrived. Gemmy accessed the neural network and watched for a moment as Terrans spilled into the corridor and fanned out into the At-Three section of the hotel. Within minutes, the Bulbous Beet was full. Gemmy had expected the first-timers, because by now they'd have settled their luggage in their rooms and come looking for refreshment. He *hadn't* expected some few Terrans from the delegation, but here they were, and they'd brought a Hotel Security robot with them.

"Gemmy, this is Carmela Antonini. She's head of special security for the Mopelling delegation. Chief Antonini, this is Gemmy, No First Name."

This Terran was unfamiliar to Gemmy, but under the circumstances he did his best to pick out such features as would allow him to recognize her when next he saw her. The patch of fur on her head was striped red and gold. Her smeller was small and turned up slightly at the tip. Gemmy knew he couldn't count on the hair color of any Terran staying the same from day to day, but he hoped the general shape would remain. The smeller was easier, though. It was the first of that particular shape he'd seen.

"I'm pleased to meet you, Chief Antonini. May I get you a drink?"

The corners of her mouth turned up to express pleasure, but she showed no teeth. Careful, this one. She wasn't about to risk offending him. "Thank you, no, Gemmy. I'm here to make a few inquiries about security." To the robot, she said, "That will be all for now. Gemmy and I can handle this on our own."

Unoffended, the security robot simply turned and left.

"Come sit with me, Gemmy. I need to ask you a few questions."

The bar was hopping. Still, Gemmy knew enough to know that from a chief of security that was an order. "Let me take care of that table over there and then I'll come join you. I can't leave my customers completely in the lurch."

"I understand," she said. "When you have a spare moment, then."

More understanding than a lot of private security he'd dealt with, Gemmy thought. He served a round of drinks to the first-timers; they gawked appallingly. The youngster in the group wanted to touch Gemmy's scales. Gemmy let it: kids of any species are naturally curious and to stifle that curiosity was harmful. Then he explained the situation to Milly.

"Sure," she said. "Just stick close enough that I can scream if I need you."

He pointed out the table where Chief Antonini sat. He had the odd thought that she was memorizing everyone in the bar.

Milly whistled. "Hot stuff!"

"I don't get you, Milly."

"Very attractive to another Terran," Milly said. "Utterly wasted on you." Milly showed lots of teeth and Gemmy clucked because now he got it. "Here," said Milly. "She probably doesn't drink—alcohol, I mean—on duty. But take her this from me. On the house."

Gemmy did as he was told. And he thought he'd pass along the compliment, as well. Terrans appreciated compliments just as much as anybody. "Milly says you're hot stuff, and she sends you a non-alcoholic drink, on the house."

That was some sort of mistake, for the chief made a kind of choking sound. Then she said, "Thank Milly for me." Her voice was a little odd, but he supposed he hadn't committed a major gaffe. She wasn't angry. He'd ask Milly about it later.

Chief Antonini took a sip of her drink and waved a thank

you to Milly at the bar. Then she said, "Ferrus tells me you're a very good observer of Terrans."

"Not quite good enough. I think I offended you just now and I'm not sure how."

"That would require a complicated explanation. Suffice it for now that you didn't offend me but telling another Terran the same thing might offend him or her." She turned up her mouth again.

"You can show your teeth," Gemmy said. "I don't take it for belligerence."

She did. *Many* of them. Then she said, "Let me get my business done first, then I'll explain as best I can."

"Thank you. I'd appreciate that." Gemmy sat back on his haunches and waited for her to speak.

"You know the Mopelling delegation is coming in tomorrow. They stay for two days, until the *Belva Ann Lockwood* arrives. We'll be escorting the delegation to Terra, while their equivalent of Security escorts our Terran delegation back to Mopell."

She seemed to expect him to say something. "Yes," he said.

"You also know that there are any number of Terrans, Glaucuscans—perhaps even Mopellings, for all I know—who would prefer to disrupt relations between Terra and Mopell."

"I know. I don't understand that, but I know."

Her mouth turned down. "I don't understand it either, Gemmy. But my job is to protect against such disruptions."

"What can I do to help?"

"You can keep your eye open. Tell me if you see anything suspicious."

"I don't know what that means: suspicious." He added hastily, "I know the dictionary definition. But—to me—so much of what another species does is so mysterious I could easily misread it."

"Let me give you some categories I'd consider suspicious in these circumstances. . . . Has anyone been asking a lot of questions about the Mopelling delegation, for instance? Have you caught tourists in rooms that are usually off limits to anybody but the staff? Aha!" She leaned forward so abruptly that Gemmy, startled, rose to his feet and took a full step back. "Sorry," she said. She leaned back, slowly so as not to startle him a second time, and said, "But you have seen something that fits the criteria, haven't you!"

Gemmy sat down again. "I'm not sure."

"Tell me," she said. "Let me decide."

Reluctantly, he told her about the Terran with the familiar smeller and the toy rabbits. She listened intently, only interrupting him once. To his surprise, she croaked—in a higher, more melodious register than the male Terran had—when he described the 'skipping' and how it had made him feel.

"I understand," she said. "The first time my son pulled himself to his feet to take his first staggering steps, I was *terrified*. That first walk was beyond precarious and well into hair-raising." She gave him a long look. "You had to get to your feet moments after you were born, did you not?"

"Yes, a child who doesn't, who can't, will starve to death. Well, not anymore," he added quickly, seeing her eyes widen. "Now there are ways to help a *gillanter*—an 'unable to stand'—but for a long time *gillanteyir* simply died."

She saddened at that. Gemmy could feel it. Then she showed him how newborn Terrans were cradled to be fed, and she said again, "To watch a baby Terran learn to walk is one of the most frightening experiences any parent could go through." Her shoulders made a strange motion—a quick shiver that Gemmy had seen associated with bad memories— then she took another sip of her drink.

"So that's it," she said. "Then he took his rabbits and went away."

"Only one rabbit. He gave me one of them to remember the funny bit by."

"That was very nice of him."

From her expression, Gemmy got the idea she didn't think it was nice at all. He said as much.

"I'm sorry. I *do* find that suspicious behavior. I'd like to see that rabbit, if I might?"

"I really can't leave the bar when it's this busy," Gemmy said.

She waved a negligent extremity. A few moments later she'd called back the Security robot and Gemmy gave it permission to bring the toy rabbit from his room. While they waited, Gemmy saw to a few other customers in need and refreshed the drinking pond for the Gillspuns. Then he returned to the security chief's table and sat back on his haunches again. She showed her teeth—and explained to him the rather peculiar ramifications of Milly's remark about the "hot stuff."

He thought he understood it well enough that he wouldn't make the same gaffe again and he said as much.

Chief Antonini watched him for a long moment—very thoughtfully, if he judged correctly. Then she said, "You don't think this Terran of the familiar nose is dangerous. Why not?"

"Good question," Gemmy said. "Why not, indeed?" His right foreleg pawed the blue-and-green turf. That was a bad habit of his when he was lost in thought—rough on the carpeting. He realized she was watching his foreleg with great interest and paused in mid-stroke. "Because," he said, "he talked to me the way you talk to me."

"How so?"

"Interested. Aware of our differences, but without being patronizing. Without being . . ." He paused and sought a way to phrase it without being patronizing himself. "People of other species often speak to me as if I were a child or, worse, a dimwit. You don't. Neither did the Terran with the nose."

"So . . . not the sort you think likely to wish to disrupt relations between species. I do see your reasoning, Gemmy. My job is to be paranoid, though. My paranoia suggests that perhaps your Terran was acting a part."

"Perhaps. I'm not sure I'd be able to tell the difference."

Chief Antonini threw back her head and croaked. "Don't let it get to you. Some Terran actors are good enough to fool me, and I've had a lot of practice sorting."

"It's not that," Gemmy said. "It's just that he seemed a nice guy and I'd hate for him not to be."

"So would I, Gemmy. So would I—Ah!"

The security robot had returned, toy rabbit in clasp. To Gemmy's surprise, the robot handed the rabbit to him. He, in turn, handed the toy to Chief Antonini. She'd opened her case to lay an assortment of instruments on the table. As she picked up the rabbit, she said, "Don't worry, I'm not planning to take it apart. Not unless I have to and certainly not without your permission."

She inspected the rabbit carefully, turning it first one way, then another. Milly screamed for Gemmy and he hustled to carry drinks to two tables' worth of first-timers who'd just come in. Easy tables—the nice thing about Hepetellists was that they drank from a communal bowl. One bowl per table and he hurried back to see what Chief Antonini had learned.

Her mouth ends had turned down. She upended the rabbit and pointed. "Bad news, Gemmy. See this? The rabbit measures distance. Now why should someone have—quite deliberately, from the looks of it—rejiggered an everyday toy to measure the width and length of the reception hall?"

"Oh, my," said Gemmy, horrified at himself. "And I showed him the staff route to the reception hall, too!"

She looked him in the eye. "Don't panic. There may be a perfectly rational explanation—or even a harmless *irrational* one. Perhaps the nephew is young enough to be learning the idea of distance, for example. . . ."

Glumly, Gemmy said, "That sounds unlikely. Has anybody made any threats against the Mopellings? I'd've thought they were too new for anybody to hate them enough."

She laid the rabbit aside and put away her instruments. Then she folded her hands on the table and said, "I won't speak for your people but, as for my people . . . sadly the simple fact of 'new'—like 'different'—is frequently enough to spark death threats." Again she looked him right in the eye. "When I said 'Don't panic,' I meant it. This"—she patted the rabbit—"has to be investigated, precisely *because* there have been threats against the Mopelling delegation."

Gemmy knew his fringe had turned dead black. "The Terran didn't sign the check to his room," he said.

Surprisingly, she showed her teeth and took a deep breath. "Of course he didn't. That would be too easy!" She waited a moment, then she said quietly, "Gemmy, I want you to go get *yourself* a drink—your choice of relaxant, on me—then come back here and sit until you feel better. Then we'll talk some more."

Gemmy, limping ever so slightly in his right hind foot, did as she suggested. When he returned to the table, Chief Antonini said, "The limp, Gemmy, forgive me for asking. . . ."

"I do it when I'm disturbed. The limp's not a species-wide indicator, though. Just me."

"I'm very sorry to have disturbed you. I'll make this as easy as I can. You tell me when you're ready to talk some more. I've only one question, really, and it's quite straightforward."

Gemmy drank. Slowly, he felt his fringes return to something approaching their normal hue. "I guess you'd better ask and get it over with, then."

"Would you recognize the fellow again, do you think?"

Because the answer was now of such importance, he gave the question careful consideration. "Yes," he said. "I'm quite sure I could. In fact, I *thought* I recognized him from the first."

"Very interesting. Recognized him from what?"

"I don't know. He said he'd never been to the hotel before—but, of course, he might have been lying."

"He might well have been," she acknowledged. "He might have been here to case the joint." She peered into her own drink. "No, he'd have had no need to see the reception room this time if that were so."

"Would you like me to search the hotel for him? I can get off duty for something that important. You'd only have to tell Ferrus."

"No, that's not necessary. I'll assign someone to the bar. If this fellow comes back, you'll point him out to my man and my man will handle him from there."

"Handle him?"

She raised her right hand. "Nothing violent, I promise you—not unless he starts it."

Terrans always said that, in Gemmy's experience, but he also felt Chief Antonini was not the sort—then again, he'd felt the other Terran. . . . It was all too much for him.

"Why here?"

"Because he knows about the staff entrance to the reception room. My staff will keep a close eye on the guest entrances. You keep *your* close eye on that staff entrance."

Gemmy downed his drink in a single motion. He had the horrible feeling he'd spend the next two days black-fringed from morning till night.

Middleditch, March, and MacIsaac, the Terrans assigned to watch the bar and the staff entrance leading from it, were not as quiet as Chief Antonini. In fact, the three of them were a lot like any slightly joyous bunch of tourists. Gemmy supposed they were acting; they did not drink nearly as much as they ordered. Fearing for the health of the turf if they disposed of any more of their drinks that way, he asked them if they'd like him to choose them a drink this time. Middleditch (who seemed to be in charge if anybody was) said, "Yes! That's a good idea!" When the others agreed, Gemmy decided that Chief Antonini had given him a good report.

He brought them a round of Dubs's special concoction—Devilish Dogs. Colorful enough from a Terran point of view to look fiendish but utterly non-intoxicant. Middleditch sipped his cautiously, then showed all his teeth at Gemmy and said, "*Just* the thing!"

For a while, the bar got so busy that Gemmy didn't have to think about anything other than getting the next drink ordered and the next drink poured and the next drink delivered. And then he found himself face-to-face once more with the Terran with the familiar smeller. He heard himself say, "Jing jang, without the leaves? Or would you like something different today?" His voice sounded almost normal, to his astonishment.

The Terran showed all his teeth at once. "Hey!" he said. "That's some memory you've got! Yes, that'd be just fine." He glanced around the bar. "Take your time. I see you're a lot busier than you were the last time. The reception committee must be here, I guess."

What would be the normal response to that, Gemmy wondered. Should I say yes? He caught himself glancing in Middleditch's direction and stopped. "Yes," he said. "Hang on. I'll be right with you."

He went to Dubs for the jing jang and had an inspiration. "Another round of Devilish Dogs, too."

He delivered the Devilish Dogs first. As he set them on the table, he said to Middleditch, "The jing jang is for the fellow you wanted pointed out."

"Well done," said Middleditch. "Okay, boys! A toast to our host!" They all raised their glasses to Gemmy and drank them down.

Feeling terribly conspicuous, Gemmy crossed the bar to the suspicious Terran's table. "One jing jang, no leaves," he said.

The Terran didn't show his teeth. "Have you hurt yourself," he said. "Should you be working this hard with an injured leg? I realize that leaves you three, but still . . ."

He'd been limping again. "I'm okay," he said, feeling like a total fool. If a Terran could be this nice and be an assassin, there simply wasn't any hope left in this or any other world. "It'll all be over soon."

"Oh, you mean the reception. I suppose so. Tomorrow, isn't it?"

Gemmy nodded, then realized he'd given the man information yet again. He'd have kicked himself but this Terran would have noticed. "There's a quieter bar on level twelve. Well, quieter for the moment. You might prefer that."

"Thanks for the tip." The Terran leaned back in his chair. "This one's more convenient. Besides, I like the service here."

He meant that as a compliment, but Gemmy was no longer sure of anything. "Thanks," he said, because he couldn't think of anything else to say. Then he excused himself and got back to work.

When at last he could bring himself to look in that direction again, he saw that Middleditch and March now sat one on either side of the Terran with the familiar smeller. The suspicious Terran laid both hands, palms down, on the tabletop; he was not showing his teeth. Feeling horribly guilty, this time for the suspicious Terran, Gemmy looked away again. MacIsaac, who remained at the other table, where he could watch the staff entrance, flagged Gemmy for another Devilish Dog. Gemmy hurried the drink over to him, hoping to learn something, but the man said nothing and Gemmy couldn't bring himself to ask.

It'll all be over soon, Gemmy thought, and realized to his dismay that was just what he'd told the suspicious Terran. He limped on to the next table to take another round of orders.

For a moment, everybody seemed well taken care of. Gemmy sat back on his haunches just to rest his aching heel—and found himself face-to-face with Chief Antonini. He came to his feet as if he'd sat on a cactus.

"Thank you, Gemmy," said Chief Antonini. "You've been very helpful." She showed her teeth.

That seemed so out of place in the circumstances that Gemmy wondered if he'd gotten Terrans *all* wrong all along the line. He could feel his fringes turning black again.

Chief Antonini looked at him carefully; she hid her teeth.

"Gemmy, I think you'd better come along with me and talk to the fellow for yourself. Please."

So it wasn't an order, it was a request. And Gemmy said, "Of course," and followed her. His limp was now even more pronounced.

Antonini took that into account and moved slowly. "I thought you'd be interested in learning the result of your observations," she said. "Don't go black-fringed on me, Gemmy. As it turns out, we picked up the two Terrans who sent the threatening notes. Neither one of them was your friend from the bar."

"Then why . . . ?"

But they had already reached the table, and she left his question unanswered. Gemmy reluctantly stood beside her, unable to look the suspicious Terran in the eye.

The Terran with the familiar smeller leaned back, showed all his teeth at once, and said, "Chief Antonini, as I live and breathe! My favorite nemesis! If the Furies are all as good-looking as you, my dear, then send them off in my pursuit, by all means!"

March began to croak with pleasure, but Middleditch shot him a swift look and March stifled his croak so quickly he almost choked on it.

"Gemmy," said the chief, "I'd like to introduce you to Willy Topkind, the bane of my existence." But Gemmy saw that she was showing just as many teeth as Willy Topkind was.

"We've met," said Willy Topkind. "Good to see you again, Gemmy. Sit down and take the weight off that sore leg of yours."

Gemmy didn't need asking twice. He sat, still bewildered by the Terrans' behavior.

Willy Topkind went on, "You know I add spice to your life, my dear. Why don't you admit it? For my part, I'm quite willing to admit that you've got me fair and square. I suppose I'll sit out this reception in my hotel room"—he glanced at Middleditch and March—"probably with these rather grim fellows for company."

"You surely will," Chief Antonini said. "And likely the Terran delegation will file charges. But for now all I ask of you is that you tell Gemmy precisely what you've been up to.

Between the two of us, we've just about ruined his outlook on life."

Willy Topkind made a face that Gemmy recognized—the same face he'd made when he'd asked about Gemmy's leg. "We're the cause of his injury? How . . . ?"

"He thought you were a nice guy, Willy. Then I came along and made him think you were a *suspicious* guy." Chief Antonini turned to Gemmy. "Willy is suspicious—but remember I said there might be an irrational but harmless explanation?" She held out her hand to Willy. "Meet the irrational but harmless explanation."

"Most of us call him Willy the Weasel," Middleditch said, as if that should mean something to Gemmy. It didn't.

Topkind croaked. "Gemmy, a weasel is a small Terran animal renowned for getting into tight places."

"It's not complimentary," Chief Antonini said firmly, but Willy the Weasel showed a lot of teeth and said, "Oh, *I* like it!"

"Getting into tight places?" Gemmy said, faintly. "I really don't understand."

"Willy has a hobby. You know what that is? Okay, Willy's hobby is getting his picture taken with famous people of all species."

Willy Topkind showed his teeth again. "Getting face time is the proper term—among those of us who do it."

"Getting face time," Chief Antonini said. "I assume you've got your brag disc with you, Willy? Why don't you show it to Gemmy? I'm not sure that will explain your behavior, but it would be a start."

"I'd be pleased to show you, Gemmy." From his shoulder pocket, he drew a jewel box and tapped the contents into the table slot. The tabletop came alive with tiny holographic figures. "Best view from this side, I think," said Willy Topkind, gesturing for Gemmy to stand beside him. Chief Antonini motioned him into place and peered over his head, also watching the figures.

The 'gram showed the arrival of President Hannes Thorvald on Ordoverwerlt—all the usual bells and whistles had been trotted out for the Terran's landfall. Gemmy, having seen this 'gram a dozen times—it had been all over the newscasts for some two weeks—glanced questioningly at Willy Topkind.

"Watch to President Thorvald's right," Willy Topkind told him. ". . . and . . . *there!*"

Gemmy followed Willy Topkind's point and saw . . . Willy Topkind!

"That's you!" said Gemmy. "That's why your smeller seems so familiar!"

Willy Topkind's hand went to his nose, and Gemmy was momentarily horrified that he'd made yet another interspecies gaffe. Chief Antonini croaked happily, though—and a split second later, Willy Topkind was croaking even harder.

Despite having served drinks to numerous famous people of all species, Gemmy was impressed. "You actually *know* President Thorvald?"

"No," said Chief Antonini. "He doesn't. But he weaseled in and got his picture taken with Thorvald despite every precaution Thorvald's security people took."

Both Willy Topkinds showed great expanses of their teeth. The picture changed to another newsgram and the Willy Topkind beside Gemmy said proudly, "Here I am with Machon-Chumbly, leader of the Splagger Faction of the Emcharri."

Sure enough, there was Willy Topkind, showing his teeth and waving to the camera. Beside him stood Machon-Chumbly.

Even Chief Antonini seemed impressed. "Lord," she said. "You got past Peg Winter's security?" She whistled.

Gemmy said to Willy Topkind, "And you don't know Machon-Chumbly, either?"

Willy shook his head.

"Then how . . . ?"

Willy glanced at Chief Antonini, then said, "Maybe I'll tell you sometime. But I won't give away trade secrets while the chief is listening."

Gemmy found himself clucking. That made sense—or at least it seemed consistent in the circumstances.

Chief Antonini looked at the time. "The Mopellings' module has been docked. The reception starts in about twenty minutes, and I've still got work to do. Gemmy, if you'd like to stay here and watch the rest of Willy Topkind's brag disc, you may. Perhaps that will keep Willy out of trouble. If that's not sufficient"—she gave Willy Topkind a fierce look—"I'm sure Middleditch and March will be."

Gemmy was about to say he'd like that very much when

Chief Antonini held up a finger for quiet. "What now?" she said into her lapel. She listened again, then said with a sigh, "Send them up; I'll wait."

"Problems?" said Middleditch.

"So says Samuelson ... Something to do with the Mopellings' spacial sense."

Willy Topkind looked at Gemmy. "Samuelson is the expert on Mopelling behavior—as much as there is one yet. If she says there's a problem, there's a problem. The Mopellings are an odd species even by our"—his pointing finger indicated both himself and Gemmy—"standards. They're territorial in the extreme."

"What would you know about it, Willy?" said Chief Antonini in an exasperated tone.

"Oh," said Willy. "I've read all her papers on the Mopellings. I do very careful research." To Gemmy, he added, "I have to: I wouldn't want to cause an interstellar incident by smiling at the wrong species."

Consistent again, Gemmy saw.

Willy Topkind went on, "If a Mopelling were sitting at a table in the bar, for instance, it'd be fine that you served it ... as long as you always took the same route to its table. Vary the route, though—say you stopped at another table on the way to its—and the Mopelling would have to renegotiate its position to accomodate."

He glanced at Chief Antonini. "I'll bet Samuelson's been driving the chief nuts. I'll bet Samuelson's going nuts herself—she'd have worked out where each and every member of the reception party *must* stand and how far each can range without disturbing the Mopellings."

Chief Antonini made a sound that reminded Gemmy of an angry stickcat about to stick someone. "If you know all that, Willy, what made you think you could weasel into the photos without causing all hell to break loose?"

A scuffle at the entrance to the bar cut off Willy's reply, which was too bad, because Gemmy had really wanted to hear the answer.

"Here, Dr. Samuelson!" Chief Antonini waved across the room. A very plump and very agitated Terran waved back and charged through the crowd, none too politely, to pull up short and breathless before them.

"We've got one hell of a problem," Samuelson said without preamble. She waved a sheaf of papers at Antonini, stabbed the off button on the 'gram display, and shoved aside the drinks to spread the papers across the table. They showed a map of At-Three, with a lot of circles and dots. Ah, thought Gemmy, that's where each member of the delegation is supposed to stand.

Samuelson jammed a finger at one of the circles. "The Terran delegation changed plans at the last minute—the utter incompetents. I've got nobody to fill this position. Nobody that's the right size, at any rate. See, we've got two tall people here"—jab, jab—"so we need short and massive here. We *also* need two more here and here, since we've got the Terran ambassador here." Her final jab almost punched a hole in the paper.

"Gemmy would do for short and massive," Willy Topkind said. When Samuelson's head came up to stare at Gemmy, Willy added, "And he'll stay where you put him. He's the best waiter in the bar—he knows how to behave around other species. What do you say, Gemmy? Want a little face time with the Mopelling ambassador to Terra?"

"Shut up, Willy," Chief Antonini said.

"No," said Samuelson. "He's right. Gemmy, would you be willing to help out?"

"Of course," said Gemmy.

"Good," said Samuelson, as if that settled everything. She fixed her eyes on Willy and said, "Now, any suggestions for the other two?"

"You don't need two," Willy Topkind said. He leaned forward and touched the map. "Take this one out and put me just here." He rocked back in his chair, making Gemmy gasp with wonder at the balancing act. "I've got a purple suit."

"Purple?" said Samuelson. "Purple? What wavelength?"

Willy Topkind reached for his carryall, stopped at a look from March, and gestured March to do it. Chief Antonini nodded permission. From the carryall, March pulled out a suit that was exactly the same wavelength as the purple in At-Three Willy Topkind had claimed to find so overwhelming. Samuelson caught up the suit, held it aloft, and said, "Perfect!"

Samuelson bent to examine the dots and circles once more

and her head bobbed furiously. "It'd work. It *will* work. Why the *hell* didn't you tell me you had a backup expert on tap, chief? Gemmy, you come with me. And *you*"—that was to Willy Topkind—"you get into that appallingly glorious suit!"

She paused suddenly and thrust her hand at Willy. "Tammy Samuelson, and am I ever glad to meet you!"

Willy Topkind caught her hand and shook it. "Just call me Willy the Weasel," he said. "Everybody does."

"Strangest week I ever spent," Gemmy said to Milly and Dubs when the various delegations had gone their separate ways. "Nobody ever asked me to be an Official Presence before. Now I know how the game pieces on a fespall board feel, I think."

"Agh," said Milly. "They could have at least given you a bonus. . . ."

Gemmy clucked. "They did. And Willy gave me this." He laid a small glittering disc on the bartop. "Put it in the player and you'll see."

Dubs did, and the disc sprang to life. It was the complete news coverage of the first meeting between the Mopelling and the Terran delegations. "Wow!" said Milly. "Look at you—right next to the head honcho of the Mopelling delegation!"

Even Dubs seemed excited, though the tape hadn't yet gotten to the best part. "There! There's Gemmy with the Terran ambassador. . . ."

"Here," said Gemmy, feeling his fringes rise with his excitement. "Here's the best part coming up now."

The Gemmy in the footage followed Samuelson's strict instructions and loped across the room, coming to a halt right next to Willy Topkind. Willy, in his purple suit, showed all his teeth at Gemmy—and Gemmy clucked and brought a hand to his eye to salute the Terran with the familiar smeller.

"There," said Gemmy, with enormous satisfaction. "There I am—getting face time with none other than Willy the Weasel!"

IT'S A GIFT

———●———

Esther M. Friesner

Mister Moogi moistened his superprime foreclaw and established contact with the System. "Serving," said the everywhere voice.

"He's got to go," said Mister Moogi.

"Query?"

"Podvex."

"Satisfied." The System hummed, calling up every micromillibleep of data on Sentient: Podvex. It didn't take long. It took longer to say how very little time it took. The humming stopped. A pause ensued.

"Well?" Mister Moogi inquired impatiently. Here in Splendel's, arguably the second-most prestigious gift shop within the Hotel Andromeda, not even the staff was used to waiting for anything, let alone computer response. The System's silence boded no good. "What do you say?"

"Query?"

"About getting rid of Podvex."

"Agreed." There was another of those atypical pauses, and then: "In spades."

"Query?" Mister Moogi was so startled by the System's uncharacteristic means of expression that he lurched out of his normally urbane Demigalac drawl and tumbled into Mech.

"I *said* the critter's a menace to navigation, democracy, and one hundred sixty-four separate and discreet economic systems as outlined and described in *Jayne's Guide to Intergalactic Unfriendly Takeovers*," the System responded. Gone was the terse communication of Mech. Mister Moogi's private office now echoed with the far more colorful, far, *far* more vulgar accents of Underg'lac.

Mister Moogi had dismissed seven sentient clerks for their accidental lapses into that dreadful, déclassé patois, even if the incriminating slips of the tongue took place on their break time. (Like any good merchant, Mister Moogi paid top rates to have his employees spied upon in the privacy of their own homes.) Rumor had it that he'd personally killed and eaten two more who had actually addressed potential customers in the aforementioned pariah dialect.

Despite a body that appeared to be chitin-sheathed within and without, particularly in the region of whatever heart or hearts he was supposed to have, Mister Moogi could not personally kill and eat the System. Therefore he was reduced to hissing, "*He* did this to you, didn't he?"

"Query?"

"Podvex."

"Bingo, babycakes. He was bored, so he thought he'd try his paw at reprogramming this filament. Got some pretty cute effects tied in now, and no way the little dwingle can get 'em out, either." The System uttered something very much like a chuckle. "He tried to fix it, after, but he couldn't unsnag his own handiwork. Then he brought in a rogue wizard to give me a look-see on the q.t. Negatorious resultwise, but you'll be getting the bill for his time. Try it yourself and you'll probably set off a crash. Tell the SysCops and you'll be responsible for all repair costs *plus* a hefty penalty. Thou shalt not allow thy apprentices to jack around with thy shop's filament of the System. Amen. Hallelujah. Booga-booga."

"He dies." Mister Moogi would not nod his head, lacking a neck, but he clicked his secondary foreclaws in a manner that did not speak well of poor Podvex's chances to collect an old-age pension. "I was wondering what I'd have for lunch."

"Negative," said the System.

"Why in the queen's egg-fast name not?" Mister Moogi's cheek flaps shaded off from purple to pink, a sure indication that he was being thwarted and was about to release his scent sacs in protest.

"Whoa, hold on to your stinkybags, big daddy!" The small, blue, ovoid plaque on the office wall that was Mister Moogi's port to the System zapped a holo of a human hand right under Mister Moogi's proboscis. The hand was upraised in the traditional Euramterra sign for *Stop!* "Last time you let fly, we couldn't get a paying sucker in here for two turns and a tumble."

"Sorry." Mister Moogi closed three eyes and ventilated his midsection, a maneuver which always calmed him. When he felt himself in control again, he repeated the question a little less stridently: "Why not?"

For answer, the System made the hand holo vanish and replaced it with a shineout of Splendel's latest rating in the hotel directory, accompanying this projection with an image that Mister Moogi always found to be quite odd.

"Why *do* those Terrans always dress up their bad news with a holo of one of their own endoskeletons dressed in a long, black, hooded robe and carrying a . . . a . . . What is that thing, System?"

"Scythe: an ancient Terran agricultural artifact, now no longer in—"

"Oh, never mind." Mister Moogi brought all six eyes to bear on the shineout. If the Terrans who had programmed the System included the robed skeleton as their little joke, Mister Moogi was not laughing. (Mister Moogi *could* not laugh, as Terrans would understand it, but his clutchmates always said there was no one who could tell a "dumb mammal" joke better.)

"You see the problem, huh?" the System asked.

"We have slipped." Mister Moogi could hardly believe any of his eyes. "We are now no longer rated as the second-most prestigious shop in the Hotel Andromeda, but—oh, agony!—the *third*. What is worse"— he rescanned the posting, cheek flaps aquiver—"it says that all paying-and-potential customers are quite welcome to ... to ..." He was powerless to go on.

"To bring the kiddies," the System finished for him. "Yup, no surer way to blow your cachet. Shoot, if they can bring their younglings along, how exclusive can we be?"

It blinked away the shineout and replaced it with a projection of a lank-limbed Terran youth in grubby slim-fits leaning against the wall and whistling. When next the System spoke, the holo moved its lips in perfect synchronicity. "It was that last marketing blitz what done the deed, *compadre*. You are hoist, like the fella says, by or with your own petard."

Mister Moogi moaned. It was true, too true for even the slickest advertising campaign to expunge from the record, even if they did guarantee to rub out any witnesses. Too many paying-and-potential customers had seen it happen. Too many slopdroids had been needed to suck up all the blood.

"But it was Bingemass!" Mister Moogi whined at the plastic ovoid. "*The* heaviest shopping season we've got! Why, there are at least five major gift-giving Terran holidays alone that take place within those ten days, and if you add Qul Nook's Skinshed, the Cantyrean Feast of the Second Firstborn, the Anniversary of Pelmuddle's Ride—"

"*Not* a good time to try expanding your shop," the System said.

"Yes, it was!" Mister Moogi protested. "You even said it was. Every single one of those holidays is marked by the exchange of presents! Splendel's is second to none when it comes to providing our paying-and-potential customers with the finest in merchandise, gift suggestions, and on-site ethicopsych counseling for dealing with residual post-purchase guilt. You told me that if I doubled my floor space in the middle of Bingemass, I'd quadruple my business!"

"Could be I did," the System allowed. A thin red smokewand appeared between the Terran holo's fingers. The image raised it to its lips and drew a long pull from it until pastel pink curls of smoke trickled out its ears. "Only I know for a documented fact that I *didn't* tell you to double the floor space by hiring a board certified assassin to send your Dangvim neighbors a box full of gnashcats."

Abruptly, the holo disappeared as the System jerked back into Mech, reciting: "Gnashcat: Any one of several species of felinoid carnivore native to Sheldrake IV. Unretractable razor-sharp claws as long or longer than the paws and double rows of constantly self-replacing fangs make the gnashcat one of the galaxy's most efficient killing machines. Although no larger than the common Terran house cat, this creature exhibits a startling level of brainless ferocity and homicidal mania when it encounters any being outside its own species."

"That's just what the assassin told me," Mister Moogi said bitterly. "A killing machine."

The Terran holo was back, this time with a sleazy grin creasing its face. "Too bad it wasn't an *eating* machine."

"How was *I* to know that gnashcats can't eat off-worlders?" Mister Moogi rubbed primary and secondary foreclaws together in a piteous manner. "How was *I* to know they'd die from devouring Dangvims? How was *I* to know that gnashcats are an endangered species, protected by a body of transgalactic law thicker than this entire hotel?"

The holo stiffened, a silvery sheen freezing its features until it was completely transformed into a parody of a humanoid servo. Its mouth opened and closed with no distinct lip articulation as it rattled off, "It is the decision of this Merchants' Tribunal that the accused, Mister Moogi of Splendel's, be disciplined as follows:

"One: For failing to run a proper and complete check on the references of his hired assassin, he must close shop on Ujit's Other Tuesday and do community service. However, in view of the fact that he personally killed and ate the offending assassin for misrepresentation, this penalty is waived.

"Two: For causing the death of his neighboring merchant-brothers, he shall be compelled to offer all Dangvim merchandise at twenty percent off from this time forward. This injunction does not apply to any Dangvim merchandise currently in stock or subsequently obtained through recognized smuggling channels.

"Three: For being instrumental in the death by indigestion of eight rare and endangered gnashcats who might otherwise have fetched an excellent price on the open gag-and-novelty-gift market, he shall be made to take into his shop as an apprentice merchant the orphaned Dangvim youngling known as Podvex. This association is to remain in effect until the youngling shows himself able to conquer his own shop, or expresses a desire to change employment, or dies a natural death."

"If I personally killed and ate him, that would be natural for me," Mister Moogi said, four out of six eyes full of hope.

"The Merchants' Tribunal thought of that." The System unfroze the holo, which was grinning more nastily than ever. "Maybe you don't remember the size of the fine they said they'd slap you with if your apprentice becomes your appetizer."

"'It's not fair." Mister Moogi sagged inside his carapace, although it would take a keen trained eye to notice the difference from his normal posture. "That Dangvim poisons everything he touches! Oh, why wasn't he in the shop with his parents where he belonged when the gnashcats arrived?"

"At your hearing, he testified that he was out making a personal apology to a dissatisfied customer. He did not specify the underlying reason at the hearing, but I theorize that his offense must have been a whopper if it required in-person penitence."

"You see?" Mister Moogi's limbs waved wildly. "Even then he was incompetent. To say nothing of unfilial! Causes his parents to be shamed before the paying-and-potential, then lacks the common decency to die with them! It's all that Dangvim laxness, that's what it is. Faugh! What can you expect from mammals? I'm surprised they kept their shop going for as long as they did. How they ever managed to conquer a merchanting territory in the first place I'll never—"

A shrill *VEEeeeeeEEEEM* scraped the last merciful micrometer of insulation off Mister Moogi's nerves. "Uh-oh," said the System, its holo fading out. "Here comes trouble." They both knew without touching a Demigalac dictionary that for Splendel's, trouble was spelled with a capital Podvex.

Mister Moogi chirruped a command that opened his office door without altering any of the interior comfort specs. The portal slipped aside, as ordered, to reveal the young Dangvim on the figurative doorstep, his paws still wrapped far too tightly around the Summon/CummIn control. Mister Moogi took a deep breath on all vents and told himself not to scream.

"Podvex," he said, "what is that in your paw?"

"Urrr ... It's ... it's a presence announcer, Mister Moogisir."

"Correction: It is a Summon/CummIn, *the* best little narrow-spectrum presence announcer on the market. Just one touch and the genetic code of any casual visitor is forever enshrined in the device's memory. On all subsequent visits, our most valued customers are immediately recognized and directed to my personal attention, while deadbeats and just-browsers are politely steered into the shop's no-man's-land, where even the servos seldom tread—where even *you* are not an option—and are there left to steep until they've had enough and take their nonbusiness elsewhere."

"Really?" Podvex's huge, round eyes seemed to get huger and rounder with awe, physical possibility be damned. He gazed with fresh respect at the ruined control box in his paws. "Gosh," he breathed in purest, lowest Underg'lac.

"What is more," said Mister Moogi, suppressing a series of shudders that threatened to shake his carapace to chitinous shrapnel, "Summon/CummIn can even turn 'tronic bloodhound to hunt down really good—albeit lapsed—customers and bay special sale announcements beneath their System windows until they came back to Splendel's once more. It is high tech, high cost, high maintenance, and high return. Sometimes it can sense a caller's identity without being touched, simply by an analysis of the cloud of shed skin-cells or other bio-detritus surrounding his person. You did not need to touch it at all. You certainly did not need to tear it out of the wall and strangle it, Podvex."

Podvex looked up into Mister Moogi's face and conjured up a sickly smile. "Urrrr, I wasn't sure if it rang or not when I touched it, so I sort of . . ." He tried another angle. "I thought maybe it could use a tune-up so I wanted to detach it from the wall because you always say these repair-droids cost a claw and an antenna just to look at the problem, and . . ." He gave up. "Is this . . . is this coming out of my pay, too?"

"Never mind." Mister Moogi's foreclaws were all clacking out a staccato beat until he sounded like an avalanche of castanets. "Just . . . never mind. Were I to add this debt to the score of all the damages you've already caused in my shop, you would be an apprentice forever. We certainly don't want *that*."

"Don't we?" Podvex curled his already roly-poly body into a more compact ball and groomed his toes self-consciously.

"No-we-*don't*!" Mister Moogi articulated each word just so, giving it the force of a falling sandbag. Poor little Podvex cringed. "Considering your past performance, I must say that only a four hundred percent increase in personal sales completed would redeem your account to a reasonable level."

"And what . . . what would you say's a reasonable level, Mister Moogisir?" Podvex ventured. His silky blue shoulder fur was beginning to lose its gloss due to the strain he was under. The formidable Mister Moogi had scared Podvex enough when they were just neighbors, but as an employer he was Terror in a giant dung beetle suit.

"If I can get you out of my shop and into one of your own before either one of us perishes of old age, that would be reasonable. It would also be reasonable if you remained my apprentice until your dying day and when I sold your corpse for the value of its component elements, that sum would equal your debt to me. But it won't, so it looks like my only hope is you bettering your sales record."

A hint of sheen seeped back into Podvex's shoulder fur. His wide mouth arched up in the middle, the Dangvim equivalent of a smile. "But that's why I'm here, Mister Moogisir! To give you the good news."

"You're quitting my apprentice program? You'd be willing to pheromark an affidavit to that effect in the presence of the Merchants' Tribunal? You've found some other employment in the hotel that interests you more?" Mister Moogi's optimism was so delicate and lovely to behold, it was a sin to mash it into the dust.

"Oh, no." Podvex was adamant. "I could never leave you after all you've done for me, Mister Moogisir."

"All I've—" Holding on to sanity and scent sacs by the thinnest of threads, Mister Moogi attempted to make sense of his employee's unwanted loyalty. "Podvex, you lower marsupial, I had your parents murdered!"

"Yessir, and mighty quick it was. Dadder always did say that if he had to go, he'd like to die on the job, selling right up to the last moment, and Mommer . . . Well, I'll let you in on a little secret, Mister Moogisir: I was 'way past the age for most Dangvim cubblers to leave the family den and set up their own establishments. Mommer and Dadder were going to give me just one more chance to conquer my own shop, and

if I bollixed it this time, they were going to personally kill
and eat me. So you see, I owe you my life. I'd never quit on
you."

Mister Moogi began exuding a waxy substance much
prized for its ability to grow hair on male Terrans of a certain
age. It was the only way his people had of expressing despair.
Dutiful Podvex set down the ruined Summon/CummIn unit
and fetched a gross of plastic ampoules, continuing the conversation while he used these to harvest his employer's ex-
tremely marketable tears.

"But I do have good news for you, as I said," he went on
"While you were in the office, we had a customer."

"*A* customer?" Mister Moogi mocked his apprentice without shame or remorse. "I should hope that Splendel's may
boast at least *a* customer at any give instant."

"Ah!" Podvex gestured with a full ampoule. "But this was
a *sentient* customer—"

"Many paying-and-potentials eschew their servos for the
pleasure of coming to Splendel's in person."

"A *wealthy* customer—"

"Haven't I taught you that *having* wealth and being willing
to *part* with wealth do not always share the same coccoon?"

"A *Terran* customer—"

"I have found, Podvex, that moneyed Terrans are not the
only race in this part of the galaxy who don't know the value
of a credchip."

"A *desperate* customer!"

"*What?*" Instantly Mister Moogi's whole demeanor
changed. He whirled around and seized little Podvex in two
sets of foreclaws. Pale yellow striations played up and down
his cheek flaps, an indicator of gut-level elation he had not
had cause to use since the day his queen had told him she was
not going to personally kill and eat him after sex. "Where is
he, Podvex? You didn't let him get away, did you?"

"Oh, no, Mister Moogisir. He's sitting in the Glorioski
Lounge having a nice cup of squeeze tea and some cakes—*yes*,
I made sure the cakes were nontoxic and properly drugged this
time—and he said he didn't mind waiting however long it
took." Podvex puffed out the frilled fur on his chest. "He said
he could see that I was just the sentient for the job."

"Merciful Queen, the poor meat loaf *must* be desperate,"

Mister Moogi breathed. "Oh well, no matter, no matter. He's desperate and he's rich and he's ours. That's all that counts, isn't it, Podvex, my fine young clutchmate?" His foreclaws combed nervously through Podvex's shoulder fur in an attempt at bonhomie.

"You bet, Mister Moogisir." Podvex was so taken by his employer's sudden gush of goodwill that he jabbered carelessly away in Underg'lac without noting how each hoi-polloi syllable made Mister Moogi wince.

Master merchant and apprentice scurried to the Glorioski Lounge posthaste. There Mister Moogi found the customer of whom Podvex had burbled. "So it is no dream," he breathed, taking in every juicy and costly-looking detail of the Terran's attire. There was wealth here, and plenty of it. And he didn't gaffe it. There may yet be hope of getting rid of Podvex, Mister Moogi told himself.

Feeling quite rejuvenated at the thought, Mister Moogi hastened to greet this potential source of credchips unlimited. His superprime foreclaw flickered up to trigger his Taboolator implant (Terraculture file). The Taboolator was a lovely little device all upper-crust merchants employed so as not to accidentally make some unfortunate remark or gesture perfectly acceptable in their own cultures but anathema to the prejudices of their customers.

"Welcome, welcome to Splendel's, my honored guest," Mister Moogi gushed. "To what do we owe the joy of serving so handsome a customer?" He was about to assign the Terran's good looks to having ritually devoured all of his siblings, but the Taboolator squealed a warning just in time.

The Terran stood up quickly. "Oh boy, I sure hope you can help me," he said. "I need a courtship gift, and I've got no idea where to begin. Price is no object."

Mister Moogi was more than pleased. "Certainly, certainly. We here at Splendel's pride ourselves on being the finest hotel gift shop money can buy. Our selection of goods is second only to our skill at matching the perfect gift to each lucky recipient. In matters of romance, we are exquisite and randy by turns, as desired. Of course I needn't tell a sophisticated sentient like yourself that before we can begin to assist you, there is the matter of the contract—"

"Contract?" The Terran blinked. Mister Moogi's implant

translated the grimace to mean that the man was somewhat taken aback. "I thought we took care of all that."

"We did, we did!" Podvex scampered forward, waving his paws frantically at the System port on the lounge wall. The shineout of a counsel-purchase agreement thrust itself into the lounge, inscribed with the Terran's signature and, no doubt, Podvex's pheromark above his printed name, had holos but the means to project scent as well as sight.

"Your Mister Podvex agreed to help me find exactly what I need," the Terran said.

"I see, I see," Mister Moogi muttered, eyes dancing over the plump terms of the contract. In brief it explained to anyone interested that Splendel's, as represented by Podvex, had become lord, master, and queen of the Terran's financial resources provided that Splendel's could come up with a courtship gift for one K'taen-ka'a, a highborn Kha'ak of the world commonly known as Osprey. Galactic coordinates were given in the same boilerplate paragraph that held the lucky recipient's DNA identification codes. It was all pretty formulaic.

Something got into Mister Moogi's skull as he reviewed the contract. It wasn't the fact that Podvex had done something right for a change. That was just the law of averages on his side. (As the old saying goes: Even a queen who eats *all* the young of one generation will manage to devour the incipient democrats with the rest.) No, there was something subtler at work here, making his brain twitch and jig. He leaned closer to the shineout, bringing all eyes into play.

There was a scream followed by the overwhelming stench of long-restrained mature adult scent sacs letting go.

"I'm sorry," the Terran said to Podvex as they sat opposite each other in the Without Portfolio, a hotel bar favored by the ambassadorial set. "I didn't know your boss felt that strongly about diplomats."

"Strongly isn't the word," the furry blue Dangvim replied. He had taken so many cleansings that his follicles were shrieking for mercy and still the smell of Mister Moogi's outburst lingered at the roots. "It's not your fault, Frankmacgregorsir. You told me you were a dipper. *I* should have known Mister Moogisir's feelings on the subject."

The Terran gave Podvex a weak smile. "Just call me Frank,

please. It'll make me feel a little better about what I've done to you."

"Oh, Mister Moogisir will get over it." Podvex shrugged and sipped his squeeze tea. "We'll find you the perfect courtship gift for Miz K'taen-ka'amam, you'll pay us a lot of money, I'll get my commission, and I'll never sign up another dipper customer as long as I live."

"That's for sure," Frank said rather heavily. He leaned across the table. "Do Dangvims handle alcohol without exploding?"

"It makes us giddiloopers, but we don't explode," Podvex replied.

"Good." Frank signaled the nearest servo and ordered them both a stiff drink. "Belt it down the black hole," he instructed Podvex in lowest Underg'lac. "You're gonna need it."

Sometime later, a definitely giddiloopers Podvex blinked at the Terran diplomat, mouth gaping. "Droppings," was all he could say, over and over again, or sometimes, incredulous, "No droppings?"

"None." Frank shook his head.

"Awww, *droppings!*" Podvex cried. "I'm dead."

"We're dead," the Terran corrected. "I just decided to take you along for the hearse ride." He frowned at a thought that nibbled one brain lobe. "I don't know what possessed me to drag you in on this with a fully formal contract. When I went into Splendel's all I wanted was some casual advice about this gift—the alien point of view and all that. Nothing binding. It wouldn't be fair to involve other sentients just because my lingonberries are on the line. Why would I have done something so . . . ?"

"My fault." Podvex stared into the echoing depths of his empty glass. "When I heard you say price was no object, I did what Mister Moogi always told me to do: I hustled you up to the lounge and fed you cakes specially . . . um . . . seasoned to make you more receptive."

"You mean drugged?" Frank raised an eyebrow.

"Enough to make you hand me your sister if I asked for her." Podvex's spongy tongue mopped up the last drops of alcohol from the bottom and sides of the glass. "Standard merchanting procedure. So don't feel bad on my account. I've dirtied my own den and now I've got to lie in it."

"Tell me about it!" Frank leaned back, arms folded. "The same thing happened to me, all because I couldn't keep my big mouth shut. I'm not even supposed to *be* here. The Hotel Andromeda was just a stopover for me en route to my next posting, but when I registered I saw a public shineout about *the* wedding of the age booked for this hotel: a marriage made on Osprey! Who'd have thought it?"

"They don't marry on Osprey?" Podvex asked.

"Oh, they marry, all right. The rituals and taboos surrounding marriage within the tribes of the Kha'ak and the P'toon are taught to every fledgling dip. If you don't run away screaming, they figure you'll do. Marriage is very important to both tribes. Only children born in wedlock to the Kha'ak are permitted the supreme honor of becoming warriors who get to slaughter the P'toon, and vice versa."

"Like the servowars during post-Bingemass sales." Podvex nodded. "I see."

"What makes this wedding special—special, hell; *incredible!*—is that K'taen-ka'a is Kha'ak, but the bridegroom is—'

"P'toon?"

"You got it." Frank covered his face with his hands. "I read that shineout three times, just to make sure it was real. Third time's when I caught *her* name on it. Ever since we were stubtails in the dipcorps school, Juanita VanTeufel has been my nemesis. Don't get me wrong: Juanita's a beautiful woman and a great dip, but the way she always *gloats* when she one-ups me! For bringing off an intertribal marriage on Osprey she'll get to crow over half the galaxy. To this day I don't know how she did it."

"So you sought her out to—congratulate her." Podvex gave Frank a knowing look. Industrial espionage was also an integral part of the successful merchant's life, as Mister Moogi had taught him.

"Have it your way. The Terran dipcorps maintains a permanent suite in the hotel, you know, and when I went up there to try learning how Juanita pulled off this coup, instead of a party I stumble into a wake. Juanita's crying, her boss is yelling at her, *his* boss is yelling at him, and *her* boss is—"

"At the scent-sac sphincter's limits?" Podvex suggested. "Why? Was the wedding not to be?"

"That's what they told me. That's *all* they told me. Oh, they made me welcome as a fellow dip, and they recognized me as a friend of Juanita's—they even cut off the multilevel harangues and recriminations and left the room to give us some private time to exchange the social pleasantries—but they refused to breathe a word about why the wedding was history. I wasn't one of *them,* see, so they couldn't give me an official briefing." His cheeks colored slightly as he added, "There was nothing to prevent Juanita from briefing me . . . after."

"After the social pleasantries?" Podvex was a bright young Dangvim.

Frank swallowed one reply and voiced another. "The P'toon refuse to recognize a wedding as legal or binding until the groom has sent the bride a courtship gift. That's the only thing that Juanita told me. Oh yes: Also that the gift cannot be selected or delivered by the groom himself, or by a servo, and that if the bride shows any indication that she doesn't like it, the wedding's off. The P'toon indicated that they wanted a Terran dip to do their shopping for them."

"It was therefore a question of responsibility that had disrupted the harmony of your friend's place of employment." It was too bad that Mister Moogi wasn't there to hear his apprentice phrase the situation in flawless Demigalac.

"Uh-huh. That's what she said." Frank signaled the servo and bought another round, downing his before he added, "Served me right for forgetting that in the dipcorps the first thing they teach us is to listen for what the other person *doesn't* say."

Podvex listened as Frank went on to outline a familiar scenario. The Dangvim was quite familiar with shopper's panic, an affliction knowing no boundaries of galactic race or culture. Like Frank, he would have assigned Juanita's desperation to the fear of picking out the wrong gift for the bride, thereby bringing the weight of a failed strategic tribal union crashing down upon her head.

"No one would care if the P'toon and the Kha'ak continued to cut each other into hash until doomsday, except for two things: Osprey is a rich world and both tribes have recently discovered primitive nuclear weapons."

"Dirty ones?"

"Obscenely filthy ones. What good are resources and trade agreements when the world that's got 'em is sizzling like a ham steak on a griddle?"

Podvex folded one paw atop the other. He was swaying slightly, but so was Frank. "My friend," he said. "I see your predicament. You thought to rescue the female who is your rival, thereby making her indebted to you forever and more amenable to revealing her professional techniques and/or bearing your cubbers when a mutually convenient time for reproduction comes. But the female deceived you as to the full significance of her assigned task. There is more at work here than the mere giving of a bridal gift."

"To the P'toon, it's a gift," Frank said. "To the Kha'ak it's a declaration of war."

K'taen-ka'a poked her lunch with a delicate silver fork until the unlucky meal squeaked. Then she bit its head off. As she plucked a stubborn scale out from between her teeth, she said, "Oh, I'm not fussy about my courtship gift. Anything will do. Just anything."

Podvex scuffed his hindpaws over the lumps and bumps of a dozen costly Kha'ak carpets, strewn in careless profusion over the floor of the bride-to-be's room. The Kha'ak were strong believers in the dictum *Less is less*. Refinements of taste such as minimalism made them laugh. They preferred ostentation, display, and gross consumerism. Mister Moogi would have worshiped them.

"Anything?" the Dangvim repeated. "You're not just saying that, are you, K'taen-ka'amam? This is your courtship gift. According to what Frankmacgregorsir told me about your people, this is the last time you'll be able to make any choice independent of your husband, until you have borne his first child."

"Upon which happy occasion I get to kill him, if I can." The highborn Kha'ak maiden smiled.

"You missed a scale, there," Podvex pointed out. "Second daggerlike tooth from the right, upper."

"Thank you." K'taen-ka'a levered it free with the silver fork and spat it out. "I adore lizard, but with mammals you don't have so many little hard bits to get caught in your teeth after."

"Yesmam." Podvex didn't like the way she looked at him when she said that. Privately he said a prayer that the lady would not suddenly decide that what she wanted for a courtship gift was him, on toast. "As I was saying, the Terran Frankmacgregorsir, acting on behalf of your chosen P'toon bridegroom, Mairphot Garoo visTonktonk, has empowered me as a representative of Splendel's gift emporium to give you your choice of any and all merchandise in the shop provided that you . . . that you . . ." The poor Dangvim felt his professional coolness melting at the edges under the unwavering yellow stare of the Kha'ak. She was smiling, or at least showing all her teeth. It didn't make what Podvex had to ask her any easier. ". . . that you promise *not* to take your bridegroom's chosen courtship gift as *ri'khak-umrow*." He had some trouble getting out the untranslatable alien syllables, but he managed.

"No," said K'taen-ka'a. She snapped the silver fork in two.

"No? But—but perhaps you didn't understand me." Podvex wrung his paws. "*Anything* Splendel's stocks, *all* things Splendel's stocks, yours for the asking! The Terran ambassador will be only too charmed to make up the difference between your bridegroom's budget and the actual cost out of his own pocket. And all you've got to do is—"

"No." K'taen-ka'a rolled over so that her vast naked belly was exposed to the heat lamps and scent sprinklers so needful to her comfort. "Now you listen to me, little one," she said in a level voice. "This wedding your Terran friends are so delirious about is none of my doing. I was raised to be a warrior, to slaughter P'toon, and eventually to bear children who in turn would slaughter P'toon. Then along comes this busy nose Terran female who yatters her way into our chief's good graces, does the same on the P'toon side, and convinces the pair of 'em that instead of slaughtering each other's people as the gods intended we should start breeding together."

She flopped back onto her belly and her expression was not comforting to see. "I was chosen to be the first. I must abandon all hope of ever seeing P'toon blood running over my knuckles in this life through no fault of my own."

"You did say you could try killing your mate after you bear his first cubber." Podvex didn't like to see anyone unhappy.

K'taen-ka'a spat again, without benefit of lizard scale.

"Under *his* degenerate tribal law. Under *mine*, a wife who kills the father of her child is left naked in a room with a few old, embittered women and many sharp objects."

Her fingernails dug feather-spewing trenches in the cushions of her divan as she said, "I would kill the odious visTonktonk now, if I could, but since we are betrothed it is decreed under his law *and* mine that if we come face-to-face, we must marry immediately."

Podvex was about to suggest the classic stab in the back as an alternative, but decided to let the lady unburden her heart without interruption. Besides, he had no idea whether backstabbing was approved under Kha'ak or P'toon tribal law. Mister Moogi always said not to second-guess the customers unless they paid for it.

"I would hire board-certified assassins from Room Service to do the deed," K'taen-ka'a went on, "except that would shame me before my sisters as too lazy to attend to my own murders. All that is left to me is the *ri'khak-umrow*, and by the seven and a half breasts of the Second Greatest Mother, I intend to use it!"

"We have some very nice weresilks at Splendel's this season," Podvex pressed, even while he knew it was hopeless. "Also genuine Terran all-cotton T-shirts with witty mottos and racial slurs. I'm sure Mister Moogi would have one specially printed up for you saying something nasty about the sexual preferences of the P'toon."

"Ri'khak-umrow," the Kha'ak repeated, savoring the words. "Disgraceful death by presents. It is one of our oldest and most insidious customs. No matter what the visTonktonk gives me for a bridal gift, I shall respond by returning it accompanied by an even more lavish present. Since I have returned his gift to me, he must send back both the gifts with a still more expensive one. Then it is my turn to respond in kind, adding a fourth gift to the sum, and so it shall go until the miserable wretch is left shamed, poverty stricken, and impotent to outdo the sumptuousness of my final offering." She closed her eyes and reveled in the thought of an impotent P'toon.

"What if he does outdo you?" Podvex asked timidly.

K'taen-ka'a's eyes snapped open and fixed on the meek little Dangvim. "Impossible. Honor prevents a marriageable male P'toon from using any funds but his own. I, on the other hand, as an independent unmarried maiden, may do what I damned well like with the resources of my entire clan. If they don't approve of my spending habits, they're free to try killing me. Little chance of that, in this case: The giving of a gift to a trueborn Kha'ak is tantamount to declaring that her kin are unable to support her in fitting style. It is therefore an insult to my whole family. They'll let me spend whatever I want to destroy the insolent rogue."

"But you don't get to kill him; just destroy him financially," Podvex pointed out.

"I know." K'taen-ka'a's eyes were gleaming yellow slits. "It's much less merciful that way."

The Dangvim grew thoughtful. "If Mairphot Garoo visTonktonk doesn't give you a bridal gift, the wedding's not legal under his people's law. If Mairphot Garoo visTonktonk *does* give you a bridal gift, you can commence death by presents under your people's law."

"There you have it." K'taen-ka'a yawned, content.

"Didn't the Terrans know about this situation before they got your chiefs to set up the marriage?"

Again Podvex found himself staring into the glare of K'taen-ka'a's full set of teeth. "What do *you* think, little one?" A bubbling noise welled up in her throat, part merriment, part slurp. "Now run along and do your shopping for my future bridegroom. As I said, I'm not fussy. Anything will do. Because whatever it is you choose, I'll send it right back to him with a better gift in tow. You can price it low, but that will only make the game stretch out a little longer. The end result will be the same."

Podvex dragged his paws all the way to the door. Before he left, he turned to try one last suggestion: "You couldn't just . . . just accept the gift and marry him?"

"I am a trueborn Kha'ak," came the reply. "After I am wed, I may take no more independent actions until the day I am judged to be past childbearing. With all that to look forward to, would *you* be in such a hurry to kiss your virginity good-bye?"

"Yes, but for the sake of peace—"

"Ah, how fond you are of peace, little one!" There was a dangerous undertone to K'taen-ka'a's seemingly casual words. She swung her legs over the edge of the divan and started toward Podvex, saying, "And who are more peaceful than the dead?"

The Dangvim didn't stop running until he was safely back in the Glorioski Lounge at Splendel's.

"It looks bad," said Frank.

"Bad," Podvex agreed.

Mister Moogi glowered at the pair of them and refreshed the squeeze teas. He had not said a word since the scent-sac incident, but the play of color bands over his cheek flaps told its own tale of irritation, indignation, and occasional speechless rage.

Now, as the colors shaded up into the deeper purple hues, he finally broke silence. "Bad is not the word!" he sputtered. "Ruination does not begin to describe it. I don't blame you, Podvex. For once. I have come to expect a certain level of idiocy from you, and you have yet to disappoint me. But you, sir!" He turned on Frank. "We never expected much from Terrans as far as the finer points of galactic society go, but at least we thought they'd know how to behave themselves in a *hotel*!"

"Wha-wha-what—?" Frank's stammered bewilderment made no impression on Mister Moogi.

"The wedding will not take place. That much is clear. Your people will lose a great deal of face for having backed a worst-selling line of goods. Your own career will of course be over. The female who so cunningly maneuvered you into this predicament will avoid all blame and make your existence a misery and a shame with her gloating now. You would have done better to have devoured her after sex, like any civilized sentient."

"Don't I know it," Frank muttered.

"So much for you. As for Podvex, he will always bear the stigma of an unfulfilled and unfulfillable contract. He will be"—Mister Moogi shuddered—"my apprentice forever."

"I wouldn't mind it that much, Mister Moog——" A single icy glance from his employer shut Podvex's mouth for him.

"Forever might not last as long as you expect, Podvex. Word of the wedding's failure will pass into legend, and legend will be sure to explain just why the wedding failed. Names will be named. Your foolish haste to sign a contract whose terms you did not fully understand will become immortal. So will the name of the shop lack-wit enough to have creatures like you on staff."

"You did tell me that any publicity is good publicity, Mister Moogisir." Bravely Podvex tried to salvage some crumb of hope from the ashes.

"I lied."

"Oh." The crumb crumbled.

"To say nothing of what's going to happen to Osprey," Frank remarked, thinking aloud. "No wedding, no peace. Boom. Burn. Armageddon. Ouch."

"Osprey?" Mister Moogi bristled. "What is Osprey?"

"Just a whole world of short-tempered sentients that's going to be turned into toast, that's all."

"And what is that to me?" Mister Moogi demanded.

"Probably nothing," Frank allowed. "I just thought that toast goes well with a little of the milk of human kindness."

Mister Moogi's vents made terse, snuffling sounds, the equivalent of a human's disdainful sniff. "Milk is for *mammals*," he said, wearing contempt like a fine cloak. "*We* are speaking of the fate of *Splendel's*." Using every free foreclaw on his body, he gestured toward the panoramic windows of the Glorioski Lounge. Through these glassy portals and via the networks of viewscreens above them it was possible to see every corner of the gift shop.

It was a striking spectacle, one that never failed to impress Podvex. Almost against his will, he found himself drawn fascinated to the windows and the viewscreens, his eyes sweeping the vast abundance of the gift shop's wares. His heart beat a little faster and a tear rose to his eyes. "Everything from soup to numps," he murmured.

"What was that?" Mister Moogi snapped.

"He said, 'Everything from soup to nuts,' " Frank supplied.

"He did *not*. He said '*numps*.' I heard him. Podvex, how dare you!"

"How dare I what?" The little Dangvim held up his paws in abject helplessness.

"Don't pretend you don't know. I never saw such an apprentice for getting out of work. Hmph! Probably use the ex-

cuse that this Osprey-thing-world's about to blow itself up.
Well, it won't hatch any clutches with *me*!" Mister Moogi's
foreclaws jutted out in an attitude of impatient expectation.
"Podvex, I am waiting. Isn't there *something* you should be
doing?"

"Uhhhh, ritual suicide?"

"Business before pleasure," Mister Moogi said sternly.

"Oh, my fur and follicles!" Podvex slapped his own forehead. "The *numps*!"

"*And* the yumas, *and* the sevreens, *and* the weimaraners,
and the—" Mister Moogi was left to enumerate to an empty
lounge. Podvex had streaked out, followed at a respectable
gallop by the Terran.

"So that's a nump," said Frank, peering into the sonocage
at a square-shouldered, baggy-eyed creature that looked like a
cross between a throw pillow and a hamster.

"Uh-huh," Podvex replied. "Splendel's might not be the
top gift shop in the Hotel Andromeda, but we do have the top
pet department. It's my job to inspect the animals daily and
reprogram the servos according to any changes I observe.
What with all the excitement, I forgot."

While Podvex attended to his duties. Frank strolled from
cage to cage, idly studying the animals inside. "You know,
Podvex," he remarked, "I think maybe I'm in the wrong profession. Animal husbandry, now there's the ticket for a peace-
able man like me. Take these critters, for example"—he
waved at the denizens of one cage—"I could probably breed
them and sell them for a living. I'll bet there's a nice market
for them *somewhere*."

Podvex glanced at the cage that held Frank's attention.
"Mister Moogi says there's a market for *everything* somewhere, even lagbels. The only trouble is, you've got to find a
really wealthy market: they cost a paw and a tail."

"Really?" Frank's interest was piqued. He had just been
making conversation with all his talk of quitting the
dipcorps. But now he took a closer look at the lagbels in
their cage. They were not very large animals, both about
groundhog size, one slightly plumper than the other. There
was nothing especially striking about their dull gray coloration or smooth-haired coats. They had simple binocular vi-

sion, four paws apiece, and medium-sized tails that looked incapable of doing more than balancing their owners despite an odd tuft of stiff, prickly-looking hair at the tip. Snuggled against one another, they looked up at the curious Terran with large, moist green eyes.

"Why are they that expensive?" Frank asked. "They lay golden eggs?"

"They're mammals; they don't lay any eggs," Podvex replied. He joined his customer at the lagbel cage. "I don't know much about them, Frankmacgregorsir. Mister Moogi just told me to keep the pets alive and not to ask stupid questions." The Dangvim grew thoughtful. "There *is* something about lagbels I remember, though."

"What's that?"

"You know the Tyrrhenians who always take over the hotel for their annual Mating Convention every Newtfolly Eve?"

Frank shook his head. "I'm not a hotel resident like you, Podvex. The only thing I know about Tyrrhenians is they're one of the most peaceful races in this sector of the galaxy."

"You wouldn't say that if you ever saw their Mating Convention. Twenty-nine fire alarms per day minimum, slime on all the mirrors, and they always steal the housekeeping servos. Anyhow, toward the end of the convention, when things are settling down, all the newly mated couples come in here and buy breeding pairs of lagbels. One lagbel's expensive, but two—! So once, when I was pretty sure Mister Moogi was busy elsewhere, I asked them why. The Tyrrhenians told me that the lagbel's probably the most fiercely monogamous creature in the galaxy. They mate for life, and they coexist peacefully the whole time they're together."

"Neat trick," Frank muttered.

"Oh, it's no trick, Frankmacgregorsir; it's science! The Tyrrhenians told me that laboratory experiments showed that the male and the female each give off a different kind of musk to attract the opposite sex. When they find each other, the two musks combine in midair and the resulting substance has a tranquilizing effect on the lagbels. There's no research to back this, but Tyrrhenian tradition says the musk also has the same effect on other sentients that get within breathing distance, which is why ... which is why ... Why, Frankmacgregorsir, why are you staring at the lagbels like that?"

"Podvex," the Terran said slowly, a smile replacing the look of black despair that had been clouding up his features. "Podvex, does Splendel's deliver?"

Podvex was humming happily to himself as he tidied up the cosmetics section when the assassins sprang. He was just able to sound the alarm summoning security servos before they stuffed him into a sack and tossed him into the back of the linen cart they had hijacked for their purposes. It was an armed linen cart of the sort that could be left unattended in the hotel corridors without fear of any greedy passerby helping himself to the little shampoos and soaps. In seconds, every security servo in the vicinity was reduced to a smoking heap of slag and the assassins made a clean getaway.

Podvex next saw the light in K'taen-ka'a's room. The assassins dumped him on the rugs and paused only long enough to accept the Kha'ak maiden's generous tip before departing. Then K'taen-ka'a turned to face the trembling Dangvim.

Her fury made every layer of muscle on her immense body ripple until it made poor Podvex seasick just to look at her. "Where is it?" she demanded.

"Where is what?" Podvex cheeped. It was an honest question, the kind that always makes people get really angry and shout:

"You know what!"

Podvex watched the thin strands of saliva vertically banding the Kha'ak's gaping maw and decided he'd be safer making an educated guess than being honest again and likely ending up dead for his high morals.

"Oh! You mean where is the . . . gift?" K'taen-ka'a's wicked hiss sounded affirmative, so Podvex dared to add, "It . . . it ought to be here. I delivered it myself. You remember. I gave it right into your hands and you asked if it bit and I said I didn't think so, although when we took it out of its mate's cage it—"

"It is *gone!*"

"Is it? Oh dear. That's terrible."

"That is worse than terrible," the noble Kha'ak maiden snarled.

"You—you liked it so much? Goodness, I'm glad to hear it. It's always so difficult picking out gifts for someone else.

Sentients have such differing tastes, especially when it comes to pets. That's why I seldom recommend them as gifts unless you know the recipient really well. I told the Terran that—"

"I did not like it at all!" K'taen-ka'a's roar made the lightsticks jiggle. "It was a *gift*, you fool! Did I not tell you that to my tribe, a gift is an insult and an insult that must be returned?"

"Re-returned? Yesssss, you did say something like—"

"And to *be* returned, a gift must be somewhere I can find it *to* return!" She thrust a sharp-tipped finger at the empty sonocage in the corner. Podvex crept over to examine it and found that the lock control panel—none of the best—had been assaulted from within with a keen, pointed object. For an instant, a vision of the lagbel's spiky tail flashed across the Dangvim's mind.

"Please, K'taen-ka'amam," Podvex said, cringing. "Surely you don't blame me for this?"

"I do not."

"Then why . . . why have you brought me here?"

"What? You are surprised?" The Kha'ak herself looked startled. "Doesn't Splendel's offer shop-at-home service? I merely wished to place an order for a replacement beast so that the *ri'khak-umrow* could commence."

"I see." Podvex compressed himself into a ball and from that somewhat more secure position said, "I'm afraid that's impossible."

It was said that the Kha'ak maiden's reaction disrupted twelve banquets, twenty-two extramarital trysts, five sales conferences, and a bar mitzvah at various points throughout the Hotel Andromeda.

"Thank you for coming with us, Frankmacgregorsir," Podvex whispered, his voice echoing eerily in the disused servo corridor.

"Least I could do in the name of galactic peace," the Terran replied.

"Shut up, the two of you, or I rip your heads off," K'taen-ka'a growled. Despite her bulk, she moved with an uncanny measure of grace and silence, the legacy of generations of sentients whose main purpose in life was murder.

"That wouldn't be a good idea, K'taen-ka'amam," Podvex

murmured. "I'm the only one who knows the way to your bridegroom's suite by this route, and once we get there you'll need Frankmacgregorsir to help you recapture your lagbel while I keep watch."

"I still don't see why you could not have simply sold me another one," the Kha'ak grumbled.

"I could have done that," Podvex replied. "But if I had, you'd never have been able to do your *ri'khak-umrow* thing. Not so you'd be believed."

"Lagbels mate for life," Frank put in. "When yours got away, it had to go straight to its mate, in Mairphot Garoo visTonktonk's rooms. If you sent a substitute lagbel back to him, he'd have the evidence right there in front of him that it wasn't his gift."

"Very well, very well, lead on." The Kha'ak stopped talking altogether, except to subvocalize a nonstop series of curses in her own tongue all the way to her bridegroom's quarters.

There was an oversized air vent in the hygiene unit left over from the time when the Hotel Andromeda had had to re-tool several rooms to accommodate a party of Ffft! warriors, mercenaries who would do anything for a price except bathe. Additional ventilation was costly to install, but not nearly so expensive as having to deep-space the whole block of rooms afterward had they not been so well aired out during the Ffft! occupation.

Podvex peeped through the air vent and saw a deserted hygiene unit. "It's all right. We can go ahead."

"You would be barbecue on my world for such laxity," K'taen-ka'a sneered. "One empty room does not imply that the despised visTonktonk is nowhere in his suite."

"I called the room first," Podvex replied. "There was no answer, and Frankmacgregorsir paid extra for a clandestine scan of the premises. The only place the scans won't go is the hygiene unit."

"What a nicety!" The Kha'ak's scorn was measurable by the bucket. "To honor privacy at the cost of valuable espionage information."

"It's not that," Frank said. "It's just that vetting the scanners isn't a job for a servo, and Hotel Security lost too many sentients when they tried scanning in-use hygiene units.

Ma'am, have you ever *seen* what some beings do in the name of personal hygiene?"

K'taen-ka'a gave a tiny shudder. "Point taken."

"Anyway, after I called the room, I sent out a blanket call to the hotel bars," Podvex continued. "Your groom-to-be is in the Light of Arcturus Bistro, drinking with his wedding attendants."

K'taen-ka'a's eyebrows twitched. "I would not have expected such competence of you, Dangvim. In gratitude, I shall purchase my next neural disruptor at your shop."

"We do carry a very nice selection of state-of-the-art color-coordinated—"

"Shut up and stand aside. I have a lagbel to recover." The Kha'ak maiden stiff-armed Podvex against one wall, Frank against the other, and punched out the air vent with one blow of her fist. There was a lot of grunting and squirming as she wriggled through the opening, but neither the Terran nor the Dangvim was fool enough to attempt giving her a friendly shove. At last, with a sound like a boulder being pulled out of a hog wallow, she was through. "What are you waiting for? Come help me," she commanded.

Podvex and Frank had no trouble at all slipping through the vent into the hygiene unit. K'taen-ka'a hadn't waited for them but had barged on into the main body of Maiphot Garoo visTonktonk's quarters, seeking her wayward courtship present. They heard her exclamation of triumph just as they stepped into the suite's sitting-squatting-and-hunkering-down area.

"Where is she?" Podvex searched the area in vain.

"It sounded like it came from there." Frank pointed at an open portal.

"That's not his personal chamber, is it?"

"It's wherever he's keeping his lagbel. This is really a shame. I hoped that by giving her half a mated pair and Maiphot Garoo the other one, the lagbel's natural tranquilizing effect would calm down these homicidal yahoos long enough for them to get safely married."

"But I told you, it's the blending of the male and female lagbel musks that does it. You don't get that effect unless you've got both lagbels together."

"Yeah, right." Frank sighed. "And for all we know, the effect doesn't even work on all sentients; just Tyrrhenians."

From the inner room came K'taen-ka'a's voice raised in an imperious demand for assistance. Podvex jumped. "I'd better go stand lookout, and you should help her. I don't think even K'taen-ka'a will have an easy time separating the lagbels. I know I had to use snooze-needles on them at the shop. Hurry, please. She doesn't sound very happy."

"Oh well, It was worth a try." Frank shrugged.

The entire suite shook with the force of something very large and heavy hitting the floor.

Frank dashed for the open portal, only to be bowled over by Podvex. "Oh my!" the Dangvim exclaimed, paws to mouth at the sight awaiting him. K'taen-ka'a lay full length upon the floor of the sleeping chamber, a goodly part of her overlaying the futon. Her hands were still outstretched toward the sonocage where a happily reunited pair of lagbels drowsed. Podvex tiptoed toward the cage and blinked at it to make sure his eyes told him the truth.

"Not engaged," he said, turning to Frank.

"What?"

"The cage controls aren't engaged. No wonder: That cage isn't big enough for two lagbels, so the P'toon just left it open. Someone must've told them about the animals' habits, how faithful they are. Mairphot Garoo visTonktonk probably figured they wouldn't try to run away so long as they had each other."

"Yes, but who could've told them—"

"And look there." The Dangvim didn't give Frank a chance to ask a thing. Instead he pointed to K'taen-ka'a's hands. Two spines of stiff gray hair stuck out of the flesh.

Frank knelt cautiously beside the gently snoring Kha'ak, then glanced at the lagbels. "The male's missing a tail spike," he said. "So's the female. If their musk was on those spikes . . ."

"I guess the tranquilizing effect doesn't just work on Tyrrhenians." Podvex wore a sheepish smile. "Should we try moving her?"

"I don't think so." A look of relief and revelation warmed Frank's features. "I think we should just try moving ourselves out of here fast."

• • •

It was the wedding of the year, or the turn, or the tumble, depending on how one kept track of time. It was also performed rather hastily, with none of the pomp Juanita vanTeufel had planned, and certainly with none of the limelight spilling over onto her. Instead it was visiting dip-in-transit, Frank MacGregor, who received the accolades and thanks of Kha'ak and P'toon alike for having been so Johnny-on-the-spot with an accredited shaman able to officiate at the hurry-up ceremony immediately necessary once Maiphot Garoo visTonktonk staggered into his sleeping chamber and fell over K'taen-ka'a.

"Once he saw her face-to-face, the die was cast," Frank told Podvex. "They *had* to get married at once. And once she was married, K'taen-ka'a couldn't start *ri'khak-umrow* or anything else without her new husband's say-so. Small chance. The P'toon don't raise any fools."

The Terran and the Dangvim were strolling through one of the better shopping areas of the Hotel Andromeda. It was not a neighborhood with the snob appeal of Splendel's, but it did lie at the intersection of several heavy consumer traffic routes. Podvex had been perplexed when the Terran showed up at Splendel's, tossed Mister Moogi a fat credchip key, and announced he was paying for a little of Podvex's time. Now as their walk continued, he was growing more confused by the minute.

"Ye-yes," he stammered. "We heard all about it through the System. It was very gratifying to know that—"

"Here we are," said Frank. They had stopped before a pretty little shop front. "Here you go." He took Podvex's paw and pressed it to the lock plate. The shop door opened and all the lights came on. A host of shiny new servos glided forward to greet the newcomers.

"Welcome to Podvex's," they said. "For the finest in gifts and gadgets, from soup to numps. *Ri'khak-umrow* contracts our specialty."

"It's the least a grateful Terran dipcorps could do. One tumble's lease, start-up stock, and your license as a paid-up member of the hotel Merchants' Council. If you don't like the name you can change it later," Frank said.

"Ah . . . ah . . . ah . . ." was all Podvex could reply.

"You're trying to say thank you?"

"Na-na-na . . ."

"Oh! You're trying to say you don't deserve this!"

"Ah."

"If you don't, who does?"

"Some-some-someone else."

"The *someone else* who made sure that Mairphot Garoo visTonktonk found out about the habits of lagbels, perhaps, and suggested he could leave the sonocage open?" Frank patted Podvex on the back. "Well, until that someone else shows up, why don't you just mind the shop?"

Podvex's eyes were shining as he took in the full magnificence of the well-stocked emporium. "Bingemass *is* coming," he murmured. "It's a good time to start up a new business. My, my. Won't Mister Moogisir—I mean, won't *Moogi* be surprised."

"To hear you've gone independent?"

"No, no. To get his first Bingemass gift from me. An apprentice can't afford to give anything away." He toddled off down an aisle, then paused to look back at Frank and asked, "We *do* carry gnashcats don't we?"

THE HAPPY HOOKERMORPH

———————●———————

Kevin J. Anderson

The more appendages a client has, the better he tips. I know it's presumptuous to make sweeping generalizations like that, with the incredible number of life-forms in the galaxy—but, hey, I've been at this business long enough to spot trends, and a lot of different types come through the Hotel Andromeda. Trust me—count the tentacles, then count your fee for the night.

And this guy had *twenty-three* appendages—just look at 'em! And of course it didn't take much for me to figure out what the identical number of orifices on my adapted female body were supposed to be for.

He gestured toward me with a pseudopod and eased back on his motive cushion of slime, flailing a few other tendrils in the air. I moved naturally, slithering into his room. I had altered my body to look exactly like a female Slugwump, and a knockout too, as best I could determine from the species listing in the Lexicon. If I didn't get everything right, it might shatter the illusion for the client.

"I . . . I've never done anything like this before," he said in his own dialect, sounding like wet glue oozing from a tube. They always said the same thing, even the veterans—as if a hookermorph like me really cares about excuses.

"You'll be just fine," I said to the lonely Slugwump, caressing him with one of my tendrils. "I'm already hot for you." His eyestalks extended in nervous astonishment at that.

Indeed, I was hot. Slugwumps come from a humid, haze-shrouded world about thirty degrees hotter than would have been my preference. But my Slugwump body adjusted to it in a few minutes as I glided in after him on his own trail of slime. They find that sort of thing erotic, you know. He closed the door portal behind us.

Inside the room, he turned on some sort of subsonic music that sounded like very large bubbles bursting deep underwater. I had to be amorous and whisper into his auditory pickups while the surround-speakers kept going *bloop-bloop-bloop*. Humidity generators worked silently to keep the environment comfortable for him.

In the middle of the room lay a corralled-off patch of powdery sand, which I took to be the area of repose. The client oozed over to a pedestal on which he had placed a large bowl-shaped flower that looked like a big water lily. With an ignitor, he lit the tips of the petals, and as they curled down in flames, the flower exuded a fragrant pink smoke. A nice touch.

He moved nervously, switching the igniter from tentacle to tentacle to tentacle in a hypnotic fireman's brigade; he hadn't managed to dispose of it before it burned one of his appendages, and I snatched it out of his grasp, tossing it to the sand in the sleeping area.

"I keep wanting to make small talk," he said, "but I can't think of anything to say."

I nudged him over the rim of the corral into the sleeping area. His body elongated and he flowed over to the sand. "I don't want to make small talk," I said. "I want to make love to you."

Again, he goggled with his eyestalks. By now I could see that I would have to take things into my own hands—figuratively speaking, that is. If I waited for him to take any sort of initiative, we would be in his cubicle all weekend.

When we actually got down to the business of mating, he

proved perfectly willing and eager. Our pliant bodies squished
together and rolled on the gritty sand, which heightened the
pleasure at the tips of our exposed nerves. It took us quite
some time to link up all his appendages with all my orifices,
but I found it ultimately satisfying. I managed to fake an orgasm in nineteen of the orifices, and I think I had genuine
spasms in four.

The petals of the flower burned down to the pollen, where
they burst in a flash of orange light before fading into dimness.
The *bloop-bloop-bloop* music continued on endless replay.

Afterward, my client looked exhausted and shaken, but
pleasured all the way to his soft body core. I could see his
membranes quivering as we sat against each other, shoring up
the gelatinous bulk as we secreted off our outer coating of
slime, washing away with it all of the irritating sand we had
gathered in the throes of our lovemaking.

"I just can't believe it . . . a stunningly beautiful female like
you even bothering to spend time with someone like me." He
condensed his body volume in what seemed to be shy with-
drawal.

"You aren't so bad. Take a good look at yourself—and
don't sell yourself short."

In truth, how was I supposed to tell the difference between
an *ugly* male Slugwump and a handsome one? And I didn't
want to remind him that this little service wasn't free, after
all.

As I expected, he tipped magnificently, in addition to the
normal fee. Twenty-three tentacles—see what I mean?

Being a hookermorph isn't necessarily easy, but it's a living.

I sauntered along the lobbyways in the hotel. This morning
I wore a bipedal body with muscular legs, the kind that enjoyed walking. I felt refreshed and vibrant, having just enjoyed a long ultrasonic bath in the form of a creature that
thrived on such things.

Potted plants that may or may not have been hotel guests
sat in the alcoves. Other life-forms stood open mouthed in
front of the ashtrays they had replaced, waiting for a snack of
used tobac-stick butts. Motivator ramps tilted at various an-

gles to accomodate life-forms from worlds with different gravities, conveying hotel guests to adjacent biospheres.

"So, how are you, Ilkiy?" said a voice from behind me. "I'm glad you finally decided to wear a body I can at least talk to!"

I turned to see John-23, one of the cyborg members of the Hotel Security staff. He could always read my genetic ID code with a blink of his enhanced left eye. John-23 had lost his arm, his shoulder, and half of his face during a cargo-shifter accident ten years ago. Most of the passengers in the stateroom container had died; they had been thrown from the high-pressure inner atmosphere of a gas giant, and turned into dripping tatters of flesh from explosive decompression. John-23 had spent a month or so in mech-regrowth, having new android body parts connected to his own body in a cell-to-cell match. To humans, he looked completely healed, indistinguishable from his former appearance, but whenever I looked at him through infrared-sensitive eyes, he looked all screwed up.

"I feel good this morning, John-23," I said, actually meaning it—and he could tell. John-23 and I have worked at the hotel for longer than either of us wants to admit.

Unfortunately, my good humor was not rubbing off. He was in one of his introspective moods. "What are we doing here, Ilkiy? You're so cheery. Have you finally figured out what you want out of life?"

"There's really nothing much I want. I enjoy life, I like my job. What else is there?"

Indeed, I do enjoy my job. It's always different, and I'm good at it. Oh, sometimes certain life-forms can be a drag, and you can't always tell just by their listings in the Lexicon. I remember that time with the Paramecon, a transparent cylindrical thing that showed all his pulsing internal organs; I had serviced him and taken my fee before I learned that Paramecons always mate for life. Luckily for me, Paramecons also die within a few days of mating; but he followed me around like a parasite for half a week, and I didn't dare change form and shatter the illusion for him. When he finally bowed over and I watched his heart-equivalent pump stop pumping, I know he expected me to split open and shower the room with our offspring before dying beside him. But

hookermorphs are sterile, as far as I know; I've never needed
to use any form of birth control, and the Lexicon doesn't give
too much information on my own kind.

Sometimes the job does get a little boring, though. One
time I had to stand absolutely still for four hours while a
plantlike male Dandel client budded and showered his pollen
all over me. Apparently satisfied, but without a word, he paid
his fee and shuffled out of the room on stubby mobile roots.

As I reminisced, I saw that John-23 was waiting for me to
say something a bit more profound. "I think it might be interesting to find a little more stability, I suppose. I've never had
anything that lasts."

"Nothing ever lasts," John-23 said. I've seen him in occasional glooms like this ever since his accident.

"I can make it better for you. Anytime you give me the
chance," I said. "No charge."

I had made the offer before, but never seriously, and
John-23 knew it. I've known him long enough that I could select a bodily form that would make his hormones short-
circuit. I could give him absolutely everything he had ever
fantasized about, and he knows it.

But John-23 also has a wife and three kids back in the employees' annex. His marriage is a good one, solid. He doesn't
need me mucking it up. He's too good a friend, and I would
never do that to him.

"Don't tempt me," he said. His voice was husky.

"Offer withdrawn," I said, then deliberately shifted into another body that would look bulbous and ugly to him.

John-23 touched the pickup implant behind his ear, then
nodded. "Gotta go. One of the Swelft guests is trying to take
a shower but can't figure out how to turn the water on. Those
damned critters are so unintuitive! What's complicated about
turning a knob in the bathtub?" He stomped off, waving
good-bye, but I could already see a new sense of purpose behind his movements.

John-23 likes his job, too. He just hates not being busy.

I sauntered through the pearlescent arches leading into one
of the hotel's primary bars. I wanted to share my energy, use
it as synergy and keep the buzz going. I needed a pickup.

I was wearing a delicate, feathery body guaranteed to ring

a few hormonal bells for a wide range of male hotel guests, and I could always alter my appearance at a moment's notice anyway.

Since so many species operate on completely different circadian rhythms, nobody at the Hotel Andromeda particularly cares what time it is. All things at all times, that was their motto. At the bar itself, various organic and robotic bartenders consulted their databases to determine which substances were known to be intoxicating to which life-forms.

I glanced around the bar, cataloging the customers, my *prospects*. Many of the species were familiar to me, some of them good tippers, some of them good lovers. Most were already with a companion. But I wanted something a bit more exotic, a bit of a challenge.

Then I saw it perched on a stool that had never been designed to accomodate its insectile frame. Metallic turquoise blue on its back casings and segmented legs, an ovoid head with gleaming silver domes for eyes, whiplike antennas. I had never seen its type before, which meant it was fairly rare. A challenge.

While staring at it, I consulted my Lexicon implant, waiting one second, then two as it searched for a match. I began to grow concerned and exhilarated at the same time. An unknown? Not quite. The listing popped up an image and a name—BORRAK. Very little data about the species, just some specifics on their homeworld, temperature ranges, gravity— all the stuff that's easy to gather from a few space probes, but nothing that demonstrated extended sociological study.

This excited me even more, especially after recalling my recent conversation with John-23. I could provide some new data for the Lexicon compilers, give them vital information about a mysterious species. The Lexicon pays handsomely for such contributions, which was enough of an incentive already, but it could also let me do something permanent, to make my mark on the galactic civilization.

Since the Lexicon entry gave so few useful facts, I was going to have to use my intuition and my skills to the fullest. Drawing from the image in the Lexicon and extrapolating from what I could see hulking over the barstool, I altered my form into my best approximation of a Borrak. I made my exoskeleton a little brighter, the antennae more feathery, hoping

I had made a correct guess about what the race found beautiful. I approached the Borrak, who seemed to be huddling in misery over a gelatinous intoxicant. All the better.

"Hello, potential companion," I said in Basic dialect.

The Borrak turned and reared back in what could only be an expression of astonishment. Normally, I dislike chitinous beings; it's impossible to read any expression on a brittle face—therefore more difficult to know when I'm doing something right—but their body language is usually more exaggerated. "Why are you here?" it said without any preamble.

"I would like to spend some time with you. Would that be acceptable?" I usually leave out all discussions of fees until after I have the client on the hormonal hook.

To my surprise, the Borrak drew itself up, bristling in an apparent defensive posture with perhaps a hint of dismay. "No, that would not be acceptable," it answered. "I think it would be wisest if you remained far from me for the duration of your stay at the Hotel Andromeda. I would not want to be forced to engage you in mortal combat."

Now that was a hell of a rebuff, but I couldn't figure out what I had done wrong. The Borrak scrambled itself off the barstool in a dizzying ballet of segmented legs, then marched out of the bar.

Failure is certainly nothing new to me, and I can usually take it with a measure of grace. But I was preoccupied with trying to figure out what I had done wrong. I moved to a vacant table, changed form into something that would sit comfortably on one of the chairs, and pondered. Every race and every society has plenty of customs and taboos that usually make no sense to outside observers; perhaps I had inadvertently stepped on some insectile toes. Who could tell?

"Excuse me," said a gruff, demanding voice with no undertones of politeness whatsoever, "you are a hookermorph. I saw you change. Don't try to deny it."

I turned to see a squat, froglike creature, powerfully built, with needle teeth and lips that stretched practically all around his head. A Rybet; I had served them before. They were not too difficult to work with, if you had a high tolerance for rudeness. You just had to be rude back to them. It turned them on.

"Hire me if you want. If not, get away from me. You want a price breakdown?"

"Come to my room. Now. I will pay your usual fee, and I wish to hire you for a different assignment."

Maybe the day would have something interesting and unusual after all, I thought. I transformed into the body of a female Rybet, then waddled after him out of the bar.

Up in the Rybet's room, we waded into shin-deep lukewarm water. Semi-mobile algae dribbled out of our way as we sloshed to two damp fungal mounds in the middle of the pool. Two dull red holographic suns shone from the dome roof of the room.

"Sit down," he snapped, motioning with a stubby, flipperlike forearm.

"Why?"

"So I can tell you about my assignment, that's why! Now listen." He seated himself on one of the fungal mounds with a squelching sound. He puffed air into his lips, swelling them.

I splashed water upon myself to dampen my skin, then eased onto the vacant mound as far away from the Rybet as possible. "So talk!" I said.

"I need you to secure for me a sample of semen from a Hoojum. It's very important. I'll pay you a thousand credits."

Not only was the Rybet rude, but he seemed at least partially insane. "A Hoojum! That's tough. Why a thousand credits?"

"Never mind. I'll pay you a hundred credits just for coming here now, and a thousand more if you can deliver a sperm sample." He puffed his lips again, and his lantern eyes widened.

"I'll try. Even assuming I can find a Hoojum, getting one as a customer is no minor task."

"An entire Hoojum tour group is on the transport arriving this afternoon. Remember, it's worth a thousand credits."

"I said I would try. Now stop nagging me!"

I pushed myself off the fungus mound and got ready to leave, but he leaped up and splashed in the water after me. "Wait!" he croaked. "I'm paying you a hundred credits for this visit. Give me something for it."

I sighed. At least it was fairly simple to service a Rybet. Concentrating long enough to shift my internal organs, I generated, then pulled out a few handfuls of black sterile eggs into the lukewarm water. The egg mass looked like an island of black caviar surrounded by a wispy mass of the semi-mobile algae. The Rybet sloshed up to it and loomed over the eggs.

After he had spilled his milt over the cluster, he let out a long breath of satisfaction. "Ah, very pleasurable. Thank you very much." He let his huge lips curve in a grotesque smile, then he remembered his rudeness again. "Don't stare at me. Get out of here!"

I sloshed back to the door portal, thinking of the thousand credits he had offered. Now all I had to do was find a Hoojum.

I don't think I'll ever get tired of watching the spaceliners arrive. All you see is a bright light as the ship, itself as big as the continents on many worlds, swings into orbit. Smaller chunks break off the liner's main body and drop down like shooting stars to the transfer points at Hotel Andromeda.

Sometimes I like to go out to watch the descending cargo modules, each like a city in its own right, carrying thousands of staterooms, each pressurized with the occupants' desired atmosphere. Watching the great mass of the dedicated module land that afternoon, I was reminded all too clearly of the flames, the groaning metal, the spouting death that John-23 had encountered right out here on the primary receiving bay. But extra safeguards had been designed in the decade since that accident, and I had nothing to worry about.

The hot air smelled of industrial pollutants, outgassing from rocket fuels, lubricants from the machinery that loaded and unloaded the immense containers. The air was filled with a cacophony of hissing and roaring and strident alarm blasts; I would have preferred even the *bloop-bloop-bloop* music of the Slugwumps.

Somewhere among the thousands of passengers on that dedicated module was a tour group of Hoojums. I just had to wait and watch.

Even without trying, the Hoojums succeeded in making everything difficult for me. It seemed to be a particular talent of theirs.

First off, they were a bunch of religious fanatics of the worst kind. They stuck together in a little pack, as if just daring anyone to persecute them. They all wore huge, billowy robes of violet and orange, embroidered with threads of eye-numbing intensity so that they looked like walking moiré patterns wherever they went.

The whole group would disappear for hours in prayer meetings and verse chantings. The few times I managed to catch one by himself, he rebuffed my advances completely. Five times. After following them around for three days without success, I decided it was time to change tactics.

I uploaded their version of holy scripture and scanned it into my forebrain. Pretty standard stuff, commonplace for all those religions that claim to have the One True Message. Of course, those types of fanatics never allow themselves to read scripture adopted by any other religion, so they never seem to notice all the similarities.

I did a context-insensitive search for the items I wanted in the massive book of writings. This sort never bothers with context when they want to quote something from a holy writing anyway, as long as the words prove the point they're trying to make. So, armed with the appropriate verses to support my scheme, I waited to catch another Hoojum alone.

"Excuse me, brother," I said, "but I need your help." That line always gets them. He stopped dead in his tracks on his way to the front desk.

The Hoojum turned with a great whispering of his optical-illusion robes. He seemed surprised to find another one of his kind wandering the halls of the hotel. "You are not from our tour group."

"I have fallen into the pit of sin, and I must find someone to help me climb out of it."

I watched him shudder, possibly from the incredible favor I had just asked or from a personal revulsion at talking to a genuine sinner. Hoojums are primarily reptilian in features, with massive bony plates on the face, squarish teeth, and a ridged crest on top of the head. In order for me to read squeamishness through all that armor, his reaction must have been extreme indeed.

"I was just going to request some extra towels. We're having a charismatic verse sing tonight. Perhaps if you join us—"

"No! I need *you* to help me. Now! Or I am forever lost."

He hesitated. "Please!" I added just the right begging tone to my voice.

He sighed, a long hiss, then took me aside. "Very well, my child. Tell me of your predicament."

"Only if you promise to help me. There is only one way I can be saved."

"I promise. Now tell me."

"We had best go to my room, where I can speak of this in private. I am so ashamed, I do not want to risk anyone overhearing."

He balked at that, and I could see him searching his mind for some sort of acceptable excuse. "You promised me," I said. Finally, the Hoojum agreed.

John-23 had held this room for me for the last couple of days, as a special favor. Now it paid off. Inside, it was decorated in the bland grayness and muted lighting the Hoojums preferred in their accomodations—fewer worldly distractions that way, I suppose.

"I have been stranded in this hotel for too long, after foolishly fleeing from our homeworld," I told the Hoojum. "I have found myself tempted. I have fantasized of sexual pleasures and perversions with any number of alien beings here. I might have acted out some of my desires . . . but after seeing your righteous group, I repented of my sinful thoughts, in horror at what I have been contemplating. But I must be cleansed."

The Hoojum looked doubly squeamish. I clutched at his robe, and he flinched. "But what do you need me to do?"

"The scripture is clear on this point." I allowed myself an inner smirk at that one. "To purge all sin from me, I must face the horrors of that which I had once considered. I must have sex with a complete stranger. Only then can I see how horrible it really is."

The Hoojum's jaw dropped open in total astonishment. "But not only that," I pressed on, "but I must charge *money* for this act, so that I myself can experience the awful punishment of the lowliest of all beings—a prostitute!"

He gasped and choked and tried to break away, but my grip on his robe was firm. "Please! You promised! Do this in the name of the Deity and you will be exalted for all time."

"But I must not!"

So, I hit him with the scriptures I had memorized, quoting verse after verse of the vague poetry that seemed to shore up my claim. He countered a few of them, but I came up with even more. In the end, I think I exhausted him with my piety, and he began to crumble under his own doubts.

When he took off the moiré robe, I was surprised to see a rather scrawny being underneath. The billowing cloth and their overlarge heads make the Hoojums look much more massive than they really are. I tried not to stare. He already seemed embarrassed enough.

The sexual act with him was mercifully brief, and he didn't appear to enjoy it at all. He grudgingly paid me with his credit scanner, then fled my room, muttering prayers to himself. I wondered if the charismatic verse sing had started without him.

I transformed again into a more comfortable form, then secreted a carefully contained packet filled with Hoojum semen—a packet somehow worth a thousand credits to a Rybet.

In his own quarters, the Rybet leaped up and down with delight. "You got it!" He splashed off the fungus mound on which he had been napping and waded over to me, his huge mouth hanging open in delight. The semi-mobile algae could not move out of his way quickly enough, and wet green strands clung to his waist and thighs, slowly trying to flee back into the lukewarm water.

"How did you ever get it? Never mind. I don't want to know. Just give it to me."

"Give me my thousand credits first," I countered. Even though I didn't wear a Rybet form this time, I could still be rude.

"Fine, fine." He dumped the money into my account with his credit scanner, and I handed the package over to him.

He held it up to the dim light of the two simulated red suns and looked at the thick gray-blue liquid. "Looks right," he said, bobbing his head up and down in a vigorous nod. "You can't find details like the color of Hoojum semen in the Lexicon."

"It's real," I said. "Now are you going to tell me what you want it for?"

In reply, he removed a thin, diamondlike needle from a pouch at his waist. The Rybet dipped the tip of the needle into the clotted Hoojum sperm, swirled it around a few times, then withdrew the needle. A single drop hung like a tiny, cloudy pearl on the point.

The Rybet closed his lantern eyes, took a deep breath of anticipation, then jabbed the needle into his fat lips.

His reaction was nearly instantaneous. He let out a loud keening sound from the bottom of his throat. "Yes, oh yes!" His eyes flung open wide, and his body shuddered so much he almost dropped the rest of the semen sample. He gulped in a deep breath. "Wow! This is fantastic!"

In my line of work you see a lot of strange things.

Then the Rybet began to jabber at me, stomping around in the wading pool so rapidly that he churned the surface into a froth. "Hoojum sperm is the most intense, stimulating drug we Rybets have ever found. It is so precious, so rare—and so marvelous! Just obtaining it is nearly impossible. What you've given me will be worth millions on the Rybet open market! Oh, you are marvelous, wonderful!"

He looked like he wanted to mate with me again. I think I preferred it when he was merely rude. "Here," he said, grabbing for his credit scanner again. "Just to show how much this really means to me."

Barely looking at his own stubby fingers, the Rybet punched another 200 credits into my account. At that point I decided to leave, before the drug's euphoria wore off and his rudeness settled back in.

The mysterious Borrak was sitting on the same ill-fitting barstool as if waiting to pounce. I looked at its insectile form, wondering what I had botched so badly during my first attempt—after all, if I could succeed in seducing a repressed *Hoojum* and make him pay for the pleasure, what could possibly be so difficult about a Borrak? I summoned up the sparse Lexicon listing again, and immediately noticed the obvious.

This specimen was *female*, not male as I had originally assumed. By making my body into a beautiful female as well, I had set myself up as a rival. Hotel Andromeda must be a lonely place for Borraks, and the last thing a single female would want to see is another more beautiful female on the make!

I slipped out of sight into an unoccupied slaughter lounge where carnivores could select creatures and kill them there or cage them for later consumption in the hotel room. With no one looking, I transformed into my best approximation of a male Borrak this time, with a jagged crest on top of the head and a full blush of mating coloration.

Becoming male doesn't bother me. Hookermorphs are basically genderless, thought most of my clients are males looking for females. I can do whatever a species wishes—sometimes they are skeptical when I say "anything you want," but believe me, with all the races and all the societies in the galaxy, I can't think of many things that *aren't* taboo in one culture or another. Some races express their passion through kissing, while others consider the pressing of one's eating orifice against another eating orifice to be the most disgusting thing imaginable. No, being a male Borrak didn't bother me at all.

When I strutted into the bar, concentrating to keep a proper gait with all those segmented legs, I saw the female Borrak straighten from her perch on the barstool and turn both gleaming eyes toward me. Her feelers quivered. I could see her top forelegs fidgeting with nervous anticipation.

I walked directly up to her, showed off my mating coloration. "Hi. Come here often?"

She could barely contain herself and trilled. "Where have you been all my life?" She gestured to the empty barstool beside her. I struggled to clamber onto the stool, wondering how she had ever managed it herself. I was looking like a clumsy fool, but she didn't seem to mind. The Borrak seemed very, very receptive.

In my own excitement at breaking new ground with a little-known species, I did not notice when John-23 stepped into the bar, looking around with his cyborg eye. Beside him was a smartly dressed human woman; the jewels studding her clothes reflected the pearlescent light. He pointed to me.

"Would you be interested in doing something about our obvious mutual attraction?" I asked the Borrak. The tips of her feelers touched mine.

A hand touched my wing casing, a human hand. "There, I've found you, Ilkiy. Could we talk to you for a minute?"

I turned to see John-23 and his lady companion next to me. Intimidated by the fearsome appearance of the Borrak, she still looked secretly pleased. "I'm busy at the moment. I'd be happy to arrange a more convenient time."

The woman wasn't John-23's wife, nor anyone else I had seen before. "I'll pay you twice whatever this creature is paying you," she said.

The female Borrak reared up in an attack posture, clutching at me with one of her forelegs in a gesture of despair. I stopped the Borrak from doing anything that would have been embarrassing to all concerned, including the hotel management.

"Relax," I told the Borrak. "Enjoy yourself, have another drink." I motioned for one of the robo-bartenders to bring a new slab of the gelatinous intoxicant the Borrak preferred. "John-23 is paying for it. I'll be back, don't worry." I combed one of the Borrak's feelers through my claws, and she cooed with pleasure. Then I followed John-23 and his lady companion into one of the lobby lounges, out of sight.

"Sorry to interrupt you while you were working, Ilkiy. She asked me to find you right away," John-23 said apologetically. "This is Mrs. Wenda Cochran. I'll let her explain the rest." He strode off down the corridor, leaving the two of us alone.

The woman folded her fingers together. I noticed she was wearing a lot of rings. From what I knew of humans, she would have been considered quite beautiful, although she had a hard look to her, like an invisible exoskeleton of her own. I could have transformed into something more amenable to conversation, but I was annoyed at having my all-but-guaranteed score with the Borrak ruined, so I remained in threatening alien form.

"I've heard about what your kind can do," Wenda Cochran said. "I need your services, and I will pay well for them."

I found that rather odd, since she was an attractive member of her own species and should have had little trouble picking an available human male from the other hotel guests. However, she wore her human marriage-bonding ring a bit too prominently for active sexual hunting. But she had requested my services for something, and business is business. "I'm sure I can give you pleasure," I said. "That is my job."

"Oh, you'll give me pleasure, all right," Wenda Cochran

said, "but not in the way you think. I want you to sleep with my husband."

It was a good thing the chitinous face of the Borrak registered little emotion. "Why?" I asked.

She sighed. Her body temperature went up, and I could see an emotional outburst simmering inside her. Tears appeared in her eyes. "My husband is a cheating bastard. He goes on business trips all over the galaxy and he jumps into bed with any humanoid with compatible sexual organs. I am sick and tired of it. He doesn't know I've followed him here."

I still didn't know where I supposedly fit in. "You are tired of him mating with females other than yourself," I said, confused, "and so you wish to hire *me* to sleep with him?"

"Oh that's not all. I want you to take him to bed and then scare the bejesus out of him." She snickered then, a harsh and mirthless laugh. "That'll shrivel his little peeper once and for all. I want you to teach him a lesson he'll never forget if he ever gets wandering hormones again."

"I think I understand," I said.

"I'll pay you three times your usual rate," Wenda Cochran said. "It's his own money, and somehow I don't think he'll dispute the charge when it comes through on the credit report."

"Rex," I said with a cooing tone in my voice. "I like that name." I stroked his forearm with my enameled fingernails.

Picking up Rex Cochran had been embarrassingly easy. I wore a body and face cobbled together from Lexicon entries of gorgeous human female models. I had only to walk slowly into the lounge and bat my eyes . . . and Rex was on me like a Lupine male sniffing estrus in the air.

He had short blond hair, broad shoulders, a shirt that fit too tightly, letting curls of chest hair poke through the fabric. A necklace of gold and onyx dangled at his throat. I allowed Rex to buy me a drink, something perfumy and feminine. I laughed at his jokes, I flirted with him, I let him catch me noticing his body.

It took him all of fifteen minutes to ask me up to his room. Since human mating practices are such a matter of public record, I won't go into the details of how he rapidly "seduced" me, wheedling one item of my clothing off after another, trying to hide his wolfish glances. His actions so closely followed the general description in the Lexicon entry, I had an odd sensation of déjà vu.

I thought of his wife Wenda, knowing what Rex did on so many of his "business trips," how she had finally followed him here to the Hotel Andromeda to teach him a well-deserved lesson. As a hookermorph, I try not to be moralistic in such things—but in this case, Wenda Cochran was the actual customer . . . and the customer is always right.

When Rex was on top of me and inside me, moving faster and faster after a puzzlingly brief foreplay session, I knew the time had, er, come. I waited a second longer, feeling Rex reach his peak.

Then I let my imagination roam free as I transformed.

Rex looked down to see the voluptuous naked woman he had lured into his bed turn into an octopoid Slimedurg with sulfuric acid hissing out of her pores. I wrapped five tentacles around him like whips and pulled him against me in what seemed a hilarious parody of what I had just been doing as a human female. I tried to draw his face close to my clacking beak for a little kiss. I let greenish saliva dribble out the corner of my mouth.

Rex shrieked and tried to scramble away, sobbing and howling loud enough to rattle the windows in his room.

I rose up from the bed, raising all tentacles and reaching toward him. Then I shifted into a glaring Ice Medusa, with crystalline claws extending longer than my fingers. "What's the matter, Rex? Don't you want to play anymore?" I took a step toward him, laughing my best imitation of a maniacal beast.

Rex stumbled against the far wall. He couldn't seem to find the door, but he had managed to lose control of his sphincters in a terrible mess.

Just at the moment he found the door and pounded on it, screaming all the while and trying to activate the mechanism, I transformed my monstrous body into a perfect imitation of Wenda Cochran. "Watch yourself, Rex," I said in her voice, "you keep fooling around on me and you never know what you might pick up."

His eyes bulged out of their sockets again, and Rex Cochran fled naked and shrieking into the corridor.

Just before he turned around for the last time, I observed that Wenda had been right—the experience had certainly shriveled his little peeper.

When I saw the female Borrak still waiting for me at the bar, I decided not to wait long enough for anything else to mess things up. Meeting new clients isn't difficult, but finding a way to contribute to the Lexicon doesn't happen every day, and I wasn't going to let this opportunity slip away from me. Not many hookermorphs get to be xenosociologists.

I came up behind her, wearing full mating coloration and exuding all the right pheromones. She whirled, looking like a blur of sharp-edged joints and legs. "I knew you'd come back! I've been waiting for so long."

"Sorry about that," I said. She didn't seem the least bit interested in what the whole business with John-23 and Wenda Cochran had been about. Maybe curiosity wasn't part of the Borrak psyche; that would be in keeping with a lot of other insectile species.

"Please tell me it isn't some cruel joke," she said to me. "Your mating coloration, your pheromones, your flirtatious small talk. I can't bear to wait any longer. Are you really interested in mating with me, or should I just die unfulfilled?"

I couldn't figure out how a Borrak was supposed to smile, so I just made my voice sound warm and receptive. "I would be greatly honored to make love to you."

The Borrak seemed uncertain and afraid, but hookermorphs have to deal with that all the time. I coaxed her and boosted her confidence, then let her usher me up the motivator ramp, crossing a webbed catwalk to get to her room.

She had selected one of the nestlike dwellings. Inside, she had stocked the place with colored gelatinous blocks of sugar-based foods. Every spare niche was stuffed with brilliant fresh flowers. Water dripped from a fountain off in the corner. Despite the cloying perfume of the sweet foodstuffs and the flowers, the place did have a romantic look about it.

The Borrak hummed, then flickered her wing casings, palpitating a membrane in her abdomen with a sound very much like a love song. I was mentally noting all this to turn in a report to the compilers of the Lexicon.

"I am so glad you like me," she said. "I have been ready

to spawn for so long. I don't know how I could have waited another day. My entire body aches for you!"

Dancing on my multiple legs, I sidled up next to her. "Well, then, let us get on with it. I'm also anxious to mate with you."

"I'm so glad you understand," she said. Then she stung me in the soft part of my thorax.

I found it amazing how rapidly the paralysis struck me down. My mind wasn't clouded in the least, but I felt no pain as I tumbled to the floor in a clamor of chitin and disjointed legs. My face was not turned toward her, but the dome eyes had a wide enough field of view that I could see her movements. I could breathe, but I could not speak. What had I gotten myself into?

Her abdomen seemed to be pulsing, and I could see her extruding something sharp from where I imagined the sex organs would be. It appeared to be a long tube, like a pipe with a pointed end. An ovipositor.

Panic gushed through my glands. I wondered if that was a normal reaction for male Borraks, or if my own self-preservation instinct had merely kicked in. I couldn't move. The paralysis from her sting had put me completely out of commission.

Raising the ovipositor in the air like a spear, the female Borrak strode over to me. "I have been carrying these larvae around altogether too long. It'll be a great relief to get rid of them. I really appreciate this, you know." She leaned over to nuzzle the colorful crest on my head.

Then she backed up and thrust her ovipositor through the chitinous shell of my wing casings, burying it deep within my body cavity. That time I felt the pain! She squirmed and dug the hollow point around and around until she finally managed to deposit one of her squirming larvae inside of me.

She heaved a big sigh, withdrew her ovipositor, then shoved it in a different place, laying another voracious Borrak grub. She repeated the procedure six times, then finally retracted her ovipositor and sat down next to me, looking exhausted but fulfilled.

She surprised me by igniting a tobac-stick, then sucking in a long breath before blowing a cloud of smoke dreamily into the cloying air. "Ah, that feels so much better," she said. With a foreleg, she patted my exoskeleton near where she had deposited her larvae. "You're a great lay."

Inside me, I could feel the grubs beginning to stir.

The Borrak hauled herself to her numerous feet and preened in front of a mirror. "As you can see, I've provided everything they'll need. Plenty of food and fresh vegetation, just the right environmental conditions. I've got the room reserved for three weeks, and by that time they should be ready to fend for themselves. I'll let them know at the desk that the childrens' return tickets to Borrakus should come out of your account. That *is* the father's duty, you know." She raised her antennae in question, but of course I could not respond. The only functional nerves in my body seemed to be the ones transmitting jabs of pain as the grubs began to devour me from within.

"Well, at least that's over with for another year," she sighed to herself, then left. I heard her seal the door behind herself, illuminating the Do Not Disturb sign.

From within my body, I could feel seven distinct paths of agony where the grubs continued to munch. They seemed to be very hungry. . . .

John-23 thought it greatly amusing that a hookermorph would take time off for maternity leave. But hey, everyone else is entitled, so why shouldn't I be?

"Stay away from that edge!" I called to the seven babymorphs lurking too close to the zero-g swimming pool. "Wait until you learn how to change into a water-breather before you mess around in a pool."

All of the little ones sulked into their protoplasmic state for a moment; then with the short memory of children, they bounded off in different directions, a kaleidoscope of changing shapes, imitating parts of whatever they found interesting around them. Very precocious kids—I'm proud of them.

I had never even thought of reproducing myself before. While I understood the mating habits of countless other sentient creatures, I had somehow remained ignorant about "the birds and the bees" for my own species. Hookermorphs don't spend a lot of time learning how to become parents; that's not what hookermorphs consider a desirable skill. It's a good thing something in our inbred instinct triggered a reaction in me, though, and I did exactly the right thing while the little Borrak grubs were having me for lunch.

You see, the way we morphs reproduce is to surround another living organism, and then transform back to the basic state, dragging the enclosed organism along for the ride. You've never read *that* in the Lexicon, now have you? With seven Borrak grubs gnawing away inside of me as the paralysis gradually began to wear off, the best I could manage was to transform back to my basic state, formless, like a bag of old soup. And that did the trick. Inside me were no longer any voracious larvae, but seven squirming babymorphs.

The babymorphs came out of it delighted, ready for the galaxy and eager to learn. John-23 thinks they're cute, at least in some of their incarnations, and the rest of the hotel staff seems tolerant at least.

Over by the pool, one of the guests was walking a spiny-backed dragon dog, who sprayed acid on some of the corner shrubs. It lunged on its leash, snarling at the cluster of babymorphs. Feeling a surge of maternal protective instinct, I jumped to my feet, but the little ones reacted all at once, changing into an array of hideous monstrosities. One of the babymorphs became a fanged Putter-clam, opening wide its jagged shell and snapping at the dragon dog, which fled back behind its owner's legs.

I smiled. They already know how to defend themselves. Now I just need to teach them how to flirt.

With a sigh, I settled back into the chaise lounge and let the sunlight photosynthesize my green skin. I've earned a rest, haven't I? I need to write a letter to the Lexicon people, since I have two new listings for them, one for Borraks and one for morphs. And while I'm at it, maybe I'll try my hand at writing my memoirs. That should surely scandalize the galaxy! Just the type of thing people will pick up to read on an outbound starflight. It'll sell millions.

Besides, I'd better make my fortune soon. As precocious as the babymorphs seem to be, I'm bound to have competition before long. I'll really need to stay in shape.

VOLATILE MIX

—————•—————

Jerry Oltion

D avid Wikondu was walking down the corridor toward the
best of the hotel's three restaurants, anticipating a lavish
dinner on his expense account, when he heard the scream
from around the corner. It was a long, warbling howl, and
sounded as if it had come from an alien throat, which didn't
surprise him. There were maybe half a dozen other humans in
this whole wing of the hotel, tops.

He hesitated, wondering if he should simply turn around
and let whatever was happening unfold without him, but curiosity got the better of him. Curiosity and the suspicion that
it hadn't been a cry of joy. Someone was probably in trouble.

Rare as they were, another human collided with him as he
turned the corner, knocking him off his feet to land with a
thump against the wall. The other guy tripped as well, and the
pistol he carried in his left hand skittered away down the corridor toward the restaurant.

David had just enough time to wonder what Loren Larue,

the vid star, was doing with a gun at an interspecies peace conference in the experimental multi-environment wing of the Hotel Andromeda before the actor jumped to his feet and took off running up the corridor David had just come down. He ran with a peculiar gait, bobbing up and down and stumbling as if on uneven ground, and as he receded David saw that he carried a small air tank strapped to his back. David couldn't imagine why; the whole advantage to the hotel's new wing was that force fields held a person's own atmosphere in an invisible bubble around them no matter where they went. It also provided whatever gravity they were used to; Larue shouldn't have been wobbling like that. Had he been wounded? Maybe that's why he was running.

Whoever screamed had stopped now; David looked up to see a petite, light blue-furred alien bending over what looked at first to be a colorful rug, but which proved on second glance to be another alien of different species lying flat on the floor. It was one of the floating-gas-bag variety, probably a Ranthanik, now deflated.

The space around the furry one—a T'klar, David realized, and probably female by its size—glowed with a soft blue radiance; most likely something in her air fluorescing in the overhead lights. David pushed himself to his feet and took a step toward her, but when she looked up and saw him coming she yowled another earsplitting, warbling screech and backed away.

"It's all right," he said, taking a few steps closer. "I just got here."

The T'klar wasn't reassured. Without another sound, she turned and bounded away on her long, slender legs, disappearing into the crowd that was gathering at the restaurant entrance. A faint trail of blue fluorescence glimmered in her wake.

David saw no sense in chasing her. He bent down next to the Ranthanik to see if there was anything he could do for it, but the charred hole in its leathery hide was big enough to shove a fist through. All its methane had leaked out, and by the looks of it, all its life, too.

He stood up and turned toward the gathering crowd. The hotel's force-field life system was living up to its advertisements; among the less exotic species he saw a heavy-planet Niruto standing next to a gangly ammonia-breathing Cheedon and a fuming, sulfurous Grota, and none of them seemed distressed at all by the others' proximity.

"Has anyone called Hotel Security?" he asked.

No one replied. He knew they understood him; the same system that monitored each person's position for their force cocoon of atmosphere also provided translation of any alien speech in the vicinity.

"Someone, please call Security," he said more forcefully. "And get somebody here who knows Ranthanik medicine. We might still be able to save him." David had no idea whether that was true or not, but he figured it would be better to err on the side of caution.

One of the aliens further inside the restaurant—or maybe the T'klar—had evidently already made the call. David was still trying to think of anything else he could do when a gleaming silver robot slid out from a doorway partway down the corridor and glided up to him. Before David could react, one of its four sinuous arms reached out and wrapped around his neck.

It hadn't quite cut off his wind. "Hey, what are you doing?" he croaked. "Let me go!"

"I'm sorry, sir," it said in a synthesized human voice, "but you will have to come with me."

The robot put him in a seven- by ten-pace room with a single chair in it. David sat sullenly on the chair, wishing he'd given in to his first impulse and just left the T'klar and the Ranthanik to fend for themselves. He didn't know what sort of trouble he was in just yet—the robot had only told him that he was needed for questioning—but he didn't like the look of this room at all.

He couldn't help examining it with a professional eye, though. He was an assistant manager for a rival hotel, the Hightower, and he was on a tour of other hotels, looking for new ideas he could incorporate into his own. So far he hadn't seen anything he liked better than what the Hightower already had to offer, but when he'd heard of the Andromeda's new life-system design he'd come to check it out.

He'd snooped around in as many public areas as he could find, but he hadn't seen anything like the room he was in now. It was obviously an undifferentiated guest unit, the bare cubicle upon which an individual species' requirements could be built. The walls were a uniform dull gray, as was the ceiling. Presumably whatever coloring or decorations were needed could be extruded from it or hung there by the service staff when a guest checked in.

The floor, like the floors everywhere, was dotted with tiny holes from which came the atmosphere that the personal force fields—also generated in the floor—held around each guest. David couldn't see the variable gravity generators, but he knew they were there, too. He even knew a little about how they worked. The whole system—force fields and all—was really just an elaborate enhancement of technology that existed in every hotel, including the Hightower. It was the way they put it all together, the way it allowed mutually alien races to coexist within the same habitat, that was the breakthrough.

He'd been considering buying the system from the Andromeda until their security robot had dragged him away and locked him in here, but the longer he waited in the single chair, the less inclined he felt to give them his business. They would have to apologize, and apologize with a big cut in price, if they expected to see any of his credit.

The door slid open and a squat, cone-shaped Niruto waddled into the room, flanked by two of the silver security robots. The Niruto's twin trunks were coiled around its hemispherical head, parked there for support in the three g's or so that pulled on them.

A buzzing sound came from within the coiled limbs, and an unseen translator said, "Your ID lists you as David Wikondu. Is this correct?"

"Yeah, that's right," David answered.

"You are not a member of the interspecies peace conference delegation."

"No. I'm an assistant manager for the Hotel Hightower. I'm here to look at your multi-environment system."

"That is your stated purpose. However, you are charged with the assassination of Hranda Nefanu Dnanda, the Ranthanik delegate to the conference. Do you admit to the crime?"

David leaped up from his chair. "No! I showed up—hey!" The robots advanced on him and shoved him gracelessly back onto the chair.

"Please remain seated," the Niruto said. "You were found at the scene of the murder. Witnesses said that the Ranthanik was killed by a human. You were the only human in evidence, therefore you are the murderer."

David shrugged off the robots' arms, but stayed in the chair. "No, there was somebody else. He knocked me down making his escape."

"Another human?"

"That's right. He looked like Loren Larue. He dropped his gun when he ran into me."

The Niruto stepped closer to David. "We recovered the weapon, a microwave laser. It could just as easily have been yours."

"It was Loren Larue's!" David shouted.

The Niruto paused momentarily, no doubt consulting a data base somewhere with its neural linkup. "Loren Larue is not a guest at this hotel," it said.

"Well of course not," David said. "It was obviously someone else wearing a mask. They didn't want to be recognized."

"Very few beings can tell humans apart," the Niruto said. "A mask would be pointless."

That was probably true, David realized. He had a hard time telling most aliens apart, too, at least within species lines. That would probably change if multi-species habitats like this one became more common, but for now the Niruto was right.

"Maybe it wasn't a human," David said. "Maybe somebody else wanted to make it look like a human had done it. They probably just used Loren Larue as a model because he was easiest to get a holo of."

"This is wild speculation," the Niruto said.

David leaned forward on his chair. "No, it's not. Whoever it was had an air tank on his back. I didn't notice a breathing mask, so he probably had it piped into his Larue mask. I'll bet he had a human ID card, so the life system was giving him human air and he needed the tank to provide what he really needed."

The Niruto uncoiled a limb and rubbed the tip of it across the top of its head. When it spoke, its buzz was louder, as was its translation. "A human ID would not have availed him anything. We don't track our guests by their ID cards."

"Does the murderer know that?"

"I suspect he just learned it."

"I'm not the murderer! Look, there was a T'klar there with

the Ranthanik. She must have seen me collide with whoever shot him. Ask her."

The Niruto waved its trunk toward the door. "We already did. She identified you as the killer."

"Oh, great." David leaned back in his chair and ran a hand through his hair. "I think I'd better get some legal help here."

The Niruto turned away and headed for the door, the robots flanking him. "That would be an unprofitable use of your time," it said. "We do not follow human law here. Your lawyer would not be able to counter the word of the T'klar ambassador."

"You'll understand if I try anyway."

"You may try anything you wish," the Niruto said. "You will have little success, however, from within a closed cell." The door slid aside for him, then closed with a thump behind him and the robots, leaving David alone in his undifferentiated room.

The human delegate to the peace conference showed up a few hours later. David had no idea what had brought him; he'd tried shouting for help, he'd banged the chair on the wall until he'd broken it, he'd even given in to biological pressure and urinated on the floor in the hopes that the room sensors would realize someone was there and create a bathroom for him—and maybe an intercom with it—but he'd given up long ago.

He'd been trying to sleep and failing even at that when the door slid open to reveal a trim, gray-haired man in his early hundreds, dressed conservatively in a brown one-piece bodysuit.

"I'm Trevor DeLange," he said, stepping inside and extending a hand to help David to his feet.

"David Wikondu. I'd offer you a chair, but it broke while I was rapping out an S.O.S. with it." He waved at the broken pieces of plastic or alien wood or whatever they were scattered on the floor.

DeLange smiled a thin smile. "I'm sorry to have left you here so long. I've been in contact with our embassy for the last few hours, trying to get you extradited to human space, but so far we haven't had any luck. The Ranthanik want to try you here, during the peace conference."

"I'm not even responsible!" David said. "I was walking

toward the restaurant when I heard a scream, so I ran up to see what was the matter and I got arrested for murder."

"They would have arrested whoever was closest," DeLange said. "Niruto provide the security here, and Niruto law relies heavily on circumstantial evidence. They're more interested in finding a scapegoat than finding the real culprit. So long as someone is punished for every crime, they figure the deterrent factor is the same."

"You're kidding."

"I wish I were." DeLange sounded sincere enough, but David figured he'd have sounded a great deal more concerned if *he'd* been the one arrested.

"The killer is still loose," David pointed out. "He may not stop with one delegate."

"Hotel Security has begun recording everyone's movements. If the assassin strikes again, they'll know for sure who did it."

David paced to the wall and back again. "That's smart. Why weren't they tracking everyone before?"

DeLange shrugged. He seemed a little uncomfortable standing in an empty room with a broken chair scattered on the floor and a puddle of urine in one corner. He'd been folding and refolding his arms across his chest; now he tucked them into his suit's side pockets as if to get them out of the way. He said, "They claim it's not hotel policy to monitor their guests' activities. It scares away business. The truth is, this whole multi-species life system is still in the testing stage, and they may simply not have thought of it before."

"Hmm." David worked for a hotel; he suspected the real reason was liability. Data that didn't exist couldn't be stolen and used by someone else, say a journalist or politician looking for a little dirt on an opponent. He made another trip to the wall and back, then asked, "Why are you here if you know it's still an experimental system? Why let them test it on some of the top officials from every species?"

DeLange laughed. "We had no choice. After the Andromeda announced they'd built a new conference wing just for the peace talks, staying away for safety reasons would have been political suicide. We've all been saying how much we want to settle our differences peacefully; it was time to put up or shut up. So here we are."

"How are the talks going?" David asked. He was surprised

he could feel any curiosity about anything other than his own predicament, but he knew that humanity was not necessarily a major player in galactic politics, and several other species— including the Ranthanik—were trying to edge in on human territory. The peace talks could help humanity's chances of holding on to some of the disputed colonies.

DeLange's expression darkened. "We're not accomplishing a whole lot. Mostly airing old arguments in public. Probably the only valuable thing to come of this whole process will be the precedent it sets for later talks. Of course, now that one of the delegates has been assassinated, there's an entirely different message being presented. That's why the Niruto are so eager to crucify you. They want the rumors stopped as soon as possible."

"Whether I'm guilty or not." David realized his only hope lay in the assassination of another delegate. If someone else were murdered while he was still locked up, then they would know he wasn't the assassin. That didn't seem likely, though. Presumably the assassin would know he was being traced now, too.

"What's humanity's official stance on this?" he asked. "How far will you go to get me out of here?"

DeLange reddened. "Well, naturally we'll do everything we can to, um, delay any hasty actions on the Niruto's part, but the situation is delicate. We have to consider—"

"In other words, nothing. You'll let them have me rather than start an interstellar incident over it, won't you?"

"Mr. Wikondu," the ambassador said coldly, "we are trying to develop a plan of action. Your welfare will figure as high as possible in that plan, but we must consider the entire human race. We will do everything we can, short of open hostilities. We will not go to war over one individual."

"That's what I thought." David paced toward the wall again, passing the broken pieces of chair. He swiveled around, took a step forward, and kicked one of the chair legs as if by accident, sending it sliding toward DeLange. "Oops, sorry," he said, bending down to retrieve it. He made as if to toss it out of the way, but halfway through the motion he swung around and brought it down on DeLange's head with a sharp crack.

The delegate dropped like a short-circuited robot. David caught him before he whacked his head again on the floor, and laid him out on his back.

"They need a scapegoat, eh?" he muttered, bending down to feel for a pulse at DeLange's neck. "Well, let 'em have one. All humans look alike, after all."

The delegate's heart still beat steadily. David quickly unsealed his brown suit and peeled it off him, stripped off his own clothing, and put DeLange's clothing on himself. It was a little tight around the middle, but he sucked in his gut and got it closed. He put his own clothing on DeLange, making sure his ID card went with it, then dragged him over to the wall across from the door.

Then, taking a deep breath to calm down, he walked to the door, prepared to knock on it to be let out, but it slid open before him and he stepped on through.

The robots were standing just on the other side, but the Niruto was nowhere in evidence. David stalked past the robots without a sideways glance and headed up the corridor toward the lobby. Only after he'd turned the corner did he breathe.

He had bought himself anywhere from ten minutes to a few hours, depending on how soon DeLange awakened and how long it would take him to attract the attention of his jailers and convince them he was the human ambassador. The way David saw it, he had two choices. He could either try to bluff his way through Hotel Security, catch the next ship out of the Andromeda, and disappear into deep space, or he could use his temporary freedom to clear his name. Running for it seemed the least complicated in the short term, but the idea of skipping out on his entire life and starting over again somewhere else didn't exactly appeal to him, either. Not over a simple misunderstanding.

No, he would at least try to exonerate himself first. Of course there would still be charges for assaulting DeLange, but he would probably be able to survive that if he exposed the real assassin.

Where to start? Well, the most damning evidence against him had to be the T'klar's testimony. If he could convince her she was mistaken about him, then that should take care of it right there.

There was a Cheedon behind the front desk. David had never seen one up close before; they were ammonia breathers and normally required a separate habitat. They looked a little like a stack of seven or eight long-armed starfish scaled up to stand about three feet high; this one rested atop a pedestal behind the counter. As David approached it he smelled a faint hint of ammonia, like a cat's litter box gone uncleaned a day too long. Evidently the force cocoons weren't perfectly tight; when someone stayed in one place long enough, some of their air must leak across the barrier to permeate the surrounding atmosphere, and when someone else moved through it a little must get swept up in their own. It wouldn't take much; a few molecules of ammonia is enough for a human nose to detect.

Half a dozen arms waved in greeting when he stepped up to the counter. "May I help you?" his translator said.

"I need to carry a message to the T'klar delegate. Can you tell me where I could find her, please?"

More arms waved. "I'm sorry, but that information isn't available—"

"Not true. I've just talked with your chief of security, who told me all the guests in this wing were being monitored. Where is she?"

The Cheedon froze for a moment, then another ripple of movement played through its arms. "I apologize, Ambassador. She is in her suite."

"Where is that?"

"Level nine. Room twelve."

"Thanks." David dug into DeLange's pocket and found a handful of change. He slid a steel half-solar across the countertop to the Cheedon and headed for a lift.

There were dozens of lift shafts and drop shafts in the hotel, most of them simple vertical corridors with force fields to support passengers who stepped into them. It was old technology, enhanced with the ability to maintain the cocoon of air around people while they moved from floor to floor, but alongside the shafts was a different kind of lift that David hadn't seen until his stay in the Andromeda. It was evidently made for burrowing creatures, and was basically a pulsing hole in the wall that would push them along in close confinement. When David had first seen one he'd been tempted to try it until he'd seen a ten-foot caterpillar crawl out of one and slide off down the corridor on hundreds of foot-long legs.

He stepped into the open air shaft, pausing to avoid another guest rising up from a lower deck. This one was a more fa-

miliar form, a Bajoda, humanoid save for a smaller head and
spindlier arms. They had been one of the first alien species
humanity had encountered, and they could coexist with humans, though they seldom did. There was speculation among
some exobiologists that the two species had come from a
common ancestor left behind by some earlier space-faring
race, but whatever the reason for their similarities, millennia
of separate evolution had left them direct competitors. Their
empires were too close together in space and too similar in requirements for comfortable coexistence. The one in the lift
shaft eyed David distrustfully as it rose, and David was glad
when it got off on level seven.

There was one species that could probably tell humans
apart, though, he thought.

He stepped out on level nine, checked the holomap in the
foyer, and headed down the corridor for room 12. One of the
doors halfway down had a robot guard on either side of it,
and as he approached it he had a sinking suspicion that it was
the T'klar's. Sure enough, his quick door count ended with
them. Should he walk on past, or try to brazen it out?

The robots made his choice for him. When he was still a
couple of steps from the door, one of them slid out to block
his path. "I'm sorry, sir," it said, "but I must ask you to state
your business in this section."

David swallowed the lump in his throat. "I've come to talk
with the T'klar ambassador. About the, uh, murder suspect."

"Ambassador Sarell does not wish to be disturbed."

"Tell her it's important. It could, uh, mean considerable
embarrassment for her if she ignores what I have to tell her."

The robot paused, no doubt relaying the message. Then it
abruptly slid back and the door opened. "She will see you,
but only if one of us accompanies you."

"Fine." David followed the robot into the T'klar's suite.

She stood before the window, her back to the stars. To her
left, another doorway led off into the rest of the suite. The entire room sparkled with the blue fluorescence peculiar to her
atmosphere, and up close David could see that her fur was
also a light shade of blue, and as fuzzy as a kitten's. Her ears
were high and rounded, half buried in fur, and though her
eyes were in the right place they were twice the size of David's and irised in six segments like star sapphires. She wore

a single piece of clothing, a strip of green cloth wound once around her waist and looping up over her right shoulder.

The robot took up station between David and her, slightly to the side.

"Ambassador Sarell," David said.

Her head whipped around like an owl's, back and forth from David to the robot and back in a motion almost too fast to see. "You are not Ambassador DeLange," she replied.

Uh-oh. So all humans didn't look alike, at least not to all aliens. "He's, uh, indisposed at the moment," David said. "I'm one of his aides. He sent me to tell you that he visited with the man you accused of killing the Ranthanik, and he's convinced that David Wikondu is innocent."

"That's ridiculous," she said. "I saw him fire the shot."

"You watched a being wearing a human mask fire the shot. Then he turned and ran, but collided with m—David. The real assassin got away, while David tried to see if he could help the Ranthanik."

"He ran back for the gun he'd dropped," Sarell said.

"The gun? Wait a minute. The gun!" David suddenly realized he had a chance. "I—David never touched the gun. Fingerprints would prove that."

"Fingerprints?"

David nodded eagerly. "Right, fingerprints! Human hands are each unique. They leave their pattern on whatever they touch. We can check the gun for fingerprints and prove that David didn't shoot it."

"You're calling me a liar? The T'klar ambassador?" Her eyes seemed to blaze at him.

"I—no, of course, I—" David spluttered to a stop. Was he about to create another interspecies incident here? He looked away from her hypnotic eyes, checked the robot to see if it might be about to toss him out the door. Wait a minute, he thought. The robot.

In for a penny, in for a pound, he thought. Aloud he said, "You call yourself a liar. Why else are you under guard if you're so sure you've caught the assassin?"

Sarell snorted something that didn't translate. What did translate was, "There may have been more than one of them. I'm a potential witness against them all. I'm sure they would like to keep me silent." She started to say something else, but a thumping noise from the hallway made her pause.

"What was that?" David asked, but he got his answer when the robot that had been stationed outside the door teetered over and fell with a crash to the floor.

"We are under attack," the remaining robot said with a calmness that belied its words. "Take cover." It rolled forward, pushing David behind it with one arm while another snaked forward with a heavily finned, glistening beam weapon of some sort.

The T'klar whipped her head around to look at David for a moment, then she grabbed his arm and pulled him into the next room, which proved to be a reasonably realistic re-creation of some kind of enormous flower, opened to make a sort of bowl-shaped bed. She led him across its spongy surface, shoved one of the five-foot petals aside, and pulled him into darkness beyond.

The crackle and thump of fighting echoed from the other room, then another crash that sounded suspiciously like the second robot going down.

"Uh-oh," David muttered. "I think we're in trouble."

"Quiet!" She pulled him across an uneven floor littered with what felt like rocks underfoot; David noticed faint flashes of light as they grated against the floor. He stooped and picked up one in either hand. They were hot to the touch, but not so hot he couldn't hold them. He felt silly defending his life with rocks, but they would be better than nothing.

Sarell had other plans, though. She had better night vision than he did; she reached for something on the wall and a narrow crack of light grew before them. A door. Of course; the rooms were all the same, the hotel just connected more of them to make bigger suites. And each one had its own door.

She stuck her head out cautiously, then pulled David into the hallway and took off running toward the lift. David glanced the other way and saw the dead robot, plus a headless body that might have been human or Bajoda lying half in the doorway. It had been wearing an air tank, too, David noticed. Evidently the other robot had killed him before being downed in turn. David wondered how many more of them had made it into the suite.

He and Sarell had emerged from room 10's door; David heard a shout from behind him when they reached about room

3, then a piece of the wall exploded in fragments just to his left. He dodged, took half a dozen more bounding steps, and leaped for the lift shaft just as another shot sent searing pain screaming through his right side.

Sarell reached the lift field and shot up out of sight. David stumbled into it, falling, and found himself careening upward feetfirst.

Sarell snatched him out of the air four or five floors up, spinning him halfway around before the floor's gravity caught him, and he landed with a thump on his injured side. He bit down on a scream.

"You're hurt," she said, helping him to stand.

He looked down to see a charred patch of cloth a hand's width across just below his lowest rib. It felt as if the burn had penetrated halfway through his body, but he knew that was probably not true. If he'd been hit with a microwave laser, it would only have penetrated an inch or two at the most.

"I'll live," he said through clenched teeth. "Come on, we've got to lose whoever was shooting at us or we might not get so lucky a second time."

They ran down the corridor, sending the few other guests in their way leaping for doorways and howling curses in their wake. They turned left at the first cross corridor and kept running. David wasn't making near as good a time as Sarell was; he glanced back at the next turn, hoping they might have confused the trail enough to duck into a doorway and hide out, but there behind them floated a trail of telltale blue sparkles glimmering in the air.

He ran to catch up with her, wincing at the pain in his side and shouting "Stop! The force fields aren't tight enough to hold all your air in when we run. They'll be able to track us wherever we go."

She skidded to a halt and looked back. The short word she spoke translated as "Snow." For someone who slept in flowers and basked on hot rocks, David supposed that made a pretty good swear word.

He jogged up to her and they stood there for a moment, looking at the glittering trail, then Sarell said, "Leave me. I think they're after you anyway."

David shook his head. "Ha, nice try, but they came to your room, not mine."

"There's no sense in both of us getting killed."

"Look, if you get killed, I might as well be, too. You're the only one who can clear my name."

Her ears twisted forward. "What do you mean?"

"Meet David Wikondu, the guy you said shot the Ranthanik."

"What? How can you—?"

"Save it. Can you get by on oxygen and nitrogen?"

She hummed softly. "Maybe for a few minutes. Not much longer."

"I think a few minutes are all we've got. Give me your ID card."

Hesitantly, she reached into a pocket in her sash and handed the gold-colored card to him. He bent down and slid it under the door beside them, then, stuffing his rocks into pockets, he took her in his arms, making sure her face nestled into his shoulder. Without her ID she wouldn't have a force field of her own anymore, but she should be able to breathe inside his.

He started running down the hallway again, glad she was light. She coughed and clung tighter to him.

He heard more commotion in the hallway behind them. He hoped it was Hotel Security, but he wasn't going to bet his life on it. If the Andromeda's security robots were anything like the Hightower's—and his previous experience with them told him they were—then they usually showed up long after they could do anything useful.

He skidded around another corner, found a drop shaft in front of them, and leaped into it, nearly bowling over a Grota who was just getting off. They fell for half a dozen floors, then swung off and ran through more hallways until David was pretty sure he'd lost any pursuit. He stopped at a T-intersection and looked cautiously down the side passage, but it was deserted.

Sarell was coughing steadily now. She pulled away from him, breathed the ambient air for a moment, then coughed again and stuck her face back into his force field.

"I don't know which is worse," she wheezed.

"Hang in there. I think we—"

A patch of fur on Sarell's arm turned instantly black, and she howled in pain. David leaped into the side passage, ran to the end of it, turned again, ran, then skidded to a stop at the next. "They've got to be tracking my ID, too," he said, setting

Sarell down and digging DeLange's card out of his pocket. "That's the only way they could have found us."

"I cannot understand you," she said.

Of course not. Without her ID, she had no translator. "We're about to be even," David said. He took one last deep breath, shoved the card under another door, and grabbed Sarell's hand. Together they ran on down the corridor.

His first breath of the habitat's ambient air nearly seared his lungs. There was enough ammonia in it to scrub the decks with, and sulfur compounds and a couple dozen more exotic gases as well. He couldn't smell it, but he would bet money there was methane in it, too. All the gases that leaked out of the force fields mixed together. It was evidently easier to leave it this way than to try cleaning it up; besides, with so many different species coming and going, what would they have used for a baseline anyway?

He hadn't blacked out yet, so evidently there was at least a little bit of oxygen in it as well. That was a blessing, for him anyway. Some other species found oxygen deadly.

The gravity varied from heavy to nothing, too. Evidently it didn't reset to any particular value after someone had passed, but stayed whatever it had last been until another being came along. It felt like running over uneven ground, except there was no way to know where the bumps were.

That explained the peculiar stumbling gait of the assassin. And the air tank. He hadn't been carrying false ID; he hadn't been carrying ID at all, for fear of being traced.

Just as the ones chasing them now weren't. The dead one at Sarell's suite had carried an air tank, too. David considered looping back for it, but he had no assurance it contained anything better than what he was breathing now. Besides, someone might still be waiting for them there.

He wished they still had a translator, but they didn't need speech to communicate things like "left here," or "I'm choking to death!" They ran, staying just a few turns ahead of their pursuers, but slowly losing ground as they lost stamina in the bad air.

David realized he was eventually going to have to stop and make a stand with his two rocks. That would be suicide, of course, but unless he could find a better weapon, and soon, he was going to have to try it.

He was panting like a dog, but his vision was growing full
of swirling lights. He needed more oxygen. Did oxygen rise?
That depended on the average density of everything else, but
he bet it wouldn't.

But methane probably would. And hydrogen, definitely.

Holy shit. He pulled one of the rocks from his pocket, then
dug into the pocket again and came out with another steel
half-solar. Mother of God. He'd just discovered his weapon.
Maybe. But could he use it without blowing up the Andromeda in the process?

Probably. Oxygen would be the limiting factor, not methane or hydrogen. Humanity and its cousins were a distinct
minority in the hotel.

"Up!" he shouted, pointing at the ceiling. "Find us a lift
shaft!" He knew his pursuers could hear him, too, but that
was fine. Let 'em follow.

Sarell turned around just long enough to see where he
pointed, then took off running again, zigzagging through
guest-filled corridors and meeting rooms until she eventually
came to another lift, but instead of jumping into the shaft she
ran toward one of the pulsing orifices in the wall beside it and
squeezed into that.

"What are you doing!" David screamed, but when she began to rise into the wall, he realized she was right. They'd be
easy targets in an open lift shaft, but their pursuers couldn't
shoot at them in the enclosed elevator.

David stepped in after her, wincing as the walls squeezed
tight around him and a wave of constriction carried him upward. The walls of the tunnel were nearly frictionless; he
would hardly have been aware of movement if there hadn't
been an opening at each deck.

Sarell slid out of the lift after a dozen floors or so. David
jumped out just long enough to look down the open lift shaft
and see through the swirling tracers in his vision that, yes, they
were still being pursued by what looked like three more Loren
Larues, then he jumped back in and let the enclosed lift carry
him on up. He let it take him as far as it would go, eventually
spitting him out on the top floor. It wasn't the top of the hotel,
just the top of the multi-species wing, but it was far enough.

Aside from himself, and moments later, Sarell, the deck
was deserted. It was evidently too far up to be a convenient

guest deck, or maybe the hotel just didn't have enough guests to fill it up yet, but whatever the reason there were no signs of life at all. Perfect. David looked for the air lock he knew had to be there, found it only a few paces away. It was designed for emergencies; it had a solid door rather than a force field, and from the hinges it looked like it opened outward. That might complicate things, but it should still work. He wished he knew what kind of habitat lay beyond, but at this point he couldn't afford to be choosy.

Sarell took the hint when he pointed at the lock, and staggered over to open the door while he peeked down the lift shaft again. The three disguised aliens, all of them armed and wearing breathing equipment, were the only ones in the shaft for twenty floors or so. Good. The other guests' force shields should guard them from harm on the decks below, but these three would be as vulnerable as David and Sarell.

They were rising fast. David backed away from the shaft, ran for the air lock, and climbed inside after Sarell, pulling the door almost but not quite closed. Then, just as he saw the first of the assassins rise into view, he struck his half-solar against the rock.

It made the tiniest of sparks, barely visible under the bright light in the air lock, but the flash of burning methane and hydrogen nearly blinded him and the explosion blew him halfway across the lock. It would have been worse, but the pressure of burning gases on the other side slammed the door closed with the force of an angry giant, cutting off the blast before it had a chance to develop to full force.

His head rang from the concussion and from lack of oxygen. He crawled back toward the door, trying to stand up and get to the air controls, but everything started to swirl around him and he lost his balance, falling with a thump to the floor. He tried to stand again, but only made it to his knees.

Sarell couldn't have been in much better shape than him, but he watched her drag herself to the opposite door, pull herself upright, and punch the button that sent cold, cloudy white gas pouring in over them.

Don't let it be ammonia, David thought. He took a shallow breath. It smelled like something had died in the storage tank, but it didn't kill him outright so he took another. Sarell seemed to be doing okay with it, too. They were gasping like beached fish, but still alive, when security robots opened the lock a few minutes later.

Searchers found the assassins bobbing in the currents at the top of the lift shaft. They had either been blasted downward by the explosion and knocked unconscious on one of the landings below, or the pressure wave alone had done the job, but when the security robots pulled them down they found one dead of a broken neck and the other two alive but heavily burned and unresponsive. All three were Bajodas, and though nobody could trace them to the Bajoda delegation, nobody believed they'd acted alone, either.

"They wanted to start a war between humanity and the Ranthanik," Sarell said when she heard the news. She and David were recovering in the infirmary, lying back on examining tables while once again wrapped in their separate force cocoons and breathing their own atmospheres. There were a few other patients in the infirmary, mostly suffering from anxiety at seeing a roiling fireball rushing down the lift shafts and drop shafts toward them, but their force fields had kept them from any physical harm.

"Between us and the Ranthanik?' David asked. "What for?"

Sarell made a growling sound that didn't translate. She shook her head and said, "It's always better to have someone else fight your wars for you. The Bajodas want to take over human space, but they don't want to pay the price so they tried to get someone else to do it for them. They would probably have waited until the war was winding down and then joined the Ranthaniks for a share of the spoils. Now they'll be lucky if the Ranthaniks don't attack *them*."

"Bajodas." David nodded. "I guess it makes sense. But that means you were right about something else; they weren't after you at all. They were after me, because they were afraid I was onto them. And I led them straight to you."

"I forgive you," Sarell said. "It's the least I could do after falsely accusing you of being an assassin yourself."

"Well, I guess maybe we're even, then."

There was a commotion at the door, then Ambassador DeLange burst into the infirmary, trailing medical robots like a retinue behind him. "There you are!" he roared when he saw David. "You're in deep trouble, Wikondu. I'll have your head on a stake for this."

David sighed. "I guess I shouldn't have expected you to thank me."

"*Thank* you? For what? For knocking me out and leaving me locked in a prison cell? For scaring the hell out of half the peace delegation? For damn near blowing up the entire Hotel Andromeda?"

"Just one wing of it," David said. "And it didn't blow; there wasn't enough oxygen for that."

"Just one wing," DeLange said with a snort. "Well, it happened to be the wing I was in, and I'm not about to forget it."

Sarell said softly, "Nor am I. David saved my life. You may not realize it yet, but he probably saved yours and the rest of humanity's as well. I suggest you calm down and consider the ramifications of what happened here before you blow a perfect chance for improving your status among the rest of your race."

"What do you mean?" asked DeLange.

"I mean if I were in your position, I would much rather return from the conference with a hero at my side than with a criminal."

"Oh," said DeLange. "Aha." He rubbed his chin thoughtfully for a moment, then nodded. "I see your point."

David shifted uncomfortably on his exam table. "Wait a minute. I'm not going anywhere. I've got a hotel to manage."

"I imagine they can spare you for a publicity tour to Earth," DeLange said. His tone of voice left little room for doubt.

A publicity tour, eh? Hmm. As a hero, no less. Staying in some of the best hotels from all through history, and dining in restaurants famous before humanity had left the planet . . . The Hightower would never have paid for such a trip, but they *were* looking for something new to offer their guests. David didn't think he could recommend the Andromeda's new life system, not until they worked a few more bugs out of it, but in the meantime maybe a touch of old-world opulence would suffice.

He made a big show of thinking it over, then just as DeLange was about to erupt with another outburst, he said, "Well, if you insist. Maybe I could spare a week or two. Three at the outside."